Nichole Severn writes explosive romantic suspense with strong heroines, heroes who dare challenge them and a hell of a lot of guns. She resides with her very supportive and patient husband, as well as her demon spawn, in Utah. When she's not writing, she's constantly injuring herself running, rock climbing, practicing yoga and snowboarding. She loves hearing from readers through her website, www.nicholesevern.com, and on Twitter, @nicholesevern.

Angi Morgan writes about Texans in Texas. A *USA TODAY* and *Publishers Weekly* bestselling author, her books have been finalists for several awards, including the Booksellers' Best Award, *RT Book Reviews* Best Intrigue Series and the Daphne du Maurier. Angi and her husband live in North Texas. They foster Labradors and love to travel, snap pics and fix up their house. Hang out with her on Facebook at Angi Morgan Books. She loves to hear from fans at www.angimorganauthor.com.

D1589759

Also by Angi Morgan

Discover more at millsandboon.co.uk

RULES IN BLACKMAIL

NICHOLE SEVERN

RANGER GUARDIAN

ANGI MORGAN

MILLS & BOON

First Published in Great Britain 2018
by Mills & Boon, an imprint of HarperCollins*Publishers*
1 London Bridge Street, London, SE1 9GF

Rules In Blackmail © 2018 Natascha Jaffa
Ranger Guardian © 2018 Angela Platt

ISBN: 978-0-263-26583-5

39-0718

MIX
Paper from
responsible sources
FSC˚ C007454

FSC
www.fsc.org

Printed and bound in Spain
by CPI, Barcelona

RULES IN
BLACKMAIL

NICHOLE SEVERN

For my husband: couldn't do this without you.

Chapter One

"You have exactly five seconds to talk, or I start shooting." Sullivan Bishop slipped his finger alongside the gun's trigger.

"I'm not armed." The woman in his sights raised her hands to shoulder level, but didn't make another move. She might've been pretty, but in his experience, pretty faces were the best at hiding lies. And the lean dark-haired woman standing in the middle of his office had one of the prettiest faces he'd ever seen. Knowing her, she'd come armed. "I want to talk. Figured this would be the best place to do it."

He balanced his weight between both feet. His heart pumped hard as he tightened his grip around the Glock. How long had it been since Jane Reise—the legendary JAG Corps prosecutor herself—had crossed his mind? Nine months? Ten? Didn't matter. Nobody uninvited strolled into Blackhawk Security and stepped back through those doors without answering for something.

Jane had a lot to answer for.

"And you thought breaking into my private security company after hours was your best plan? How the hell did you get in here?" Sullivan closed in on her one inch at a time while he listened for movement on the rest of the floor. How had she gotten past his security system? Blackhawk Security provided top-of-the-line security measures, including cameras, body-heat sensors, motion detectors and more. Whatever the client needed, they delivered. Sometimes those services included personal protection, investigating, logistical support to the US government and personal recovery. They did it all. But right now, his gut instincts were telling him Jane wasn't standing in his office for some added security around her town house.

"Would you believe me if I said I came to hire you?" She swiped her tongue over her full bottom lip. Dropping her hands to her side, she scanned the rest of the office and widened her stance. Moonlight, coming through the wall of windows looking over downtown Anchorage, splayed across one half of her face. It washed out the brilliant color of her hazel eyes he'd studied from her file all those months ago. She was far more beautiful in person—no argument there— but the cord of tension stiffening her neck darkened her features.

"You're kidding, right?" This was a joke. Had to be. Sullivan stopped no more than five feet from her, a quick burst of laughter rumbling through his chest. The gun grew heavy in his hand. He lowered it to his side but wouldn't holster the Glock until he was certain she'd come unarmed. "I'm the last person on this planet who'd help you."

Jane scanned the office a second time, looking everywhere but at him. Even in the dark, Sullivan swore the color drained from her face.

"I never meant…" She cleared her throat, determination wiping away the momentary fall of her features. "You have every reason to laugh in my face and shove me out the door, but I don't have anywhere else to go. The police don't have any leads, and I can't get the army involved. Not yet."

"Involved in what?" Flipping on the overhead lights, Sullivan saw what she'd tried to hide by sticking to the shadows of his office. She squinted against the onslaught of brightness. Dark circles had taken up residence under her eyes, a sort of hollowness thinning her cheeks. Her normally athletic and lean frame seemed smaller than he remembered from her photos, as though she'd lost not only weight but any muscle she'd gained from her current stint in the army. The white T-shirt and black cargo jacket washed color from her skin but didn't detract from her overall beauty. Still, something was wrong. This wasn't the same woman who'd stood in front of a judge a year ago and ripped apart his family.

"I'm being watched." The corner of her mouth twitched as though she were biting the inside of her cheek. Her shoulders rose on a deep inhale. "Stalked."

The fear in her voice twisted his insides—would twist any man's insides—but Sullivan didn't respond. It was a counterintelligence tactic. Keep your mouth shut, and the target was more likely to fill the silence. If she was lying, he'd know by the way her eyes darted to the left or how she held her arms around her middle.

"They've been in my house and my car. I don't know where else." Jane brushed a piece of short dark hair behind her ear and the strong, confident woman he'd studied from the surveillance photos and video taken during the trial disappeared. "If the army knew about this, they'd limit my security clearance, and I could lose my job. I called in an anonymous tip to the police, but—"

"The case isn't high on their list." He understood the way the Anchorage Police Department worked. Until there was an actual threat on Jane's life, they had more important cases to work. That'd been one of the reasons Sullivan had founded Blackhawk Security in the first place. Aside from providing investigative services for government officials and witnesses to crimes, his team protected victims law enforcement couldn't. Or wouldn't. But taking on Jane's case...

She wasn't lying, at least not from what he could tell, but helping her wasn't exactly high on his priority list either. "Do you have proof?"

With a quick nod of her perfectly angled chin, she drew her cell phone from her jacket pocket, swiping her finger across the screen. A few more clicks and she offered him the phone. "I found this picture of me sleeping in my bed yesterday morning. It's dated two nights ago, around midnight."

He took the phone from her and his index finger brushed against the side of her hand. The lack of warmth in her skin caught his attention, and he pulled back. Studying the photo taken with her own phone, Sullivan fought the urge to tighten his grip on the device. The idea of a man—any man—taking photos of a woman without her permission built pressure behind his sternum. A woman shouldn't be afraid, shouldn't have to look over her shoulder. Not ever. "Any ideas of who could've broken in?"

"No." Her defeated answer wisped out from between her lips, drawing his attention up. Eyes wide, she shook her head slightly. "I live alone."

Then, barring a random break-in, she most definitely had a stalker. Handing the phone back to her, Sullivan ensured his fingers didn't touch hers again. His insides had already caught fire from an intruder breaking into his highly secure office. He didn't need anything else clouding his head. "Does anyone else have a key to your apartment? Maybe an old boyfriend who hasn't gotten the idea you two are over?"

With another shake of her head, her hair swung slightly below her earlobes. "No. I don't…" Jane cocked her head to the side as she shrugged. "I don't have any old boyfriends. Not since I went into the army."

Which was five years ago, according to her military record. Sullivan's fingers twitched at his side. "And what about your case files? Anyone not—" he ground his back teeth "—*happy* with the way you handled their case?"

Aside from him, that was.

Her lips thinned as she rolled them between her teeth. "Not that I know of, but I have all the files for the cases I was assigned back at my house if you want to go through them."

Not going to happen. He shoved the Glock into his shoulder holster, the adrenaline rush draining from his veins. Despite getting past his security system, Jane wasn't a threat. Yet. "That won't be necessary."

"Okay, what then?" She rolled her shoulders back but didn't move otherwise. Did she realize how much he blamed her for what happened and didn't want to take the chance of getting close? He liked to think so. She'd prosecuted dozens of devoted soldiers—men and women who'd sworn to protect this country, men like him—and she wanted his help? The woman was insane.

Captain Jane Reise was responsible for his brother's suicide. She didn't deserve an ounce of pity from him.

Spinning toward his desk, he grabbed a pad of paper and a pen. "This is the name of another security consultant to handle your case. I suggest you give him a call and get out of my office."

"I came here because I need *your* help." Hints of that legendary prosecutor he'd studied bled into her voice. Her sweet scent of vanilla climbed down into his lungs and he forced himself to hold his breath. "Isn't that what Blackhawk Security does? Help people?"

"Yes." Sullivan ripped the note from the pad and handed it to her. He spun away from those far too intelligent eyes and headed for the door. Turning the knob, he swung it open and motioned her out. "But not you."

Crossing her arms, Jane leveled her chin to the floor and sat back against the desk. Every cell in his body stood at attention as fire bled into her gaze. "I'm not leaving until you agree to help me."

"Move. Or I'll throw you over my shoulder and dump you in the hallway." He liked the visual. Far too much. He shouldn't, but damn it he did. All that soft skin, her lean frame wrapped around his, her hair tickling him across his back. Sullivan shut down that line of thought. Didn't matter how fiery or intelligent she was or how much she begged for his help. Wasn't going to happen. Ever. He crossed his arms over his chest, parroting her movement. Even from this distance, he noted her throat constricting on a slow swallow. "Get out."

"I can pay you." She pushed off from the desk. "Anything you want."

"This isn't about money." Sullivan dropped his hold

on the door. Marching across the room, he shortened the space between them until she had to look up at him.

Her chin notched higher as she held her ground.

The woman had stood up to all kinds of criminals and soldiers over the years. She wasn't intimidated. Damn if that wasn't the sexiest thing he'd ever seen. But he knew better than to trust her.

Chest almost pressed against her, he quirked one corner of his mouth. There were other ways to get her out of his office. He pushed his palms on either side of her on the desk, leaning down. "Unless you're talking about something other than money…"

Her lips parted, a sharp exhale of air beating against him. Jane studied his face from top to bottom but didn't move to escape the box he'd created around her. She locked that striking gaze on his, eyes determined and wide. "Dollars and cents, Lieutenant Bishop. Nothing more."

"Then you'll want to leave before I put in a call to your commanding officer and have you disbarred for harassing the family of one of your victims." He shoved himself away from the desk, away from that intoxicating scent of hers, and headed toward the door.

"I can make you help me," she said.

Another rush of heat overwhelmed his control, and he stopped dead in his tracks. What part of his answer didn't she understand? He spun back toward her. If it was a fight she was looking for, fine. He had no problem taking down the woman who'd destroyed his family. He might even enjoy it. "I'd like to see you try."

"All right." Jane straightened her spine as though she was preparing for battle. That same fire he'd caught a glimpse of during his brother's court-martial encroached on the darkness embedded in her features. "I know who you really are. And I know what you've been hiding."

"YOU DON'T KNOW anything about me." Sullivan Bishop seemed so much...*bigger* than he had a moment ago. Caged by his body against the desk, she felt his heat tunnel through her clothing. Hatred had burned in those sea-colored eyes as he'd pressed his chest against hers.

Jane swallowed as he stretched his shoulders wider. What had she been thinking to try to blackmail a man like him? Blackhawk Security's CEO wasn't an administrator over a team of highly trained ex-military operatives. He *was* ex-military. He'd been a SEAL, capable of the worst kind of violence. And she'd just threatened everything he'd ever worked for.

He closed in on her a second time. His clean, fresh scent whispered across the underside of her jaw as he spoke.

The hairs on the back of her neck stood on end. Every word out of his mouth promised she was going to wish she hadn't gone down this path, but Jane didn't have any other choice. Gliding her tongue across her bottom lip—a movement his eyes locked onto—she stood her ground. There was no turning back. He was the best, and she needed his help. One way or another.

"I know Sullivan Bishop isn't your real name." Every muscle in his body tightened in warning, and Jane forced herself to breathe evenly. She pressed her lower back into the desk. "And the people holding your company's military contracts might be interested to know why you changed it. A few of your classified clients, too, I imagine."

"You're blackmailing me?" A low growl reverberated up his throat and hiked her blood pressure higher. The shadows angling across the dark, thick stubble darkening his jaw shifted, but those sea-blue eyes never left hers. The veins in his arms popped as he leaned into her, the butt of the Glock in his shoulder holster pressing into her arm. "Are you sure you want to go down this road, Captain Reise? It won't end well."

"I'm willing to do whatever it takes to survive." A shiver chased up her spine, but Jane held her ground. She couldn't live like this anymore. The late-night phone calls, the feeling of being watched, the sick photo in her cell phone of her sleeping. And there was more. Going back several weeks. "Have you ever been hunted like an animal, Lieutenant Bishop?"

The suffocating bubble of tension he'd built around her disappeared. The edge to his features softened. She breathed a little easier. Putting some distance between them, Sullivan relaxed his hands to his sides, but the strong muscles flexing the length of his arms promised he was fully capable of violence. "Yes."

"Then you know what it's like to constantly be looking over your shoulder, to feel so helpless you don't seem to have any control of your own life." She crossed her arms over her chest, fully aware of the loss of body heat he'd forced through her with his proximity. Her hands shook as the terror she'd tried keeping to herself crept through her. "To feel like every second you're alive could actually be your last."

The lines running from the edge of his nose to those perfectly crafted lips deepened. She couldn't read his expression, but the tension in his neck and shoulders released.

"How did you get through it?" she asked.

Sullivan's chest expanded on a deep inhale. At least he wasn't crowding her anymore. She could actually breathe again, but the cold fist tightened in the pit of her stomach. "I have people I trust to back me up no matter what the situation calls for."

She nodded. That was what she was counting on. Why she was here in the first place. Sullivan had the reputation for committing himself to every job he took on, and while it was a risk to rely on the man she was blackmailing, she hoped his reputation proved true. "Well, I don't have a team. I have you. And if it's going to take blackmail to get you to help me, then so be it."

Silence pressed in on her as Sullivan studied her from head to toe. A scorching trail of awareness skittered across her skin. What did he see? A woman who couldn't protect herself? Or the woman responsible for his brother's death?

"I'll give you twenty-four hours of my time," he said. "After that, you can go back to your cold, empty existence and leave me the hell alone."

He was just like the rest of them: her peers, the men and women she prosecuted to protect citizens of the United States, even her commanding officer. She'd earned her reputation as the Full Metal B, she supposed. Her job required an almost ruthless approach to the cases she'd been assigned, but this was the first time her rib cage tightened at someone's assessment of her. Which didn't make sense. She didn't care what Sullivan Bishop thought of her. She didn't care what any of them thought of her. Her insides twisted. She didn't care. Jane shoved off from the massive desk he'd trapped her against moments before. Uncrossing her arms, she stepped toward him. "So you'll help me?"

"I don't have a choice, do I? Isn't that how black-mail is supposed to work?" Sullivan rounded his desk. The thick muscles across his back flexed through his shirt. She forced her attention to the sway of his gun rather than the way he moved, to prove she could take her eyes off him. Lean waist, strong legs, hints of his trident tattoo peeking out from under his T-shirt. Such a dangerous man shouldn't be that attractive. "We'll take my car."

Jane straightened. Okay. They were doing this. "Where are we going?"

"To your town house. I'll brief my team on the way." He unholstered the Glock from his side and dropped the magazine into his hand. After a glance at the rounds, he replaced it with efficient, sure movements and chambered a round. He raised that piercing gaze to hers. "I have a man on my team who used to work forensics for the NYPD. If your stalker has been in your house like you claim, he'll find the evidence and we can all move on with our lives."

She ran her cold palms over the front of her jeans and took another step toward him. He was actually going to help her find the man trying to destroy her life? A knot of hope pulsed from deep in her chest. "And if he does find evidence? What then?"

Sullivan came around the desk, his wide shoulders blocking out the magnificent view of the Chugach mountain range behind him. Nearly pressing against her, he stared down at her. At six foot four, it wasn't hard, but the intimidation had drained from his body.

He stalked toward the office door. "Then you'll have the proof you need to take to the police."

"What?" Jane wrapped her hand halfway around his massive biceps and spun him around to look at her. He'd let her. She didn't have the strength to move a mountain like him. She was at the end of her rope, and she hadn't come here to admit defeat. Her leave ended in a week, and she'd come no closer to discovering her stalker's identity than she was three months ago. Desperation held her tight.

She glared up into those sea-blue eyes of his, her throat constricting. "I thought I made myself perfectly clear. Either *you* help me find the person stalking me or I go to the government and your clients with what I know about you. And your family."

Facing her, oh-so-slowly, Sullivan towered over her, and she fought the urge to take a step back. He leaned in close, mere centimeters from her mouth, as though he intended to kiss her. "Then let me make myself perfectly clear. The only way you get my help is if we do this my way, and I plan to get you out of my life as soon as I can."

Jane flinched, but he didn't wait for her to answer, heading for the door.

"Let's go," he said.

This was a mistake. She should've known how deep Sullivan's hatred for her flowed, but she'd run out of options. Jane followed on his heels toward the elevator, allowing a good amount of distance between them as they crowded into the small space on the way down to the parking garage. Neither said a word. His clean scent wrapped around her, and she gripped the handrail to clear her head. In less than a minute, he led her out of the elevator and across the empty parking garage toward a black SUV.

Tingling spread across her back—an all-too-familiar feeling—and Jane turned back toward the elevator, heart in her throat. Darkness surrounded them. Everyone in the building had already gone home for the day. She'd made sure. Everyone except Sullivan and a few security guards, but someone else was here. *He* was here, watching her. She felt it.

"Jane." Sullivan's deep timbre flooded her nerves with relief, but she couldn't shake the feeling they were being watched. "Jane," he said again.

She stared at him. It was her imagination. Had to be. There was no way anyone could've followed her here. She'd been too careful, but still, the sensation between her shoulder blades prickled her instincts. "I'm coming."

Sullivan ripped open the driver's-side door of the large black SUV, his eyes sweeping across the parking garage as she moved to the other side. Once she was safely inside the car, the sensation disappeared and Jane breathed a bit easier. Nobody had been watching her. The constant paranoia had just become a habit.

Sullivan slammed the door behind him and started the engine. Black leather and dark interiors gave her a false sense of security, but having him in the driver's seat eased some of the tension on either side of her spine. At the exit, he lowered the window and scanned his key card. Nobody went in or out of the garage without a card. He swung the SUV north through an area of warehouses and railroads, as though he knew exactly where they were headed.

The SUV plowed through the wet streets of downtown Anchorage, spitting up water and snow along the way. The heater chased away the ice that'd built inside her over the past few weeks. She was reminded of Sullivan's heat back in his office. The same heat rolled off him in waves now. She watched him from her peripheral vision. He wore only a T-shirt and jeans in these temperatures, a human furnace. It'd been too long since she'd felt anything but fear.

"I know what you've heard about me, what they called me in Afghanistan. I'm not as cold as you think." Sitting straighter in her seat, Jane stared down into her lap to counteract the need to explain herself to Blackhawk Security's CEO. "I didn't want to dig into your history. I needed—"

"We're not doing this right now," he said, one hand on the wheel. He still wouldn't look at her. Typical alpha male, determined not to talk. Sullivan pressed his foot on the accelerator as they rolled onto the bridge across Knik Arm, the shallow water almost motionless with a few inches of ice across the top.

"All right." She wiped her clammy hands down her thighs. "Tough crowd."

A light falling of snow peppered the windshield. Nothing like the storms Anchorage usually saw this time of year, but just as beautiful as she remembered growing up in Seattle.

The high screech of peeling tires broke their self-imposed silence, and Jane swept her gaze out the window. Blinded by fast-approaching headlights, she shoved away from the door as a truck slammed into her side of the SUV.

Chapter Two

The loud groan of a truck's engine brought Sullivan around.

"Reise?" Pain. In his skull. Everywhere. He blinked to clear his vision and ran his hand over his left cheek. Something warm and sticky coated his hand. Blood. He fought to scan his body for other injuries. Hell. They'd flipped.

Cracks in the windshield spidered out in a dendritic pattern, blocking his view of the other driver. Had they survived? Been injured? He depressed the seat belt button and collapsed onto the SUV's roof. Broken glass from the window cut into him. He pounded his fist into the roof and locked his jaw. "Damn it!"

He swiped blood from his eyes. Where was Jane? Twisting inside the crushed interior, he spotted her. Sullivan crawled through debris and around the middle console, ignoring the pain screaming for his attention. The seat belt held her in the passenger seat, upside down. Couldn't search her for injuries here. They needed to get clear of the wreck. "Captain Reise, can you hear me?"

She didn't respond, unconscious.

Bracing himself, Sullivan released her belt and

caught her just before she hit the SUV's roof. He pressed his palm against the glistening gash across the right side of her head to stop the bleeding, then checked her slender neck for a pulse. Thready, but there.

Burning rubber and exhaust worked down into his lungs. Crouching low to see through the passenger-side window, he kept pressure on her wound. But couldn't hold it for long. The yellow tow truck's tires screeched again as it made another lunge straight for them.

"You've got to be kidding me." His fight-or-flight instinct kicked into high gear. Heaving Jane across the cab, he pulled her through his shattered driver's-side window with everything he had. They cleared the SUV, but his momentum catapulted them down the steep embankment surrounding the shallow water of Knik Arm.

The world spun as snow and mud worked under his clothes and clung tight to his skin and hair. His arms closed around Jane, the movement as natural as breathing as they rolled. They slammed into a nearby tree, mere feet from the ice-cold water of the river. Positioned on top of her, he scanned her once more, panting. His vision split into two and he shook his head.

He leveraged his weight into the palms of his hands to give her more breathing room, his heart pumping hard. "Captain Reise, wake up. We need to—"

The second crash forced Sullivan's gaze up the snow-covered hill. The SUV's headlights flickered a split second before the entire vehicle started to slide down the slope, heading right for them. There was no time to think. He dug his fingertips into Jane's arm and spun them through the snow and weeds to the right as fast as he could. The SUV sped past, breaking through the six inches of solid ice at the edge of the river.

Hell. This wasn't some freak accident. Someone wasn't just stalking Jane. They'd now decided they wanted her dead. He studied the cut across her head, then her sharp features. She'd been telling the truth. Sullivan exhaled hard. Puffs of breath crystallized in front of his mouth. "Come on, Jane. We have to get out of here."

Jane? When had he started calling her by her first name?

Screeching tires above echoed in his ears as the tow truck hauled fast away from the scene. *Damn it.* He hadn't seen the driver at all. He could still catch up. He could—

Jane moaned as she stirred in his arms. Her lips parted. Such soft, pink lips. Pulse now beating steady at the base of her throat, she fought to focus on him. She lifted one hand toward her face, but he wrapped his fingers around her small wrist. "What…happened? My head—" She locked her fuzzy gaze on him. "Did you just call me Jane instead of Captain Reise?"

He swallowed. She'd heard that? "You hit your head pretty hard against the window when the truck slammed into us. Must've heard me wrong."

Sullivan shoved a strand of her hair out of her face to see her wound better. Her features softened as she closed her eyes. She was okay as far as he could tell, but the spike of adrenaline had yet to drain from his system. Whoever had been driving that truck had made a very dangerous enemy. Not only had he gone after an unarmed woman, he'd tried killing the CEO of the government's most resourced private security contractor. No way Sullivan was going to turn Jane's case over to Anchorage PD now. That bastard was his.

"What happened?" Those brilliant hazel eyes swept over the embankment, and he noted exactly when Jane caught sight of the totaled SUV. Every muscle down her spine tightened as she dug her heels into the snow to sit up. "Somebody tried to kill us."

No point in denying the facts. Her stalker had gone from hunting Jane in her own home to outright attempted murder. "Looks that way. Can you stand?"

She nodded, rolling her upper body off the ground, but grabbed for his arm. Stinging heat splintered through his muscles where she touched him, his bare skin exposed to the dropping temperatures.

"It'll be light soon." Sullivan tugged his arm from her grasp as he scanned their surroundings. They hadn't made it too far from downtown, but he couldn't take the chance of taking her back to the office. Her stalker had known exactly where to find them, as if he'd been waiting. Might've been on her tail when Jane had broken into Blackhawk Security. Whoever it was, the guy was willing to kill bystanders to get to her, which meant they couldn't go to her town house either. "We don't want to be caught out here overnight."

"There's nowhere we can hide." Her teeth chattered together as she wrapped her arms around her midsection. She stared at the half-sunken SUV, shaking her head. "I was careful. I made sure no one was following me when I went to your office. I made sure…" Her words left her mouth quick and breathless as she finally looked at him. "He wants me dead."

His insides flipped, and Sullivan reached for her without thinking. He pulled her into his chest. At about five foot three, Jane barely came to his sternum, but she fitted. Fragile, vulnerable, but strong. His back molars clamped together, jaw straining. She'd ripped apart his family. She was even blackmailing him into protecting her, but the fear darkening those eyes had urged him to lock her body against his automatically. Her job might've made her a few enemies, but not even the army's most revered prosecutor deserved to be hunted like an animal. No one did.

Tremors racked through her—most likely shock—but he dropped his hold. Wisps of her sweet scent replaced the smell of exhaust and burned rubber seared into his memory, and he inhaled deeply to clear his system. They had to get moving. "Whoever this guy is, we'll find him."

The shivers simmered. Sliding her hands between their bodies, she placed them above his heart and tilted her head back to look up at him. "Thank you."

Heat worked through his chest, a combination of dropping temperatures and the rage he held for her fighting for his attention. Her nearly dying at the hands of a crazed psychopath wouldn't change the past between them. Nothing could.

"For getting me out of the SUV, I mean." Cuts, scrapes and dried blood marred her otherwise flawless skin, a small bruise forming on the right side of her face. A strand of short black hair slid along the curve of her cheek, but he wouldn't brush it away. "You could've left me there to take care of your blackmail problem, but you didn't. I appreciate that."

He kept his expression tight. Right. Jane Reise had the power to bring down his entire company with one phone call and had made it perfectly clear she was willing to use it. How could he have forgotten?

"Yeah, well, whoever you pissed off tried to kill

me, and you're the only lead I have to hunt him down."
Sullivan put some much-needed space between them.
She'd most certainly lived up to her reputation in the
last hour they'd been forced together. He curled his fingers into his palms to douse the urge to comfort her.
The woman who'd destroyed his family—the woman
blackmailing him for his help—didn't deserve comfort. And she wouldn't get it from him. He had control. Time to use it.

"Right." Jane's throat constricted on a hard swallow.
She shoved her hands into her jacket pockets and sur-
veyed their surroundings. "I'd say call a tow truck, but
I think your SUV is beyond saving."

Cracking ice pulled his attention toward the river.
The SUV was sinking. In less than five minutes, the
entire vehicle would be submerged in the icy Gulf of
Alaska. Treading through six inches of muddy snow
toward the vehicle, Sullivan registered her confident
footsteps behind him. He hauled the tailgate above his
head and tossed the false bottom of the trunk to his
right. "Now we're on foot. Take this." He thrust the
lighter duffel bag from the trunk at Jane. He grabbed a
thick coat and the heavier bag for himself. Boy Scouts,
SEALs and Alaskans all had one motto in common:
Never Get Caught in the Wilderness Unprepared.

She unzipped the bag he'd handed her. "Food and
guns. You're officially the man of my dreams."

She'd meant it as a joke, but, hell, the compliment
forced him to pause.

"Wait until you see what's in this bag. Between us,
we'll be able to survive out here for at least three days."
He didn't bother closing the tailgate. Some civilian
would drive past and put a call in to the cops, or the

SUV would sink. Either way, he and Jane weren't sticking around to find out. He couldn't take the risk of her stalker coming back to the scene to make sure the job was done. "We're heading northeast." He pointed toward the thick outcropping of trees as he pulled on his thick coat. "It's a three-mile hike. We need to leave now in case your stalker realizes he didn't finish the job."

"Where are we going?" She brought up the hood on her cargo jacket. Smart move. The Alaskan wilderness wasn't any place to screw around. They had to stay warm and dry or risk hypothermia.

Sullivan covered his head to conserve body heat. A gust of freezing wind whipped one side of his body as he headed into the forest. "Somewhere no one will find us."

HE'D CALLED HER Jane back on the embankment. Not Captain Reise. She'd heard him clear as day. Because even in the midst of suffocating unconsciousness, Jane had locked on to his voice. The man she was blackmailing had brought her out of the darkness. Why? He had no allegiance to her.

Sullivan cleared a path through the thickest parts of the forest with one of the extra blades from his duffel bag a few feet up ahead of her. Shadows cast across his features from the beam from his flashlight. Snow had worked down into her boots, turning to slush. Her jeans were soaked through. How long had they been out here? An hour? Two? Three miles didn't seem like much until deep snow and freezing temperatures added to the misery. Not to mention it was dark and difficult to see. Her toes had gone numb long ago, fingers following close behind, but Jane kept her mouth shut.

They had to be close, right? She swiped away a few drops of water from her cheek, wincing as pain radiated up toward her temple. The sooner they made it to their destination—wherever that was—the better.

Distraction. She had to keep her mind off her frozen limbs. "Bet you've never had to walk through the Alaskan wilderness with a client to escape a crazed psychopath before."

"You're right." He laughed, a deep guttural rumble she felt down into her bones. It was real, warming. Swinging his arm out, he held back a large branch so she could pass. He stared down at her while she maneuvered around him, those sea-blue eyes brightening in the muted beam from his flashlight. "I usually reserve these kinds of trips for people I've been assigned to hunt down."

"Is that a nice way of putting that you've killed people for a living?" She instantly regretted the words, and her heart rate rocketed. "I mean, I read your military record during the trial. I know you used to be a SEAL, one of the best. You don't have to lie to me or sugarcoat anything."

"Once a SEAL, always a SEAL. You never really retire. It stays in your blood, makes you who you are. Forever." Defensiveness tinted his words as Jane followed in his sunken footsteps. But, faster than she thought possible, he latched onto her arm and spun her into his chest. The hard set to his eyes said Sullivan Bishop could be a very dangerous enemy, but she'd known that before throwing his secrets in his face. Right now, in this moment, her instincts said he wouldn't hurt her. She'd learned to trust those instincts to get her through the past few years. "And, as a prosecutor, you of all people should understand that the best defense against evil men is good men who deal in violence."

Jane took a deep breath. One, two. She couldn't get enough air. Staring up at him, she noted the gash across his cheek he must've suffered during the wreck. He'd protected her back there because she was a lead. Nothing more. He'd said as much, but why did being this close to him change her breathing patterns? "And what about now?"

"What do you mean?" Sullivan narrowed his eyes, his features turning to stone.

"Do you still 'hunt down' people for a living?" she asked.

Seconds ticked by, then a minute. Something in her heart froze. Sullivan was a killer. It'd been part of the job description, part of his past, but Jane couldn't keep track of how long he held her there as snow fell from branches around them. His mesmerizing gaze held hers, but Jane had a feeling he wasn't really seeing her at all. His fingers dug into her, keeping his hold light enough not to bruise. He wasn't trying to hurt her. Maybe…he didn't want to let her go.

"Isn't that why you blackmailed me into helping you?" The demons were evident in his eyes, but Sullivan released his grip on her arm and put a few inches of freezing Alaska air between them as he turned his back on her and pushed forward.

"No. I blackmailed you to find the man doing this to me so we can turn him over to the police." Her skin tingled through her thin coat where he'd latched onto her arm. Phantom sensations. There was no way he could affect her like that. Not in these temperatures. She studied him from behind, the way his back stretched each time he took a step, the way he carried himself as though nothing could get through him if a threat arose. "I'm sorry. I didn't mean to…"

What? Pry into his life? Doubt his reasons for doing what needed to be done overseas and here in the United States?

Pushing on up ahead, he worked to clear branches. After a few seconds, Sullivan halted in his tracks, turning back toward her. Stubble speckled with ice and snow, he swayed on his feet. Good to know she wasn't the only one suffering from exhaustion. He scanned over her from head to toe. "Don't worry about it."

"I appreciate everything you've done for your country and what you're doing now. I'm sure every American does. It's admirable." She fought for a full lungful of air. Despite the dropping temperatures, her skin heated when he looked at her like that. Like she was a threat. She stepped over the remnants of a few branches he'd demolished along the way, nearly losing her footing. In that moment, something between them shifted. An understanding of sorts. No messy blackmail. No psychotic lunatic trying to run them down with his tow truck. Not even security consultant and client. Just two people trying to survive in the middle of the Alaskan wilderness. Together. "You don't have to do all this work yourself, you know. I can help."

"You're more than welcome to…" His mouth went slack as though he couldn't get enough oxygen. Probably couldn't. Freezing temperatures didn't discriminate against SEALs or lawyers. Mother Nature treated everyone equally.

"Are you okay?" she asked. "Sullivan?"

They'd crossed at least two and a half miles of

heavy snow and growth, maybe more. She was tired and couldn't feel her toes, but her instincts urged her to get to him. Now.

Sullivan doubled over, dropping his gear before he collapsed onto his side.

"Sullivan!" Jane discarded the duffel bag and lunged toward him. Her feet felt like frozen blocks of ice, but she fought the piling snow with everything she had. Hands outstretched, she checked his pulse. Weak. "No, no, no, no. Come on. Get up."

Gripping his jawline, she brought one ear to his mouth. Still breathing. Would anyone hear her out here? "Help!"

Sullivan Bishop was a SEAL, for crying out loud. This shouldn't be happening. He'd trained for situations exactly like this. Her heart beat out of control. She dived for the duffel bag he'd been carrying. Food, more guns. There had to be a—

"Yes!" She ripped the first-aid kit from the bag, fought to break the seal on the space blanket, then covered him completely. The hand and foot warmers were easier to open with her stiff fingers, but they wouldn't be enough. One look at Sullivan's normally full, sensual pink lips said she was running out of time. She had to get his body temperature up before hypothermia set in, but the blanket and a few warmers wouldn't cut it.

"You are not allowed to die on me. You hear me? I can't do this without you. You're going to listen to my voice and wake up so I don't have to carry you." Scanning the thick trees ahead of their location, Jane narrowed in on a clearing. And across that? A small cabin set into the other side of the trees. Had to be Sullivan's safe house. Had to be. If not, they'd at least have some protection from the elements while the owners called for help. "You're going to make me drag you there, aren't you?"

She didn't have time to wait for an answer. Leaving the duffel bags, Jane fisted her numb grip into his jacket and pulled. The snow eased the friction underneath him as she hefted Sullivan toward the clearing, but her strength gave out after only a few hundred feet. She collapsed back into the snow, fingers aching, heart racing. Hours upon hours of training kept her in shape in the army, but this? This was different. And the security contractor at her feet wasn't exactly a lightweight. "Come on, Sullivan. Think lighter thoughts."

The trees passed by in a blur. She couldn't focus on anything but shoving one foot back behind the other. Minutes passed, hours it seemed, and they hit the clearing. Only a few hundred more feet and faster than she thought possible, the heels of her boots knocked against the steps leading into the cabin. She tried the door. Locked. Pounding her fists against the door, she listened carefully for movement, but no one answered. In a rush, she searched for a fake rock, anything that would get her inside. She hunted around the bushes and flitted over something that was most certainly not natural: a key taped to one of the thick branches. Shoving the steel into the dead bolt and turning, she sighed in victory.

Heat enveloped her in seconds, thawing her fingers in a rush until they burned. No time. She spun back to Sullivan and slid her grip under his arms. An exhausted groan broke free from her lips as she hauled him inside. Fire. She had to start a fire to get him warm.

"Almost there. Hang on." Throwing off her coat,

Jane ran toward the fireplace and got a small fire going. She'd add more to it in a few minutes, but right now, Sullivan's wet clothes and his own sweat were doing his body more harm than good. She stripped off her coat, socks and jeans, staring down at the peaceful expression settled across his strong, handsome features. Then it was his turn.

"Sorry, Sullivan. You might hate me even more after you wake up." Crouching at his feet, she untied his boot laces and unbuttoned his pants. Jane hefted her own shirt over her head, adding it to the pile of clothes at her feet. Tugging him up into a sitting position, she stripped him down to nothing. "But it's going to save your life."

Chapter Three

Dying hurt like hell.

Heat blistered along his forearms, neck and face. His entire body ached in places he hadn't thought about since his SEAL days. He hadn't been on active duty for over a year now, but Sullivan still trained as though he were. Had to be ready for anything his clients might throw his way. Even the beginning stages of hypothermia. Damn it, he should've known better. Groaning, he cracked open his eyes, stomach still rolling. A fire popped a few feet from him.

At least he knew where he was. The cabin was sparse: one bedroom, one bath, a living room and small kitchen. He mostly came out here when he wanted to be alone, needed to get away from people, the city or both. No neighbors, no one to encroach on his business. And he'd never brought anyone here before. He'd kept this place under his mother's maiden name in case he'd needed a safe house. It couldn't be traced back to him if Jane's stalker—or anyone else—had the inclination to investigate. But how in the hell did he get here?

Sullivan raised his head. He wasn't alone.

Endless amounts of warm, smooth skin stretched out beside him under the heaviest blanket he kept on hand in the cabin. A head of black hair rested against his right arm. Jane? He had to be dreaming. Skimming his fingers across her shoulder blade, he sank into how very real she felt. Nope. Not a dream. But why would she… The lapse in his memory filled almost instantly. The last thing he remembered was the look on her face as he…collapsed. Terrified. Hell. Had she dragged him all the way out here on her own?

Her shoulders rising and falling against him in a slow, even rhythm said she was fast asleep. He couldn't have been out for long. An hour—two, tops—from the amount of moonlight coming through the front room window. He'd messed up out there, but her sultry vanilla scent spared him a few ounces of guilt. It dived into his lungs, and he took a deep breath to keep it in his system as long as possible. His heart rate dropped to a slow, even thump behind his ears. He closed his eyes, all too easily seeing himself burying his nose in her hair for another round.

Nope. Not the time and definitely not this woman.

Sullivan shifted his hips away from her backside. If Jane woke up now, there'd be no hiding what was going on downstairs in that moment. His brain might have control, but with the expanse of soft skin along his front, his body had other ideas. He scanned the living room and spotted his clothes hanging from fishing line around the open rafters by the fireplace. He'd gotten out of some real complicated situations in the navy. There had to be a way to unwind himself from this warm, coldhearted woman without waking her.

He leveraged his weight into his toes and stretched out his arm. A soft, guttural moan worked up Jane's throat. Something primal washed through him. He froze. There was a stalker on the loose and he'd nearly died out in the wilderness, but all Sullivan could think about was what he wouldn't give to hear that sound again.

She shifted against him, wrapping her leg around him as though she sensed he was trying to escape. What the—

The breath Sullivan had been holding crushed from his lungs. He settled back where he'd been, pressed right against her, his front to her back. "You're awake, aren't you?"

Rolling into him, Jane startled him with a wide, gut-clenching grin. The dark, sultry look of her gaze constricted his throat, and a shiver chased down his spine. Her pupils expanded. For an instant, he swore he saw desire blazing in her eyes. Or maybe the hypothermia had done more damage to his brain than he'd originally thought. "I couldn't wait to see your reaction when you woke up and found a naked woman under the blanket with you. Surprise."

"Did I meet your expectations?" Sullivan was proud of the fact his voice sounded steady and calm. Especially considering how very far from calm he felt at the moment. Aware of how naked he was and how she couldn't possibly miss the show going on at her lower back, he held his weight away from her.

"Absolutely priceless. And, as a bonus, I got to see you naked." That amused smile of hers did funny things to his stomach, and he couldn't help but clench the blanket in his grip for some piece of control. Resting her hand on his chest, Jane pushed herself up to a sitting position, taking the blanket with her as she stood. Cool air rushed down his body, prickling his skin along the way. "Don't worry, big guy. It wasn't anything sexual. You were dying and I had to get your body temperature up."

Her long legs peeked out from between the folds of the blanket as she walked, the fire glinting off her bright red toenail polish. Not exactly the color he'd visualized for the woman he'd blamed for his brother's suicide this past year. Black maybe, something to match her soul.

But Jane had saved his life out there. Even if she was only using him to track down her stalker, that counted for something in his world. Her reputation said she was the JAG Corps prosecutor willing to do anything and everything to convict the men and women who interrupted her crusade for justice. He scanned over his clothing hanging from the rafters. The Full Metal Bitch had only kept him alive to fix her stalker problem. Nothing more.

There was a lot he didn't know about her, even more he couldn't trust. One thing he did know? He would've died out there today if it hadn't been for Jane. So, for now, he would choose to see a woman in danger, a woman who'd lost her grip on everything she thought she could control. Not someone who could turn on him at any moment.

She smiled over her shoulder at him as she pulled her clothing from the makeshift laundry lines.

Pulling a pillow from the couch across his hips, Sullivan cleared his throat. "Thank you for saving my life out there. Can't imagine what it took to get me through that door. Couldn't have been easy."

"Guess that makes us even, doesn't it?" Her hair flipped around her head as she headed straight for the single bathroom on the other side of the cabin and shut the door tight. The sound of the lock clicking into place shut down any hint of something between them.

It wasn't going to happen. Not now. Not ever. She might've saved his life out there a few hours ago, but Jane had a lifetime of steel running through her veins, steel that'd gotten his brother killed. She was the reason he didn't have any family left in this world. Besides, she was a client, and Blackhawk Security operatives were never to get involved with their clients. No exceptions.

Which reminded him—he had to fill his team in on their new case. Because even without blackmail hanging over his head, the bastard terrorizing Jane owed Sullivan a new SUV.

He tossed the pillow back onto the couch and dressed in a hurry. She'd hung his clothes up by the fire to dry them out, and the warm fabric chased away the chill of Jane leaving his side. How could he have been so stupid out there? Rule number one when in below-freezing temperatures: stay dry, stay warm. He usually had enough sense to slow down and ensure he wasn't sweating. What had changed?

The bathroom door clicked open and his attention slid toward Jane as she stepped back into the main room. He pulled his shoulders back. There stood his answer. He hadn't exactly been in the right frame of mind after nearly getting run down by a tow truck. He'd wanted to get Jane to safety as fast as possible. Stupid. She'd proved she could take care of herself, had even saved his life in the process. Aside from a few bumps and bruises, she was no worse for wear.

"This is a nice place." She scanned over the small

cabin, fingers stuffed into her jacket as he opened one drawer of his massive desk. "Not great security, though. A key taped to a bush? Thought you security consultants were better than that."

"Sometimes there's beauty in simplicity. Anybody breaking in here would expect some kind of elaborate security system, all the while wasting time looking for it. Gives me time to counter." Another one of those debilitating smiles overwhelmed her features, and he couldn't help but smile back. Sullivan flipped one of the many burner cell phones he'd unearthed from the desk over in his hand. The sensation of lightness disappeared, however, the longer he studied her. Eyes narrowing, he tried justifying the last few hours since she'd broken into his office. Why him? Why now? "What are you doing here, Jane?"

A small burst of laughter escaped from between those rosy lips. She motioned toward the front door. "Well, I couldn't very well leave you here alone after—"

"No." Sullivan closed in on her, the hairs on the back of his neck standing on end. "I mean why did you break into my office tonight? You had other options. Any number of bodyguards or private investigators in Anchorage would've jumped to help you for the right price. After all, you were ready to offer me anything." He halted no more than a foot from her, reading those deep hazel eyes for any sign of hesitation. "Why come to me?"

"Isn't it obvious?" She tried backing away but hit the wall beside the front door. "I had dirt on you and your family, and I knew I could use it to force you to help me. Saved myself a hell of a lot of money in the process."

Heat prickled under Sullivan's skin, crawling up his neck and warming his face. Only Jane crossed her arms across her chest and the strong pulse at the base of her neck beat unevenly. She didn't believe a word she was saying. And, thinking about it now, she'd only pulled the blackmail card when he'd refused to help her the first two times she'd asked. "You're lying."

Color left her features, a telling reaction he'd noted back in his office. Jane curled her fingers into the palms of her hands, stance wide as though she intended to run straight out the front door. Nervousness? Embarrassment? Difficult to tell when she wiped any kind of emotion from her features so fast.

"What do you want from me?" He stalked toward her. No. She wasn't going to hide behind that hardened exterior this time.

"I guess after what happened on the road, you deserve the truth. It seems stupid now, but I didn't have anyone else I could trust." She licked her bottom lip, but Sullivan refused to let the motion distract him this time. Answers. That was all he wanted. He'd risked his life—twice—for her. Now he needed to know why she'd pulled him into this mess. She cocked her head to the side. "I came to you because I saw how protective and dedicated you were to Marrok during his trial. And after I uncovered that photo in my phone yesterday, I needed a little bit of that in my life." Raising that beautiful gaze to his, she let her shoulders deflate and she exhaled hard. "I needed *you*."

"I NEED TO brief my team." His gravelly voice played havoc with her insides, but Sullivan turned away from her, phone in hand. Refused to even look at her.

Every nerve in Jane's body caught fire. That was all he had to say? Watching him, she noted the strain around his eyes, the slightly haggard expression on his features as he spoke into the phone in whispered, clipped responses. She was used to it. In their line of work, she'd learned anybody could be listening in. Phone taps, parabolic mics. Without an idea of who her stalker was, why they'd come after her or what resources they had access to, she and Sullivan couldn't afford to be careless.

She headed into the kitchen. When had she eaten last? Her stomach rumbled. Too long ago. Sullivan turned toward her at the sound. The weight of his gaze slid across her sternum. Head down, she focused on her hunt for anything edible in this place. No luck. He obviously didn't stay here often. The walls were bare, the counters covered in dust. She ran her fingers over the cream granite, but ripped her hand away at the low temperature.

"I sent my forensic investigator, Vincent, to your place with some backup." Sullivan tossed the cell phone he'd been using onto the granite. Exhaustion played across his features, darkening the circles under his eyes. He hadn't gotten much sleep after nearly dying. Neither of them had, but Jane was too wound up and too anxious to figure this mess out. "If your stalker has been there, Vincent will find the evidence and call me back. Could be an hour, could be tomorrow. Just depends."

"Okay. What do we do until then?" She couldn't sit around waiting for some maniac to make the next move. There had to be something in her case files, something in her work for the army that could point them in the right direction to an ID of who'd T-boned them back at the bridge.

"We dig into your cases." Sullivan slid onto the bar stool on the other side of the granite countertop as though using it as a barrier between them. Probably a good idea. Because those heated, confusing minutes of them under the blanket in front of the fire together hadn't exactly gone as Jane had expected. His skin had pressed against hers from chest to toes, his very prominent arousal at her lower back, and the way he'd feathered his fingertips over her shoulder... Jane swallowed back the memories. His touch had felt good, real. Then again, she'd lived the past few months as a hermit and wouldn't know the difference between her own arousal and the simple need for human contact. Jane shivered. No. That wasn't it. She'd recognized the difference. She just hadn't felt that kind of drowning heat in a long time. Her insides burned to close the distance between them for another passing glimpse of it, however fleeting.

But Sullivan's reaction had been simple biology. There'd been a naked woman pressed against him and his body had responded. He didn't want her. Because no matter how many heated moments they shared, how many times they laughed together or how long they talked, Sullivan blamed her for his brother's suicide. Plain and simple.

"I'm already having the files brought from your town house by another operative on my team," he said.

Pressure built behind her sternum. Sullivan might not use all of his training from his military days for Blackhawk Security, but from what she'd read of him, he never missed a clue. She cleared her throat, stuffing her hands into her sweatshirt pockets. "Good idea. I've already gone through most of them, but another set of eyes might uncover something I missed."

Jane's stomach growled again.

"You need to eat and rest before Elliot gets here with the files." Sullivan stood, his wide shoulders blocking her view of the living room and the fire popping and cracking in the fireplace. Muscles flexed across his chest and arms, and Jane swallowed the rush of saliva filling her mouth. "I don't come up here often so I'm sorry to say there's nothing more than a few MREs lying around, but there should be enough in the duffel bags we brought to last us three days." He searched the living room. "Where did you put the bags after I tried to kill myself out there? I'll make us something to eat."

Jane's responding smile to his willingness to feed her disappeared. Exhaling, she ran her hand through her hair. Crap. "I left them outside. I wasn't thinking after I pulled you in—"

"Don't worry about it." He stepped right into her, that massive chest of his brushing against her. Staring down at her, Sullivan bent at the knees to look her right in the eye, his hands posed above her arms as though he didn't dare touch her. And she didn't blame him. The difference in height between them was laughable, but she appreciated the even ground now. His hands rested around her upper arms. Her insides flipped as his body heat spread through her, but she didn't pull away. "You had your priorities straight. You saved my life. I'll get them. About how far did you drop them?"

Good. He'd just go get them. Her breathing eased the longer he kept his grip on her, but it took a few seconds to clear her head of his proximity enough to answer. "Beyond the tree line. I don't think it snowed enough to cover my tracks. You should be able to follow them to the bags."

"All right. And when I get back, we'll call Anchorage PD to have them put an APB out for that tow truck." He dropped his hold on her, spinning toward his discarded gear drying over the fireplace. A shiver rushed through her, but Jane held her ground as Sullivan donned his shoulder holster and thick coat. He reached under the built-in desk where the keyboard drawer clicked into place and removed a Glock, disengaged the magazine and pulled back the slide to check the chamber. He moved in quick, confident steps to reload the magazine and put a round in the chamber as though he'd done the same moves a thousand times before. Which he probably had. "I shouldn't be gone more than five minutes." He checked the batteries in the flashlight next. "If anything happens while I'm out there, use the burner phone to call the last number I dialed. It'll put you directly through to my guy Elliot. He's the closest right now, and he'll get here as fast as he can."

Jane nodded. He wouldn't be gone more than a few minutes, but she pointed toward the gun. "Do you have an extra one of those for me? Just in case." They'd already proved anything could happen. For crying out loud, a tow truck had blindsided them on purpose. She wasn't about to make it easier for this psychopath to get to her.

A smile lit up his features before he turned toward what she assumed was the only bedroom in the cabin. Mere seconds later, he handed her another Glock. "This is my service weapon from the SEALs and my favorite gun. If you have to shoot it outside for any reason, make sure there's no snow in the barrel and that you've warmed it up. Otherwise, it might blow up in your hands."

"I went through weapons training, too, remember? I know how to handle my guns in cold weather." Jane hit the button to disengage the magazine and pulled back the slide to clear the chamber, just as Sullivan had done with his own gun. Faster than she thought possible, the guarded curiosity in Sullivan's eyes changed to something dark, primal. She clenched her lower abdomen. Air stalled in her throat. She focused on the gun in her hand. "Besides, you won't be gone that long. I'm sure I can manage to take care of myself for five minutes."

"Of that—" he secured the Glock he'd taken from under the desk in his shoulder holster, eyes scanning her from head to toe "—I have no doubt." Sullivan disappeared out the door without looking back.

The goose bumps along her forearms receded the longer Jane stared after him. There was no denying it now. She'd seen the way he'd looked at her, the way he'd held on to her earlier. He wanted the intel she'd called in a few favors to get, the one with his real identity inside. Because there was no way that man wanted her for any other reason. No matter how deep he'd buried his past, she'd uncovered the truth and she'd known the second she confronted him with it, she would pay for using blackmail. What was he going to do? Torture her with desire until she gave him everything she had on him and his family?

Jane leaned against the countertop, Sullivan's service weapon comfortable in her grip. Now that she thought about it, torture by desire was one of the better ways to go. Especially with a six-foot-four, muscled, powerfully built SEAL. A smile pulled at her lips. Crap, she imagined that outcome between them all too easily. The heat, the explosion of passion, the—

The front door slammed open and her muscle memory hefted the gun up. She aimed, ready to pull the trigger. Adrenaline pumped fast through her veins as Sullivan swung his head around the thick, wooden door. Jane dropped the gun to her side, heart beating a mile a second. She could've shot him. "You scared me to death. Do you always barge into a room like that?"

Sullivan stomped his boots on the mat at the door, then headed straight for the burner phone on the kitchen counter. He brushed against her, but instead of heat penetrating through her jacket like before, she only felt cold. Something was wrong. Stabbing the pad of his thumb into the keypad, he brought the phone up to his ear, those sea-blue eyes glued on her. Darkness etched into his expression, and Jane took a step back to give him some space. "The bags are gone."

Chapter Four

The guns, extra ammunition, food, tracks, everything was gone. Looked like Jane's mysterious stalker had tracked her back here after all. The phone rang once in his ear before Elliot Dunham, his private investigator, picked up.

"Go for Dunham," Elliot said.

Sullivan checked his watch. "How far out are you?"

"Five minutes."

"Make it three. The bastard knows we're here."

"See you in two." The revving of a car engine echoed in the background before the line disconnected. As an operative on the Blackhawk Security team, Elliot would understand to come in hot—armed and ready for a fight. Sullivan had swiped the private investigator off the Iraqi streets right after Sullivan's discharge from the SEALs. The man had a knack for finding and recovering classified documents, digging into a person's life, discovering those secrets his target didn't want the world to know about. Like a pit bull with his favorite chew toy, Elliot never gave up and never surrendered. Most likely a side effect of his con artist days; each case a long con. With a genius-level IQ, he dug deep, he got personal. At least until the job was done. Then he disappeared to start fresh. It hadn't been difficult to recruit him either. Only a few phone calls that could put Elliot back into an Iraqi jail cell.

His next call was to Anchorage PD to report the tow truck that'd nearly rammed them into the Gulf of Alaska. A minute later, Sullivan tossed the phone onto the counter and rubbed at his face.

"Is Elliot bringing supplies?" Jane stared up at him, arms wrapped around her small midsection. Her shoulders hunched inward as though she felt the weight of someone watching her. Which Sullivan bet was familiar by now.

The same weight pressed in on him, too, but they only had to wait a few more minutes. Then they could get through her case files and find out who exactly had turned Jane into a target. After that, they'd come up with a plan. "I make every member of my team carry extra guns, ammo and food in case of emergency."

"Do you think whoever is after me is out there, right now, watching us?" Jane's voice trembled. She was scared. And rightfully so.

Whoever had taken their bags had wiped any evidence of their existence from the snow. There weren't a whole lot of men who possessed that kind of skill, Sullivan being one of the few. His father had ensured his sons knew how to hunt their prey properly, before the old man had turned into the sick psychopath he became known for. But right now, in this moment, Sullivan wasn't the hunter. He felt like the prey.

A soft ringing reached his ears, and Jane extracted her cell phone from her jacket pocket. Frowning, she put the phone to her ear. "Hello?"

He couldn't hear the response from this distance

and, while eavesdropping on his client's phone calls was technically part of the job, Sullivan wouldn't crowd her. *I needed you.* Those three small words had been circling his brain since they'd left her mouth.

"Who is this?" The color drained from Jane's features.

Sullivan's instincts prickled at the alarm in her voice. He stepped into her personal space, forcing her to meet his gaze, then reached for her phone. He hit the speaker button, holding the phone between them. "Who the hell is this?"

"He can't protect you, Jane," the voice whispered across the line. Her name on the bastard's lips tightened the muscles down Sullivan's spine. "You're going to pay for what you've done."

Memorizing the number on the screen, Sullivan gripped the phone tighter. He couldn't peg an accent due to the whispering, no dialect to pinpoint where her stalker originated from. "Come within three hundred feet of her and I will tear you apart. You tried to kill her once. Won't happen again. Understand?" His voice dropped low—deadly—as he studied the fear skating across Jane's features. "Don't call this number again."

He moved to hang up the call.

"Always the protector… *Sullivan*." Laughter trickled through the phone.

Sullivan's thumb froze over the end button. A shiver spread across his shoulders. The line went dead, only static and crackling from the fireplace filling the silence.

In a split second, one of the burner phones he kept on hand was at his ear, ringing through to Blackhawk Security's head of network security. The line picked up. "Elizabeth, trace this number." He recited the number he'd memorized from the call. "I want a location as soon as possible. Send it straight to the number I'm calling you from."

"You got it, boss," the former NSA analyst said.

He hung up. Sullivan's gaze lifted from the phone as Jane backed away. The terror etched into her expression urged him toward her. Without hesitation, he reached for her. "Jane…"

Eyes wide, mouth slack, she shut down her expression, and Sullivan dropped his hand. "He's here. He's *watching* me. He knows you're with me."

That had always been a possibility. Stalkers liked to keep tabs on their targets. The bastard had most likely been the one responsible for taking their gear, too. She'd known the risks going into this, but Sullivan wouldn't remind her of them now. In this moment, he needed her head on straight. Focused. "You hired me because I'm good at my job. He's never going to get close to you. You have my word."

"Thank you." Her chin notched higher. Jane shifted her weight onto her toes as though she intended to kiss him, and right then, all too easily, Sullivan imagined how it'd feel to claim that perfect mouth of hers. Would she taste as good as she smelled? Damn it. Why couldn't he keep himself in check around her?

Three knocks on the door ripped him back. The thick wood swung inward, and Sullivan shoved Jane behind him. Her fingers clenched the back of his shirt as he unholstered the Glock at his side. The man hunting Jane most likely wouldn't knock, but maybe there were polite stalkers out there in the world.

"And here I thought I'd get to shoot someone when I got here." Elliot Dunham's wide grin shifted the dark stubble across his jawline. The lines at the edges of his stormy gray eyes deepened. The private investigator holstered his own weapon underneath a thick cargo jacket and kicked the door closed behind him. "Good news for everyone. The perimeter is clear, and I won't get blood on my new shirt."

"We wouldn't want that. I'd have to hear about it all night." Sullivan couldn't help but smile as he clapped Elliot on the back. "Did you bring the files?"

"Got them in the truck along with extra munitions and snacks. But I have to be honest, I ate all the nuts on the way here. This place is in the middle of nowhere." Swiveling his head around Sullivan, Elliot caught sight of their new client. Jane. The con-man-turned-investigator sidestepped his boss, something close to intrigue smoothing out his features. "And you must be Jane. Your picture doesn't do you justice."

"You're kidding, right?" Jane asked. "*That's* your opening line?"

"Oh, I like her." Elliot's smile made another appearance.

Sullivan clamped a hand on his investigator's shoulder. Elliot had absolutely no interest in their new client, but something inside had tightened at the thought of another man coming anywhere near her with that look on his face. What did he care? He'd taken her on as a client, however forced. He didn't have any kind of claim on her. "How about you do your job and get me those files from the truck?"

"Sure thing, boss." Elliot half saluted Jane, then spun back toward the front door and disappeared.

A tri-chimed message tone brought the burner phone back into his hand. Sullivan read Elizabeth's message, then dropped the phone onto the hardwood and stomped on it. The screen cracked under his boots, pieces of plastic skating across the floor. "My team couldn't trace the number. We weren't on the line long enough to get a location."

"And you felt the need to take it out on your phone?" she asked.

"Can't be too careful." In reality, he'd been thinking ahead. If this case went south and the man hunting Jane expanded his crosshairs, Sullivan wouldn't leave any evidence behind that could lead to his team.

"So that's your private investigator." Not a question. Jane's arm brushed his as she passed him heading into the living room. A shot of awareness trailed up Sullivan's arm. He slapped a hand over the oversensitized skin, but she didn't notice. Head in the game. Standing in front of the fire, her bruises and cuts illuminated by the brilliant orange flames, Jane still held her head high. There was a target on her back, but she hadn't fallen apart. She didn't trust him with her emotions. Didn't seem to trust anyone.

"Elliot is the best private investigator in the country." He closed in on her one step at a time, giving in to the urge to have her nearby in case her stalker took a shot through the front windows. He'd already tried to kill her once. No telling what he'd do next. At least for now. "Used to be a con man. Elliot can read people. He has the resources to dig into their lives and a genius-level IQ to see three steps ahead. He'll find whoever's targeting you."

"What if he can't?" Turning toward him, Jane gave him an exhausted smile. Her shoulders sagged as though she'd collapse into a puddle on the floor. "I've been through those files a dozen times. I know them better than anyone, and I couldn't pick out any potential suspects." She massaged her temples with her fingers. "I just want my life back."

"Look at me." Sullivan closed the small space between them. He pushed every ounce of sincerity into his expression, his gaze, his voice, but didn't move to touch her this time. "I don't give my word lightly. You might've blackmailed me into it, but I promised to protect you, and I will." The small muscles in his jaw tightened. "We will figure this out."

She nodded. "I believe you."

"Good." Four hours ago, he'd tried kicking her out of his office. But now... They were in this together. He'd saved her life. She'd saved his. And he wouldn't let some nutjob with a sick obsession get close to her again. No matter how much he blamed her for Marrok's death. "You're dead on your feet. Why don't you go lie down in the bedroom? I'll wake you if we find a lead."

Jane nodded, her eyes brighter than a few moments ago. "I'll also expect that meal you promised when I come out."

A laugh rumbled through his chest as Sullivan watched her disappear into the bedroom. Flashes of those long legs peeking out from under his blanket skittered across his mind, and his gut warmed. He stared after her a few seconds longer, but the weight of being watched pressed between his shoulder blades. His neck heated. *Damn.* "How long have you been standing there?"

"Long enough to see you're going to break your own rule if you're not careful." Elliot dropped the box of Jane's case files and laptop onto the built-in desk and raised his hands in surrender. "Okay, now you look like you want to kill me."

No way was he going to talk about this with his private investigator. Or anybody. Ever. "What did you find when you went through the files?"

"I've narrowed it down to two possibilities within the army after you said the guy erased his tracks after taking off with your supplies. That takes a lot of skill, and not many of the people she has regular contact with have any kind of training like that." Elliot shoved the lid off the box and extracted three manila file folders. "Your girl took some damn fine notes on the cases she worked. Made my job easier."

His girl? Not even close. But Sullivan didn't correct his investigator. He took the files from Elliot and scanned over the extensive notes inside. Must've been Jane's handwriting. Precise, to the point. Nothing fancy. But the purple and pink Post-its stuck through the files surprised him. Just as her red toenail polish had. He scanned over the first file. "Staff Sergeant Marrok Warren."

Something sour swept across his tongue.

"Now, that guy is a piece of work. There's only one problem." Elliot leveraged his weight against the desk and crossed his arms over his chest. "Jane prosecuted him for sexual assault of three female enlisted soldiers, but—"

"He's dead." There it was. Stamped across Jane's case file in big red letters. *Deceased.* Sullivan's ears rang. He discarded the file back into the box, his body strung as tight as a tension spring. His brother might've had the skills to pull off blindsiding them in the SUV and taking their supplies without leaving behind a trace, but it wasn't possible. Marrok Warren was dead. Sullivan had buried him ten months ago almost to the day.

"That would be the problem. I tied him to Jane's case because of the guy's father." Elliot pulled a bag of peanuts from his jacket pocket. "Ever heard of the Anchorage Lumberjack? Killed twelve victims, all with an ax. With Staff Sergeant Warren dead, could be a close family member coming after Jane now, maybe one of those psychopathic groupies I'm always hearing about. Wonder what they're like…"

Sullivan crumpled the files in his hand, the tendons in his neck straining. He locked his attention on Elliot, then took a deep breath, forcing himself to relax. "Who else do you have?"

"We've got her commanding officer." His private investigator nodded toward the second file in Sullivan's hand, ignoring the obvious tension that'd filled the room. "Major Patrick Barnes is Jane's CO. He'd know her daily schedule, her routine, and have access to all of her files. He would know her whereabouts while on tour, and he's the one who grants permission for her to go on leave."

"It's not Major Barnes," a familiar voice said.

Twisting around, Sullivan locked on to Jane, the grip around his rib cage lightening at the sight of her. As long as she was in his sights, she was safe. He tossed the files onto the desk. "You should be resting."

"Couldn't wind down. Besides, this is my case. I should be helping." Jane shoved off from against the doorjamb and sauntered forward. Reaching for Major Barnes's file, she scanned through the pages, her proximity setting Sullivan's nerve endings on high alert.

She tossed the file on top of Marrok Warren's and crossed her arms over her chest. "I owe Barnes my life. He tackled me to the ground after an IED exploded in the parking lot outside my office in Afghanistan two months ago. He wouldn't have done that just to turn around and come after me himself. And he has no motive."

"All right. Then we take a tour of your life outside the army. The only other name that stands out to me is Christopher Menas." Elliot handed the file to Jane, but shifted his gaze to Sullivan before settling back against the desk. Hesitant? "He's won a few hunting awards, but that's about all I know aside from his criminal record. I can't find any employment records, no college degree, no military record, nothing that says he's changed his name, or a death certificate attached to this guy. Menas simply dropped off the grid after skipping bail, but you two had a complicated past and that's why I'm pinning him as a suspect."

"I can't believe this." She stared at the name on the edge of the folder, her eyes panicked and wide. She slipped her index finger between the yellow card stock but didn't move to open the file. "I haven't thought about Christopher in years."

"Jane?" Warning bells rang in Sullivan's head as he closed in on her. "What are you thinking?"

Tearing her attention from the folder, Jane lifted her gaze to his. "It's him. He's the one doing this to me."

CHRISTOPHER MENAS.

Flashes of his face, of those cold brown eyes and dark skin, lit up the back of her eyelids. Jane bolted upright off the bed, out of breath, surrounded by pure darkness. She'd been in love—outright smitten—with the quarterback of the University of Washington Huskies football team. And it'd all been a lie.

She couldn't see anything with the bedroom door shut, but her instincts screamed she wasn't alone. The silhouette of a man shifted in her peripheral vision. She slipped her hand under her pillow, curling her fingers around the gun Sullivan had lent her when she'd gone to bed.

"I'm not armed." A chair creaked to her left before the mattress dipped with added weight. Her hand relaxed from around the Glock. Sullivan. The light on the nightstand flickered to life, bathing his stern features in warmth. "Tell me about Christopher Menas."

"What?" She squinted into the brightness. "What time is it?"

"Just before dawn. You were talking in your sleep earlier. About Christopher Menas." Every muscle in her body tightened at that name. Sullivan's voice remained soft, coaxing. "I read the police report on him. He sexually assaulted two women while you two were dating. Your roommates, right? Right before he came after you."

A shiver chased up her spine. How could this be happening again? She'd moved on with her life, joined the army, made something of herself. She'd left that part of her life—left Christopher and everything that reminded her of him—behind.

"Is that why you went after my brother so aggressively? To make Marrok pay because your college boyfriend got away with his crimes?" Sullivan stared at her, stone-like. The muscles in his jawline flexed as though he was grinding his back molars, but Jane still forced herself to meet his gaze.

"Are you really accusing me of corruption, or is this because I prosecuted your brother for sexual assault?" She regretted the words the second they left her mouth. Clenching the sheets, she steadied her nerves. No. This was his job; this was why she'd blackmailed him in the first place. He got the job done, no matter what it took. And if Christopher was the man behind this, she'd make sure her ex paid this time. With Sullivan's help. "I'll tell you anything you need to know about Christopher, but believe me when I say this has nothing to do with you or your brother."

"How can I trust you?" Sullivan's calm, collected exterior broke around his eyes and mouth. "You charged my brother with these exact same crimes, which led to Marrok committing suicide. You're blackmailing me into helping you now. And you purposefully left out a credible lead."

What? "I never—"

"You told me you didn't have any ex-boyfriends who would hold a grudge against you. You're the one who turned Menas over to the police all those years ago. You knew he'd skipped bail. All this time you didn't think he was the one who might be after you?" Standing, Sullivan ran his hands through his hair. Shadows threw his features into sharper angles and brought out the darkness he'd kept under control up until now. "Damn it, Jane. I could've gotten people on him the second we left my office and none of this would've happened."

"How do you know it's him stalking me or he's the one who ran us off the road? You said it yourself, whoever took the bags didn't leave any evidence, and you never got a look at the driver." Jane threw her legs over the edge of the bed and stood, thankful she'd chosen warmer attire tonight rather than her usual T-shirt and panties. None of this made sense. Why would her ex-boyfriend come after her now? That was a lifetime ago. The statute of limitations had run out on his charges and he'd never gone to prison. What could he possibly hold against her now?

"Weren't you the one who said, 'It's him. He's the one doing this to me,' out there?" Dropping his hands, Sullivan faced her head-on, body still tense.

She didn't know how to respond. The idea of Christopher coming back into her life after all this time...

"Anchorage PD recovered the vehicle. The tow truck that blindsided us was recovered from behind a gas station just inside town." Sullivan pulled a hand through his short hair. "My forensics guy has been working with Anchorage PD. They've confirmed the black paint on the fender is from my SUV. Jane, the registration is filed under Christopher Menas's name."

The air in her throat froze. They had a lead, proof. Christopher had come to Anchorage. For her. Locking her teeth together, Jane tugged her sweatshirt off the edge of the bed, then shoved her feet into her boots. She'd gone into the army because of her ex, learned to protect herself against men like him. But no more running. Christopher wanted revenge? He was going to have to work for it. Heading for the door, she gave into the sudden rush of determination pumping through her. "Then what are we waiting for? Let's go."

"Go where?" he asked.

Wasn't this man a SEAL, trained to think two

steps ahead of everybody else to get the upper hand in any situation? "To Christopher's. He must have a safe house, a hotel room or an apartment—something around here if he's stalking me, right?"

"We can't go barging into the man's private residence, Jane." Sullivan shot to his feet and wrapped his hand around her arm, but she wrenched away. He seemed to be doing a lot of that in the last twenty-four hours, touching her, but now wasn't the time to analyze the contact. Despite the fact he'd accused her of corruption, they had a stalker to find. "We're not the police. We don't have a warrant. The best thing we can do is put surveillance on him for the next couple days. Then we can go from there."

On any other case, she'd agree. She'd taken an oath as a lawyer. She was supposed to play by the book, but this case had turned more personal than she'd imagined. "I don't have a couple of days. I need my life back *now*." Throwing the door open, she stalked straight toward Elliot, who was asleep on the couch. "I need your car keys."

Elliot's feet lifted off the couch as he dropped his arms away from his forehead. A yawn twisted his features as he rubbed sleep from his eyes. "Well, good morning to you, too."

"Keys." Jane extended her hand. "Please."

"I take it you told her about the tow truck," Elliot said to Sullivan over her shoulder. He sat up, digging into his jacket pocket before dangling the car keys in front of her. "Have a nice field trip, sweetheart. Call me if you need me."

She swiped the keys from his hand.

"If we're going—" Sullivan fisted both his hands in

Elliot's jacket and hefted him from the couch "—then you're coming, too."

"We don't have much time. Christopher is smart. He probably left that truck there for us to trace back to him, but I doubt he's going to stick around and risk arrest." Jane took a deep breath to clear her head and handed the keys back to Elliot. A rush of cold air slammed against her as they stepped back into the freezing Alaskan wilderness. It took a few seconds for her lungs to catch up with the change in temperature, but she refused to slow down. They had to catch Christopher by surprise, but the sun would be up soon and they'd lose their cover of night.

Once they were all within the safety of the truck, Elliot put the shifter into Reverse but didn't move. "What exactly is our plan here?"

"You're a private investigator. I assume you already know where Christopher is hiding." Jane buckled herself into the back seat. "I want to surprise him and get some answers. That's the plan for right now."

"And if he's armed?" Sullivan turned around, his gaze glued to her.

"Isn't that why I hired you?" Throwing his own words back in his face wouldn't smooth the tension between them, but Jane still couldn't believe he'd implied she'd had anything personal against his brother during the court-martial. Sure, Marrok's charges were nearly identical to Christopher Menas's, but she'd always strived for compartmentalization and professionalism when prosecuting a case. She couldn't practice law if her emotions got the best of her. Hence that damn nickname. No emotion. No attachment. Jane cringed inwardly and crossed her arms over her chest as they pulled away from the cabin. But that wasn't her. Not anymore.

The truck barreled through the snow as they headed back toward Anchorage without signs of an ambush, but Jane still kept an eye out for any rogue tow trucks waiting for them at signals through town. According to Elliot's research, Christopher Menas had been renting an apartment near Taku Lake. Within twenty minutes, the private investigator parked the pickup two blocks from their destination.

The apartment complex wasn't anything special— two levels, blond-wood balconies with white stucco on the sides. Trees and shrubs gave the complex a lighter feel, but as Jane stepped onto the pavement, a ball of dread fisted at the base of her spine.

"He's in apartment 310." Sullivan stayed on her tail as she headed down the street and for the third building to her right. Dressed for warmer temperatures, he showed off long lengths of muscle down his arms, and the flood of apprehension gripping her disappeared. "May I remind you this isn't a good idea? We have no idea what's waiting for us on the other side of that door."

Right then, she didn't care. "I'm putting an end to this. For good."

Screeching metal filled Jane's ears as Elliot extracted a long steel tube from the bed of his truck. Both Sullivan and Jane spun, staring at him. "What?" He hefted the small battering ram over his shoulder. "It's in case we want to commit a felony."

The breath she'd been holding rushed from her. She couldn't believe any of this. She hadn't thought of Christopher Menas in years. But here she was, climbing up the steps to her ex-boyfriend's apartment to find out why he was trying to kill her.

Sullivan maneuvered in front of her, using his body to shield her from the door. Her throat tightened as his fingers smoothed over her jacket. He couldn't have meant what he'd said back at the cabin, could he? After everything they'd been through the last twenty-four hours, he couldn't think so low of her. She'd saved his life. Didn't that count for something? Pounding on the door, Sullivan stepped back and pulled his weapon. As did Elliot with his free hand.

No answer. No sounds of movement inside.

It was barely sunrise. Surely her stalker could have had the decency to be home when she came to confront him.

Sullivan pounded his fist against the wood again. Nothing. "Are you sure you want to do this?" He nodded toward Menas's front door. "We can still go back, come at this from another angle."

Go back? She couldn't go back. She couldn't walk away now. Jane swallowed the hesitation screaming at the back of her mind. "I'm sure."

"All right. Breaking and entering it is, Counselor. Just promise not to charge us, since you're the one giving the orders." He stepped aside, ushering Elliot forward. "Have at it."

"Once we're in, be sure not to touch anything. Someone's about to call the police." Elliot slammed the head of the battering ram into the thick wood, and the door frame splintered. He hit it a second time, buckling the hinges, and within a minute, they were inside.

"Let's go. We don't have long before the police or a curious neighbor show up." Sullivan stepped inside first, Glock in his hand, body tense. Like the good security consultant she'd blackmailed him to be.

Jane's insides clenched as she followed close behind him. Whether it was from their conversation back in the bedroom or the situation, she couldn't tell. She hadn't seen Christopher Menas in nearly a decade.

Sullivan flipped on the lights with his elbow, and Jane leveraged her weight against one wall to clear her head. The inside of the apartment was…normal. No foul-smelling decaying bodies, no bloodstained carpets. The two-bedroom apartment had been decorated in a Southwestern theme—where Christopher was from—and looked like it'd been that way for a while. No quick getaway for him. Their suspect intended to stick around.

"Are you sure we have the right information?" Jane smoothed the hem of her coat sleeve over the back of the black leather couch. "This place doesn't exactly scream psychopath."

Searching the kitchen, Sullivan used a napkin to open drawers, go through receipts and sift through photos. He held up a business card for her to see, as Elliot checked out the back bedrooms. "We're in the right place."

She took the card from him, not entirely stable on her own two feet. "Menas Towing. Why didn't that show up in Elliot's research?" Jane scanned the rest of the apartment, taking anything—everything—in. There had to be something here that pointed to Jane as a target. According to the profilers she'd worked with on dozens of cases for the army, stalkers usually kept mementos of their victims. Trophies. But from what Jane could see, they'd made a mistake. There was nothing here. So if Christopher wasn't her stalker, then who was? The only evidence they had to go on was the tow truck registered in his name. "Who would be stupid enough to hit us with their own truck?"

"Nobody." Sullivan locked those mesmerizing eyes on her for the first time since accusing her of corruption. Her heart rate skyrocketed when he looked at her like that, like a puzzle he needed to solve. "Unless we're supposed to be here. What about the voice on the call? Did it sound like Menas?"

"I couldn't tell from the way he was whispering. And it's been so long since I've talked to him, I'm not sure I could identify it as his anyway." She ran through Sullivan's words a second time and half turned toward him. "Do you think somebody is setting Christopher up?"

"Not likely." Elliot stepped back into the main room and hitched a thumb over his shoulder. "You need to see this."

"What did you find?" Jane sprinted after the private investigator, heart in her throat. Had he found the evidence? Found Christopher? The hallway passed in a blur as she hurried after Elliot toward the back bedroom. She halted at the door frame. Her jaw slackened. She couldn't breathe. The world tilted on an axis, but she managed to stay upright.

"What the hell?" Sullivan's words echoed her own thoughts as he brushed past her and moved into the room.

Jane shook her head, clinging to the door frame with everything she had. "I don't think we're in the wrong place anymore."

Chapter Five

No matter where he turned, Jane was there.

"There has to be hundreds of photos of me here." Jane's voice shook as she stepped up to one wall.

Something deep in his chest urged him to reach out for her, but Sullivan stood his ground. This wasn't the time. There were more photos than the one on Jane's phone of her sleeping. These showed her eating. In court. Right outside her home. His insides raged as he scanned over the closest wall a second time. In the shower. From the look of it, the past three months of her life had been documented in pictures taped to four plain white walls. Rage burned hot under his sternum. The sick freak had stolen precious moments from her life—too many to count—and Jane would never get them back.

She slid her fingertips over a handful of photos, seeming not to even breathe.

And he couldn't take staying away any longer. Sullivan took a step toward her, hand outstretched. "Jane—"

"This is my life. He…" Her lips parted on a strong inhale. She dropped her hand, turning toward him, and he froze. Swallowing, Jane covered her mouth. She rushed past him, her vanilla scent thick on the air. "I think I'm going to be sick."

She fled the room. A few seconds later, a door slammed down the hallway and he shut his eyes against the onslaught of surveillance her stalker had collected. One inhale. Two. The protector buried deep inside of him clawed its way to the surface for a breath of fresh air. Christopher Menas was a dead man. Whatever game the bastard had going on with Jane was over. Sullivan was coming for him. Opening his eyes, he spun toward the hallway. "Elliot, document everything. We're leaving."

He had to get Jane out of here. The police were most likely on their way from when Elliot had brought down the door. She couldn't get wrapped up in their investigation. The second the report went live, the army would limit her security clearance and she'd be at risk of losing her job. Stalking down the hall toward the bathroom, gun in hand, he listened for signs of movement. He was sure their suspect wasn't in the apartment, but a man who could cover his tracks in the Alaskan wilderness had to have a few more tricks up his sleeves. And Sullivan wasn't about to make a mistake on this case. Not with Jane's life on the line.

With three light taps on the bathroom door, he leaned against the wood. "Jane?"

No answer.

His heartbeat rocketed into his throat. He squeezed his free hand around the door handle, but didn't move to open it. Yet. Fanning his grip over the Glock, he scanned down the hallway. "Are you okay?"

Still nothing.

"All right." Backing up, Sullivan cradled the gun in

both hands, prepared to kick in the door if he had to, to get to her. "I'm coming in."

The door swung open on silent hinges, and the torn woman in front of him hurried to swipe salty streaks of tears from her face with the back of her hand. In a split second, she locked her emotions away as though she hadn't fallen apart out of his sight. "I'm fine. I just needed a minute."

"You don't have to hide from me, Jane." His throat tightened, but he released his suffocating grip on the gun. Every cell in his body urged him to stand as a pillar of comfort for her, and he straightened. Forget the past. Forget the rules for a few seconds. Jane was falling apart and it was his job to hold his client's life together. Even if she'd blackmailed him into it. Closing in on her slowly, he brushed a stray tear from her face, careful to leave space for her to escape if she wanted. Hesitation shot down his arms and into his chest, but this time he didn't pull away. Didn't feel the need. Those hazel eyes closed as she leaned into him for support, and he set his chin onto the crown of her head. Her short black hair tumbled forward against his chest and his fingers tingled with the urge to shove it behind her ear so she'd look up at him. "I'm sorry you had to see all of that. You don't deserve this."

For the first time since Jane had broken into his office last night, he meant every word. Her body heat tunneled through his jacket, sinking into his muscles, his bones. The tension throughout his body relaxed second by second. All Sullivan could think about in this moment was taking her back to the cabin and shielding her from what was to come. Men willing to kill the object of their obsessions didn't give up easily. But she couldn't run. Not from this.

Sullivan inhaled deep. He smelled…smoke.

"Do you smell that?" Jane pulled back.

"Elliot." Panic wrapped a tight fist around his heart. Clamping his hand around hers, Sullivan tugged Jane after him down the hallway. After discovering Menas's sick collection, he wasn't about to let her out of his sight. Black smoke escaped out from under the second bedroom door. Had he closed it behind him? He dropped his hold on her and kicked in the door. Bright flames climbed up the walls where Jane's photos used to hang. Covering his face and eyes in the crook of his arm, Sullivan avoided the majority of the smoke but couldn't see anything worth a damn. There was too much smoke. Too many flames. "Elliot!"

"Sullivan, there!" Jane latched onto his arm, pointing to one corner of the room. Without waiting for him, she launched herself through the flames consuming the door frame.

"Jane, no!" He grabbed after her but missed her jacket by mere centimeters. She couldn't pull Elliot out of there on her own. Not with flames consuming the walls on every side. The roar of the fire drowned out any sounds of Jane or his private investigator. Lunging into the heart of the fire, he kept low, searching for her, searching for Elliot. "Jane!"

"Over here." A cough led him toward the back of the room. The crackling of the flames nearly drowned out her voice, but he homed in on the uncontrollable coughing coming from his right.

"Jane." Within seconds, he'd wrapped his hands around her arms and shoved her back toward the bedroom door. He covered his mouth and nose with the crook of his arm as smoke worked into his lungs. Squinting from the heat, he fought to see the door. "Get out of here. Get outside."

She'd found Elliot knocked out near the west wall. Hiking his private investigator over his shoulder, Sullivan narrowly avoided a falling rafter as he wound through debris and flames.

Outside, he breathed in as much clean air as his lungs allowed, nearly collapsing as his muscles weakened from oxygen depletion. Jane ran forward, eyes wide, hands outstretched to catch them both. The three of them fell in a pile of limbs and heavy breathing as sirens filled the night. In less than seven minutes, fire crews sprinted to put out the blaze. Staring up at the damage, Sullivan noted the entire building had caught fire.

"How many—" His lungs worked overtime to expel the smoke he'd inhaled. He didn't want to think about the casualties. There was no way the fire had been a coincidence. Christopher Menas had known they were there. The fire had most likely been set to destroy the evidence he'd left behind. Maybe to hurt them, to hurt Jane.

"I got them all out." Jane cradled Elliot's head in her lap, her palms on both sides of his slackened jaw. "When you pushed me out the door, I pulled the fire alarm."

Streaks of soot lined her jaw and forehead, enhancing the bruises and scrapes from the car accident, but Jane had never been more beautiful than right in this moment. She'd charged into that bedroom to save one of his men's lives. And ended up saving many others in the building. What was it about the woman he blamed that compelled her to keep saving lives?

A nasty gash bled freely from the right side of Elliot's head. Knocked unconscious. Damn it. They'd walked straight into Menas's trap.

Sullivan shook his head. He couldn't breathe. Couldn't think. Until he saw the blood streaking down Jane's cargo jacket. Reaching across Elliot's unconscious body for her, he inspected the wound. "Are you okay?"

"Nothing a few stitches won't fix." She twisted her arm so she could see it better. "I'm kind of sad about this jacket, though. It's my favorite."

Squealing tires and red and blue lights claimed his attention. He tightened his hold on Jane, unwilling to let her out of his sight yet. But that gash wouldn't stitch itself.

EMTs rushed to their side, hefting Elliot onto a stretcher and prying his eyes open. But not before Sullivan lifted Elliot's phone from his private investigator's jacket pocket. Elliot had documented Christopher Menas's collection in that bedroom, and the cops weren't about to stick it in some evidence room before Sullivan could review the photos. Evidence tampering be damned.

Elliot was in good hands. Sullivan's instincts said Menas wouldn't come after him. But Jane? That was another story. They couldn't stay here. Menas had been watching them. Could still be watching them. "Are you okay to move?"

"Would you throw me over your shoulder like you did with Elliot if I said no?" Lean muscle flexed down the backs of her thighs as she stood, and Sullivan fought a smile. "I'm fine. Really. And I'm glad those pictures didn't survive."

"You went in that bedroom for Elliot. Looks like I just might owe you again." Freezing gusts of wind beat against him on one side as he hiked himself to his feet, blistering heat from the burning apartment on the other. EMTs closed in on them, two leading Jane to an ambulance and another swinging a light in front of his face. He shoved the technician away. He was fine. Minor case of smoke inhalation. Nothing Sullivan hadn't lived through before. His breath sawed in and out of him as bright orange flames licked up the side of the apartment building.

They could've died in there.

Two Anchorage police units rolled up as Sullivan messaged his team from Elliot's phone. Keeping Jane in his peripheral vision as medics looked her over on the back of the ambulance, he headed toward the officers to give his statement. While Anchorage PD would run their own investigation, he had no intention of leaving Jane's case in their hands. They'd already failed to take her claim seriously. He had far more resources to bring this particular arsonist down.

Within five minutes, another Blackhawk Security SUV pulled into the scene. Sullivan caught sight of his weapons expert as the six-foot-five-inch wall of solid, sunglass-loving muscle stepped out onto the pavement. Anthony Harris surveyed the scene from behind his favorite pair of sunglasses, chest wide, fingers relaxed at his side. The thick beard covering the former Ranger's jawline hid his expression, but Sullivan sensed he was calculating the chances of another attack and where it'd come from. Always ready for the fight, always on alert. That was what made Anthony one of the best men on the Blackhawk Security team. "Need a ride?"

"Jane." Sullivan pushed through the EMTs blocking his path to her and offered her his hand. "We're leaving." Her long fingers slid across his palm without hesitation, and he pulled her to her feet. They had to get her off the street. Most stalkers willing to take out their targets in daylight—in public—loved watching the aftermath of their work. She wasn't safe here, even with three EMTs and two Anchorage PD officers. But his team could protect her. *He* could protect her. "I've got you."

He wasn't sure where the words had come from, but Jane nodded once, setting his racing heart at ease. Hand wrapped tight around hers, he headed toward Anthony and the safety of the SUV. She'd been through hell—again—and he fought the urge to wrap her in his arms. Holding her back in that apartment, just before it'd burned to the ground, had comforted him as much as it had her. He'd overstepped the boundaries he'd set between them. Didn't seem as important then as it did now. Jane. She'd been all that'd mattered.

Shoving her into the back of the SUV, Sullivan climbed in after her. "Go," he ordered Anthony, and the SUV spun around before he shut the door.

"Where are we going? Christopher knew the tow truck would be recovered, and that we would come here." Voice soft, Jane swept her gaze across the back window, knuckles white from her grip on the edge of her seat. "He was waiting for us."

"We're going on lockdown. I've already called in the rest of my team to meet us." Sullivan studied the rooftops as they sped through downtown. Water kicked up along the side of the SUV, but he forced himself to keep his senses on the possible threat rather than the smell of smoke coming off her skin. Unholstering the Glock at his side, he cleared the chamber and loaded another round. Just in case. "Look on the bright side. You didn't have to drag anyone out of that building."

Jane's resulting laugh dissolved the knot of tightness behind his sternum, and it became easier to breathe. His smile vanished. This wasn't right. He shouldn't be trying to make her laugh, to help her cope with the situation. Shouldn't want to hike her into his side like he had some kind of claim.

"We're here." Anthony swung the SUV into Blackhawk Security's parking garage. The gate locked down behind them the second the bumper cleared. Four other vehicles had been parked close to the elevator doors. The rest of the team had already arrived and were waiting for orders. Good. The sooner he wrapped up Jane's case, the better. He might've led some of the blackest operations the US government had ever ordered during his time as a SEAL, but Sullivan only had so much control when it came to the woman determined to surprise him at every turn.

"Stay behind me. Use my body as a shield." He locked his gaze on those beautiful hazel eyes before Jane could climb out of the SUV. "If you feel threatened in any way, run for the emergency exit next to the garage door and don't look back."

"Okay." Her hair hid one side of her face. His fingers itched to put it back where it belonged. But he wouldn't. No matter how many times he'd thought of touching her, getting mixed up with a client—with *her*—only complicated the situation. He wasn't about to take that chance. For her own safety and his brother's memory, he couldn't do it. "What about you?"

Sullivan cleared his head. *Keep her safe. Eliminate the threat. Nothing more.* "Don't worry about me. I can take care of myself."

"As you clearly showed on the way to your cabin." A smile brightened her features.

"I knew you were going to throw that almost dying thing back in my face," he said.

Her smile disappeared. She shot her hand out to rest on his arm before he could climb from the SUV. Sullivan sat paralyzed, hypnotized, as an uncontrollable rush of desire raced up his arm. Despite their past, he was beginning to like it when she touched him. Too much. "Promise me something before we get out of the car."

One hand on the door handle, the other on his weapon, Sullivan narrowed his eyes. "Anything."

He meant it, but he swallowed hard. What was coming his way?

"As a lawyer, I took an oath to uphold the law. Promise me we're going to bring this guy to justice." Determination unlike Sullivan had ever seen sharpened her jawline, and a chill swept down his spine. "Legally."

"That is the one thing I can't promise, Jane." He stepped out onto the pavement. He controlled *his* actions. God-given agency prevented him from doing that for someone else. So whether or not Christopher Menas saw the inside of a jail cell rather than the inside of a coffin was up to him. Not Sullivan.

He took point, with Jane close on his heels and Anthony taking up the rear. They moved as one toward the elevator doors, the only way into the main building from the garage. Blackhawk Security was one of the most protected buildings in the world. Then again, Jane had walked right into his office last night without setting off the alarms.

Which begged the question, how had a JAG Corps prosecutor gotten past his security? And how had she uncovered his true identity to blackmail him in the first place?

SOMETIMES MEMORIES WERE the worst form of torture.

Jane dropped her head against her palm and brought her knees into her chest while she sat on the couch outside Blackhawk Security's main conference room. Sullivan's team had been holed up in there for two hours now. Coming up with a plan. She had wanted to be part of the meeting, but Sullivan wouldn't budge—Blackhawk agents only.

She closed her eyes against the flashes of all those photos on Christopher Menas's wall, photos he'd taken of *her*.

Her stomach rolled. Exhaustion tore at her from the inside, her clothes smelled of smoke and she hadn't eaten in over twenty-four hours. How much more before the nightmare ended? She wanted her life back.

Raised voices—male voices—penetrated through the glass doors. Jane studied movements between the closed blinds just as the door to the conference room swung open. She straightened.

A thin woman with long blond hair and stiletto heels threw her a sad smile as she sauntered down the hallway in her pencil skirt. She carried files with her, but hollowness in the woman's cheeks and the dark circles under her eyes kept Jane from asking if the files pertained to her case. Grief, thick and strong, clung to the woman, and Jane wouldn't stop her in the middle of her escape.

A handful of Sullivan's team trickled past the door frame and down the hall. She'd met Anthony, the tall, silent statue of muscle who wouldn't spare her a glimpse from behind those dark sunglasses of his, but the others weren't familiar. Another woman, this one with shoulder-length brown hair and a strong jawline, kept her head down in her own files as she followed the blonde. Had to be Elizabeth, the NSA analyst Sullivan had called to trace the call to Jane's cell phone. The lone man left behind—muscular, handsome with wild brown hair and tan skin—headed straight toward her.

Sullivan trailed the group out of the conference room, staring at her as she stood. "Jane, this is Vincent Kalani, our forensics expert."

"Nice to finally meet you." His Hawaiian accent surrounded her in a trusting vice as Vincent offered his hand. The peacoat he kept drawn up around his neck attempted to cover the dark tattoos flowing artistically down his neck but failed. Deep lines creased his forehead as he studied her from head to toe. Not sexually, but almost as though he'd been waiting for this moment between them for a long time. "I feel like I know you already."

"Oh?" Jane took his hand. Rough. Worn around the edges. Just like his dark brown eyes. Dropping his grip, she crossed her arms over her midsection. Something about Sullivan's forensics expert raised her defenses. Like he really did know her…and all of her secrets.

"Vincent is the one I sent to your town house to collect evidence your stalker had left behind after breaking in. He worked for the NYPD, so he's familiar with cases like yours." Sullivan maneuvered to her side, his hand planting on her lower back, and she couldn't help the tiny flood of comfort from his touch. "Tell her what you found."

"Aside from the fact you hide massive amounts of chocolate-chip cookie dough in a drawer at the back of your fridge," Vincent said, straight-faced, "nothing."

"What?" Jane uncrossed her arms. Pressure built behind her sternum the longer the forensics expert refused to elaborate. "What do you mean 'nothing'? He was in my house. I have the proof on my phone—"

"Everything in your home has been wiped clean." Handing her a manila file folder, he nodded toward it. "No fingerprints. No hairs. Nothing in your carpets left from shoes. No fibers left around." Vincent shifted his weight as she read the file, lowering his voice. "Not even yours."

"That's not possible." She snapped her head up. Checking the address at the top of Vincent's report, she closed the file. Her gut instincts kicked into overdrive. She didn't have to read the rest of the report to figure out where this was going. It was written all over the forensics expert's face, in the way he'd held her hand a little too tightly a few moments ago, in the way he studied her now, looking for a crack in her expression. She was a lawyer. She'd attended her fair share of interrogations over the years. Pointing the report toward Vincent, she leveled her gaze with his. "You think I'm hiding something."

Not a question. She'd heard part of an argument from outside the conference room while the Black-hawk Security team deliberated what to do about her next. Her grip tightened on the folder, and she slid her attention to Sullivan. Did he trust her? Or Vincent? "And you? I assume you read the report. After everything we've been through the past day and a half, the accident, the fire, what do you think?"

"I can't forget you kept Christopher Menas's name from us." Arms crossed over his chest, stance wide, Sullivan's expression turned defensive. He exhaled hard, but refused to look at her, attention on Vincent's report. "I have to look at every possibility and, as of right now, we don't have the evidence to confirm Christopher Menas is after you. Both the tow truck and the photos could've been used to frame him." His eyes shifted to Vincent. "This could be someone's way to get back at Menas for skipping his sentencing and not paying for what he did ten years ago."

Not someone. Her. An invisible knife twisted in her stomach. Jane held her ground, but she wasn't sure how much longer she could stand there. She rolled her fingers into the center of her palm to keep the betrayal working up her throat at bay. "I see. So I hired someone to T-bone us in that intersection, putting my life at risk, took all those photos of myself and hung them in his apartment, then set the fire while you and Elliot weren't looking?"

"You're a smart woman, Ms. Reise," Vincent said. "Top of your class at University of Washington School of Law, instant promotion during your enlistment. It's not difficult to imagine a scenario where you might want revenge on a man who ran from his crimes." He took a single step toward her, most likely trying to intimidate her with his six-foot-plus frame, but it wouldn't work. She was the Full Metal Bitch. Her gaze flickered to Sullivan, and Jane's insides froze. It wouldn't work. "Is that why you came to Blackhawk Security?"

"It's *Captain* Reise." Jane notched her chin higher, her voice more confident than she felt inside. "And I have no idea what you're talking about. I already told Sullivan why I came to him. He has the skills to catch whoever is doing this to me."

"See, now, I think it's more than that." Vincent shoved his hands into his coat. "As Sullivan has just informed us, you were the lead prosecutor on Marrok Warren's case. You hated the fact Sullivan blamed you for his brother's death, and now you're here to make it look like you're the victim. Or is it a coincidence you moved to Anchorage shortly after Sullivan was discharged from the navy?"

Her jaw wobbled, but Jane clamped it tight. This wasn't about Marrok. This wasn't about her and Sullivan. This was about survival. Turning to Sullivan, Jane pushed every ounce of strength she had left into her voice and stared straight into those sea-blue-colored eyes, the eyes she'd started to trust. Foolishly.

"If blaming victims is how you insist on running your security firm, then I made a mistake in relying on you for help." Jane headed for the elevators down the hall, but stopped alongside a fake ficus tree and turned her attention over her shoulder. "Run my phone records, check my email or get my financials. Do whatever you have to do. Do it and then call me when you figure out who's trying to kill me."

Sullivan's eyes widened a split second before she turned, forcing her feet to slow as she headed toward the elevators. He followed after her. "Where are you going?"

"I'm not standing around here waiting for whoever is after me to find me again. I haven't slept or eaten in over a day." She punched the button for the elevator to take her to the main floor but refused to look back at him. Instead, she watched the red LED lights shift into different numbers and focused on keeping her eyes dry. "I'm going home. Don't follow me."

Chapter Six

Jane wasn't responsible for any of this.

He'd known the second she'd given his team permission to run phone records and financials, and to sift through her laptop. Vincent had pushed too hard, but questioning her motives had been the only way to clear Jane's name from the suspect list. There'd been too many coincidences so far in this case and too many ways it'd gone south. How had Menas known to wait for them at that light? How had he found them at the cabin? And how the hell had he gotten the upper hand on them at the apartment?

A short growl resonated deep in his chest as Sullivan pounded his fist into the door three times, his face square in the peephole's focus. Interrogating Jane had been the last thing on his mind when he'd stepped into that conference room, and he'd made that perfectly clear to his team. But the evidence—or lack thereof—spoke volumes. They were dealing with a professional.

The door ripped open. And time froze. Damn, she was a sight for sore eyes.

"I thought I told you not to follow me." Jane leaned against the door, showing off her lean, athletic shape and a hint of skin from under her T-shirt, which she realized and straightened.

"Can I come in?" His insides vibrated with the need to touch her, to ensure he hadn't broken the trust they'd forged over the last couple days, however ridiculous that sounded.

"Let me guess." She crossed her arms over her chest, accentuating the fact she wasn't wearing a bra, but didn't move to let him past the door. "You're here to tell me you uncovered something else that points to me framing Christopher Menas so I can have my own sick revenge."

"I'm sorry about before." And Sullivan meant it. "You've officially been taken off our suspect list. It won't happen again."

Nodding once, Jane moved aside to let him in.

Mentally punching himself in the face, he pushed past her and scanned the town house for signs of forced entry. A window, the back French doors, anything. But Jane had everything locked up tight. The three-bedroom, two-and-a-half-bathroom rental reflected a vibrant personality. Lots of color, fake flowers, geometric-style pillows. Nothing like the bare walls of his cabin or the emptiness of his office. The thick scent of vanilla surrounded him. The entire house smelled of it. Of her. He spun back toward her, determined to say what he'd come to say and get out before he didn't have the mind to leave. "If it makes you feel any better, I had Elizabeth scour your records, and everything checks out."

A loud beep filled the living room. She brushed against his arm on her way toward the kitchen and opened the microwave. "Someone has tried to kill me two times in the last two days. Nothing short of my stash of cookie dough will make me feel better, if Vincent didn't steal it."

Slamming the microwave door closed, she stuck a fork into whatever she'd nuked and blew on it to cool it down, which shouldn't seem so damn sexy, but right here, right now, Jane was home. She looked relaxed in her sweatpants and T-shirt, hair slightly wet. He'd obviously caught her coming out of the shower. Too bad his own self-hatred had kept him parked outside her house until a few minutes ago. He could've—

"How is Elliot doing?" she asked.

"He'll pull through. He's too stubborn to let a little blow to the head get the best of him, but that's not why I'm here." Resting his hands on his hips, Sullivan focused on her eyes instead of the way her sweatpants hung off her hips. "I need to know how you broke into my office two days ago and where you got your intel on my real name."

Her gaze snapped to his—alarmed—but she covered her surprise faster than he thought possible for a woman who chased the truth for a living. "Because you still think I'm bent on revenge or you're genuinely curious?"

"I've installed a top-of-the-line security system, rigged hundreds of cameras and have around-the-clock security on every floor in that building." Sullivan slowly closed the space between them. His heart rate sped up as though he'd just run a marathon, and he couldn't slow it down. She held her ground but tilted her head back to stare straight up at him without giving anything away. Her sweet scent washed over him, and Sullivan couldn't help but lean into her further.

He'd been shot at, tortured, endured physical night-mares and watched men on his team die right in front of him. All without his pulse raising a single beat. How was it possible Jane affected him like this? "There's no way you could've gotten past that system without trig-gering one of my alarms. Not to mention I buried the files on my old life and my family so deep, not even the CIA could get their hands on them."

"You're right. You have the best security in the world. It's impossible. But the files? That didn't take very much digging at all." Those hazel eyes stayed glued to him, her voice rich and gravelly with exhaus-tion. A playful sweep of her fingertips across his shoul-der froze the air in his lungs. "But I'm not about to give away all my secrets until I can trust you."

Sullivan straightened his spine. "You seem awfully confident for a woman who was accused of orchestrat-ing her own stalking a few hours ago."

"If you believed Vincent's report that I set this whole thing up, that I moved here to change your mind about me—" the playfulness disappeared from Jane's expres-sion "—then you wouldn't have stood up for me against your team in that conference room."

He couldn't argue with that. The instincts that'd been beaten into him during his enlistment in the navy screamed her innocence. She didn't have anything to do with Christopher Menas or whoever was behind this trying to make her life a living hell. She was the victim here.

"Now, if you're hungry, I have more microwavable mush in the freezer. Unless you're into peanut-butter-and-jelly sandwiches." Putting some distance between them, Jane held up a thin black tray with what looked like chicken nuggets, mashed potatoes and a warm brownie. "That is, if you don't want to go back to sitting in your SUV all night, eating beef jerky."

"You saw me?" Tingling spread across his chest. Another smile pulled at the corners of his mouth as Sullivan drove his hands into his jacket pockets. Of course she'd seen him. This wasn't just any client he was dealing with. This was a woman who'd received death threats every day of her career. That brand of work required her to keep her instincts on alert and a gun under her pillow. *His* kind of woman. "And here I thought I had good surveillance skills."

"I've been stalked across the world by a crazed psychopath for the past three months. I'm bound to notice one of your SUVs parked for a couple hours two blocks down the street. Besides, I'm not stupid. I wouldn't have come home and let my guard down long enough to shower if I hadn't known there'd be backup." Jane shoved a forkful of dessert into her mouth, eyes bright, her delectable mouth curling into a smile. "Would you judge me if I said I only bought these meals for the brownie?"

Sullivan straightened. "Across the world?"

Her smile didn't last long. "Guess I left that part out, didn't I?" Lowering her fork back to the plastic dish, she wiped her fingers across her mouth. "Vincent wasn't totally wrong about my moving to Anchorage." Alarm flooded her features. "I mean, I didn't move here in some sick attempt to get you to forgive me for what happened to Marrok. I came here because I started noticing things missing from my quarters back in Afghanistan. At first, it was little things. One of my hair ties, some pieces of clothing." She set her food on the edge of the small round kitchen table a few feet away and crossed her arms under her breasts. "Then my service weapon was stolen. A .40 Smith & Wesson. I asked to be put on leave for personal reasons and came to find you. And to blackmail you if you wouldn't help."

"Your stalker tracked you down in Afghanistan, then followed you to the States?" Sullivan made a mental note to check Menas's travel records, phone records, credit cards, anything that could put him in the Middle East the same time as Jane. Would've been good information to know from the start, but they hadn't exactly gotten the chance to dive deeper into Menas's life before it'd literally gone up in flames.

"I can't think of anyone who would hate me this much. Aside from you." Jane crossed her arms over her chest once again, the strength in her forearms apparent. The apprehension clouding those beautiful eyes singed him right down to the core. "Hey, maybe you're the one stalking me."

"I tried hating you." Sullivan noted the flash of sadness across her features and locked his jaw tight. "Didn't stick after you saved my life back at the cabin. Then ran into a wall of flames to save my private investigator."

Her features brightened as she picked up her forgotten dinner. "Then since you're not here to turn me into the police and I'm not telling you how I broke into your office or uncovered your real name, why are you still here, Sullivan?"

"You're not safe here. This guy knows you. He knows things he shouldn't—"

"Doesn't seem like I'm safe anywhere right now. At

your cabin, on the move. I might as well find a small bit of comfort in my own house as long as I can." Yellow lighting reflected off the line of water welling in her lower lash line. Her shoulders sagged as she tossed her meal back onto the table. "It doesn't matter where I go. Whoever wants me dead is going to find me."

"Not if I have anything to do with it." The darkness in her beauty compelled him to close the small amount of space between them and he stepped into her. Sullivan framed her sharp features with calloused hands, those troubled eyes of hers widening. His blood pumped hard through his veins as he breathed her in. His last memory of his brother pulsed at the back of his mind. But right then, all he could think about was chasing the shadows from Jane's gaze. Stupid really.

"We should get some sleep." Jane pulled back, mere centimeters between them, breathing heavy. "You're welcome to take the couch and anything in the fridge."

He clamped his grip around her arms, not willing to let her leave yet. She was soft but strong, the kind of woman who could hold her own in a fight. "Even the cookie dough?"

"Sure. I guess you deserve it." Her lips curled into a smile. "But I'm still not telling you how I broke into your office."

Sullivan used every ounce of control left in his body to take a step back. Damn, he was a sucker for pain. Getting involved with a client—with Jane at all—was possibly the worst idea he'd ever had. But the sight of her when she'd opened the door had unleashed everything he'd tried to bury since he'd pulled his gun on her two nights ago. Desire. Hope. Life. "Give me a clue?"

"All right. I'll give you one clue, but that's all you get." She hooked her hands behind his neck and pulled herself into him. Shifting her weight to her toes, Jane raised her mouth to his ear, her exhale tickling his already sensitized skin. "It wasn't as hard as you might think."

JANE ENTERED HER bedroom with slow, determined steps and shut the door behind her. But no amount of space from Sullivan eased her racing heart. Had she really imagined kissing him?

She leaned against the door and thunked her head a little harder than she intended. Pain radiated across the back of her head and down her neck, but still didn't dislodge the rampant desire flooding her veins. Offering Sullivan her couch for the night probably wasn't the best idea. It'd been at least ten minutes since he'd taken her face in his hands, but the heat in her lower abdomen still hadn't cooled.

But she couldn't go down that path. Her life depended on her keeping her emotional distance. She exhaled his clean scent from her system and immediately felt better. Swiping the hair out of her face, Jane wrenched the bifold door of her closet back and punched in the six-digit code to her firearm safe. She'd meant every word when she'd told Sullivan that her stalker would find her.

Because she intended to let him.

It'd been the reason she returned home. Whoever was doing this to her had already shown a willingness to harm bystanders. She only hoped Sullivan had the resources and the manpower to protect her neighbors and to get the job done since she'd vastly underestimated the man coming after her. They both had. But not anymore.

No place was more comfortable and familiar to her than her own home. Yes, her stalker had broken in. Had probably searched the place. But she was the one who lived there and knew every detail of her town house.

It was much better than trying to lay a trap somewhere new.

Wrapping her fingers around the .40 Smith & Wesson—similar to the one her stalker had stolen in Afghanistan—she dropped the magazine out, then slammed it back into place. The drill had been burned into her muscle memory for years. She could strip down and reassemble any weapon in the US military arsenal, but her own personal firearm would have to do for tonight. The steel warmed in her hand. It'd been a long time since she'd had to shoot first and ask questions later, but tonight was about survival.

Not the fact that Sullivan Bishop was downstairs on her couch.

"Keep it together a little while longer, Reise." Jane placed the gun under her pillow, brushed her teeth and climbed into bed. The cold sheets raised goose bumps along her arms. Nothing like Sullivan's hot, hair-raising touch. Her mind raced with different ways she could make that particular fantasy come true. All she had to do was go down to her living room.

Nope. Not going there. Tossing onto her side, Jane stared into the lens of the small camera she'd installed a few minutes before Sullivan pounded on her front door. Her stalker had already broken in once. Wouldn't happen again. Stay awake. Finish this once and for all. Get on with her life. And Sullivan…

She shoved her nose into her T-shirt and inhaled deep, clinging to the remnants of his scent on her clothing. They could cross that road when there wasn't blackmail and a life-threatening stalker hanging over their heads.

Visions of his magnetic blue eyes danced across the back of her eyelids. Exhaustion pulled at her, her body aching for sweet relief. It'd been more than twenty-four hours since she'd had the chance to lie down, but she couldn't give in to sleep yet. The camera would catch her stalker on video—give them concrete evidence Christopher Menas was behind this—but the gun under her pillow would put an end to this sick game.

DEAFENING SILENCE WOKE HER.

Jane rubbed her eyes with the heels of her hands. Crap, she'd fallen asleep. Reaching for the S&W tucked under her pillow, she sat up straight. Fog clouded her brain, but not so much as to not realize what was missing. Where was her gun? She spun for the lamp on the nightstand and twisted the knob, checking the rest of the bed.

A crisp white piece of paper lay beside an all-too-familiar .40 S&W handgun on the pillow. She'd recognize that gun anywhere. Her stolen service weapon.

Her heart hiccuped.

Five words in block letters. "You're going to need this."

He'd been here. In her house. Maybe even touched her.

She couldn't breathe. Couldn't think. Covering her

mouth with the back of her arm, Jane fought the bile climbing up her throat. This was what she'd wanted, why she'd come home, but the reality gutted her from the inside. How had her stalker gotten past Sullivan? Snapping her attention toward the cracked bedroom door, Jane wrapped her hand around the gun and threw off the sheets. "Sullivan."

If something had happened to him, she'd never forgive herself for dragging him into this mess.

The soft echo of the front door closing propelled her out of bed. The intruder was still close by. Grip tight on the gun, Jane ripped out of her room and ran after the shadow disappearing through the front door. He wouldn't slip away this time.

Freezing November air slammed against her, but she pumped her legs hard without missing a beat. No more games. No more fear. Gravel cut into her bare feet as she chased after the figure up ahead. He passed under a streetlamp, heading south. Thick black jacket, Huskies ball cap, short brown hair. She was too far away to get much else and ground her back molars as she pushed herself harder. Her stalker ducked into a short alley between two single-family houses, but he wouldn't lose her that easily. "Christopher!"

The breath that heaved in and out of her lungs crystallized into large, white puffs in front of her mouth as she slowed. Her skin tingled with the sudden change in temperature, but Jane wasn't going back to her town house. Not yet. She pressed herself into the wall outside the alleyway. She'd memorized this neighborhood and every escape route the day she'd moved in. Her stalker obviously hadn't taken the same precautions. The alley ended at the back of a Chinese restaurant with no other access unless he broke into the large factory directly north of there. There was nowhere for him to run.

Jane angled her head around the corner, but moonlight and streetlamps cut off at the top of the houses. She couldn't see anything. Surveying the rest of the street, she took a deep breath. Hints of spicy aftershave hung on the air, pulling at memories of first love, suspicions, then terror. She remembered that aftershave from college, from Christopher's skin. But why come after her now? It didn't make sense.

With another look down the alley, her instincts screamed for her to go back home. No sign of the man who'd run from her. Something wasn't right, like Christopher had lured her to this point for a reason. But why?

"Jane!" Sullivan pounded up the street toward her.

The tension running down her spine lessened. He'd chew her out for running after a crazed stalker on her own, but a small part of her was relieved he'd followed her. And he wasn't hurt.

Lowering her weapon, Jane relaxed in defeat and sunk her weight against the house. She glanced one last time into the alley. Christopher was still just playing games with her. Trying to keep her scared, confused. Vulnerable. And it'd worked. He'd lured her out of the house. She shook her head as though she could rewind the past few minutes. She'd let emotion get in the way of catching the man responsible for turning her world upside down. How could she have been so stupid? Shoving off from the wall, she stepped toward the road to head Sullivan off. "Over here—"

"Hello, Janey." A hand clamped around her mouth,

then another around her waist, pulling her against a wall of muscle.

Jane struggled against her attacker's grip as he dragged her into the depths of the alleyway, darkness closing around her.

Chapter Seven

Sullivan was either going to kill Jane for running out the door with a loaded gun by herself or kiss her. He'd decide when he found her. He stumbled out the front door, gun in hand, but the world tilted on its axis. He hit the ground hard. Whatever drug he'd been injected with still hadn't cleared his system. The intruder had come through the front door. No forced entry—like they'd had a key. Every second played in his mind on slow repeat. Sullivan had shot up from the couch, clicked off the safety on his weapon and took a single step forward. But whoever had broken in had been two steps ahead of him. The syringe had emptied into his neck before he'd even had a chance to counter. He'd crumpled right there on the floor. Paralyzed but alert. His mind had gone to a dark place while he'd watched Jane run out the door and he lay there. Useless.

What the hell had he been shot up with? A mild paralyzer?

Menas had come into Jane's home, had terrorized her for the last three months. The bastard was going to find out exactly what kind of monster Sullivan had kept locked up the past decade.

Adrenaline pumped hard through his veins as he

burst through the foot of snow in Jane's front yard, only the sound of his breathing loud in his ears. A cramp shot up his right calf muscle, curling his toes inside his boots, but he pushed through. Pain, exhaustion and stiffness clawed at him from the inside, his vision blurry, but he wouldn't stop until he found Jane alive.

There were no other options.

Shuffling down one of the alleys to his left claimed his attention. The man behind these mind games wasn't an idiot. He'd known Sullivan would be there to protect his target and had drugged him to keep him out of the fight. Wasn't happening. Sullivan fanned his grip around the gun, index finger planted beside the trigger. Anticipation vibrated down his spine. This was what he did best, what he enjoyed doing. For his country. For his clients. For Jane.

What was it about her that he couldn't seem to hate? After everything she put him through—was *still* putting him through—she deserved it. But he couldn't hate her. Not such a strong, intelligent, vulnerable woman. She needed his help. She needed *him*. And nothing would stop him from getting to her.

Back pressed to one of the houses, Sullivan checked the alleyway. No sign of movement, but that didn't mean anything. Her stalker might've knocked Jane unconscious or— No. Sullivan wouldn't go there. Shoulders pulled back, gun up, he kept low and moved fast. His right foot dragged behind slightly, the last of the paralysis taking its sweet time leaving his system. Would've been easy to finish the job back at the town house with Sullivan unable to fight back, but apparently Jane's stalker didn't want him dead. Which he fully intended to take advantage of.

But where was Jane? Sullivan held his weapon steady, closing in on the alleyway one slow step at a time. "I'll give you three seconds to show your face before I start shooting. There's nowhere left to run. We know who you are and why you're doing this. And I'll hunt you down as long as it takes to put you behind bars."

Another round of shuffling said he was in the right place, and he swung the gun to his right. Pain shot up his neck and spidered throughout the base of his skull. He fought to stay upright and keep his weapon level.

But a wall of flesh slammed into him.

He hit the side of the building, the air knocked from his lungs. The gun slid across the pavement as blow after blow rained down on him from the shadow armed with a metal pipe. Sullivan held his forearm out to block the hits. Heart thundering in his ears, he swept one leg out and unbalanced his attacker.

The man went down, landing on his left arm. The crack of bone filled the few short seconds of silence just before deep groans reverberated off the walls, but it didn't keep his attacker down for long. A glint of metal flashed. The man had traded his pipe for a knife.

Sullivan pushed to his feet, pulling out his own knife, which he kept strapped to his ankle, and flipped the blade outward. He swung it parallel to his wrist and moved in, legs spread, torso angled to make himself a smaller target. His attacker did the same, and Sullivan hesitated.

Christopher Menas didn't have military training according to his records, yet this man almost mirrored Sullivan in his movements. The first swipe came fast, but Sullivan blocked it and shoved his attacker's arm down, striking out with a fist to the man's face. Shadows played across his attacker's black ski mask as Sullivan countered, slicing the blade across the man's chest.

Another groan filled the alleyway, but the injury didn't slow his opponent. He charged at full speed.

Sullivan kicked out, slamming his boot into the man's kneecap to keep from getting tackled. He barely registered the remnants of the drug in his system, but another swipe from his attacker's blade landed home. Stinging pain lanced through his biceps, but disappeared as his body's fight-or-flight response surged through his blood again.

No more games. Jane could be anywhere by now. Could be hurt.

He lunged forward, shoulders low, and hiked his attacker over his shoulder and into the alleyway wall. Hard. An elbow slammed into his spine. Two times. Three. Sullivan's knees buckled, and he forced all of his momentum into rolling his attacker over his head. With one foot planted in the man's stomach, he tossed the masked assailant as far as he could, using his attacker's momentum to roll himself on top.

Only his attacker had the same idea.

Sullivan's vision blurred as he spun, landing pinned under his opponent against the cold, wet asphalt. In the span of half a breath, his attacker plunged the blade down toward Sullivan's sternum, but Sullivan caught his wrist a split second before the knife hit home. His muscles burned as he held the blade above his chest. Sullivan was stronger, but whoever was on top of him leveraged everything he had into putting that blade into his chest. Sweat dripped into his eyes, the air in his lungs frozen.

He wouldn't lose this battle. Not when Jane's life depended on him. Sullivan hiked his right knee into his attacker's rib cage, dislodging the man's hold on him. He slipped out from under the knife and shot to his feet. He wrapped his hand around his opponent's neck, flipped him over and planted his knee into the man's spine. Moonlight glinted off his blade as he placed it at his attacker's throat.

Convulsed breaths echoed throughout the alleyway.

"Where is she? Where is Jane?" The words left his mouth as a growl. The urge to tear, to rip—to protect what was his—surged through his blood. And the man pinned beneath him looked a lot like prey. Sullivan clenched the man's ski mask and ripped it over his head. Pulling his attacker into the circle of light from the streetlamp, he swayed on his feet. He breathed through his nose, slowing down his heart rate to keep his head on straight. His fingers went numb for a moment as he studied the man in his grasp. A hard exhale rushed from him, but he tightened his grip on his attacker. "You're not Christopher Menas. Who the hell are you?"

Bubbling laughter filled the alleyway. An older, darker face, nowhere close to Menas's thirty-four years of age, contorted in pain as the man in his grip fought to look up at Sullivan, a crooked smile spreading across his face. "I don't kill and tell."

"A contract killer. Great." He should've known. No way Menas would've been able to defend himself like that. Jane's stalker was a tow truck operator. No military experience. But none of this made sense. How did

Menas even get in contact with a mercenary? Shoving the blade under the man's throat, Sullivan leaned in close. "Where is Jane?"

A sniper's laser sight slipped over the mercenary's shoulder, and Sullivan reacted by instinct. He dropped the knife and swung the man in his grip around. Two bullets ripped through his attacker's back, the shots rocking Sullivan with two strong thumps.

A glint of moonlight reflected back toward him from the roof of the warehouse across the street, but disappeared a split second later. Another slow exhale worked to bring his heart rate under control. A scope. Had to be another contracted mercenary cleaning up the loose ends. But where did that leave Jane?

Sullivan discarded the man he'd used as a human shield and stepped over the body. Sweeping his weapon into his hand, he stalked toward the factory at the north end of the alleyway. With a single tap on the device lodged in his ear, he had his weapons expert on the other line. "We've got new players. One of them just took a shot at me. Warehouse north of Jane's town house. Bring the shooter to me."

"Done." Anthony hung up. No time to waste.

Loud pops cracked in Sullivan's neck as he wrenched his head from side to side. Didn't matter how many mercenaries Menas had hired to protect himself. The bastard could have an entire army behind him for all Sullivan cared. It wouldn't stop him from getting to Jane.

JANE THREW HER elbow back with as much force as she could but hit solid muscle and Kevlar. Digging her fingernails into her attacker's wrist, she swung her legs wide and threw her weight forward in an attempt to unbalance him. Didn't work. The man squeezing the air from her chest was so much bigger and so much stronger than she was. No amount of escape attempts seemed to faze him as he pulled her across the wide expanse of the factory.

"Did you think you could get away from me that easily? I'm not the man you claimed you loved back in college anymore, Jane. I've changed. Traveled. Killed people. Made some new friends." The eerily familiar voice closed in on her right ear and sent a shiver down her spine. Christopher Menas. "Besides, I've been waiting too long for this chance."

"Christopher, please. It doesn't have to be like this." Her bare heels caught on chunks of broken cement as she struggled to loosen his forearm grip around her collarbone. The sour scent of cigarettes dived deep into her lungs with every panicked inhale. He'd already dragged her halfway through the sheet metal factory, weaving between large pieces of machinery she'd never seen before. Any deeper and Sullivan wouldn't be able to track her. Because he was coming for her. She had to believe that. Stall. Get Christopher to slow down. Give Sullivan a chance.

"Sure it does, Janey." Her insides flipped at the nickname he'd used for her all throughout their relationship, but not in the way it used to. He didn't sound the same, didn't feel the same as she remembered. Christopher pulled up short and swung her around to face him.

His dark brown eyes flashed as a stream of molten metal poured into a base a few feet away. It was late. Usually only a few factory workers kept an eye on operations overnight, but the unhinged mania in Christopher's gaze said it all. He'd kill anyone who got in his way. She couldn't risk dragging innocent lives into this. Sweat glistened down his stern features as he stared at her. He was right. He wasn't the same man she'd given her heart to all those years ago. Familiar angles and planes of his face were still there, but he'd filled out. A lot. The Kevlar vest he'd strapped on struggled to rein in the muscle underneath and intensified the in-depth story of tattoos covering every inch of his now-massive arms. Scars interrupted the thick five-o'clock shadow across his jaw, as well as his eyebrows, and his hair had receded several inches. The man staring her down with hell in his gaze was dangerous. Perhaps psychotic. Definitely not the tow truck operator she'd had in mind when she and Sullivan had pinned him as her stalker less than twelve hours ago. "And don't worry about your bodyguard. My friends certainly know how to show a guy like him a good time."

Friends? Her heart sank. *Sullivan.*

"What did you do?" She ripped out of his grasp and, surprisingly, Christopher let her go. No point in running. He'd wound them through a maze of machinery she had no idea how to escape. Probably for that reason alone. He'd catch her without trying, and she'd have wasted precious time in getting to Sullivan.

At least four knives and just as many handguns peeked out from under his jacket and from the pockets of his cargo pants. What had her ex turned himself into? A mercenary? Flipping his wrist over, he read his watch. Christopher reached for her again and hauled her into his chest. Her sternum hit his Kevlar with a thud. "We've got such plans for you."

We?

"Are you going to kill me?" *Keep him talking. Keep him distracted.* Jane snaked her hand around to his closest pocket. Loud hissing sounds from the nearest machine drew Christopher's attention to his left and he reached for one of the many sidearms haphazardly packed into his gear. Not in control. Too easy to scare. Dangerous. Her fingertips scraped over the butt of a large blade in his pants, but Jane couldn't wrap her hand around the grip without tipping Christopher off. Her throat tightened, his cigarette breath fanning across her cheek.

"Not yet." He slid back from her. Jane let his own movements draw the knife into her hand. "First—" wrapping his bruising strength around her arm again, he shoved her ahead of him "—we've got a chopper to catch."

"I'm not going anywhere with you." Jane swung fast, arcing the blade straight across Christopher's face. He doubled over to the side as she hit her target, his scream nearly bursting her eardrums. Fleeing, Jane pumped her legs hard, exhaustion from the insufferable heat around her already pulling at her muscles. Grip tight around the knife, she mentally ticked off the different machines Christopher had dragged her past on the way in. There had to be a way out of this maze.

The factory's windows had been blacked out. No sign of an exit. No idea which way they'd come in. She couldn't just run from a crazed maniac until she lucked out with an exit. She needed a plan. The aggressive hissing and movements of the machines covered any sounds Christopher might've made from following her. Jane checked over her shoulder. She couldn't see him but ducked behind one of the larger machines for cover. Air dragged through her windpipe as her heart fought to keep up with the rest of her body. She'd kept in shape over the years, but running on pure adrenaline would only take her so far.

Okay, luring Christopher to her town house hadn't been the best idea. But then again, she hadn't expected him to be a mercenary either. None of Sullivan's or his team's research into her ex had hinted as much. Although, now that she thought about it, there was a piece of her that always believed she'd see his name on the FBI's Most Wanted List someday.

"Janey…" he said, taunting. Her name on his lips pooled dread in her stomach. "That wasn't very nice." He sounded close all of a sudden—too close.

Her spine straightened, and she pressed her back into the machine behind her. Heat seared her skin, but Jane clamped her mouth shut. She couldn't call out, couldn't give away her position. If she had to guess, she'd ended up at the south end of the building. She studied the blade in her hand, the edge tinted red. There wasn't an exit on the south end. At least, not one she'd noted mapping out her neighborhood when she'd first moved in.

Where was Sullivan? She had no doubt the former SEAL could take care of himself, but neither of them had calculated the addition of Christopher's "friends."

Footsteps echoed nearby, and her surroundings came into a sharp focus. She breathed deeply, evenly, as a deadly calm descended over the factory floor. Sweat dripped from her eyebrows. The blade's handle grew slick in her hand. She needed to get to the exit, needed to find Sullivan.

"Janey." A shadow passed in front of her faster than

she thought possible. Christopher knocked the knife from her hand and clamped his grip around her throat. Shoving her hard against the machine at her back, he let the skin across her shoulder blades sizzle from the blistering heat for a few seconds. Searing pain lightninged throughout her upper body, but Jane couldn't scream with her air supply cut off.

She fought for breath, vision blurry, but this close, she realized she'd slashed a deep cut into his right cheekbone. And the look in his near-black eyes along with the hand still around her throat said he intended to make her pay. But the second she gave in would be the end of her. She wasn't getting on whatever chopper he had waiting for her. No matter what. Mentally checking off all the ways to counter an attack, Jane unclamped her hands from around his wrist and went for his eyes. She dug the fingernails of her thumbs into his eye sockets, then kneed him in the groin.

Christopher's grip lightened but didn't let go as another scream ripped up his throat. And before she knew what was coming, his other hand slammed into her jawline. "You shouldn't have done that. I promised to bring you in alive. Not untouched."

She hit the heated cement floor—hard—sparks and hot metal brightening up the dark edges of her vision. His rough exhales drowned out the overwhelming pounding in her head. A single kick to her rib cage pushed the air from her lungs and shut down any other ideas of her fighting back. Jane rolled into the fetal position to prevent another hit, but the damage had already been done. Pain unlike anything she'd experienced washed over her, her vision going white for a few seconds. She couldn't breathe. Couldn't think.

"You've got a lot more spunk in you than I remember." Christopher crouched over her, slipping the blade she'd stolen from his pants back to its rightful place. "Where was this girl when we were dating? I might not have had to go after your roommates if you'd shown me a little bit of a challenge."

Her lungs spasmed out of paralysis from the kick to her midsection, gulping down heated air. She couldn't stop fighting, couldn't let him take her. Because, from the deadly look in his expression, the chances of her getting out alive were not in her favor. A single name crossed her mind as tears welled in her eyes. Where was he? Was he alive? "Sullivan…"

"Dead," he said.

No, no, no, no. Not Sullivan. "No."

"Yes." Christopher's scarred features closed in on her as he slipped a strand of her hair behind her ear. Her mouth filled with bile at the intimate gesture. The world spun as he wrapped his calloused hands around her arms and hiked her over his shoulder. He straightened, locking her knees against him and her hands in his grasp. "Nobody's coming for you, Janey. You're finally mine."

Chapter Eight

When Sullivan finally reached the factory, Jane was slumped over a heavily armed man's shoulder. He'd found her.

Tearing across the slick cement factory floor, Sullivan sprinted harder than he had in years. The navy had trained him for any kind of combat, taught him how to successfully shoot his Glock and hit the target from two hundred yards, but risking Jane's life in the process wasn't an option. Unbearable heat dived deep into his lungs, and he inhaled fast to keep oxygen pumping to his extremities. "Jane!"

Thick doors slammed behind the man with Jane in his arms as they disappeared out the west exit. Sullivan pushed himself harder, sweat dripping into his eyes and down his neck. The longer he lost sight of them, the smaller chance he had of recovering her unharmed. He rammed his left shoulder into the steel, slamming the door open into the concrete wall behind him. His heart pounded behind his ears as his lungs devoured the cold, fresh air.

No sign of Jane.

"Jane!" Sullivan ran a hand across his forehead to dispel the sweat now freezing to his skin. No response.

Damn it. He couldn't have lost her already. It was impossible. The factory's brightly lit parking lot didn't offer anything in the way of cover. Whoever had Jane couldn't have disappeared with a 120-pound woman that fast on foot. Unless...

Headlights drifted over the right side of his face a split second before a black Audi Q7 barreled straight toward him. Sullivan dived for cover, swinging his gun up and over. He squeezed off four rounds, none of which penetrated the SUV's windows. Bulletproof. The SUV sped across the parking lot, heading for the main road.

He tapped the earpiece connected to the most combat-experienced asset on his team and vaulted after the vehicle on foot. He wouldn't get far on his own, but he wasn't about to give up on Jane either. "Forget the shooter. The package is in a black Audi Q7 heading east toward Seward Highway. License plate is—"

A Blackhawk Security GMC screeched to a halt in front of him, and Sullivan lunged inside. Anthony Harris, his resident weapons expert, slammed on the accelerator, not waiting for Sullivan to shut the passenger-side door. He twisted the steering wheel, flipping around. "Your shooter is in that vehicle. Hold on to something."

Momentum pinned Sullivan to the back of his seat, and he braced himself against the roof of the SUV as they raced over the speed bumps set throughout the parking lot. Red taillights flashed at least a quarter mile ahead as the Audi spun onto the highway. "Faster, damn it. We can't lose them."

Anthony didn't answer. Always one for taking orders without question. The GMC's engine growled as he pushed it harder, and within seconds they were approaching the highway. They skidded into oncoming traffic, horns and headlights penetrating through the thick cloud of pressure inside the SUV.

"There." Sullivan pointed at the Audi weaving in and out of both lanes of cars. He leaned forward, hoping to catch a glimpse of Jane's outline through the dark tinted windows. No such luck. Majestic snow-covered mountains edged up against the freeway, but it was too dark to see much of anything else. Something wet and sticky tickled the underside of his arm as they maneuvered through traffic. Blood glistened across his skin with the help of the headlights of other cars.

"There's a first-aid kit under your seat," Anthony said, eyes never leaving the road.

Sullivan put pressure on the wound across his arm with his gun hand. "I'm fine. Just find a way to get me closer to the SUV." He would jump on the car's hood if he had to. Although, shooting out the tires should be enough, as long as they weren't armored, as well.

The Audi cut through two lanes of cars. Motorists swerved to avoid hitting others, effectively causing all traffic to skid to a halt. Anthony slammed on the brakes. Bracing himself for impact, Sullivan kept his focus on the SUV now turning onto International Airport Road, one of the only roads leading to Ted Stevens Anchorage International Airport. If her stalker got Jane onto a plane, Sullivan would never see her again. And that wasn't an option. Not today. Not ever.

Screeching tires filled his ears as the GMC skidded at a twenty-degree angle until his weapons expert veered off-road and cut west.

"They're headed for the airport." Sullivan pushed

the button to release his seat belt and then climbed into the back seat and unearthed the heavy-duty case of ammunition that traveled anywhere Anthony went. Dropping the magazine out of his Glock, he replaced the expended 9 mm rounds he'd wasted on the bullet-proof SUV and slammed the magazine back into place. He flipped open another case that stored three black Kevlar vests and geared up. Two more knives and an extra magazine of rounds fitted into the vest. "I'm not going to even ask if you're armed."

"Don't worry about me," Anthony said. "Get ready. We're going in hard."

Through the windshield, Sullivan watched the distance between the two vehicles shrink fast. Anthony closed in on the Audi's bumper, slamming the back driver's-side quarter panel. The hit rocked through the vehicle, and Sullivan pitched forward between the two front seats. "Hit them again."

The GMC lurched forward and cut off any maneuvering the driver of the Audi had in mind. This was it. No way would that SUV reach the airport. Anthony spun the steering wheel and slammed into the Audi. The SUV fishtailed until the vehicle hit the GMC perpendicular. The tires caught on the pavement and the Audi flipped, two times, three. Air rushed from Sullivan's lungs.

Anthony slammed on the brakes to keep from ramming into the underside of the SUV, but Sullivan was out of the vehicle before the GMC came to a full stop.

Boots heavy on the pavement, he palmed the Glock in his right hand and unsheathed a knife with his left. The sounds of broken glass and heavy breathing consumed his attention, as someone fought to leave the vehicle. Jane was strong, a survivor like him, but the hand clawing its way through the debris wasn't hers. He couldn't think about that right now. Mercs were known to shoot first and ask questions later, and he had to do the same. *Neutralize the threat. Then get to her.*

A car door slammed behind him.

Sullivan clicked off the safety of his gun and aimed without looking back at his weapons expert. The former army Ranger could take care of himself and understood the directive: get the client to safety. At any cost.

The first shots forced Sullivan to take cover behind the GMC's open passenger door. He returned fire, hitting the shooter multiple times. The thick tree line on either side of the road provided deep cover, but Sullivan wasn't about to let any strays escape. The shooting stopped. Nothing but the sound of the wind rustling through the trees reached his ears. This wasn't over. Not by a long shot. He maneuvered around the door, weapon raised, muscles tight.

Two more heavily armed men climbed from the wreckage. Neither had the chance to lift their weapons in defense as Anthony closed in on the vehicle. Seconds passed in silence. Minutes. Where was Jane?

Another round of gunfire spread over the pavement, and Sullivan hit the ground.

"Sullivan!" a familiar voice screamed.

He snapped his head up. "Jane."

Tracking the rushed movements of two shadows as they ran down the road—one with short dark hair—Sullivan pushed up from the asphalt and took off after them. Menas's contract killers had nowhere left to run. The tree line was thinning, the airport was still five miles away, and the woman he held on to only slowed him down. His heart thundered in his ears. Or was that something else?

"Boss!" Anthony called.

A pool of light materialized over Jane and her kidnapper, illuminating the road and the mercenary's identity with blinding light. Christopher Menas. Sullivan clenched his jaw and leaned into the run as the black EC725 Super Cougar helicopter descended over its target—Jane.

Choppers. Mercenaries. Who the hell was this guy?

A spread of bullets flew over his head from behind, but Anthony's attempt to keep the helicopter from landing was in vain. Cougars were built for war, made to repel anything weaker than a Hellfire missile.

If Jane got onto that chopper, he couldn't follow. With a three-hundred-mile range at his fingertips, Menas could take her anywhere in the country, and Sullivan would lose her forever. Not an option.

"Jane!" He swung his arms hard, anything to force his legs to go faster. He was within shooting range to stop Menas but wouldn't risk Jane's life in the process.

She swung her elbow up and back into Menas's face, buying Sullivan a few more seconds, but a backhand to her face knocked her out cold onto the pavement.

A growl worked up Sullivan's throat as he lunged for Menas. He collided with solid muscle and Kevlar but held on to his gun. Straddling the enemy, Sullivan pulled the trigger, but Menas shoved his wrist aside. The bullet hit the asphalt next to Menas's head, and a blow to Sullivan's left side wrenched him off her kidnapper.

Menas straightened, blood running down his cheek

from a deep gash. "You must be the great Sullivan Bishop. Heard a lot about you, Frogman."

Sullivan caught the kidnapper's boot as he kicked out and flipped the bastard onto the pavement. Rolling Menas's head between his thighs, he squeezed with as much pressure as he could, taking hit after hit to his kidneys. Outside the pool of light, Anthony collected Jane and ran to the GMC. Mission complete. Time to end this. The pilot of the chopper rushed to help Menas, but Sullivan put one round in each of his legs before the pilot could pull his weapon.

"I have a strict no-abduction policy when it comes to my clients, Menas." Sullivan twisted Menas's arm until a snap sent a shiver down his spine, but, to the bastard's credit, Menas didn't scream. He'd finish this now. For Jane.

A spray of bullets ricocheted off the asphalt at his feet, and Sullivan swung his gun up as he jumped to his feet. He fired three rounds at the second SUV barreling toward the chopper from the other direction. Damn it. Menas must've had another team waiting at the airport. The Glock clicked as he squeezed the trigger. Empty. He discarded the gun across the road and spun for cover. Tires screeched ahead of him as he took position behind the chopper, return fire whizzing past him to his left. Anthony had him covered, but as two mercenaries exited the SUV and closed in on Menas—raining a nonstop storm of bullets on the GMC—Sullivan recognized the window on ending Jane's nightmare closing fast.

Menas remained motionless in the chopper's spotlight as two members of his team clamped on to his arms and dragged their leader across the pavement to-

ward their escape vehicle, all the while spraying rounds
right at Sullivan. He didn't have any other weapons,
no way to stop Menas from getting away.

The Blackhawk Security GMC rolled up beside him,
Anthony positioned out the driver's-side window to
keep the mercs at bay in case they returned fire. Sullivan fought to catch his breath, the aches and pains of
fighting overwhelming. Doubling over, he clamped a
hand over the gash in his arm, then straightened. Satisfied they were in the clear—for now—his weapons
expert leaned across the cab and pushed open the passenger-side door. "Boss, we gotta go. She's not looking good."

Sullivan ignored the open door and slid in beside
Jane, attention on the second SUV hauling away from
the scene. The brake lights dimmed in the darkness.
Menas was gone. Wrapping his arms around her, he
checked her pulse and wiped the blood from her skin.
Her moan rumbled through him, hiking his heart into
his throat. She was alive, but this was far from over.
"I've got you, Jane. I've got you."

Soft pulses of sound echoed in her ears. Her eyelids
felt heavy, like she could sleep for a few more hours.
But that beeping…

Jane ran her tongue across her bottom lip. Dry.

Cracking her eyes, she fought against the sudden
onslaught of the fluorescent overhead lighting. She
blinked to clear her head. White walls. White floors.
White bedding. And an IV in her forearm. A strained
groan vibrated up her throat. A hospital.

"Hello, gorgeous." Elliot stepped into her clouded
vision, a bright smile plastered on his face. "I was hop-

ing you'd wake up on my watch. There's something about those few short seconds of watching someone realize they're not dead after all."

"Hi," she said, her voice gravelly. Putting her hand to her throat, she tried massaging the dryness away, but it hung tight. "When did you get released?"

"Here, this'll help." Handing her a clear cup of water with a straw, he helped her adjust to a sitting position and fluffed her pillows before she relaxed back into the bed. "I checked myself out as soon as I heard about what happened at the sheet metal factory. Couldn't sit there and let you and Sullivan have all the fun."

"Yeah, fun." Stinging pain radiated across her shoulders as she struggled to sit up, and she wrenched forward with a hiss. She angled her head over her shoulder. White gauze and tape covered the burns under the thin hospital gown, but she was all too aware of how they'd gotten there in the first place. Christopher Menas. The sheet metal factory. The helicopter. And Sullivan. She scanned the room for those sea-blue eyes, but her stomach sank. "How long have I been out?"

She took a long, slow sip of water. Her muscles relaxed as the liquid did its job in her throat, and Jane set her head back against the pillows. Couldn't have been more than a day or two, right? Where did that leave them? "Is Christopher dead? Is it over?"

"Not by a long shot, beautiful. But come on now." Elliot sat in a padded chair he'd pulled next to the bed and laced his fingers behind his head, still smiling. He looked awfully chipper for someone who'd had his head nearly smashed in by a tow-truck-operator-turned-mercenary. "You know that's not what you want to ask me."

She didn't dare ask about Sullivan. Asking meant

she'd be breaking one of her own rules that she'd set when she'd decided to blackmail a former navy SEAL: no getting emotionally attached. "How long have I been out?"

"Two days," Elliot said.

Inhaling some of the water, Jane coughed and spit until she cleared her lungs.

Elliot shot forward and took the cup from her, as she covered her mouth with one of the sheets. Sitting back down, he waited until she took a full breath, then sat forward. His deep brown eyes studied her, that infectious smile gone. "He knows what you did, Jane, offering yourself up as bait. He found the camera in your room."

"Oh." She sat back again, swiping one hand through her short hair and running the edge of her sheet under her fingernail with the other. She focused on the bedding and not the disappointment in Elliot's eyes. Why she cared to give Sullivan's private investigator an explanation, she had no idea. But the words fell from her mouth anyway. "We were out of leads, and I needed to know who was doing this to me. It didn't make sense that Christopher might be stalking me all these years later. I'm not a threat to him anymore. The statute of limitations ran out a year ago." She took a deep breath to counteract the painful reminder of her and Christopher's reunion at the factory. "There's something else going on here. Menas said something…" A headache pounded at the base of her skull. "But I can't remember what."

"Elliot, get out," a familiar voice commanded from the door.

"Sullivan." Jane shot her head up. The dread that'd

pooled at the base of her spine spread thin, and she straightened a bit more. Pure rage tightened the small muscles controlling his expression, and he suddenly seemed much more dangerous than she remembered. Didn't matter. He was here. He was okay.

"Hey, look at that, my shift is over. By the way, I've been eating your chocolate pudding for the last two days. I'll pay you back when you're out of here." Elliot somehow gracefully maneuvered around his boss and escaped down the hall as though he'd done this before.

And by the serious lines carved into Sullivan's features, Jane bet he had.

Seconds ticked by, possibly minutes. She couldn't tell. One part of her wished Sullivan would step completely into her room and help her forget the horrible memories of the past few days. The other part demanded she keep her head on straight and remember why she'd blackmailed him in the first place. To bring her stalker to justice.

"You could've been killed." He rolled his fingers into fists. "You almost were."

And he'd been hurt by the look of his arms and knuckles. The air rushed out of her as she scanned the cuts and bruises marring his tanned skin. Christopher Menas had gotten in a few good hits. Because of her. She'd screwed up any chance of catching her stalker by running out her front door without any idea of what waited on the other side. "Sullivan, I'm sorry. I had no idea Christopher would have backup—"

"That's right. You had no idea. We were supposed to investigate the leads together, Jane, but this is what I find instead." He shoved a hand into his jeans pocket and tossed the small camera she'd mounted in her room onto the bed. Broken into several pieces. "You put me and my entire team at risk by going after Menas yourself."

Jane didn't know what else to say, her throat closing as she fought to hold on to the last remnants of her emotional control. She fisted her hands in the sheets. Rolling her lips between her teeth, she bit down to stay in the moment. She couldn't fight Christopher and his team of mercenaries on her own, but she hadn't meant to put the Blackhawk Security team's lives at stake either. They deserved more. Sullivan deserved more. "You're right. I wasn't thinking clearly."

He stalked toward her like a soldier, his grip loose at his sides, ready to go for his weapon at a moment's notice. He walked with power. The edge of her mattress dipped under his weight, his body heat tunneling through the sheets on her bed and down into her bones. Jane couldn't think about her awareness of him right now. Because something had changed. He was looking at her differently. Like he actually would've cared had Christopher gotten her onto that helicopter. "Do you know what would've happened if Menas had killed you?"

The memories flooded in with no one to stop them from overtaking the small amount of control she'd built up. Jane blinked back the tears welling in her lower eyelids. "Well, you definitely wouldn't have had to worry about me blackmailing you anymore."

"That's not my priority right now, Jane. You're a survivor. Like me. Setting up the camera, going after Menas…" He exhaled hard. "As much as I want to be angry at you for it, you did what you felt like you had to do, and I respect you for it. You're strong, you're used to taking care of yourself, but you hired me to protect you, and I can't do that when you're running your own agenda on the side. Understand?" He slid his fingers into her hair, caging her between his massive calloused palms. Those mesmerizing blue eyes bored deep down into her as though he could bare every inch of her with a single look. Sullivan's tone dipped into dangerous territory. "If Menas had gotten you onto that helicopter, I would've spent the rest of my life hunting him and every associate involved until I put them all in the ground."

She blinked to restart her circuits. "I've upended your entire life. Twice. Why would you care what happens to me?"

"Because you put aside your own well-being to save my and Elliot's lives." Sullivan dropped the pad of his thumb to the crack in her bottom lip, and something hot and sensual rushed through her. He thought all that about her? "And because Menas won't stop coming after you, and I'm eager to personally introduce him to a world of disappointment."

He housed shadows—downright darkness sometimes—but he was also honorable. He gave his word and followed through. More than she could say about any other man in her life.

"You think highly of yourself, don't you?" And with damn good reason. SEALs were the principal special operators of the navy. With sea, land and air in their blood, they could operate in any kind of environment, hostile or not. The edges of his dark trident tattoo peeked out from under his T-shirt sleeve. Dryness set up residence in her throat again, and it had nothing to do with the drugs the hospital staff had given her over the last two days. But she sobered almost instantly. "Everyone who gets close to me ends up hurt. All my friends…my family."

No one had understood why she hadn't come back from college the same, why she couldn't move on from what Christopher had done. She didn't have anyone left.

"Then it's a good thing I can take care of myself." Sullivan set one hand beside her hip and leaned in, totally and completely focused on her. He teased her senses in every possible way. His fingertips streaking softly down her bruised jawline, his clean, masculine scent filling her lungs, the sound of his uneven breathing. Every cell in her body stood at attention, wanting him to kiss her, needing him. He traced over the cuts along her arms and collarbone, then pulled away. Air rushed from her lungs, her head clearing fast. "Menas is going to pay. I promise. I have Anthony tracking his movements since his team pulled him off the highway as we speak. We're going after him."

She didn't want to think about that right now, not with him this close, not with him chasing back the pain her body still clung to. Then his words registered. Wait. What? Jane straightened, the burns along her shoulder blades pulling a hiss from her lips. "Sullivan—"

"That's not my name." He pulled away, but the remnants of his touch would stick with her long after they finished their investigation and went their separate ways. "I want to hear my real name on your lips. I need to hear you say it, just once."

Her brows drew inward. "But you're not that man anymore."

"You don't know that," he said. "You don't know anything about me."

A weak smile pulled at the corners of her mouth. If this was some kind of test, proof that she knew who he was and what he'd done, Sullivan Bishop was in for a rude awakening. "All right, *Sebastian Warren*, you want to go after Menas? Fine. But you're taking me with you."

Chapter Nine

Another Fine Navy Day.

Or, in other words, not so much.

Sullivan rolled his head back, stretching the stiff muscles in his neck. The second trip to the cabin hadn't been nearly as exciting as the first. Of course, had Jane been *his* target, he would've struck while she lay unconscious in the hospital. But Menas had to be licking some wounds right about now. His attention drifted to the closed bedroom door. Jane had taken the single bedroom in order to clean up and rest, but he couldn't sleep.

Not with an entire group of mercenaries coming after her.

The stitches in his upper arm stretched as he pushed himself off the couch for yet another perimeter check. He wasn't taking any chances this time. The investigation had gone from gathering intel on a tow truck operator who couldn't let the past die to defending Jane against an armored attack. Sullivan parted the blinds hanging in the front window, his favorite Glock in hand. The gun wasn't his only line of defense this time. He'd made sure Anthony had visited over the last few days to turn the cabin from his getaway spot to a fortified bunker. If Menas and his band of mercenaries came within a hundred yards of the cabin, Sullivan would know.

"Couldn't sleep?" Her husky voice straightened his spine. Those hazel eyes brightened as Sullivan looked her over in the overlarge T-shirt and sweatpants he'd lent her from his dresser drawers. His private investigator had dropped off a duffel bag of clothing and shoes for her but had somehow "forgotten" Jane's sleepwear. Her long fingers stretched around the mug of coffee he'd made her when they'd first arrived. She was the epitome of perfection—more beautiful than he'd imagined—and his mouth went dry. "Me neither."

Sullivan cleared his throat. "How are you feeling?"

"Everything hurts and I'm dying." A rush of laughter burst from her chest, but she grabbed for her bruised jaw. The swelling had gone down, but the pain obviously hadn't subsided just yet. Even so, her smile warmed parts of Sullivan he'd almost forgotten existed. Flashes of threading his fingers through her hair, of bringing that delectable mouth to his, streaked through his mind. "But I can't complain too much. I'm alive, right?"

Thank heaven for that. "It wouldn't bother me if you did." Sullivan replaced the gun in his shoulder holster and rested his hands at his sides. "You've been through a lot the past few days."

"We both have." Setting the mug on the countertop to her left, Jane tucked her short hair behind her ears. Her lean frame drowned in his clothes, but something deep inside him wouldn't dream of dressing her in anything else. Because as he'd watched Menas haul her toward that chopper, he'd realized just how far he was willing to go to keep her safe. She'd gone up against a mercenary alone. And survived. How many of Christopher Menas's victims could say the same?

"Sullivan, listen." One hand leveraged on the counter, the other on her hip, Jane rolled her lips into her mouth, a tell, he'd noted, of when she was nervous. Her gaze rose to his, a hint of pink rising up her neck and into her cheeks. "I can't begin to tell you how sorry I am for what happened at my town house. The camera…" She shook her head, eyes closing briefly as though she could undo everything over the last two days. "It was stupid. The whole thing was stupid. I should've told you what I was doing." She centered on him. "I'm sorry I didn't trust you enough to tell you what I'd been planning. It won't happen again."

Sullivan's fingers twitched at his sides. He'd thought about that particular piece of information a lot over the course of the last two days as he and Elliot took apart Christopher Menas's cover piece by piece. She hadn't trusted him to get the job done, to protect her, but Sullivan wouldn't let the sting sink too deep. Despite her reputation, he saw her distrust for what it really was. Survival. Jane waited for his response, her teeth digging into that split bottom lip of hers. He'd tell her the truth. "If it hadn't been for you luring Menas in, we probably never would've uncovered his real profession."

"As a mercenary." The words left her mouth as a whisper, as though she couldn't believe her college boyfriend was so adept at violence.

"We confirmed it a little while ago. Makes sense when you think about it. You said it yourself. Christopher Menas likes to hurt people. He doesn't have any regard for authority and doesn't believe in the justice system. The sexual assault against your roommates while you two were in college was only the beginning." Sullivan had come across a few mercs during his time as a SEAL, had even been asked if he'd wanted to get in on the ground floor of a new private security company that specialized in Menas's kind of work not too long ago. His brother, Marrok, saw the career potential before he'd died—he swallowed back the tightness in his throat—but Sullivan only killed to survive or protect. Not for a paycheck. "Unfortunately, clients will pay a lot of money for traits like that."

"I take it since you've added a few new security measures to the cabin you still think he's a threat." Jane shifted on her feet. "You were going to kill him, weren't you? Even after I asked you to have him arrested and tried."

"Yes." Plain and simple. She'd asked for the justice system to punish Menas for his crimes, but in those rage-induced seconds of Sullivan fighting for his life— fighting for *hers*—he'd made a choice. He took a deep breath. "Men like Christopher Menas don't give up. They get off by making others suffer. I couldn't watch that happen to you."

"I understand." She ran a hand up and over her shoulder, where the worst of Menas's damage had been cleaned and bandaged. The burned skin would scar but could never detract from Jane's beauty. A weak smile sharpened the angles of her face. "I might not be able to sleep for a few days. But that's nothing new. Christopher's been stalking me for a while. I should be used to it, shouldn't I?"

Sullivan opened his mouth, wanting to assure her

this was the safest place for her to be, that he could protect her from any kind of danger. But he had a sense the fears Jane talked about weren't entirely physical. And he could relate. The brightness in her gaze dimmed slightly, and he couldn't help but close the distance between them. He notched her chin higher to have her look straight at him. "When this is over, the nightmares will get better. It'll just take time."

He studied the slim navy-blue box on the bookshelf over her shoulder, the one with the custom-made pen he'd kept after all these years. A gift from his mother. Identical to the pen she'd given Marrok when he'd turned twelve. "Someday, you'll wake up and they won't be the first thing you think about in the morning. After that, you won't remember them."

"Was that how it was for you?" Nothing but the pure need of reassurance radiated in her eyes. "After what happened with your dad?"

Yes. Violence left a stain, one that took a long time to bleach out. That single incident at age fifteen had changed the course of his life. It'd taken every penny he owned to have a new identity forged. He'd had his birth name declared deceased and gone into the military a few years later, desperate to get away. Joined the SEALs. Founded Blackhawk Security. Dropping his hand to his side, Sullivan focused on the warm, far too intelligent woman in front of him. He wasn't about to tell that particular story. Because it wouldn't end the way she hoped. "You should eat something. Get some rest. We have a lot of work ahead of us."

He turned away.

"You asked me to call you Sebastian in the hospital. Right after you…" She inhaled sharp and clear, the feeling of his hands on her smooth skin still so clear. "Do you remember that?" Soft footsteps padded toward him, and before he was ready, she slid her long fingers over his bare arm to turn him around.

"I remember." He remembered everything since setting sights on her in that damn hospital bed. The way her eyes lit up at the sight of him. The way her lips had creased when he'd slipped his thumb over her mouth. The undeniable rage to tear Christopher Menas to pieces as he'd traced her injuries. Another round of tension stiffened his muscles. No man had the right to hit a woman, but Menas wasn't a real man. He was a gun for hire. Any kind of morality had gone out the window long before their run-in on Seward Highway.

Sullivan closed his eyes. Heat ran up his fingers and into his shoulders. His skin tingled where she touched him. Desire stirred in his gut, kicking up speed the longer Jane held on to him. He turned toward her, nothing but her vanilla scent in his lungs. How could she possibly still smell so good after what she'd been through? "You think I'm not that man anymore."

"Am I wrong?" Jane maneuvered her hand over his chest, her heat tunneling through his T-shirt and down beneath his sternum. Down to the spot where his soul resided. "I read the papers. I know you were only a teenager when you—"

"Killed my father for murdering my mother and eleven other women?" There. He'd said it. He'd drawn blood at the tender age of fifteen and hadn't looked back. Not even for his younger brother. Sullivan squared his shoulders. "Release of that information might lose me the business I've built from the ground up, but the Anchorage Lumberjack was a serial killer who started with women who wouldn't agree to his advances and ended with my mother. So if you're looking for some kind of guilty plea, you're not going to find it, Counselor."

"I'm not looking for a guilty plea." Jane fanned her fingers over his chest. "I just want to get to know the man taking on an entire mercenary ring for me."

Get to know him? This woman wanted to face off with years of his personal demons? A laugh rumbled deep in his chest. Having her this close, with nothing but honesty and desire in her expression, Sullivan couldn't back away. As he should. Never mind that she'd blackmailed him into this mess in the first place, but Jane had single-handedly brought down the only family he'd had left.

But she hadn't forced his brother to commit suicide, had she? Marrok had pulled the trigger himself. And the blackmail... Well, he was a SEAL, damn it. He had held live grenades in his bare hands, had prevented an attack on civilians in the Middle East, could hold his breath for more than three minutes without releasing a single bubble underwater. Blackmail didn't compare to the last twelve years of nonstop training and missions he'd successfully completed. If anyone could battle the monsters hiding in his closet, the Full Metal Bitch had the best chance of survival. "Are you sure you can handle it?"

"I've faced dangerous, military-trained criminals every day of my career, survived two attempts on my life by a mercenary and dragged your deadweight through the Alaskan wilderness by myself." Her mouth turned up into a gut-wrenching smile that clenched his insides and destroyed his excuses. "Why don't you give me a challenge?"

WHY DID HER heart insist on getting involved in things it had no business interfering with? Its job was to pump blood. That was it. Get to know the real Sullivan Bishop? That should've been the last thing on her mind. But at the moment, Jane couldn't remember why. His eyes had settled on her, and the pain, the exhaustion, the alarm bells sounding off in her head all disappeared.

He shouldn't have touched her in the hospital. Because now all she could think about was having those hands on her again. And, hell, if that didn't send her thoughts on tangents everywhere but where it should be: on bringing her stalker to justice.

The shadows across the rough ridge of his nose shifted as Sullivan closed in on her. The action, so simple, set off an explosive chain reaction that stole the air from her lungs. Skin heated, heart racing, her fight-or-flight response kicked into high gear. He'd almost kissed her back in the hospital, but this, the desire raging in his gaze, was something completely different. Like he'd finally come to a decision about her.

Long-dormant longing flooded through her, but she stepped out of Sullivan's range. She had been fed, had rested, felt safe here in his cabin, everything that said she was supposed to be ready for an intimate relationship according to Maslow's hierarchy of needs, but she couldn't do this. At least, not with him.

Take care of the threat. Get her life back.

Mind over matter. That was all it'd take.

They'd only known each other for four days—albeit four of the most intense days of her life—but people got hurt when they insisted on staying in her life.

"Jane?" Confusion chased the desire from his expression. "What's wrong?"

Good question. She'd been with a handful of men in the past. Nothing serious. But it was like riding a bike, right? Except this bike was inexplicably protective of her, had taken on a group of mercenaries to save her life and stared at her as though he intended to devour her. Sullivan was a good man. And despite her original intentions when she'd broken into his office, she wouldn't let him throw away his life for her. Because guilt was the unwanted gift that just kept on giving.

"Everything." Jane ran a hand through her hair, then crossed her arms over her stomach and leaned against the back of the couch for support. Her knees locked to keep her upright when all she wanted to do was collapse into Sullivan. All the oxygen disappeared from the room. The three small lines between his eyebrows deepened, and she clenched her jaw to keep herself in the moment. Why was her chest so tight? "I blackmailed you into helping me, Sullivan, but after what happened with Christopher... I have no idea how to get you out of this."

"Get me out of this?" Sullivan widened his stance, crossing his arms over his chest. "What gave you the idea I'm looking for a way out?"

"You beat Christopher Menas until he was unconscious to save me on the highway. In my experience, mercenaries like him aren't going to forget about something like that and move on. He's turned you into a target, too." She inhaled deep, savoring his masculine, clean scent. "I know what you said about taking care of yourself before, but people who've gotten close to me over the years always end up hurt. And for some stupid reason, I don't want that to happen to you."

Silence stretched between them, a living, breathing thing.

Slowly, dangerously, Sullivan stalked toward her, a predator closing in on his prey. Before Jane had a chance to escape, he caged her between his massive arms against the couch, just as he had back in his office. The ice in his gaze melted, warming every inch of her body. "Do I look like the kind of man who's willing to back down from a fight?"

Not in the least.

"Stop looking at me like that." Jane straightened—at a loss with him practically wrapped around her—but she didn't get far. Didn't he understand? Nothing could happen between them. Ever. Christopher wasn't going to stop. He'd hunt her down until he got whatever kind of revenge he sought from her. There was nowhere she could go that didn't put them both in danger. Clearing her throat, she stood up against him. Fine. He wouldn't back down voluntarily? She'd make him see reason. "You should hate me for what happened with your brother, for what I did to force you to help me."

"I tried. It didn't work." The cage he'd constructed around her disappeared. The muscles in the right side of his jaw ticked off a steady beat. "Do you want me to hate you? Is that it?"

It would sure make them going their separate ways easier after they finished with Christopher and his friends. But what if they never found him? She'd have to leave her job with the JAG Corps. Change her name. Move again. Jane exhaled hard, but the tightness in her chest didn't lessen. What if her stalker got to her again and Sullivan wasn't around the next time? Rapid flashes of what'd happened in the factory took over, and the burns across her back tingled. Without Sullivan, who knew what would've happened to her had Christopher gotten her onto that chopper. Dread curdled in her gut. She didn't want to think about it.

"We've gone up against some of the most violent men in existence, Jane. Men most people would run from. But you…you held your ground. You've fought like hell for yourself and for me since you broke into my office." Sullivan stared down at her. "You might be the Full Metal Bitch, but I can't hate you."

Her insides warmed, relaxing her muscles.

This should've been easy. She'd planned everything down to the letter. She'd blackmail him into tracking down her stalker, the police would take over and she'd have her life back. Sullivan wasn't supposed to take on a clan of mercenaries for her. She wasn't supposed to consider what might happen to them after the job was done.

Oh, no. No, no, no, no. She did not have feelings for him. She couldn't. First rule of blackmail: don't fall in love.

Jane inhaled deep, swiping her tongue across her bottom lip. Her heart pounded loud in her ears. She couldn't get enough air. She took a deep breath to steady her nerves, but it didn't help. "Then where does that leave us?"

"Jane, my brother made his own choices. I honestly don't know what kind of man Marrok turned out to be, or whether or not he assaulted those women, but I do know you. I left that life behind—I left him behind—and while I will regret that for the rest of my life, I have every reason to believe you did your job." Wrapping his strong, calloused fingers around her upper arms, Sullivan slid his thumbs over her skin in comforting circles. Goose bumps prickled down her arms, the combination of cold and hot fighting for her senses. "You might've brought up the charges against Marrok, but nobody forced him to eat his gun. And—" his wide, muscled chest expanded on a deep inhale "—from what I've learned about you over the last few days, I don't think you'd do something like that without cause."

Jane blinked. "You don't?"

"No," he said. "Because we're a team, and I do everything in my power to back up the people on my team. And if you can believe it, that even includes Elliot." His smile vaporized the knot of apprehension that had set up shop in her chest.

Jane sank into him, setting her ear against Sullivan's chest. The steady thump of his heart settled her fried nerve endings, but the silence before the storm wouldn't last long. Christopher was still out there, still hunting her. Sullivan slid his hands up her back, thankfully avoiding the burns across her shoulder blades. "Someday, when all this is over, you're going to have to tell me what Elliot did to land in your good graces."

"Only if you tell me how you got into my office." He set his lips against the crown of her head.

"Did you think it would be that easy?" A laugh escaped from between her lips. How could she have wanted to push Sullivan away? The man was a SEAL for crying out loud. He took on the most dangerous

threats to the United States with green paint on his
face and a motto on his lips.

All in, all the time. For her.

Chapter Ten

Splashes of pinks, greens and purples wove intricate designs overhead. Aurora borealis. One of the most beautiful things he'd had the privilege of experiencing in his life. But nothing compared to the woman next to him. Three days ago, she'd survived what would probably be the most brutal attack of her life, yet here she sat, stunning as ever.

Puffs of air crystallized in front of his mouth as Sullivan exhaled. The temperature had dropped significantly over the last fifteen minutes, but he didn't dare move. Not with those vibrant colors lighting up the snow before the heavy tree line, and not with Jane bundled this close into his side.

"I've never seen the northern lights this clearly before." A fresh mug of steaming coffee gripped in her hand, she stared up at the sky. Her pupils lit up as the shifts in color played across her face. She huddled deeper into her coat, setting her head against his shoulder. "Never thought I'd get the chance to sit here and enjoy it. It's nice."

Sullivan took a sip of his own black coffee, every high-strung muscle relaxing one by one. There was something about watching the northern lights, enjoying a cup of coffee, feeling a woman's heartbeat against his side that washed the tightness from his chest. When was the last time that'd happened? A year? Two? A decade? There'd been women. Nothing serious. But this—*Jane*—was different.

The Glock he'd strapped under his jacket pressed into him. Well, he wasn't completely relaxed. Menas could show up uninvited anytime, but the merc wouldn't touch another hair on Jane's head. Ever. Sullivan's gaze followed a line of bright pink up and over the thick tree line surrounding his property. "I come out here when I need to get away from everything and everyone, or my back needs actual support from a bed instead of my office sofa night after night. Clears my head." A smile tugged at one corner of his mouth as he took another drink of his coffee. This cabin had saved his life and his sanity more than once over the years, given him the solitude he craved. He lowered his voice. "Now, if I could get rid of you, it'd be perfect."

The muscles around her spine tightened as she rammed her elbow back into his solar plexus, and Sullivan couldn't help but flinch. The woman was strong, a lot stronger than she looked, the kind of woman he'd be proud to have at his side in the middle of a fight. Jane tipped her head back to meet his eyes, a gut-wrenching smile on her lips. "Tell more jokes like that. I've got all night."

"Jokes? What are you talking about? I was completely serious," he said.

"All right." Jane shoved away from him, hurrying across the snow-covered deck as flakes quickly replaced the ones her footsteps disrupted. Doubling over, she scooped up a handful of snow and packed it between her hands. "You want to play it that way? Let's do this."

She wound her arm back and let the snowball fly.

Sullivan saw it coming but couldn't move fast enough without spilling his coffee. He dived to the other side of the bench, but it was too late. Snow plastered against his neck and melted down into his heavy jacket, setting his skin on fire. Coffee surged over the edge of his mug and spilled down his jeans. A small growl reverberated through his chest. Slowly, carefully, he set the coffee down, stood and brushed off the remnants of pure white snow.

"Are you sure you want to go down this path, Captain?" Taking a single step forward, Sullivan mentally prepared his attack, always thinking ahead to the next move and the one after that. "Because I don't know if you're aware of this, but I've been known to handle myself in tough situations. Some fairly recently. And I wouldn't want you to get hurt."

"I played varsity softball in high school and college, even helped win the army's annual softball tournament while on tour. I think I can take care of myself." Jane tossed another ball of snow a few inches up in the air and caught it bare-handed. "Unless you're scared to take me on?"

"Oh, you're going down." Sullivan lunged.

Her eyes widened a split second before she turned tail and ran as fast as she could for the tree line. He appreciated the view as high-pitched laughter drifted over the deep snowbanks she tried plowing through, but Jane couldn't outrun him. Hour after hour, he'd trained in this forest, mentally mapped out every tree, every rock, anywhere the enemy could hide. She didn't have a chance. Snow kicked up around her as she darted toward the trees, and time seemed to slow.

All his life he'd fought for control. Relentless command over his body, his mind, his life. Growing up in a psychopath's house demanded nothing less, especially for Marrok's sake. But it was the military that had beat self-reliance into him. Nobody would control him, no one would hurt him like his father had hurt their family. But the warmth blossoming in his chest right now wasn't under his control. The second Jane had broken into his office, something had changed.

Four days. That was all it'd taken for her to melt his steel heart. Saving his life in the wilderness, putting her own at risk for Elliot when the fire broke out in Menas's apartment... None of it had lined up with her reputation. Could've been intentional, Jane's way of going the extra mile to secure his services, but Sullivan's instincts said that side of her never really existed in the first place. It'd been her defense mechanism, just as solitude had been his. Sullivan took a deep breath. Dozens of men had tried to stop his heart, but Jane could actually hurt him.

The thought knotted a tight fist of anxiety in his chest, but that didn't stop Sullivan from balling a handful of snow and nailing Jane in the middle of the back. The stitches in his arm stretched, but he pushed the discomfort to the back of his mind. She'd started this fight, he'd finish it. Sullivan bent over to gather more snow, but when he'd straightened, Jane had disappeared.

The smile pulling at his mouth vanished. Dead silence surrounded him, the tree line clear. He struggled to level out his racing heartbeat but took a deep breath.

Vanilla infused the light breeze cutting through the trees. She hadn't gone far. Darting for the patch of snow he'd last seen her, Sullivan tracked a set of footsteps toward the tree line. If Menas had gotten a hold of her...

A wall of coat-padded woman tackled him to the ground.

His heart rocketed into his throat as Jane's soft groan transformed into a trail of laughter and eased the tension hardening his muscles. He stared up at her, those sharp features surrounded by pinks, greens and blues in the dancing night sky. How had she managed to sneak up on him like that? He was a SEAL. Nothing got past him.

"Easy there, soldier. You don't want to make any sudden moves." Straddling him, Jane raised a snow-filled hand. Her smile lit up his insides and chased the remnants of the small adrenaline rush from his veins. "This snowball is deadly cold, and I'm prepared to use it."

Scanning the spot where he'd seen her positioned last, Sullivan rested his head into the snow. The sensitive skin on the back of his neck burned as he fought to catch his breath. "Where the hell did you come from?"

"Sneak attack from the trees." She'd lowered her voice as though she were telling him a secret, those perfect, kissable lips spread wide. Straightening, Jane washed the smile from her features. "Silence!"

Setting one hand on his chest, Jane let drops of melted snow fall against his neck. The beads of frigid water panicked his nervous system, and he struggled underneath Jane as though he couldn't bear the thought of torture. "I warned you, Sullivan Bishop. I am very good at this game and I'm serious about winning. Now, it's my turn to ask the questions."

An interrogation. Interesting.

"You got me. I'll tell you everything." Sullivan raised his hands in surrender, but with her strong thighs gripping his hips—every man's dream—he had no intention of cooperating with her demands. No. He was going to drag this out as long as he could.

"Good. And you shall be rewarded for your cooperation." She tossed the snowball to the ground and fitted her hand around his neck. Cold penetrated deep under his jacket as she leaned in close, her lips mere inches from his, but Sullivan didn't dare move. "Tell me, if you could go anywhere in the world right now, where would you go?"

He rested his palms on the tops of her knees, the denim covering her legs thin enough he could feel her body heat. The strong muscles under her clothing urged him to slide his hands higher, but Sullivan kept himself in control. He wasn't an animal. He wouldn't take until she offered. However long that might be. "I'd be stupid to move an inch right now."

"Yes, you would be, but that's not what I asked. And now you must be punished." The edges of her mouth turned upward, and before he understood what she'd meant, she held another handful of snow over his face and neck. Freezing water trailed under his coat and T-shirt, and Sullivan had had enough.

He maneuvered one foot behind hers and bucked with the opposite hip. Jane fell to the side, and he rolled on top of her, pinning her into the snow. He was back in control. And she was his. Snowflakes peppered their clothing, but soon they'd be too cold to do anything but run for the closest hot shower. Maybe together. He held his weight off her, careful of her wounds, grip loose around her wrists, giving her the chance to escape if she wanted. But the surprised look in those hazel eyes said she planned on staying right where she was. "Now it's my turn to ask the questions."

"All right," she said. "Shoot."

"Are you going back into the army when this investigation is over?" He shouldn't have asked, didn't have any right, but Sullivan hadn't been able to think of anything else since he'd checked her out of the hospital a few hours ago.

Any evidence of playfulness disappeared from her features. "I haven't thought about it. After what happened at the factory, I didn't think I'd make it out alive."

Nothing but their combined breathing filled the silence, as a fresh wave of snow fell from the sky. Hell. He hadn't meant to resurrect those memories. The past few minutes with her had put them, and the man responsible, to the back of his mind. Freeing him from responsibility, revenge, rage. Sullivan lightened his hold on her and pulled back to give her some room.

"You are not what has happened to you, Jane." He tamped down on the strange ache growing in the middle of his chest. Sullivan had never been the relationship type, but right now, with Jane pinned underneath him, he could see himself following her down that path when this was over. If she let him. Because the thought of losing her in the middle of that highway had nearly killed him. "You're what you choose to become. Remember that."

Her mouth parted, breathing slightly uneven. "Are we really going after Christopher?"

"I like to finish what I start," he said.

Jane pushed her weight onto her elbows to sit up, with him still straddled across her legs. A shiver rode across her chest. "Do you think we'll survive?"

"I don't know." Better to tell her the truth, but as her features fell, Sullivan let the urge to protect her rage through him. His hands fisted in her thick jacket, pulling her toward him. "But I'm sure as hell not going down without a fight."

SULLIVAN BISHOP WASN'T the knight in shining armor, the one who had never been to war. He was the knight with tarnished and dented armor who knew how to win the fight and keep her safe. He'd taken Christopher and his band of mercenaries down once before. He could do it again.

But what if he couldn't or, worse, didn't survive?

Her gaze snapped to his. Jane clenched her jaw, refusing to let her thoughts sprint down that path. Because, if she was completely honest with herself, she'd rather run from Christopher for the rest of her life than let Sullivan become another casualty in this mess.

"Jane?" Concern deepened his tone.

Forget the frigid temperatures and the falling snow. Her body urged her to close the small space between them. She wanted to kiss him. More than wanted. *Needed* to. Puffs of frozen air solidified in front of her mouth. And the longer Jane studied his shadow of a beard, the sea-blue eyes that revealed his true intensions, the way his forehead creased when he was thinking something over, that need strengthened. "Don't talk. Just…"

Heat spread behind her sternum, lifting her up,

pressing her against him. The burns across her back protested, but the dull sting wouldn't stop her. Only the sound of their combined exhales reached her ears, her heartbeat steady, calm. Cold seeping through her jeans demanded her attention, but anticipation for the feeling of his lips against hers—of finally tasting him—drowned out her body's survival instincts.

Sullivan's patience disappeared.

Gripping the back of her neck, he crushed his mouth to hers. The cold reaching down into her bones melted away as the rich taste of him spread across her tongue. Black coffee, peppermint and something smoother. Like a dark scotch. The elaborate combination heightened her senses to another level. The pressure at the back of her neck lightened, but Jane didn't move away. Tilting her head to the side, she opened wider for him, invited him to take more. Take all of her.

But Sullivan took his time. Nibbling, nuzzling, going slow. So slow. Her insides flooded with need as he nipped at her bottom lip, a spike of desire rushing through her blood. He threaded his fingers through the nap of hair at the base of her neck, pulling her harder against him. Her nerve endings fired in little electric pulses each time his lips moved against hers. The aurora above her, the snow below her, Sullivan around her. Jane never wanted to move.

But the Alaskan wilderness wasn't kind.

A shiver chased across her skin, and Sullivan pulled away. A burst of laughter rumbled deep in his chest. Didn't matter she'd worn her thickest coat from the duffel bag Elliot had dropped off. He ran his palms up and down her arms to generate some heat. "You're freezing."

Danger loomed ahead, but the man straddling her in the middle of his snow-covered property smiled. Her heart rate kicked up, and it had nothing to do with her mind telling her this couldn't happen. Sullivan Bishop, former navy SEAL burdened with years of death and destruction, looked happy for the first time since Jane had broken into his office. Melted snow had penetrated through her clothing but, in that moment, she didn't care. The world had changed. He'd changed. And she couldn't help but smile back. "I don't know how. You're like a furnace. Your body heat could keep us both alive for days."

"Yeah, but it was yours that kept me alive out here the first time." He pushed to his feet, offering her a hand to help her up. "Which I intend to repay you for."

"You've saved my life plenty since I pulled you out of the snow." She reached for him without hesitation, sliding her fingers across his calloused palms. Not harsh, but worked. Like him. The colors of the northern lights blended together as Sullivan pulled her into his chest, but they bled into the dark night sky the longer they stood together. Mother Nature's show had faded, but Jane would never forget these last few minutes. Never forget Sullivan when this ended. She fingered the zipper on his dark coat. "But if you want to pay me back, I have a couple things in mind."

Jane tugged on his jacket until his mouth met hers once again. She wasn't gentle. She wasn't careful. She meant to conquer, to banish the last few days. Pushing every bullet missed, every patch of skin burned, every second she felt like she was being watched into her kiss, Jane reveled in the feeling of lightness overwhelming her body. She breathed easier, sinking into

Sullivan as she broke their connection. "That is, if you're up for it."

"I have a lot of unchecked frustration built up from the last few days. You might be the perfect person to help with that." The predatory desire raging in his eyes bolted straight to her core. Another round of heated arousal flooded her system as Sullivan wrapped his large hand around hers and tugged her after him. Snow kicked up into her boots, but Jane didn't slow as they vaulted up the front porch stairs.

A wall of warm air slammed into her, and Sullivan kicked the door closed behind them. Then his hands were on her. Pulling down the zipper on her coat, shoving the thick layers to the floor. His coat fell next, as Jane kicked off her boots, lost in his masculine scent, the mountain that was his rock-solid body. Her heart pounded loud in her ears, but nothing like in the factory as she'd run for her life. She was safe here. Sullivan was safe.

"You should get out of those wet clothes." He dropped his mouth to her neck, licking, nipping, hiking her arousal to levels she'd never experienced before. Her insides burned, every inch of her skin aware of only one thing: him.

But Jane planted her hand on his chest. All of this, the northern lights, the snowball fight, the kiss, it was everything she could hope for. But what about when it was over? Her leave was due to end in a week, and Sullivan had a business—a team—to run. Neither of those things left much room to explore this beyond tonight, but maybe that didn't have to be a bad thing. Maybe it was for the best. Because no matter how many people she'd cut herself off from, those who got close to her always ended up getting hurt. She stared straight up at him, almost a foot shorter but determined to hold her ground. "Before we do this, I need to know something."

"Ask me." He slid his hand over hers, his calluses scraping against her oversensitized skin. Sincerity cooled the flood of desire in his gaze. "I'll tell you anything you want to know. No more secrets between us. I trust you."

"You do?" Her throat went dry, but the steady thump of his heart against her hand chased the surprise to the back of her mind.

"Yes." Sullivan stared down at her hand on his chest, stroking the back of her hand with his fingers. "You might've blackmailed me into helping you, but I'm glad you did." A laugh rumbled under her hand, and Jane couldn't help but smile. "I can't remember the last time I felt this good." His hand on her hip pinned her in place. "You already know my secrets. I don't have to hide from you like I do from my team. I don't have to be so controlled. It's…freeing."

The backs of her knees weakened, and Jane fisted his shirt to keep her balance. "Wow. You really know how to sweep a woman off her feet."

"That's the plan." A gut-twisting smile deepened the laugh lines around his mouth. Sullivan spread his fingers across the bare skin beneath her T-shirt. His touch battled the waves of debilitating coldness and won. In seconds, he'd warmed her more than an hour-long hot shower ever could have. "But what did you need to ask me?"

Ask him? Right. Shaking her head, Jane fought to focus over the desperate urge to mold herself to him. She pulled her bottom lip between her teeth, that knot of concern holding her tight. People might've gotten hurt because of her in the past, but Sullivan had made it perfectly clear he could take care of himself, had even proved it over the last few days. So maybe letting herself have feelings for the former navy SEAL she'd blackmailed wouldn't get him killed.

Jane checked the distance to the single bathroom over her shoulder, then turned back to him. "I need to know how long it's going to take for you to get me into a hot shower."

Faster than she thought possible, Sullivan buried his forearms behind her knees and lifted her into his arms without regard for the stitches in his arm. The cabin blurred in her vision, but he remained steady, a constant. The warm swirl of desire in his eyes tightened Jane's hold on his T-shirt. "Why don't we find out?"

Chapter Eleven

Jane was asleep in his arms. Warm. Soft. Everything he'd ever imagined when he'd let his mind go down that path. Hope. Unquenched desire. And more. But the sun climbing over the Chugach Mountains claimed his attention. Sullivan dropped his nose to the crown of her head and breathed deep. Last night had been perfect in every regard, but, unfortunately, they were out of time.

He reached for his phone on the nightstand and swiped his thumb across the screen. A knot of tension chased back the peace running through his veins. The latest surveillance from Anthony and Elliot revealed Menas and his mercenaries gearing up in an abandoned construction site just outside the city. Sullivan knew the area but flicked through the brief's attached photos and the official report of Menas's history anyway. After skipping bail for the assault of three women in college, the seasoned hunter had realized he could make a living off doing what he did best: inflicting pain. Anthony's report started with a few jobs Menas had picked up working security for a Seattle company under an assumed name, then sped through the mercenary's climb to the private sector. From there, the money got better, the guns got bigger and Menas had put together his own team of mercenaries.

Right now, he had a team of three remaining, including himself, all highly armed with military-grade weapons and gear. Then again, the chopper landing in the middle of Seward Highway had already given Sullivan a clue. He dropped the phone to the sheets as Jane shifted in his arms, careful not to wake her. He'd had run-ins with mercs before, but not a single one of them had access to the kind of gear Menas had strapped to his hunting party. Despite not having anything to do with the military, Menas must have some kind of inside connection. Because stealing that grade of weapons and ammunition took a lot of bullets and skills that Sullivan would've heard of before now.

Something else must be going on here. Maybe Jane had been right back in the hospital. The statute of limitations to prosecute Menas for sexual assault had run out in the state of Washington several months ago, which meant the mercenary had no reason to come after her now.

Unless Menas and his team were only doing something that they'd been hired to do.

"How long do we have before we have to get out of bed?" The huskiness in Jane's sleep-filled voice raised the hairs on the back of his neck. Along with other things. Her fingers trailed across his chest, resurrecting overused nerve endings and sending a shiver across his chest. There was nothing like her touch. No one had brought his body to the brink over and over again like she had.

He pressed a kiss to her forehead, raptured with those hazel eyes staring up at him. Checking his phone again, he hit the silence button and rolled into her. "We have about fifteen minutes before Elliot walks through the front door."

"Mmm." Jane pressed her lips to his. The kiss was oddly sweet and full of promises he'd die trying to keep. He'd never been the sweet type. But promises? He intended to live up to every single one of them. For her. She maneuvered on top of him, chest to chest, the wrinkled sheets bunching over the small of her back. Soft skin surrounded him from almost every angle, and Sullivan wouldn't budge an inch. Dropping her chin to his sternum, she smiled. "Tell me he doesn't have a key and we can stretch those fifteen minutes out as long as possible."

For the first time in longer than Sullivan could remember, he laughed openly. Wrapping the top of his foot around hers, Sullivan flipped her onto her back and tossed his phone to the floor. He intended to bury himself in her warmth all over again, kissing her with everything he had left. "He most certainly does not have a key."

"Good," she said.

Fifteen minutes later, pounding on the front door pulled Sullivan from heaven. He shoved his legs through his jeans and laced his feet into his boots, closing the door behind him as Jane dressed. His heartbeat returned to a steady rhythm the more he distanced himself from her. Damn, that woman could do things to him with a single look, but last night and this morning? She'd turned his brain to mush and him into a grinning idiot.

"Right on time, Elliot." *Unfortunately.* Sullivan

ripped open the front door, every cell in his body running cold.

Elliot wasn't standing on his porch.

A solid kick to the stomach knocked Sullivan to the floor, but he rebounded fast as adrenaline dumped into his blood. He lunged for the Glock in the shoulder holster hanging off one of the dining table chairs. Two pricks of pain embedded into the muscles along his bare back, then fired with white-hot electricity. Soft clicking reached his ears as the Taser wiped out his central nervous system. His body spasmed, curling his toes in his boots and his fingers into his palms. Jaw clenched, Sullivan fought in vain to reach the gun as current after current of electricity washed over him. The spasms rolled him onto his back, but he failed to dislodge the Taser's probes.

Christopher Menas stalked through the door, two members of his team on his tail, weapons up and fingers on triggers. A cruel smile split open the slash Jane had cut into the mercenary's cheekbone, and Sullivan couldn't help but smile back. Must've hurt like hell. They fanned out into the living room. Searching. "Check the bedroom. She's in here somewhere."

Jane was smart. She would've heard the commotion and gone out the bedroom window as fast as possible. Seconds ticked by. One of Menas's teammates kicked in the bedroom door when he couldn't open it manually, but the resulting silence said there was no sign of Jane. Sullivan kept his attention on the lead mercenary, the uncontrollable spasms lessening. She'd gotten out of the cabin. Relief flooded through him, but it wasn't over. He'd give her the time she needed to escape. Even if she had to leave him behind.

Menas's expression hardened as he focused those dark eyes back onto Sullivan. The mercenary lunged, wrapping a strong hand around his throat, and brought Sullivan to his feet. The probes ripped from his skin as Menas discarded the Taser and replaced the weapon in his hand with the M16 slung over his shoulder. One pull of the trigger, and the best medical examiner in the world would have a difficult time identifying Sullivan's insides. "Where is she?"

"You know something? I'm glad you're armed this time." Sullivan knocked Menas's hand away from his throat and threw a punch right into that gash on his face. The merc doubled over; Menas's trigger finger was too twitchy. Bullets sprayed across the floor, up the far wall and straight through one of his men, who hit the floor. Sullivan kicked the M16 away, but a fist to the right side of his face forced his vision to go dark for a split second.

Another kick to the torso threw him out the open front door and down the two short stairs on the porch. Blistering cold spread across his bare chest as he hit the snow.

Menas charged full force and caught Sullivan around the ribs, hiking him up and over his shoulder.

Sullivan threw two elbows to the spine. Three. Menas dropped him. Clutching the mercenary's jacket, Sullivan pushed the bastard backward, aiming punches for Menas's kidneys along the way. Sullivan blocked the first attempt to knock him out, but not the second. He stumbled back, out of breath, as Menas took a second to compose himself. Snow kicked up around him, but he barely felt the temperatures now as anticipation pumped hard through his veins. The teammate Menas hadn't killed watched on from the porch, weapon aimed to finish the job in case his superior lost the fight. Because this was between him and Christopher Menas.

Menas rolled his fists in a circular motion as though he'd done a few rounds of illegal bare-knuckle boxing before becoming a gun for hire. Wouldn't surprise Sullivan. The mercenary came at him with a straight blow to the head, which Sullivan blocked with his forearm, spinning his attacker ninety degrees and shooting an elbow straight into the back of Menas's knee. The mercenary's screams filled the small clearing as Menas shifted most of his weight to the opposite leg.

Time to end this.

"I warned you not to come after her, Menas." Sullivan clutched the mercenary's jacket, lining him up as he pulled back his elbow for one last hit. Jane wanted her stalker turned over to the authorities, but there was no stopping men like Christopher Menas. He leaned over his attacker. "You should've listened."

"My man over there will shoot you the second my heart stops beating. Then he'll go after Jane." The mercenary stared up at him. A line of blood dripped from his bottom lip but didn't stop him from pulling his mouth up into another crooked smile. "Is that what you want?"

Sullivan glanced toward the assault rifle targeted at him. "Doesn't matter what I want anymore. You went after Jane and tried to kill me in the process. No one is going to remember your name when you're dead."

A glint of sunlight flashed off the blade cutting toward him. Menas moved fast, faster than Sullivan thought possible after the energy they'd both expended, and sliced through muscle along his side. Searing pain spread across the left side of Sullivan's body. Blood seeped down into the waistband of his jeans and stained the bright white snow around him.

Repositioning the blade in his hand, Menas hiked himself higher in order to stab down at him. Sullivan crossed his forearms, barely holding back the blade's tip from his face. Menas was strong, but Sullivan was stronger.

He threw a knee into the mercenary's midsection and watched as the blade landed in a snowbank a few feet away. "Any other surprises you want to try before I break your neck?"

Sullivan's breath heaved in and out of his lungs. He was losing too much blood to keep this up for long, but Menas wasn't recovering as quickly either.

"This isn't over with me, you know." Menas bent at the waist, holding his side. Most likely a few broken ribs. Maybe Sullivan was lucky enough one of them had punctured a lung. "I'm not the only one he hired."

Sullivan's heart stuttered. "What did you just say?"

The mercenary lunged again, and Sullivan widened his stance for the hit.

A single gunshot exploded in the small clearing.

Both Menas and Sullivan turned toward the shooter across the property, as Menas's teammate swung his assault rifle toward Jane.

"Get away from him, Christopher." She held Sullivan's favorite Glock straight up in the air, but, closing a few feet of space between them, she aimed straight for Menas. "This is between you and me."

HER WORDS SOUNDED a whole lot more confident than Jane felt. She held the gun steady, relying on the countless hours she'd forced herself to brush up on her skills at the range. Her heart drummed too fast in her chest. Muscle memory kicked in after a few heartbeats, but these were mercenaries she was dealing with. Not some muscled jock of an ex-boyfriend who hadn't been able to get over the past. He'd turned himself into a professional killer.

"Jane, what are you doing? Get out of here." Sullivan doubled over. Blood dripped from between his fingers on his left side. He was injured. Damn it. What had Christopher done to him? Her protector didn't stay down long. He raised that intense gaze to her, expression stone-like, the muscles in his jaw frozen. "Get out of here. *Now.*"

He was too stubborn and too strong.

But Jane wasn't going anywhere.

"Once again, the army is coming to bail the navy out of trouble." Not a time to make jokes, but her gut instincts were telling her all she needed to do here was stall. Elliot was on his way. Wasn't that what Sullivan had said earlier? She only hoped the private investigator had thought to bring backup.

"No," she continued. "I'm getting you out of this mess. Once and for all." She focused on Christopher. Sullivan had done his job. He'd found her stalker and she could take care of the rest. "Attempted murder. Stalking in the second degree. I could keep going. You have a lifetime of prison ahead of you, Christopher."

"Janey." Christopher limped two steps toward her, hands in the air as though he was about to surrender. Jane knew better. The last thing on the mercenary's mind was giving up. He took one more step. "We both know you're not going to shoot me. You're a lawyer, remember? Not a killer."

Jane dropped the gun a few inches and pulled the trigger. The bullet disappeared into the snow at Christopher's feet. "I might be a lawyer, but I still know how to use a gun." She directed him to the right. "Now, have your friend join you over there by Sullivan and drop your weapons."

Christopher's smile burned straight through her soul. Pure evil. "Janey—"

"Do it!" She fired another round near his right foot. Her hand tingled from the kickback, but Jane was prepared to fire a lot more shots if he forced her.

"Guess we've got to do what the lady says." Shrugging at his teammate, the mercenary tossed his remaining guns and blades into the snow at his feet and maneuvered closer to Sullivan. The second mercenary followed suit, losing his gun in the snow. "What now, sweetheart? Going to wait until the cavalry shows up? Because I've got bad news for you, Janey. This will all be over before they can even get here."

Where the small muscles in her face slackened, she noted all of the wonderful muscle in Sullivan's body went rock hard, even from this distance. His eyes widened. "Jane!"

Strong arms wrapped around her from behind, picking her up off her feet. Jane threw her head back, hitting solid bone, but whoever had her wasn't going to let a broken nose stop him. Sullivan lunged for her, but Christopher landed a hit to the gash in his side, and the SEAL went down. Sullivan's groan echoed all around her. She struggled inside the suffocating grip squeezing the oxygen from her body, her arms and legs fighting her brain's commands. Her vision blurred, and the gun fell from her hand.

"I'm a killer, Jane, and I've been doing this a long time now. I learn from my mistakes," Christopher said. Both mercenaries collected their weapons. Christopher planted a boot along Sullivan's spine, pressing his bare chest into the snow-covered ground, and widened his arms straight out to his sides. "You chose an ex-navy SEAL to protect you. I chose to bring a hell of a lot more men." He brushed the snow from his handgun and pressed a muddy boot into the side of Sullivan's head, taking aim. "And now, because of you, he's going to die."

"No!" Jane rocketed her elbow back into her attacker's stomach and then straight into his face when his grip lightened. She grabbed the fallen Glock at her feet and pumped her legs, the air in her lungs freezing. The mercenary at Christopher's side ran to head her off. The distance between them closed fast. She wasn't strong enough to take him alone, but Jane had run out of options. Sullivan wasn't going to die because of her. Not ever.

A sniper shot echoed from beyond the tree line, then ripped through the oncoming mercenary's collarbone. Jane watched as his face contorted into painful surprise and he dropped to his knees. In her next breath, he fell face-first into the snow, as another bullet took care of the contract killer rushing up behind her.

"Too late, Janey." Christopher squeezed the trigger. Sullivan's body jerked as the mercenary crouched low, desperation to survive bright in his dark eyes.

"Sullivan!" He'd been hit. Jane lunged. Her left shoulder slammed into Christopher, and she pushed as hard as she could to get him off his feet. The world spun as they rolled together through the snow. Once. Twice.

Christopher dug his fingernails into her arms, keeping her close, controlling her movements. She fought to dislodge the gun from his thigh holster, but couldn't get her arms free. He pinned her to the ground and smiled. He had her right where he wanted her, and her stomach revolted. "Just like old times, Janey. Remember?"

"Get your hands off her." Christopher's weight disappeared as Sullivan ripped him back. The mercenary stumbled but straightened fast. Blood dripped down Sullivan's side and from the bullet wound in his opposite shoulder. No normal man could survive that much damage and still have the strength to fight a contract killer.

But Sullivan Bishop was no ordinary man.

He swung, connecting with Christopher's face, his kidneys, his spine. The mercenary kept trying to block the hits, but Sullivan didn't let up, like a boxer who knew it'd be his last fight. Christopher wobbled on his feet, mouth hanging open, one eye swelling shut.

Jane stood, collecting her discarded Glock from the snow. Blood rushed to her head, but she stumbled after them as they neared the tree line. Those sniper shots that'd taken out Christopher's team said the Blackhawk Security team was close. If Sullivan knocked the mercenary out long enough to restrain him, Elliot or Anthony could haul him in while Jane got Sullivan to the hospital. His strength wouldn't last forever. Already, his punches weren't having the same effect, and Christopher realized it.

And then Christopher produced something in his

hand. The mercenary ran forward, shoving a blade up and under Sullivan's rib cage.

"No!" She ran hard as Christopher dropped Sullivan to the ground. No. This wasn't happening. "Sullivan." Her senses sharpened. Jane was already raising the gun. Her finger was on the trigger as Christopher limped toward her, Sullivan's blood on his hands. And she fired, hitting the vulnerable flesh just below his Kevlar vest.

The mercenary froze in his tracks, mouth still open.

She fired again and again and again. Blistering cold worked to freeze the tears streaking down her cheeks, but Jane emptied the magazine until the gun merely clicked in her hand.

Christopher collapsed into the snow. Dead.

Her shoulders dropped. Rushing past his worthless body, she fell at Sullivan's side. He stared straight up into the sky. "No, no, no, no. Sullivan, come on. Stay with me."

"You did it, Jane." His voice strained, something wet and guttural choking his words.

"*We* did it. It's over." She'd pulled him through the Alaskan wilderness once. She could do it again to get him the help he desperately needed. "Come on. We need to get you inside before you freeze to death."

The trees to her left shifted, and Jane raised the gun. She'd emptied the magazine into Christopher. No time to go for Sullivan's stash of weapons in the cabin. Without any rounds left in the Glock, she couldn't stop more attackers in their tracks, but Christopher's men weren't taking her from Sullivan. She might be a lawyer, but she'd kill everyone who tried before leaving him to die here alone. Two figures burst from the tree line, both heavily armed, and Jane's arm sank with the weight of the gun. Elliot and Anthony rushed forward, the weapons expert already barking orders into the radio in his hand.

"Jane." Sullivan wrapped his fingers around hers, his pupils growing bigger until limited amounts of the sea blue she'd started falling in love with remained. Bringing the back of her hand to his mouth, he kissed the sensitive skin there and a chill swept through her. "Go."

"I'm not leaving you." Hot tears fell onto his chest, smudging lines of blood. "This is all my fault."

A soft thumping reverberated across the property, but Jane had attention for only the man who'd nearly died to save her life. The man she'd blackmailed into this. Her hair whipped in front of her face. Where had the wind come from?

"Jane, you need to get out of the way." Rough hands wrapped around her upper arms, but she shrugged them away. She wasn't sure who'd grabbed her. Didn't matter. "The EMTs have to get through."

"Help him." She held on to Sullivan's hand tighter. "Please, help him."

"Jane, come on." Elliot's voice filtered through the fog around her brain. He tugged her free of Sullivan's grip as a team of EMTs closed in a tight circle around him. "You don't want to see this."

"This is all my fault. I'm sorry." Jane couldn't think. Couldn't breathe. Legs weak as Elliot dragged her against him and carried her away, Jane kept her eyes locked on Sullivan's motionless hand against the spreading red snow. "I'm so sorry."

Chapter Twelve

Bullets. Blood. Scars. Some things never changed.

A groan vibrated through Sullivan's chest as he straightened in the hospital bed. Hell, that hurt. But the pain and haziness disappeared as he caught sight of a beautiful head of short black hair sprawled across the white sheets on one side of his bed.

Jane.

He sat forward, brushing a strand of soft hair away from her face. Her breathing sped up, and a smile pulled at one side of his mouth. He'd never get used to the way she reacted to him when he touched her. She'd wrapped her long fingers around his before falling asleep, and he didn't dare pull away. With her fast asleep, the nightmares of the last five days had slipped from her features. The bruise along her cheek had lightened, the cut across her head healing without stitches. Not an ounce of fear pulled her expression taut. She looked peaceful. For once. He'd traveled the world, experienced the most amazing and destructive forces of nature, but Jane Reise was by far the most amazing.

And his.

This isn't over with me, you know. I'm not the only one he hired. Menas. Sullivan tightened his grip around

Jane's hand. The mercenary had deserved every bullet she'd emptied into him, but this was far from over. Whoever had hired Menas and his team wasn't finished. Not until Jane's heart stopped beating, which wouldn't happen. Because he'd take another hundred stabs to the torso by another dozen mercenaries if it meant she got to walk away from this. And she would. They both would.

"I don't think I've ever seen you smile at another human being like that. A piece of chocolate cake, yes. Not a woman." Anthony Harris's forest green eyes—free of sunglasses—locked on to Sullivan. The former Ranger buried his hands deep into his jacket pockets as though he didn't know what to do without a gun in his grip. Which was probably why he kept scanning the room for potential threats. Anthony cleared his throat. "If someone made me happy like that, I'd fight like hell to keep her with me, too."

The number one thing Sullivan could count on his weapons expert for? The blatant truth, even when his trigger-happy best friend should keep his mouth shut. "How long has she been here?"

"She hasn't left your side since the EMTs brought you through the front doors. Wouldn't let the technicians look at her until they got your stats stable." Anthony rolled his wrist to check his watch. "Going on thirty hours. She's been asleep for about two."

Jane. Always putting others first, even when Menas had a gun aimed at her head.

Sullivan swallowed as the memories of the final battle with Menas flashed across his mind. He'd almost lost her. Again. But this time, it'd been his own fault.

"Tell me how we missed the fact Christopher Menas was contracted to come after Jane."

"I've worked with guys like him and his team." Anthony shifted in his seat. "They've got the resources and the motives to create entire identities that hide what they do for a living. Some have two or three they cycle through to keep governments off their backs. Technically, they don't exist. No families. No friends. They're good at what they do. But Menas. Man, this guy is something else."

"He used his real name." Sullivan's gaze flickered to the rise and fall of Jane's chest. Why would a mercenary take the chance of being identified? He rested his head back against the mountain of pillows behind him. "He wanted Jane to know he was coming after her."

To throw off suspicion of the real threat?

"How did Menas manage to escape your and Elliot's detail?" he asked.

"He knew we were there. He sent a four-man team straight at us as he and three others sped from the construction site." Spreading one hand over his beard, Anthony let his eyebrows hike higher, a telling sign of stress. "I tried calling, but you never answered your phone."

Because he'd tossed it to the floor to have a few more minutes with Jane. Damn it. This whole thing could've been avoided had he just been able to keep his hands off her. He'd put her in danger. He'd *failed* her. Sullivan studied the rise and fall of Jane's back. She'd gone up against a mercenary. To save his life. Again. Shaking the disbelief from his thoughts, he dropped the back of his head to the pillows propping him up. He could really fall for this woman. He ran his free hand down his face. Hell, maybe he already had.

"Call Elizabeth. I want a list of Menas's associates, his phone records from the cell you recovered from the cabin, his laptop if you can track it down, travel records and anything else she can get her hands on. Jane said the stalking started while she was on tour. Find out who else on our suspect list has made a visit to Afghanistan." Sullivan ripped the IV out of the catheter in his inner wrist. Stinging pain radiated up his arm, but he pushed it to the back of his mind. He'd survived worse. "Get it to me as soon as possible."

Anthony speed-dialed Blackhawk Security's resident former NSA analyst and shut the door behind him. They wouldn't have the intel for at least another hour. Enough time for Sullivan to put a new plan in place. With Menas's team out of commission, they were back at square one. But the question had changed from who was stalking Jane to who wanted her dead enough to hire a contract killer?

A soft moan whispered from between her lips, and Jane's hold on his hand tightened. He stroked his fingers along the inner line of her wrist, bringing her around slowly. She lifted her head, a smile pulling at the edges of her delicate mouth. Those hazel eyes brightened as she studied him. "You're awake." She pulled her hand from his and pressed her palms into her eye sockets. He'd never tire of the huskiness in her voice when she woke, an experience he intended to live over and over. She sat back in the chair, stretching her neck to one side, then the other. "How are you feeling?"

"I'll live. Thanks to you." He hadn't been okay with her stepping between him and Menas at the time, but without her rushing the mercenary at the last second, Sullivan would've died from high-speed lead poisoning. He owed her his life. Again. "How many times have you saved my life now? Two or three?"

"Three." A flash of straight white teeth deepened the laugh lines around her mouth and Sullivan's heart stuttered. "Should I make another reference to how the army comes in to save the day or let it be this time around?"

"I knew you were going to go there. You grunts never could take a win humbly. Got to let the whole world know you saved the day." He shook his head, but had never felt so relaxed, so…at peace than he did in that moment. Anthony had been right. Jane made him happy, gave him purpose beyond running Blackhawk Security, and a reason to look forward to the future. And he'd fight like hell to keep her.

"You always know what to say." Jane slid her hand back into his, a few cuts and bruises decorating the thin skin along the top of her hand. Her smile disappeared. Connecting that beautiful gaze with his, she rolled her bottom lip between her teeth. Not a good sign. "My leave is due to end in two days, Sullivan. The army was generous enough to give me these last few months off, but with the threat gone—" she inhaled slowly "—with Christopher gone, I need to get back to work. In Afghanistan."

The pad of his thumb stopped midstroke against the back of her hand. *Afghanistan?* "You're leaving."

Not a question. Sullivan rested his head back against the pillow, staring up at the ceiling. How could he have been so stupid? Of course she'd planned on going back to Afghanistan. Her life was there. Her job was there. At least, until she was reassigned.

"Unless…" she said.

He straightened. "Unless, what?"

"Unless I put in to be reassigned here in Anchorage." That gut-wrenching smile of hers returned, and Sullivan couldn't help but hang on every word. "There's an opening at Joint Base Elmendorf-Richardson, and I'm thinking of taking it. It'd be a step down in salary for me, but Anchorage could be my last assignment before I have the option of discharge in about a year. My CO has already said the position's mine. All I have to do is ask."

"Then ask." The words were out of his mouth before he had a chance to think about what he was asking of her. He exhaled hard, but the tendons between his neck and shoulder strained. Sitting up as best he could, Sullivan ignored the pain shooting throughout his torso and brought Jane up onto the bed. Damn if he popped a few stitches. Jane was worth every ounce of agony. "I'm not going to lie. I'm not going to play games with you. I want you to ask for the transfer. I want you to stay here, with me."

Her heart beat fast against the soft column of her throat. He'd caught her off guard. Good. Smoothing her fingers over his arms, she studied him from the waist up. "Great. Because I already put the call in to my CO while you were passed out. He's sending me the papers in the morning."

Sullivan threaded his fingers through her hair and brought her mouth to his. He drank her in, memorized her in ways he'd never experienced before. He kept the kiss soft when all he wanted to do was claim her. She was staying. For him. For them. Tilting her head to the side, she opened her mouth wide, inviting him, nipping at him. She pressed herself against him, but the leads connected to strategic points on his body were determined to block his access to her. The EKG pounded loud in his ears, an echo of his own heart rate, and Sullivan couldn't drown the laugh rumbling through his chest. He gently framed her jaw with both hands, calluses against silk, and put a few small centimeters between them. "Any more of this and the nurses are going to run in here thinking I'm having a heart attack."

His hospital room door opened, but he couldn't focus on anything but her. His Jane.

"As much as I'd like to leave you two to go at it like rabbits," Anthony said, "I've got that new intel you wanted."

Sullivan's stomach sank. Right. The world wouldn't stop just for them. "Anything we can use?"

"New intel?" Jane studied Anthony, then turned back to him, eyebrows drawn inward. She checked the clock on the wall. "Oh. If this is another case, I can go. I'm supposed to give my statement to Anchorage PD in a few minutes anyway." She gathered her jacket in one hand and stood. "Then I need to go home and change."

Sullivan clamped his hand around her arm, staring up at her without any idea how he would tell her the truth. He owed her an answer, owed her far more than that, but his instincts screamed he was about to lose Jane all over again. Right when they'd agreed to give this a shot. But if she discovered the truth on her own? He'd never see her again. "It's not a new case, Jane." He licked his bottom lip, a nervous habit of hers he'd obviously inherited since setting sights on her in his office. "It's your case."

"What do you mean? Christopher is dead. My case is closed." Her eyes narrowed as seconds passed. Confusion slipped over her perfect features. "I shot him seven times, Sullivan. He's officially been declared dead."

"Christopher Menas was paid to take you out, Jane." He clamped his hand around hers, desperate to keep her within arm's reach. Not for her—Jane was strong—but for his own selfish need to hold on to her. "And whoever hired him is still after you."

"WHAT?" PANIC THREATENED to overwhelm her. No. The nightmare was over. She was supposed to get her life back. She'd put in for the transfer to Anchorage to start over. She and Sullivan were going to try to make this work. The room spun and Jane gripped the sheets for balance. Someone had hired Menas to come after her? "Who...who would hire a mercenary team to take me out?"

She was one woman. A lawyer for the army with no record of sending innocent soldiers to their deaths, not someone with a highly politicized agenda. She mostly dealt with divorces, immigration and passport issues, and reenlistment questions when she wasn't assigned to prosecute cases. She wasn't important.

"That's what I'm trying to find out. Anthony has worked with men like Menas before. I'm hoping we can get a hit off a source in one of his circles. I also asked my NSA contact to pull phone records." Sullivan wrapped his strong, steady hand around hers. "Menas would've had contact with whoever hired him. We're going to find out how."

This wasn't happening.

Christopher was dead. Despite her initial intentions to bring him to justice, she'd *killed* him and almost lost Sullivan in the process. Her hands shook as she dropped her hold on the sheets and fisted a handful of her own hair instead. Thirty hours. That was all the relief she'd had with Christopher's death. What was she supposed to do now?

Slivers of blood seeped through Sullivan's bandages. A bullet wound, a knife to the gut and a slash across the arm. She couldn't remember how many stitches the doctor had told her they'd had to sew in to keep him together, but he couldn't go through that again.

"Jane, I need to know what's going through your head, baby." Sullivan rubbed small circles into the back of her hand. The weight of those captivating sea-blue eyes studying her was almost suffocating. "Tell me."

She couldn't go home. Couldn't go back to work. And she couldn't keep putting the man she'd started to fall for in harm's way. Not for her.

Whoever'd hired Christopher Menas and his team had done their research on her, and if Christopher was reporting back, they knew she'd recruited Sullivan to keep her safe. She exhaled hard. Sullivan had done his job. He'd found her stalker. Her muscles tightened. Now she had to learn to protect herself. Jane stood, slipping out of his grasp a little too easily. He'd let her go. Because that was the kind of man he was. Considerate. Caring. Never one to thwart her own agency. She headed for the door. "I have to go."

"For how long?" he asked.

The rough edge to his tone revealed exactly what she'd feared, and Jane stopped cold. He'd either read her mind or read her expression, she didn't know. It didn't matter. She had to get out of here. Away from him. Away from the whole Blackhawk Security team. The nightmare wasn't ever going to end. They were all still in danger as long as she stuck around. Anthony waited in front of the door, capable of keeping her here if Sullivan ordered. But he wouldn't. She had to believe that.

"Jane, we can fight this thing together. You don't have to run." His voice washed over her in comforting waves, and it took everything she had not to turn back around. "Please. I don't want to lose you."

"Then you know exactly how I feel." Jane turned, her heart overriding every logical thought speeding through her mind. She should've kept on walking, should've shoved Anthony out of the way and left this all behind. But she couldn't end things with Sullivan like this. Not after everything they'd been through. Five days, that was all it'd taken for her to fall for him. How was that possible? "Do you know how hard it was for me to watch you bleed out after Christopher was finished with you?"

She fought back the memories, her throat closing.

Sullivan straightened in the bed. "I can imagine."

"Those were the worst two minutes of my life, Sullivan." She hugged her jacket into her middle when all she really wanted to hold on to was lying in a hospital bed only a few feet away. "I warned you what happens to people who get close to me. And look where you are. Look at your body." She motioned to the darkening bandages taped all over his chest and shoulder.

"But how is it going to end the next time? Or the time after that? I care about you, about what you want and need, and this isn't it."

"Jane, I can—"

"Take care of yourself," she finished for him. "I know. But you did your job. Christopher is dead. Now it's time for me to take care of myself." Jane headed toward the door, her insides twisting harder than ever before.

Sullivan hissed behind her, the machines he'd been hooked up to going haywire.

The look on Anthony's face as he lunged for the hospital bed spun her around. Ripping out the catheter and leads, Sullivan fought to stand beside the bed. His weapons expert offered a hand, but the stubborn SEAL brushed him off.

Her eyes widened, but Jane couldn't close the space between them. She'd fought too hard to get even this far. "Sullivan, what are you doing? You're going to rip your stitches out."

"Then I'll rip them out. I'm not letting you do this alone." He used the bed for support and shuffled forward. The hospital gown molded to him, a little too tight and too short for his musculature. "If that means we need to leave now, then we leave now. Anthony, go get the SUV. We'll meet you at the front."

"No. You're not going anywhere." The constant beeping from the machines would call the nurses and doctors in here in a few seconds, but even with their medical orders, Sullivan wouldn't stop until the job was done. Wasn't in his nature. She had to admire him for that, given that was exactly why she'd blackmailed him in the first place, but this time, Jane wouldn't stand by helpless when whoever hunted her caught up. And she wouldn't let Sullivan risk his life for her again, even if she had to go to extremes to stop him. "Do you remember what I said back in your office when you refused to help me?"

Fire consumed his gaze, almost hotter and wilder than when he'd taken on Christopher at the cabin. He fought to stand on his own, leaning against the bed rails, but Sullivan had lost a lot of blood. He wouldn't get far. "You wouldn't."

Jane stepped backward toward the door.

"Jane…" He pushed off from the bed, the muscles in his jawline ticking away with his erratic heartbeat. "Don't do this."

"You did your job, Sullivan. This is the only way to keep you safe. I'm sorry." She ripped open the door and shouted down the hall. "Police!"

Two uniformed Anchorage PD officers spun toward her from the end of the hall. She'd known they'd be there, waiting for her to give her statement. Both sprinted toward the room, hands on the butt of their guns, and hurried inside. "Ma'am?"

"This man isn't who he says he is. His real name is Sebastian Warren." Jane maneuvered closer to the door as they came inside the room, dread pooling at the base of her spine. This was the only way. "There's a warrant out for his arrest for murdering his father, the Anchorage Lumberjack, nineteen years ago."

The officers moved in, but Anthony constructed a barrier of hardened muscle before Sullivan set a tense hand on his weapon expert's shoulder and pushed him back. Fluorescent lighting glinted off a pair of handcuffs as the officers moved Sullivan back into the bed, but the SEAL only had attention for her.

The fire in his eyes had simmered, the remaining ashes full of…heartbreak?

A tight knot of hesitation spread through her, but Jane shoved her arms into her jacket as the officers started questioning Sullivan, and she slipped out the door. The cell phone she'd stolen from one of the officers was in her hand, her eye on the exit. She fought back the tears blurring her vision as she dialed the number she'd memorized for circumstances like this a few months ago. Never could be too careful. Off the grid. Leave everything behind.

"Jane!" Sullivan's voice echoed down the hallway, but she wouldn't turn back.

She unburied her own phone from her jacket pocket and tossed it into the garbage can against the wall. First thing Sullivan would do after posting bail would be to track her through her phone. He wanted to help, but she wouldn't lose him. Not the man who'd given her a reason to fight.

Keep moving. Don't look back. Bringing the stolen phone to her ear, she counted off the rings on the other line. Two. Three. The line picked up.

"Hey, it's me." Jane checked over her shoulder to make sure Sullivan hadn't ordered Anthony to follow her. Two nurses bolted into his room behind the Anchorage police officers as he shouted her name over and over again. She clutched the keys she'd taken off Anthony as he'd rushed to help Sullivan stand and focused on the double glass doors leading to the parking garage. Tears welled in her lower lash line, but Jane pushed them back. Turning him in might solidify her reputation, but her leaving ensured the safety of the one man she couldn't bear to lose. Sullivan. He was all that mattered now. "I need your help."

Chapter Thirteen

"How didn't we see this coming?" Sullivan threw all of the team's research into a file box and shoved it across his desk. Pain shot up into his shoulder and across his rib cage as the box hit the floor and scattered the files from Jane's case across his office. The phone rang for the hundredth time in the last hour since he'd been released from Anchorage PD custody, intensifying the headache at the base of his skull. He pointed a finger at Elliot with the hand not strapped into a sling. "You're the private investigator. You're the one who should've been able to uncover Christopher Menas's true motive before this all blew up in our face."

"The guy was good at his job, Sullivan. I don't know what else you want me to say." Elliot collapsed back in one of the many leather chairs positioned in front of the CEO's massive oak desk, cell phone in hand. The brightness of the screen highlighted the stitches in his forehead from the fire at Menas's apartment, and regret flooded through Sullivan. In reality, they were lucky Elliot hadn't been killed, considering what Menas did for a living. "Besides, I think we all learned something very valuable here. Never trust the system. Everything you need to know is in a person's routines and daily life. Had we surveilled Menas before he'd tried killing us, I could've told you everything you'd needed to know."

"Who screwed up their job the most doesn't matter right now." Elizabeth Dawson, Blackhawk Security's head of network security, tossed a handful of manila file folders onto the gleaming desk between them. "We've got a client on the run, one who's probably scared out of her mind, and we have no idea who is after her. I'd say that qualifies as our first priority." The former NSA analyst nodded toward the pile of research. "Here's everything I could get my hands on for Christopher Menas. Phone records, emails, instant messages, bank accounts, payroll for his team, surveillance photos of Jane. I had to pull a few strings, so you owe me."

Every muscle in Sullivan's body tensed at the sound of her name. Damn it. Now wasn't the time to let emotion rule. His wrist still chafed where the Anchorage PD had cuffed him while they questioned him in that hospital bed for over twenty hours. The only reasons he'd been released after Jane's attempt to keep him off her case were a heavily funded bank account and the high-priced lawyer Blackhawk Security kept on retainer. But the nightmare wasn't over.

He'd killed his father before the psychopath could hurt anyone else. Sullivan had known this day would come. He locked his jaw. But, despite the possibility of spending the rest of his life in prison, he had more important things on his mind. First things first: find Jane. If he could talk to her—

"None of it tells me who might've hired Menas." Elizabeth leveraged her weight onto her hand against the desk, wide brown eyes only giving a hint of the off-the-charts intelligence behind them. "Either Christopher Menas was lying when he told you he'd been contracted to take Jane out, or the guy behind the curtain is one of the best shadow agents I've ever come across. And trust me, I know a few."

"He wasn't lying." Sullivan straightened. Head in the game. Get Jane to safety. "The entire reason he'd used his own name was to throw us off the scent of the real threat. Any word from Anthony?"

"Jane hasn't gone back to the town house, and there's no report from her CO either." Elliot held up his phone, waving it from side to side. "I went back through her bank records. No activity on her credit or debit cards, no withdrawals from her account. She has to be getting some kind of help to stay off the grid this long. As of right now, she's gone."

"Not acceptable." He'd never lost a mission or a client in all his time on this earth, and he wasn't about to start now. "We're just going to have to find the threat responsible for the price on Jane's head—" Sullivan ground his back molars, her name still sweet on his tongue "—before he finds her."

"This woman turned you over to the police and endangered the entire company. She doesn't want you on the case anymore, Sullivan." Vincent Kalani turned around from the other side of the office, uncrossing his arms. The forensics expert hadn't said another word this entire meeting, keeping to himself in the corner, but Sullivan read the resistance across his dark features. Shadows crossed Vincent's stern expression. Of all the men and women Sullivan had hired to create the Blackhawk Security team, Vincent had the uncanny ability to bring him back to earth when he was in over his head. But not this time. "Are you going to put yourself—put *us*—back in this guy's crosshairs to save someone who doesn't want our help and who sold you out?"

"Yes." Because a man never gave up on the woman he loved. Sullivan ignored the burn of pain down his side. He inhaled deep, hoping to catch her vanilla scent in the air, but disappointment gripped him. Jane was running from whoever'd hired Menas, but also from him. She didn't want him in a position that would get him killed, but she didn't understand. He'd been in that position his entire life. First with his father, then the SEALs, now as part of the foremost private security consultancy in the United States. All of those moments had forged him into the man he was now, the man who could save her life. She'd just finally made the risk worth it.

"I built this company—and hired every single one of you—to save lives, and that's exactly what we're going to do. Save a life. Doesn't matter if we trust our clients. Doesn't matter if we like them. We have a responsibility to the people who walk through those doors, and today I only have attention for one of them. Jane Reise." Sullivan shifted his attention to Vincent. "But if you won't do the job I hired you for—" he nodded toward the double glass doors on the other side of his office "—there's the door. I don't have the time to question whether I can rely on you right now."

The phone rang again, attempting to break the tense silence descending between him and his team. Sullivan picked up the receiver and slammed it back down. He didn't have time for distractions either.

"Well, you got my vote, boss." Elliot stood, slapping his hand into Sullivan's. "But mostly because I'm terrified you're going to send me back to the prison you found me in if I don't comply."

A laugh rumbled through Sullivan's chest. "Don't you forget it, con man."

Elizabeth collected the files he'd tossed onto the floor and reorganized them across the desk. "I'll start combing through possible suspects in Jane's life again, targeting military personnel. Do you want me to call in Kate for another profile?"

"No. We can handle this without her." Blackhawk Security's profiler deserved all the time she could get after losing her husband to a random shooting two months ago. Sullivan wouldn't ask her to come back until she was ready. He ran over Elizabeth's words a second time. "Why target military personnel?"

"Someone this good at hiding his identity is a professional. At first I thought whoever hired Christopher Menas might've been former NSA, maybe current, but that doesn't add up. You said Jane was stalked in Afghanistan. The NSA hasn't had any assets there in over a year." Elizabeth brushed a piece of short brown hair behind her ear. Not quite as short as Jane's, but it accentuated her heart-shaped face and warm brown eyes, where Jane's gave the angles of her face more of an edge. "Without contacts within the intelligence community, our target wouldn't have been able to hire a mercenary team. On top of that, he knows her, he knows every detail of her life and has been following her across the globe. She doesn't have any relatives she's close to, so I've narrowed it down to three possibilities." Elizabeth ticked them off on her fingers one by one. "Our suspect is either her commanding officer, another lawyer who's worked with her or a criminal who's been prosecuted by her. All military."

"That's still a giant suspect pool, and Jane swore her CO didn't have anything to do with this when we first brought him up." Sullivan swiped his uninjured hand across his face, then focused on the hundreds of photos of Jane staring up at him from his desk. She'd disappeared twenty-four hours ago. She could be anywhere in the world. And so could her stalker. Hell. Sullivan curled his fingers into his palms, needing the small bite of pain to keep him focused. They didn't have time to make any more mistakes. "It'll take us weeks to sort through them all."

"I'll take her commanding officer." Vincent stepped close to the desk and motioned for Elizabeth to give him the file. The tribal tattoos climbing up his neck and down his arms stretched with the action. "He'd know her routine, her close friends in the JAG Corps and which defendants might want to take revenge. It's as good a place to start as any." He lifted his toffee-colored gaze to Sullivan.

"Thank you." Didn't matter that Jane had sworn up and down her CO had nothing to do with this. They'd run out of leads. Slapping his hand across Vincent's back, maybe a little too hard, he nodded. He rounded the desk and picked up one of the many photos Elliot had recovered from Christopher Menas's apartment before it'd been burned to the ground. "Now that only leaves about fifty more people we need to dig into, and any one of them could already be three steps ahead."

He didn't like those odds.

Sullivan studied the photo in his hand, his eyebrows

drawing inward. It was a photo of Jane in court. Her hair was a little longer, nearly brushing her fatigues emblazoned with the JAG Corps insignia pinned to her chest. The walls were simple, bare, only two flags standing tall on either side of the judge. The American flag and the US Army flag. No other American insignia on the walls, which meant it probably wasn't an American courtroom. Could've been Afghanistan. There was no way to tell for sure, but Christopher Menas hadn't taken the picture. Jane would've recognized him in a heartbeat if her ex-college-boyfriend-turned-mercenary had sat a few feet from her.

"Boss?" Elliot asked. "Everything okay?"

From the angle of the photo, the picture had to have been taken by the defense's side of the courtroom. But why would a defendant or an attorney snap a picture in the middle of court, and where had Menas gotten the picture in the first place? Jane stood near the witness stand, not looking at the person who'd taken the photo. A surveillance photo. His stomach sank, but Sullivan rotated the photo in order to get a good look at the papers sprawled across the desk, any evidence that could point them in the right direction. A name. An official charge. A rank.

Something else caught his eye.

He brought the photo closer. The pen on the desk. Dread pooled at the base of his spine. He'd seen it before. But…

His cell phone chimed, and he read the incoming message from Anthony.

Subject has returned home.

He put the screen to sleep and shoved the phone into his pants pocket.

"I know who hired Christopher Menas." Sullivan snapped his head up. It didn't make sense, but he wasn't about to second-guess his instincts. Setting Jane's photo back onto the desk, he pulled his top desk drawer open and shoved his favorite Glock into his shoulder holster. There wasn't any time left. They had to get to Jane's town house now. "And I know why he's doing this."

CHRISTOPHER MENAS HAD gotten exactly what he'd wanted.

Captain Jane Reise of the United States JAG Corps no longer existed.

She stared down at the new passport, birth certificate, driver's license and Social Security card on her lap, not sure why she hadn't gotten out of the car yet. The photos had been taken from her old passport, but the name, date of birth and address beside it had transformed her into someone completely different, thanks to a friend in the FBI's witness protection program. Sliding the airline ticket out from behind the thin leather, she memorized the information all over again. Her flight out of Ted Stevens International Airport to LAX left in two hours. Enough time to collect the cash she'd stashed beneath the floorboards under the right side of her bed. She couldn't use the money in her accounts. Too easy to trace. With that money, she'd have a fresh start. And there'd be no trace of her old life to follow.

The dropping temperatures were showing her breath, but Jane sat there, surveying the street for the hundredth time. No sign of an intruder, of a mercenary waiting for her to open the door. No sign of another Blackhawk Security vehicle either. Jane exhaled hard as pressure built behind her sternum. Sullivan hadn't come after her.

She pulled back her shoulders. She recalled the details of her new life. Now she was Rita Miller, a criminal defense lawyer from Los Angeles, California, who worked for a large firm right in the center of the city. She had no idea how her friend in the FBI had managed to pull that off, but did it matter?

She craned her head over her shoulder toward the town house again. So, in reality, the rental wasn't even hers anymore. All of the furniture, her clothing, the small possessions she'd collected from her travels over the last few years would be sold off in some estate sale. Her father and his new family wouldn't want them and Jane wasn't allowed to pack and ship them to her new address in California, according to the rules. Leave everything behind. Leave *everyone* behind.

The rules. A small burst of laughter had her setting the crown of her head against the headrest. Frayed wiring dangled from the control panel centered above the rearview mirror. Sullivan really should've been more careful about concealing the tracking devices he'd installed in his vehicles. Or at least have a backup. Staring up at the SUV's ceiling, she closed her eyes. She'd worked her entire life sticking to the rules, bending them to fit her or her clients' needs, but never breaking them, and she'd done a good job.

Until five days ago.

She'd broken the first rule she'd given herself when breaking into Sullivan Bishop's office: don't fall in love. And look where breaking the rules had landed her. Sitting outside her own town house in the middle of the night in freezing temperatures because she couldn't bear the thought of what she might find inside.

Or who.

Her lower lash line burned. She swiped at the runaway tear streaking down her face. This was stupid. Sullivan hadn't followed her. He wasn't waiting inside for her to come home. Jane dropped her chin to her chest, opening her eyes. "Screw the rules."

This was the only way to start over, to save the man she'd blackmailed into protecting her.

She tossed the new passport into the passenger-side seat and jammed her shoulder into the door of the Blackhawk Security SUV she'd borrowed from the hospital garage. She'd take the SUV to the airport, then let Elliot or Anthony know where they could pick it up. There was a good chance she'd change her mind if she talked to Sullivan again. Although, with how she'd left things between them in the hospital, him in handcuffs, her running out the door, he might make it easier than she imagined.

Jane jogged across the street, keeping an eye out for any movement, any glare of headlights coming to life. The key was already in her hand, in case she had to get inside in a hurry. She twisted the key in the lock and pushed the door inward. A wall of hot air rushed against her, relieving some of the tightness in her lower back. She tossed her keys onto the table by the door, as she did every day, and closed the door behind her, locking it. Her throat went dry. It still smelled like him. Her attention shot to the makeshift bed on the couch where Sullivan had slept, and she shuffled toward it.

Slumping down onto the couch, she stared at what remained of the space she used to consider a safe haven.

The town house had been tossed. Clothing, books, photos, all destroyed. She couldn't imagine how many people had trudged through her personal belongings, picked apart her life since she'd run off into the middle of the night after a murderer. Police, Sullivan's team, Christopher Menas. But, here, surrounded by the scent of the man she'd unwillingly surrendered to, her muscles slowly released. It was over. For now. The man who'd turned her life upside down for the past couple of months—who'd tried to kill her—was dead. Of course, someone had hired Christopher's band of mercenaries in the first place, but she couldn't think about that right now. A few more minutes of relief was all she needed. Then she'd get the cash and lock up for good. No looking back. A fresh start.

There should've been some relief in that thought, but all Jane could think about was the look on Sullivan's face when she'd called for the police. Christopher Menas would've killed her had it not been for Sullivan. And she'd thrown it in his face. She'd hurt him—badly—and she wasn't sure if there was any way he'd trust another woman again. Or forgive her.

She rubbed her fingers into her sternum to counteract the pain spreading through her chest. Sullivan had forgiven her for her part in Marrok's suicide, but he had every reason to hate her now. Tears welled in her eyes again, but Jane wiped them away.

She couldn't believe what she was about to do.

She was going to find Sullivan. Witness protection could wait. She had to fix this. No matter how long it took or how many times he slammed the door in her face, she'd make this right.

Because she couldn't imagine another day of her life without Sullivan Bishop—or Sebastian Warren—in it. She loved him. Threading the sheets between her fingers, Jane relaxed back against the couch. She loved him. Why had it taken her so long to realize it? She was an idiot. Of course she'd fallen for him. Sullivan protected people for a living, protected her. He stood against the evil in this world and smiled while doing it. He'd committed himself one hundred percent to the job and refused to stop when the chances of dying skyrocketed. But the best part? The way he'd looked at her while he did it, like he could've loved her back. The way he held her, ready to take a bullet to keep her safe... Jane thunked her head against the back of the couch. And wasn't that a kick to the stomach? She ground her back molars.

She'd made a mistake.

Hefting herself from the couch coated in Sullivan's clean, masculine scent, she stepped over the debris toward her bedroom. The damage extended up the stairs and through to the main bathroom, but Jane didn't have the energy to start cleaning. Wasn't any point now. After she saw Sullivan, she wasn't coming back. Every muscle in her body ached. Take a shower. Call the hospital, the police department, Blackhawk Security, whoever she had to call to track Sullivan down. In that order. She discarded her jacket onto the ottoman at the foot of her bed and turned. She hit a wall of solid muscle.

"Tell me, Captain Reise, does this rag smell like chloroform to you?" a voice from the past asked. A hand clamped a white rag over her mouth as another grabbed the back of her head to keep her in place against his chest. "Shh. It'll all be over soon."

Jane threaded her hands between his arms and looped them wide. The cloth over her mouth disappeared, but an acrid taste spread across her tongue as she lunged for the bedroom door. Her fight-or-flight response kicked into high gear. This wasn't possible. Searing pain spread over her skull as he fisted a handful of her hair and pulled her back into him. Her fingers automatically shot to her head to relieve the pain, and he clamped the soaked rag over her mouth again.

Jane kicked and kneed at him, grabbing onto his wrists to dislodge his hold. But he was strong. Too strong. And she'd lost too much energy over the last few days. She couldn't control her breathing, the poison working down into her system too fast for her to keep up the fight. The edges of her vision darkened. *No. Stay awake. Leave evidence.* Sullivan had to know…

Her grip lightened, her muscles protesting the orders her brain gave. Jane wrapped her left hand around the closest thing she could grab from her attacker's button-down shirt pocket. A single pen. Her legs gave out.

"That's it." He led her to the floor but refused to remove the rag from her mouth. "Just relax. You're in good hands."

Her arm arched up above her head, and she let the pen slip from her hold. It rolled under the bed. Staring up into the face of her attacker, Jane couldn't move, couldn't keep her eyes open as the darkness closed in. The shadows across his sharp, angled jawline shifted as he pressed her into the floor. She'd recognize that face anywhere. Her eyebrows drew inward as she squinted away the blurriness closing in. "Not…you."

"That's right, Jane. Me." He bent low over her, the scars across his eyebrows and chin deeper than she remembered. His breath snaked across the underside of her neck. She tried to pull away, tried to run, but couldn't stay awake. Her eyelids sagged closed. "And now it's my turn to torture *you*."

Chapter Fourteen

Sullivan clutched the only piece of evidence he and his team had recovered from Jane's town house as he sped down the highway: the pen. It'd rolled under her bed, but his instincts screamed that Jane had been trying to leave him a clue as to who'd taken her.

And there was only one place her stalker would hide to get his attention. The cabin.

"I'm coming, Jane. I'm coming." He'd promised to keep her safe, and he intended to keep every promise he'd made to her. Murky water kicked up along the SUV's windows as he pressed his foot harder against the pedal. The wipers crossed the windshield in the same rhythm his heart tried to beat out of his chest. This whole thing hadn't been about Jane, at least not entirely. His past had come back to haunt him, too. He just didn't have all the pieces yet. Sullivan rotated the wheel to the left, taking the SUV down the snow-coated trail. Pain zinged through his arm and side, but he only gripped the steering wheel tighter.

Clouds and short bursts of wind dumped flakes onto the windshield. The closer he got to his destination, the less he could see, nearly everything in sight a complete whiteout. Rubbing the inside of the windshield clear of fog, Sullivan squinted through the snow. He should be coming up on the cabin any second now—

A black blur appeared directly in the SUV's path.

"Damn it!" He spun the SUV to the left, straight into the tree line, and slammed on the brakes. Adrenaline flooded into his veins, heart rate rocketing. The back end of the GMC fishtailed, and time seemed to slow. Sullivan turned into the spin, breath frozen in his throat. He fought to keep control of the vehicle. The back end of the SUV missed an unconscious Jane by mere inches, but he couldn't correct in time.

The GMC slammed into a thick tree, and he hit the steering wheel hard. A cascade of snow fell over the crumpled hood as the engine died. Shoving himself back in his seat, he brushed his fingertips across his forehead. Blood dripped down the side of his face. It was a miracle he hadn't lost consciousness. His breath sawed in and out of his lungs, but he clamped on to the door handle. "Jane."

Shoving his recently stitched shoulder into the door, Sullivan suppressed a scream as agony washed over him. He tumbled out of the SUV. His boots slid along the compacted snow, and he collapsed against the GMC. The pain dissipated, slowly, but he had to push it to the back of his mind. *Get to Jane. Neutralize the threat.* He kept his breathing shallow, even, and opened his eyes.

Hands tied behind the back of a chair, Jane sat slumped over her legs, unconscious, about twenty feet away. She hadn't realized he'd almost killed her coming to save her life. Relief, however fleeting, flooded through him, and he took the magazine out of his Glock and shoved it back into place. But he didn't make a move toward her. Nobody put a victim in the middle of the road like that unless they intended to take the high ground to watch the chaos unfold. Dread coiled a tight fist in the pit of his stomach. There was only one way this could end. Her kidnapper wanted a show? Sullivan would give him one.

"I know you're out there," he shouted over his shoulder. Sullivan pressed his back into the SUV for cover, finger on the trigger. His head throbbed, heart beating loudly, but the soft crunching of snow reached his ears. His target froze in his tracks, approximately ten yards to the southeast, just on the other side of the road. "Let's finish this."

Sullivan bounded away from the SUV and swung his gun up and around.

And froze.

"Hey, big brother." Acrid smoke filled the air around Marrok Warren. He tossed the lit cigar into the snow and stomped it out with his boot, the butt of a gun peeking out from under his jacket. Thick brown hair covered the scars Sullivan had witnessed cut into his younger brother's chin by their father when they'd been younger. Deep lines wrinkled the top of Marrok's forehead as he unholstered the weapon at his side. "Guess you never expected to see me again."

"Not after I buried you next to Mom. No, I did not." His recovery of the pen their mother had given Marrok when he'd turned twelve had told Sullivan exactly what—*who*—to expect on the wrong end of his gun, but Sullivan swallowed hard. He shifted his stance wide and readjusted his grip on the Glock. "You faked your death in order to torture Jane for prosecuting you."

"What's a little revenge among friends? I certainly

had a good time terrorizing her the past three months. Then she hired you, and I had to up the stakes. Playtime was over." Marrok circled to his right, putting him in the center of the road. "Sebastian Warren. My big brother. Always the *savior*. Always the hero."

"So now you're blaming me for keeping you alive for all those years Dad came after you?" A burst of laughter exploded from between Sullivan's teeth. He shook his head, gun still aimed as he counteracted his brother's movements. "You're sick, Marrok. I can get you help."

"Thanks for the offer, big brother, but I wouldn't be the man I am now had it not been for Dad's influence. If I hadn't followed in his footsteps, I wouldn't have the connections or the money I do now. And, let me tell you, it was all worth it. Only difference between Dad and me? My tastes are a little more…" Marrok's dark eyes flickered past Sullivan. To Jane. One scarred edge of his mouth turned upward. "Refined."

The muscles surrounding his spine hardened one by one. Sullivan had buried his brother as a hero, put him to rest next to their mother in their hometown cemetery. He'd believed in his innocence for over a year. "Jane was right about you all along. You assaulted those women while you were on tour."

Marrok drove his hand into his jacket pocket, extracting a small black device. "You can't win this fight, Sebastian. Don't forget, I know you better than anyone else. You're just using a different name now." His younger brother wiggled the device for Sullivan to see, then raised his gun and took aim. At Sullivan's heart. "I know you won't kill me because you can't stand the thought of killing your own brother, but I also know you'd do anything to save an innocent life. Especially one you've been taking to bed."

"I know you, too, little brother. You're not going to shoot me." Sullivan fought to relieve the searing pain spreading down his side. Marrok had been watching them this whole time? A sick feeling rolled through him. His brother was right. He wouldn't kill Marrok, but that didn't mean he couldn't make him pay for what he'd done. He tightened his grip around the gun as he backed up a few feet to where Jane sat. Sullivan tipped her head back and his stomach sank. Pressing his fingers to her throat, he counted off the slow, uneven rhythm in his head. Her lips had turned blue, the blistering cold slowing down her heart rate, but the bomb vest strapped to her chest kicked his up a notch.

"No, Sebastian. You *knew* me. Then you abandoned me for the navy, leaving me behind to deal with the aftermath you caused after killing Dear-Old-Dad, and never looked back. Even changed your name so I couldn't track you down. Now I find you're protecting the one person I hate most in the world. *Jane Reise.*" Her sweet name growled from between Marrok's lips as he nodded toward Jane. "So you're right. I might not put a bullet in you, but I sure as hell won't feel guilty if you're caught in the crossfire."

"Marrok." Sullivan took a single step forward, his ears going numb from the pounding wind. "Everything I did, I did for you, to protect—"

"You can save the speech, big brother. I know the truth. You've always wanted to escape the life we had, and killing our father gave you a way to do it." Marrok held up the device in his hand, pointing it toward Jane. "You're a SEAL. You know what this is and what will happen if you're anywhere close to her when that bomb blows."

"Jane, baby." No answer. He brushed her hair back from her face, then straightened. "Can you hear me?"

"You don't get a choice in this, Sebastian, and you're running out of time." Keeping the gun aimed at Sullivan's chest, Marrok walked backward down the road slowly. "It's over. She gets what she deserves and we all move on with our lives."

"No." The growl reverberated through him. Move on without Jane? A small burst of wind dislodged the piles of snow lining the tree branches, whiting out visibility between them, and Sullivan had his shot.

"Jane *is* my life." He sprinted with every bit of energy his battered body could produce, the icy air filling his lungs. But the wind died too fast, and he found himself out in the open. Still, Sullivan didn't slow.

Eyes wide, Marrok squeezed off one round, which went wide. Then another, hitting Sullivan in the right arm. A third round lodged in his upper thigh. He didn't care. Blood dripped down his fingers, but he wouldn't stop. Because he loved Jane. Didn't matter when it'd happened. Didn't matter how. All that mattered was that it'd happened. He'd fallen in love with the one woman he'd vowed to condemn for the rest of his life.

Sullivan's jaw strained against his body's screams for relief. But without that detonation device, he'd lose everything. He rammed his shoulder under Marrok's ribs, tackling his brother to the ground. He pulled back his elbow, only the slightest hesitation gripping him. Enough time for Marrok to take advantage.

"You shouldn't have gotten involved, big brother." Marrok slammed the butt of his gun into Sullivan's head.

Scalding pain spread over his skull as Marrok kicked him backward. Sullivan hit the ground, cushioned by two feet of snow. Memories of countless nights, of holding a baseball bat or a knife or a gun in the back of their shared closet to protect his younger brother, flashed across his mind. He'd done what he'd had to, to protect his family. But the one person he'd never counted on turning on him had lost his damn mind. His gaze shot to Jane as her head fell to one side. She was coming around. And she needed him to protect her now.

"You were right, though. I don't like the idea of killing you either. There's a reason Menas drugged and Tasered you first." Marrok shifted his finger over the trigger of his gun. "But I will end you now if you choose Jane Reise over your own flesh and blood."

Sullivan pushed to his feet and maneuvered into the middle of the road, right between Marrok and Jane. The gun was pointed straight at him. A blast of wind kicked up snow as it swept across the clearing beside his cabin. His right arm and thigh burned from the two rounds Marrok had squeezed off. No major damage, but enough to pull at his attention. He was a SEAL, hardened and trained in every kind of environment. He didn't need to see the threat to neutralize it. A glint of sunlight off glass caught his attention from the tree line, and a smile pulled at one side of his mouth. "If you know me so well, then you know I don't stop until the job is done. And we're not done."

"I thought you might say something like that." Marrok shrugged, gun in one hand, the detonator in the other. With one click of a button, his younger brother would take everything from him. "Just like I know you brought your team to take me out in case things went south."

Marrok's gaze flickered over his shoulder as Anthony and Elliot burst through the trees, each armed and ready to neutralize the threat on Sullivan's orders. "Well, guess what, big brother? Things are about to go south." Raising the gun to Sullivan's head, Marrok compressed the detonator. "I'll see you in hell, Sebastian."

"No!" Sullivan lunged, focused solely on the detonator and not the gun aimed between his eyes.

As Marrok pulled the trigger.

THE GUNSHOTS HAD brought her around. All too familiar.

"Sullivan." His name barely whispered from her lips, her body fighting her brain's commands. Jane struggled against the rope at her wrists and ankles, but couldn't move. The brightness of the snow blinded her. Had Marrok Warren finally killed her?

She had to warn Sullivan.

Her eyelids were heavy, but Jane managed to roll her head to one side. Either hell had frozen over or she was actually strapped to a chair in the middle of the Alaskan wilderness. What had Marrok planned for her? Leave her to the wolves? Not very original.

Catching sight of two dark gray rocks half-buried in the snow beside her, she curled her fingers into her palms. She couldn't move. Couldn't scream from the effects of the chloroform. Couldn't protect herself. But she'd be damned if she didn't go down fighting like Sullivan had taught her.

Get out of the chair. Get to Sullivan. She twisted hard, tipping the chair into the snow. Air crushed from her lungs as she sent flakes above her head. Her fingers brushed against the rough edges of one rock and she stretched her hands as far as they would go to grab it. The ties were too tight, and her body was so tired. Marrok would get what he wanted, and Sullivan… No. She couldn't think about that. Her fingertips brushed against the rough surface of one rock. *There.*

Relief flooded through her as she grabbed the rock and hacked away at the rope. The ties fell from around her wrists, and she maneuvered out from under the chair. Bending to cut through the rope at her ankles, Jane caught a flash of red across her abdomen and, for a moment, she assumed it was blood. But the color was off. Brighter. And the flash disappeared, then reappeared. She squinted at the message glowing from the display, her mouth going dry. *Armed.* More colors claimed her attention. These ones long and thin. Red, blue, green and white. Wires. Oxygen rushed from her lungs as she hastily cut through the rope at her feet.

Marrok had strapped her into a bomb vest? Running her and Sullivan off the road, trying to burn them to ashes in Menas's apartment and sending a mercenary detail after her in the first place hadn't been enough. He had to blow her up, too? All because she'd done her job.

Jane clawed at the vest but couldn't find a zipper or Velcro or anything to get her out of it. A guttural groan reached her ears and she spun toward the sound. Sullivan landed backward in the snow, and the man standing over him… "Marrok."

She didn't have a weapon—unless she counted the new piece of apparel strapped across her chest—but ran toward the fight anyway. The cold had drained energy from her muscles, but she pushed on even as Anthony and Elliot burst through the tree line and surrounded the man behind all of this. Sullivan shoved to his feet, and she nearly collapsed before leveraging her weight onto a nearby tree trunk. Shoving her hair out of her eyes, she breathed a little easier. He was okay. Marrok couldn't escape now. The army would take custody of him, and this whole thing would be over. She'd have her life back. She could go back to being Jane Reise.

But in the blink of an eye, Marrok Warren raised the gun to Sullivan's head. The world stopped spinning. Her hands tightened, her insides churned. No. This wasn't how this was supposed to end. Not him. Not because of her. Jane stumbled forward, closing the vast distance between them as fast as she could. Every cell in her body fought against the desperation clawing up her throat to push herself harder. She'd only taken three steps. "Sul—"

A bullet exploded from the chamber of Marrok's gun as Sullivan reached under his heavy coat. Then two more gunshots echoed throughout the clearing, each stealing more of her hope.

Sullivan dropped his backup weapon into the snow, reaching out for his brother, but it was too late. Marrok Warren collapsed to the ground, his own weapon falling from his grip. The breath she'd been holding rushed from her lungs. She'd seen too many of those kinds of injuries on tour. There was no saving his brother now.

Only the tree beside her kept Jane on her feet. Tears welled in her eyes. Her stomach rolled. Not for Marrok but because of the way Sullivan hovered over his brother's body. Nobody deserved to watch someone they loved die right in front of them. Hadn't Sullivan been betrayed enough? Jane pushed off from the tree, her arms tingling to wrap around him as he grieved.

A series of beeps rang from the vest.

Jane stopped cold. The message stretched across her chest had changed from *Armed* to a series of numbers. And they were counting down. She shot her head up, her survival instincts paralyzed. No. No, no, no, no. This wasn't happening. She wasn't an active bomb. An invisible elephant sat on her chest, and she couldn't think. Couldn't breathe.

"Jane!" Sullivan's features cleared through the fresh tears streaming down her face.

She stumbled back. No. She didn't want to die, but she wasn't going to be responsible for taking his life. Not Sullivan. Jane surveyed the trees. She wasn't an expert with explosives, but she was smart enough to know the closer he got, the more danger he was in. If she could get some distance, he might have a better chance of surviving the blast. Throwing her hands out, she backed toward the tree line. "Stay back! It's armed!"

He didn't listen, running straight at her. Those sea-blue eyes never left her as he closed in fast. "Elliot, get your tools!"

The private investigator ran for one of the Blackhawk Security SUVs.

She stumbled back into the tree she'd used for support mere moments ago and fell. They were going to try to disarm the bomb. They were going to put their lives on the line. For her. Jane checked the display. Less than two minutes. She lifted her gaze back to Sullivan. Blackmailing him, revealing his true identity to the police in an attempt to save his life, it'd all been a mistake. He had to know that. She'd never meant for any of this to happen. "I'm sorry. I'm so sorry."

She didn't know what else to say.

Sullivan dropped to his knees beside her. Darkness consumed his features, and her insides flipped. He moved in close, his hands sliding along the underside of her jaw. He threaded his fingers through the hair at the base of her skull, and goose bumps rose along her skin at his touch. With him this close, the surrounding air filling with his reassuring scent, she wanted nothing more than to sink into his hold. But they were running out of time. Literally. "Are you okay?"

Chaos and concern tinted Sullivan's words. Not a good combination.

"I'm fine." And it was the truth. At least in her last two minutes on earth, Jane had what she wanted. Sullivan Bishop. She framed his jawline with one hand. "But you need to get away from me. This thing—"

"Isn't going to blow with you in it." A growl vibrated through Sullivan's chest. "I promise."

"Okay." Any promise Sullivan made, he kept, but the tightness in her tendons connecting her neck and shoulders refused to believe him. Lacing her fingers between his, Jane nodded. They didn't have much time left before he had to start running. And she wasn't about to make any more mistakes with the man she'd fallen in love with. "I'm sorry. For everything. Breaking into your office, blackmailing you, going after Menas on my own. All of it. I'm sorry I dragged you into this. I'm sorry about Marrok."

Elliot slid onto his knees on her other side, out of breath but smiling. "Hello, gorgeous. Not dead again, I see. Always a plus." He pushed at her shoulder, putting her flat on her back. "Hand me the wire cutters," he said to Sullivan. "I'm going to need you to hold very still. You are literally a ticking time bomb, and any movement could set it off early."

"I'm not sorry." Sullivan thrust the cutters into his private investigator's hands. A slow smile spread across Sullivan's features as he squeezed her hand. "I thought the Full Metal Bitch had broken into my office, but, in reality, it was my future. You're my future, Jane, and I'm not going anywhere."

"I can't think when you're expressing your feelings, boss. It's unnatural." Elliot's voice held a word of caution as he sifted through countless wires and traced them to different points on the vest. "That was beautiful, by the way."

Did that mean Sullivan loved her, too? The remnants of cold drained from her body at his words. But Jane still unwound her fingers from his hand and shoved him back. "You need to run."

"The last time I left your side, my brother strapped you to this damn thing." He wrapped his hand in hers again and kissed the sensitive skin along the back. "I learn from my mistakes. And the police already know who I really am, so you have no other leverage to get rid of me. Ever again."

"There are too many wires." Elliot sat back on his heels. "We've got less than thirty seconds. Boss—"

"Then we're going to cut her out of it." Sullivan reached for the serrated blade tucked inside his boot. The world blurred as they flipped her onto her front. "I'm not giving up."

Blistering cold spread down into her bones as sounds of ripping fabric reached her ears. Adrenaline dumped into her veins and rocketed her heart rate higher as she prepared for the explosion. But she couldn't move on to the afterlife without telling the man she'd blackmailed how she felt. Jane reached for him. "Sullivan, no matter what happens, I need you to know... I love you."

He hesitated for a split second, his gaze softening. Sullivan tugged on the vest, cutting down the back. "I've got it!"

Sullivan hauled her upright. The weight of the vest pulled her to the ground, but she extracted her arms from the sleeve holes. The clock was still counting down. His grip tightened around her arm. He tossed the active vest far into the woods and tugged her after him. "Take cover!"

The rest of the Blackhawk Security team scattered behind the SUVs or the long line of snowbanks. Sullivan dragged her across the road and then pushed her ahead of him. "Get behind the tree line!"

A faint hum echoed through the trees.

Then the explosion erupted. The flames shot out behind them, the blast tossing them into the air. Terror ricocheted through her as Jane hit the ground and rolled. Twice. Three times. Smoke worked deep into her system when she came to a stop. She'd lost sight of Sullivan as darkness closed in around the edges of her vision. She stared up into the trees as mountains of snow fell from the branches above, burying her deeper while blackness closed in.

"Jane..."

Chapter Fifteen

Probation and over two hundred hours of community service. Sullivan might've lost half of Blackhawk Security's clients thanks to Jane having him arrested for murder, but he also had the rest of his life to hold it over her head.

And he intended to do just that.

The hospital's white walls blurred together at the edges of his vision as he stalked toward Jane's room, the only room with an ex-Ranger stationed outside the door. It'd been a precaution in case his psychopathic brother had hired any other hit men who hadn't heard the news: Jane Reise was off-limits. And *his*.

"Hey, man." Nodding at Anthony in acknowledgment, Sullivan wrapped his hand around the doorknob. And froze. His nervous system flipped, a ball of tension gripping his stomach. The stitches in his arm and thigh where Marrok had shot him stretched, but it wasn't the pain keeping him in place. The birth certificate, Social Security card, driver's license and passport with Jane's picture she'd left in the Blackhawk Security SUV all said she'd planned on starting a new life. In California. What if, even after they'd neutralized the threat, even after he'd beaten murder charges, she hadn't changed her mind about leaving?

"I don't think I've seen your skin that shade of white before." Anthony might take refuge behind those sunglasses, but his apparent amusement stretched across his expression. "Boss."

"Do you blame me? Every time I'm around her, someone is either shooting at me or trying to blow me up." Not the truth, but Anthony didn't need to know differently. The possibility of Jane saying no to staying in Anchorage, of her taking back those three words she'd blurted when her life was in danger, constricted his hold on the doorknob. A slight sting in his side from where Christopher Menas had tried to gut him like a fish claimed his attention. He forced a smile. "I never thanked you for watching out for her. I appreciate it."

"You've always said you'd do anything to protect the team, and every one of us feels the same." Anthony shifted his weight and, for the first time, Sullivan noted a beaten gold ring hanging from around Anthony's neck, tucked behind the Kevlar vest. Glennon's ring. Anthony Harris, ex-Ranger and Blackhawk Security weapons expert, had been holding on to the love of his life all this time? He'd never said a word. Sullivan's heart sank. Surveying the hospital corridor, Anthony shoved the gold band under his shirt without making eye contact. "We don't agree with you keeping the fact she blackmailed you into all this from us, but if you love her, Jane Reise is part of this team. And we'll fight for her."

"Thanks again." The knot of tension in his gut dissipated. Not completely, but there was only one way to fix that. Because Sullivan wouldn't hang on to Jane like Anthony held on to the woman who'd walked out on him, never finding closure, always wondering if she was safe, but not being part of her life. He twisted the hospital room door handle, shouldering his way inside.

And all the air rushed from his lungs.

Jane pushed her arms through her jacket beside the hospital bed. He closed the door softly and watched her. The burns and cuts along her creamy skin had started healing, the dark circles he'd noted when they first met lighter than before. Her addictive vanilla scent filled the room, and Sullivan couldn't help but take a deep breath, holding on to her as long as he could. His Jane.

"You can stop staring at me any second now." Leveling that hazel gaze on him from over her shoulder, she smiled. Jane fixed her collar and turned toward him. "Unless you're here to tell me you're busting me out of this place a second time."

"I'm sure something could be arranged." In truth, her doctors had already cleared her to leave, but Sullivan shoved his hands into his jacket pockets and leveraged his weight back against the door. A few more minutes with her. That was all he needed. "Surviving a mercenary and my brother certainly looks good on you."

The brightness in her eyes dimmed for a split second, and that loss resurrected the gutting pain he'd felt when Menas had planted a knife in his rib cage.

"I'm so sorry about Marrok, Sullivan. You have no idea how much I wish he hadn't been involved. I never meant for any of this to happen." She rolled her lips between her teeth, her expression simply lost. She fidgeted with an invisible speck of dirt on her jacket. "You told me you didn't hate me before." She wrapped her arms across her midsection, almost as though she were preparing herself for the worst. "Have you changed your mind?"

"You deserve the truth." Sullivan closed the space between them slowly, giving her a chance to back away if she wanted. He could almost read her mind as the muscles along her spine sagged. Guilt. Shame. Regret. "Everything since that night has changed. For the first time in nineteen years, the world knows who I really am. And what I did. Because of you."

The color drained from her face. Her jaw slackened. Jane swiped at her face, her attention on the door over his shoulder, then moved to maneuver around him. "I understand."

"No, you don't." Sullivan clamped a hand around her arm and spun her into his chest. For the first time, she didn't fight, and he took that as a good sign. Staring down at her, he locked her in his hold. She wasn't going anywhere. At least, not without him. "If you understood, you wouldn't keep running away from me. None of this was your fault, Jane. You can't control other people's behavior. You did your job like you were supposed to."

Spreading his fingers along her jaw, he fought back the memories of Marrok in his final moments. And the thought of almost losing Jane to the bomb his brother had strapped to her chest. It shouldn't have gone down like that, but there'd been no way to see the real threat before discovering his brother's pen in that photo. "As much as I hate to admit what he was capable of, Marrok made his own decisions, and he paid for them."

"And what about the fact I turned you in to the police for murder?" Her voice was so soft, soft and vulnerable, and Sullivan's insides contracted. She refused to look at him, setting her palms against his beating heart. "Is the Full Metal Bitch going to be credited with bringing down Blackhawk Security's CEO? Because…" She picked at his shirt. "I'm not that person anymore, Sullivan, and I don't want you, of all people, to believe I am."

"I'm not in love with a heartless woman who would do anything in her power to bring down hardworking soldiers. I'm in love with *you*, the real Jane Reise." He moved a strand of hair off her cheek, hugging her closer. "You're determined, yes. Willing to do whatever it takes to get what you want, but I think that's what I love about you the most. You're caring and brave. And I can't imagine a better woman by my side."

A smile stretched across her features. "Don't forget saving your life two more times."

"How could I? Lucky for you, the district attorney and I came to an agreement. No prison time, considering the circumstances of who my father was and Marrok's second death." Sullivan breathed a little easier at the thought but still tightened his hold on the woman in his arms. He might never have laid eyes on her again had the DA not taken recent events into account. "He hit me with community service and probation as long I promise not to exact vigilante justice again."

"A little late for that, isn't it?" A small puff of laughter burst from her lips, as she finally looked up at him. Fisting the collar of his jacket in her hands, she shoved against him and pulled him back in. "Is that a promise you think you can keep?"

"I keep all my promises. You know that." He traced his fingertips across her jaw. Jane's breathing pattern changed. Because of him. Because of his touch. And his body hummed with the possibility of experimenting with her reactions for the rest of their lives. "But if I have to break that promise to keep you safe, Jane, I will. Whether there's a possibility of me going to prison or not."

"All right. Then I'll make a promise, too." The darkness in her beauty vanished, replaced with warmth, hope and so much more. The burden she'd hung on to for the last few months had been lifted, and Sullivan loved the effect. "Whatever happens after we walk out those hospital doors, I promise never to blackmail you into helping me again."

Whatever happened? She'd meant it as a joke, but confusion closed in on him, and Sullivan backed off a step. "If by 'whatever happens,' you mean you walking out those doors with me and signing the paperwork for your permanent transfer to Anchorage."

"Sullivan…" Jane let her hands fall to her sides, and everything inside him went cold. "Haven't you learned your lesson yet? Forget prison. Loving me is a *death* sentence. And I'm not going to be the one responsible for taking your life. I think I've screwed it up enough."

She couldn't be serious. Not after everything they'd been through. Sliding his hands through his hair, Sullivan turned away to hide the obvious fire burning through his veins. Because he couldn't stand the thought of her walking away from this. From him. "So saying you loved me when Elliot was trying to disarm that bomb strapped to your chest was some attempt to… What?" He took a deep breath, trying to clear her scent from his system, but she was all around him. She was in his veins. "Put my mind at ease in case you died?"

"No—" she swiped her tongue across her bottom lip, and his heart rate kicked up a notch "—of course not. I—"

"What you do with your life is up to you, Jane. I would never force you into anything you're not comfortable with. If you don't want to stay here in Anchorage, fine. That's your choice." He stalked toward her, craving the feel of her against him, but he caged the desire racking his nervous system. He pushed every ounce of raw passion he held for the woman who'd blackmailed him into his voice. "But just because you're holding on to your guilt with everything you have does not give you the right to make the decision of what I do with my life or who gets to stay in it."

Sullivan rolled his fingers into fists when all he wanted to do was grab her by the arms and commit every inch of her body to memory all over again. His heart worked to beat out of his chest. He took a deep breath. Two. The fire simmered to a slow burn. There, but manageable. He relaxed his hands, trailing the pad of his thumb across her full bottom lip, the one she always licked when she was nervous. "When I said everything has changed since that night under the aurora borealis, it's not that I changed my mind. It's that I'm scared as hell to love you, Jane, but here I am, in love with you anyway."

Sliding one hand into his jacket pocket, he extracted the documents she'd had made under a different name and tossed them onto the bed without taking his eyes off her. "Now all you have to do is stay."

STAY?

Her lips parted as she caught sight of the documents, and her mouth went dry. The pulse at the base of her neck quickened. She closed her eyes for a split second. She'd left them in the Blackhawk Security SUV she'd stolen from Anthony at the hospital. Sullivan's weapons expert must've recovered them and handed them over to his boss after Marrok had taken her.

The hair on the back of her neck stood at attention as the memories flashed across her mind. The bomb's beeping as Marrok had set the countdown into motion played over and over in her head. Pressing her fingers into her eye sockets, she attempted to relieve the pressure building behind her eyes. But the look of horror on Sullivan's face as he realized what his brother had done had ingrained itself into her mind. Forever. "I need…"

What did she need?

"Jane," he said.

His voice slid through her, drowning out the nightmare that'd brought them together, and she couldn't help but step into his arms. His body heat worked down through her clothing, deep into her bones, as she set her ear against his heart. She interlaced her fingers at the small of his back, terrified to let go. "I need…you." Her own words echoed throughout her mind as she recalled her reasons for seeking Sullivan out in the first place. "I need you."

"You have me. But I can't live the rest of my life wondering what would've happened if I let you walk away now. I love you. I want you to stay." He set his cheek against the crown of her head, his clean, masculine scent surrounding her, working down into her pores. "So what is it going to be, Jane?"

The tension hardening the muscles along her spine dissipated as he wrapped his thick arms around her, and she sank further into him. Was this how it would always be between them? This give and take, this passion to keep each other from getting hurt?

From the second she'd broken into Sullivan Bishop's office, she swore not to let her heart rule her decision making, but the rules of blackmail had gone out the window one by one over the past days. He'd saved her life, protected her from a group of mercenaries for crying out loud and put his future at risk. All for her. And in her last perceived moments on this earth, she'd trusted her gut to tell him exactly what her head refused to acknowledge. She loved him.

She wasn't sure when it'd happened, maybe only now, but she'd decided she wanted him more than she was afraid of losing him.

His heart pounded hard against her ear, strong and reliant. He was a SEAL. And he could take care of himself. No matter the threat, Sullivan Bishop protected those he cared about and always seemed to stay alive in the process. Jane tightened her hold on him. And that would have to be enough. "I love you, too."

He pushed her back a few inches, trying to fight the smile curling at the edge of his mouth. Sullivan gripped her around the waist. His eyes brightened as the smile overwhelmed his expression, and Jane's heart stuttered. "Really?"

"Yes. And I'm staying. With you." She nodded. Her gut instincts said this was the right choice. This was where she wanted to be. "Unless you need someone to drag you to safety through the middle of the Alaskan wilderness again, then you're on your own."

Sullivan framed her jawline between his strong hands and crushed his mouth to hers. She tried to breathe around the rush of desire flooding through her. He'd worked his way under her skin, branded himself on her soul, and her body's response to him slipped further and further out of her control. He caressed her lower back and lifted her off her feet, pressing her against him as though he intended to make them one. And she might've had a few ideas herself on how to make that happen. Injuries be damned. This was where she wanted to be.

He swept his tongue inside her mouth, laying claim. He kissed her with a wild, desperate passion and Jane took everything he gave. Arms wrapped around his neck, she clung to him as months of fear and paranoia drained from her muscles.

She had her life back. Because the one man she'd needed the most had kept his promise. Because of Sullivan.

"Is it necessary to hold that woman so tight?" a familiar voice asked.

They turned toward Elliot in the door frame, cheeks pressed together, but Sullivan kept her in his arms. A growl vibrated from deep in Sullivan's chest as he eased her back to her feet. "This better be important."

Pressed against him, Jane enjoyed the funny things that growl did to her insides but wiped at her mouth and pulled her T-shirt down over her jeans' waistband. Heat worked up her neck and into her face the longer the private investigator smiled at them.

"The police want your statements about what went down at the cabin." Elliot hiked a thumb over his shoulder. "Should I tell them to give you another thirty minutes?"

Another growl echoed throughout the room.

"Okay, okay. Forty-five minutes." Blackhawk Security's private investigator spun on his heel and wrenched open the door. How she hadn't heard him come in in the first place, Jane would never know.

"You know, Jane, I was actually worried you would be too late in telling him how you felt, and we were all going to die." Elliot turned back before hitting the hallway, and that crooked smile of his warned Jane she wasn't about to like what came out of his mouth next. "I'm glad everything worked out for the best."

"Come again?" Narrowing his eyes, Sullivan stepped toward the private investigator with fire burning hot in his gaze, but Jane held him back.

"Wait a second. Do you mean to tell me you knew which wire to cut prior to Sullivan cutting me out of the vest? And the only reason you waited was because I hadn't told him how I felt yet?" Heat surged through her. Forget about Sullivan beating Elliot to a pulp. She'd kill him herself. Jane crossed the room. Grabbing the private investigator by the collar, she hauled him close. "Are you insane? We almost died!"

"I knew you'd do the right thing when it came down to the wire. No pun intended." That crooked, cocky smile deepened the laugh lines around Elliot's mouth, but, as his attention shifted over Jane's shoulder—to Sullivan—the smile disappeared.

She didn't have to turn around to know her SEAL was considering ways to use his tightly honed skills in torture on his private investigator. Tension filled the hospital room, and she didn't see any way out for Elliot other than resigning from his job and going into hiding for the rest of his life. Jane unclenched her hold on his collar and moved out of the way. "You better start running now."

Elliot's coffee-colored eyes widened as Sullivan closed in.

"Now, boss, we're friends, right? I owe you my life. I was using the bomb as an incentive." Elliot backed toward the door, hands held up in defense, but Jane didn't hold her SEAL back this time. "Keep in mind I gave you plenty of time to cut her out of the vest in case she didn't want to express how she felt."

"The next time I see you better be on a plane to Iraq, Dunham." Sullivan stalked after him, danger and rage rising in each step.

Elliot ran out the door as fast as he could. No looking back. Probably a good decision on his part. His voice slid through the crack in the door as he bolted down the hallway. "You should be thanking me!"

The tightness remained across Sullivan's back, but Jane couldn't help but thread her arms around his waist.

"Give him a head start before you kill him." A laugh bubbled from her lips as Jane sank into the comfort of Sullivan's strong, muscled back. He spun in her grasp, pinning her with those sea-blue eyes she couldn't get enough of.

"There's still one thing we need to get clear on before we walk out those doors together." His expression sobered as he stared down at her, and Jane tightened her grip on him. "And after what happened with Menas and my brother, I think I have the right to know."

"Are you sure you're up for another interrogation? I seem to recall me winning the last one." Caution narrowed her gaze. She didn't have any more secrets. At least, none that would get them killed. But she trusted him with her life. If he wanted to interrogate her before jumping into the most dangerous assignment of his career—a relationship with her—all he had to do was ask. Echoes from the PA system filtered into the room, but Jane had attention for only the wide expanse of muscle under her fingertips. "I'll tell you anything."

"That's a good start. Because I have ways of making you talk." His voice was deep and dark, and it sent an instinct of warning down her spine. But then Sullivan raised his hand a split second before he dropped a piece of ice down her T-shirt.

Freezing water dripped down her spine. Jane screamed, trying to dislodge the ice cube, but it'd caught in her sports bra. "Where the heck did you get ice?"

"I paid Elliot five dollars to come in and tell you that whole thing about the bomb as a distraction so I could lift a piece of ice from your side table." A gut-wrenching smile spread across Sullivan's features as he wrapped her in his arms.

"So what he said wasn't true?" she asked.

"No." Sullivan shook his head. "I'm pretty sure I would've already broken my promise to the district attorney had any of that been true."

The ice fell from her shirt, and she slapped at his shoulder. "Oh, this isn't over. When we get back to the cabin, you're going to need me to save you from the brink of death in front of the fire again."

"Mmm. I like that idea." He purred into her ear, the

tip of his nose tracing the most sensitive part of her neck. "But, really, tell me how you broke into Blackhawk Security. I've had my network security team run diagnostics on my entire security system—three times—and they haven't come back with a single loophole. Either you paid someone to let you in, which your financials can't prove, or you're more than what you seem, Counselor."

"All right, Frogman, you want to know?" He'd fought like hell for her, nearly died for her—more times than she could count—and lost a brother all over again in the process. At this point, she'd give him anything he asked for. And not just the truth. Everything she had. Everything she was. And she would fight like hell for him for the rest of their lives.

"More than anything," he said.

"It's really eating you up inside, isn't it? Okay then." She crooked her finger at him, putting her mouth right next to Sullivan's ear as he leaned in. His scent washed over her, and she took a deep breath. He wanted answers, but Jane wanted more. She wanted forever. With him. A smile spread her lips thin, and she dropped the ice cube down the back of his shirt. "Did you think it was going to be that easy?"

Sullivan jerked away, his laugh loud enough to echo down the hall. Locking that enthralling blue gaze on her, he stalked toward her, all SEAL, all predator. All hers. "Oh, this is going to be fun."

* * * * *

RANGER
GUARDIAN

ANGI MORGAN

Thank you, Amanda! Thanks for the encouragement and the major kick in the behind—just the right amount of both. And a special thanks for being such a great person to model a character after!

Prologue

Eight Months Ago

Heath Murray rushed through the emergency room doors. Yes, he'd used the entrance for the ambulances. Yes, he'd parked his truck next to the building, practically on the sidewalk. And yes, he'd taken advantage of having the Texas Ranger badge he carried.

What did anyone expect? His three-year-old daughter was there. It was the only thing he knew for sure. The message from his wife had stated only what hospital they were heading to.

Life was good. Life was perfect. He couldn't imagine life without his baby girl, Skylar Dawn, in it. He couldn't imagine life without his wife, Kendall. Six years ago, if you'd asked him if his life would be full of anything except law enforcement, he would have answered no.

Now?

Life was full of pink frills and satin sun dresses. Along with brand new ponies—plastic and real. And all the disagreements about whether Skylar Dawn was old enough to own a pony. Yep, life was full, and he was blessed several times over.

He rushed to his mother-in-law, who stood up from a waiting room chair. Her eyes were red but not swollen. Her old-fashioned handkerchief was twisted and streaked from her mascara. She looked like she'd been pulled straight out of a church service, but Naomi Barlow looked like that every day. And she didn't go to church.

"Where is she?"

"Kendall is with her. She's going to be fine. It's not a break that will require surgery."

"What kind of an accident were they in?"

"Accident? Did you think they were in a car accident?" Kendall's mom asked, then laughed.

What the hell? Why was she laughing?

"Where are they?"

"Oh, honey, you poor thing. Skylar Dawn just fell on the playground at day care. That's all. She'll be fine." Naomi's eyes darted toward a set of double doors. "Only one person can be in the room with her."

He didn't need her response. What he did need was for the attendant to open the doors from the other side.

"Excuse me." He headed straight to the front desk and flipped his badge so the person at the window could see it. "I need to get through."

"May I see your credentials?"

Heath shot his ID through the slot and managed to keep his toes from tapping the linoleum while he waited. "Thanks," he added politely to the man whose turn he'd interrupted, then paced back to his mother-in-law and handed her his keys. "Give these to the green-faced Texas Ranger who comes inside in a minute. My partner, Slate Thompson will take my truck home."

"Here you go, sir. I can buzz you through now."

He heard the door lock open and hurried to pull on the handle, but it opened at a snail's pace on its own. He rushed down the hall, glancing through the small windows. Then he heard her.

A quiet, polite cry for a child of three.

He rounded a corner and took a deep breath. *Okay, they*

really are all right. He hadn't processed that information when Naomi had told him. He couldn't believe it until he'd seen with his own eyes.

So he took a second. They'd be upset as it was. He didn't need to add to the situation by not appearing calm. He shook his shoulders, slowed his racing pulse, became the dad instead of the Ranger who'd driven ninety across Dallas to get here.

"There they are." He thought his voice sounded excited to see them, instead of like the frightened-to-death man who'd just had his heart ripped from his chest.

"See, I told you Daddy was on his way."

"Daddy!" Skylar Dawn tried to lift her free arm to him. "I want Daddy."

"It's better if you stay where you are, baby. Mommy's got you." He honestly didn't think his shaking arms could hold her steadily.

Kendall tilted her cheek up for a kiss. He rubbed Skylar Dawn's strawberry blond hair. One day it would be as thick as her mother's and out of the small pigtails.

"How 'bout I sit down here so you can see me?" He sat on the floor, pulling himself close to his wife and daughter, just about ready to cry from the gratitude he felt at them both being alive and safe.

There was no tension in Kendall. She seemed far calmer than her message had implied. She mouthed, "Sorry."

His wife could probably tell how frantic he was. She'd always been good at picking up on the nuances that gave away his emotions. In fact, she was practically the only person who had ever been able to see through the wall he'd built.

A wall that had been breached several times over by Skylar Dawn.

"Let me see." He leaned closer and puckered his lips for

a loud smack without ever touching the skin of her arm. "Does that feel better?"

Skylar Dawn shook her head. "I broke it, Daddy. Does that mean we have to throw it away?"

He refrained from chuckling. "No, baby girl. The doctors can fix this all up. And you'll be as good as new."

"Oh, that's a relief." She perfectly imitated her mother.

"I've been explaining that her arm isn't a toy." Kendall smiled.

"No throwaway arms," he said.

Skylar Dawn dropped her head to Kendall's chest. "Just close your eyes for a minute, sweetheart," said Kendall. "I'll wake you up when the doctor comes back."

He placed a hand on Skylar Dawn's back and could feel when her body relaxed into sleep. *Nice to be a kid.*

"What took you so long?" Kendall whispered.

He followed suit, whispering back his answer. "We were in west Fort Worth. I did ninety most of the way. Slate thought he was going to puke."

"I just… I'm sorry about the wild message. The day care called without a lot of details. Then they told me I couldn't use my cell phone back here. I should have had Mother call with an update. I know it scared you."

"I'm good. All's good."

He listened to the details of Skylar Dawn climbing the section of the playground her age group wasn't allowed on. One of the older girls—probably about five—had helped her. Skylar Dawn had fallen.

They whispered about the X-ray and doctor's analysis. Just a hairline fracture, but they could go to the pediatrician for a cast in a couple of days.

The love Kendall had for their daughter radiated like sunshine. How awesome would it be to have another little girl as precious as this one?

The doctor came and went. Heath took Skylar Dawn

from Kendall's arms and cuddled her against his chest. Her head had a special baby smell that he especially noticed when she first fell asleep. It was something he already knew he'd miss whenever she got too big to be rocked.

"Hey, for a couple who never wanted children, I think we're handling this pretty well." Kendall smoothed Skylar Dawn's hair while they waited on their release paperwork.

"Want to have a couple more?" he said, then gulped.

"What?" Kendall's eyes grew big. "Where does this come from?"

"It was just a thought. I mean… I love you guys. I love our family. And you're right. I think we're pretty good at this."

"I do, too."

Were those tears?

"Honey, what's wrong?" He opened his free arm and pulled her in for a hug.

Special Agent Kendall Barlow was full-blown crying, silent tears running down her face. And it took a lot—like the birth of their daughter—to bring them on. Heath never expected his spontaneous suggestion to affect her this way.

"I was… I was…" she tried.

"It's okay, babe. Everything's perfect the way it is. Nothing's wrong with our family."

"But I was just thinking the same thing, Heath. I'd love another baby."

He kissed her. As much as he was able to with his arms full of their daughter.

"I am definitely looking forward to getting you home and getting this one in bed." He waggled his eyebrows at her.

Kendall dabbed at her eyes. "We can't start this afternoon, silly. I'm helping Jerry with his cyber-fraud case. It's going to take weeks. Maybe months."

"You want to wait?" He was surprised. Seriously surprised. And then an ugly voice shouted in his ear, *How many cases will be more important?*

"Whisper, please?"

"Sure." He lowered his voice to match hers. "Why would finishing cases be more important? It's not like you'll still be trying to move up the FBI ladder."

"I beg your pardon?"

"Well, if you have another baby, aren't you quitting?"

The words were there before he could mentally slap himself and stop them from forming. Mistake. It was the wrong thought to let out of his mouth.

"You want me to quit my job and stay home? What? Do you want me barefoot and pregnant in the kitchen, too?"

He tucked his bottom lip between his teeth. He wasn't going to say a word. Not a dad-blasted word. It wasn't the time. It wasn't the place.

Then she stiffened and pulled away from his arm.

Dammit.

"Kendall, we thought having any kids in day care whose parents are both in the line of fire wasn't a good idea. It's still not a good idea. But two? If you're pregnant, they'll call you out of the field anyway. Right?"

"For a few months. Just like last time. But I'm not going to give up my career. You stay home with the kids."

"I worked hard to be a Texas Ranger."

"And I worked hard to become an FBI agent."

It was the loudest whispered arguing they'd ever done. It gave him a bad feeling, like something ominous was about to happen.

"Maybe we should talk about this at home." He kissed his daughter's forehead. "When the munchkin is in bed, we can list the pros and cons."

"Or we could be honest with each other."

"I think I've been honest enough."

"Oh, that's a relief." She crossed her arms in typical Barlow fashion, after her sarcasm had a chance to sink in.

"It's going to be a long night, isn't it," he said. Fact, not a question. Just like he knew they were stepping outside into the backyard to have an extended argument once they got home.

"We both need to really think about your expectations for me. This is serious, Heath. I… It's not something I can take lightly and just forget that it happened."

"I'm sorry for jumping the gun." Apologizing was the easy part. Understanding what he did wrong would take a little longer.

Six weeks of continuous arguing began to take its toll on her family. Kendall sat at her office desk staring at the picture of Heath carrying Skylar Dawn on his shoulders. She missed him. Ached for him. Longed for someone to invent a time machine so she could take back the words she didn't even know if she meant any more.
Just when Kendall thought things were getting better, her mother overheard Heath say he didn't understand why her work was more important than a family.

She didn't know which hurt worse—what he'd said or the fact he had talked to someone else and not her. He'd always been the strong silent type. Definitely a man of action and few words.

When Skylar Dawn complained of tummy aches, Kendall suggested counseling. If they couldn't communicate on their own, maybe a third party could help.

She'd never forget the stabbing pain she'd experienced when he said, "My world has pretty much crashed down around my ears by not keeping my mouth shut." To keep from hurting their daughter, Heath packed a bag. He made a drastic, solitary decision.

If he was gone…they couldn't argue. So to solve the

problem he moved into the spare room of Slate Thompson's house on a small ranch just east of Dallas. He worked in the barn and helped with riding lessons to pay his rent.

Or at least that's what she thought. They hadn't really spoken since.

They seemed to avoid each other by staying busy with their jobs. But he never failed to call Skylar Dawn at six each evening. When her caseload picked up, he stayed at the house two nights a week.

Her mother had objected to her marriage from the beginning. For some reason, her encouragement had always been for a career. Not necessarily the FBI, just something with a title and advancement.

"How did we get this far down the rabbit hole? Yeah… Where's that time machine when you need it?"

Chapter One

Heath Murray was feeling just how crowded the small house he lived in had become. He slipped away to the rodeo every weekend, attempting to give Slate some privacy. But, man, come Sunday nights he needed to rest his weary old bones on a soft couch.

He needed to pop the top on a bottle of beer, prop his feet up on the coffee table and listen to sports while he drifted off into blissful slumber.

That never happened.

He didn't mind having his partner's mom cook. Saved him the trouble of constantly eating out. He didn't mind having Slate's new girlfriend sneak back up to the main house after not catching the front door before it slammed shut at four in the morning. Neither of them knew he hadn't really slept in months.

He didn't mind returning to his real bed twice a week to spend time with his baby girl. Skylar Dawn loved it. Kendall tolerated it. They both agreed it was better than the nights he didn't see their daughter at all.

He could deal with all that. He'd been dealing with it for almost six months. But this…

"Dammit, guys. Do you always have to be making out when I open the door?"

"Oh, man. Is it already five? I'm supposed to go see my brother tonight. I should go get ready." Vivian Watts, his roommate's girlfriend, tugged her T-shirt to her waist, making sure it was in place. She gave Slate a quick kiss and ran past Heath.

"Thanks for making her feel bad," Slate said.

"Don't mention it." Yeah, he was being sarcastic. Yeah, he didn't mean to be. Hell, maybe he did. His attitude sucked, and his side hurt. The bronc he'd been thrown from had kicked his ribs. The skin had begun turning colors before he'd started for home.

"Well, I sort of am." Slate took his hands from his back pockets and crossed his arms in a move of determination. "You know she's had a really hard time lately. They told her it's going to be at least another six weeks before they'll think about clearing her brother to leave the center."

"Sorry. I didn't mean it and I'll apologize." He would. He'd probably screw up again, though. "Maybe it's time for me to find my own place?"

"That's not what you need to do," Slate said with a certain look on his face.

The same frustrated look his friends and fellow Rangers had at least once a week. Maybe even a little more often. Like each time they tried to get him to open up about his situation with his wife. Yet if he couldn't talk about it with her, he shouldn't talk about it with his friends. Their separation was a private matter.

"You, me, Wade and Jack are tight. We're more than just Rangers, and we're more than friends. We're brothers. We've got each other's backs. I'm telling you the truth. You should call her," Slate urged.

"I will. Tuesday."

"You are such a stubborn son of a...cowboy."

At that, Heath tipped his hat off his head and let the Stetson flip into his hand. A trick his little girl loved.

"You better head on out if you're going to catch Vivian and drive her to her brother's."

"Call your wife, man. Make up. It's been six months, for crying out loud. Tell her you don't think your job is more important than hers."

"You don't think I've told her? I haven't ever lied to her. I thought she knew that. But for some reason she still can't believe me." He pulled a beer from the refrigerator, glancing at the plastic containers full of home-cooked meals. He was too sore to eat.

"Dammit, Heath." Slate stuck a ball cap on his head. "Think hard about what you're willing to give up." He stomped to the door and slammed it shut behind him.

Alone.

It was how he liked it. Right?

"Right," he spoke out loud and tipped the beer he'd wanted for the past hour between his lips and swallowed.

Another couple of minutes, and he could call Skylar Dawn before Kendall put her in the bathtub. She was almost four years old, and it had been six months since he'd destroyed any chance at a normal father-daughter relationship.

He went through the motions, just like he did every night. Nothing there comforted him like it had when he was married. There was no one to talk to about the bronc ramming him in half.

No one to joke with about the young women hanging around the edge of the stalls. Or how he'd felt too old to notice. But they'd had fun with their wolf calls when he'd bent over and showed his backside. Kendall had gotten a kick out of coming up and laying a big, luscious kiss on him when that had happened before.

That had been before she'd gotten pregnant and the barn smell had made her nauseous.

Another sip of beer. It was almost gone, and he wanted another.

Was this what life was going to be like? Waiting around

while Kendall—and her mother—made all the decisions about their life? He'd been ready for months to talk with her and apologize again. He just wanted their old life back.

Was that even possible?

Completely aware that pressure against his side would be painful, he went back into the kitchen, filled a couple of sandwich bags with ice, wrapped them in a towel and shoved it against his ribs.

The stinging cold brought him to his senses. He was getting too old for this routine. Too old to be afraid to talk with his wife. Too old to insult Vivian and Slate or any of his other friends because he was miserable with his own life.

It was time to make some changes.

Good or bad...he needed to talk with Kendall face-to-face. Soon. Maybe it would turn out better than he feared. Maybe it wouldn't. All he knew was that it was time to move forward.

Good thing he had a light load at work. He was mostly focused on court and testifying and paperwork right now. He set the ice on the table, then slid his shirt free from his belt. He tucked it up close to his armpit before looking closer at the bruise.

That was going to be a big boo-boo, as baby girl would say.

Yeah, it was time. Slate was right about that. Time to apologize and move on. How long could a woman stay mad?

Something in the back of his mind warned that *his* woman could stay that way a very, very long time. Especially with a mother whispering in her ear who hated him. Hell, his mother-in-law had shouted to the world that he'd never be good enough for her daughter.

He clicked on his phone, stared at the picture of Kendall holding a super pink baby girl and swiped to dial. He would talk to his wife face-to-face. Tonight, he'd read to his daughter.

"Hey there. How's my favorite munchkin?" He reached for the children's version of *The Wizard of Oz*.

"Daddy!"

"JERRY, I KNOW it's Sunday night. That's why I'm calling. I need more people. I know I'm close to a breakthrough." Kendall Barlow didn't back down. Her supervisory special agent should know that. She heard the house phone ring in the background, as it did every night like clockwork.

In six months' time, Heath hadn't missed calling his daughter once. And not one time had he made a serious effort to reconcile. He was a man of few words—for everyone except Skylar Dawn.

"Kendall. It's been months and you've got nothing to show for it. You know we're shorthanded. Dallas Police Department is worse off than we are. You aren't going to get more qualified personnel for the joint task force than the people already assigned to it."

"If I had another competent person who knew their way around computers, I know I could prove that Public Exposure is fraudulent. We're close. Very close."

"Oh furgle. Our resources have been tapped out. Run with what you've got, and get me something to show for your time. Of course, there is one person already on your task force you haven't tried."

"Special Agent Fisher, I've asked you not to use that word. I've looked it up and it's inappropriate. It was fine in *Catch-22*, but come on. You know it doesn't mean what you think." She was tired of this conversation. Or was he trying to distract her? Did he really think that she needed something to justify the investigation? Couldn't he think of one more possible agency to check? "Jerry?"

"Yes? I promise I'll behave. I just love that word."

"Please don't—"

"You should talk to your ex. Ask him if he's heard anything about your case."

"That's a clear conflict of interest. No one would allow him on the team."

"Seems like that's my decision now. I'll allow him to help out until the Rangers can find a replacement. Use the taxpayers' money wisely. See you in the office."

The line disconnected, and she could once again hear the exclamations of surprise from her daughter as her father read about flying monkeys and sparkly red shoes. Had she mentioned to Heath that their daughter had outgrown two pairs of those red slippers while he'd been gone?

Skylar Dawn was sitting on the couch holding the main phone extension. Her grandmother listened on an additional handset just outside the door. Heath knew about the eavesdropping even if her mother thought it was a secret. He accepted it as part of his "punishment for whatever he blamed himself."

As if living away from their precious little girl wasn't punishment enough. Why he thought he needed to be punished, she didn't understand. And no matter how she tried, her mother wouldn't stop.

Constant jabs at Heath kept an undercurrent of tension in the air. Kendall wanted to avoid the subject and leaned toward avoiding her mother in the evenings when she helped out with Skylar Dawn.

Heath wasn't her ex, and finalizing their separation wasn't high on her priority list. So far there hadn't been any squabbles about how to do anything. He'd taken only a few of his things and the horses.

Other than a picture or two of Skylar Dawn, he'd managed to leave everything looking exactly like it had been when he'd walked away. Or when she'd driven him away. She could remember exactly when things had come to a pivotal breaking point. Most of that argument had to do with her mother.

Her mother's standards had been high her entire life. Heath had a father exactly the same way. But what had turned Heath into a strong man who held his opinions to himself—or himself and his horse—seemed to be turning her soul bitter.

I can't be my mother. I can't do that to Skylar Dawn.

"Do you have to say goodbye, Daddy?"

Kendall waited for the familiar "Good night" and "I love you." Her daughter clicked the red button on the phone and her mother followed a second afterward. She crossed her arms, enveloping the phone between a breast and a well-toned limb.

Her mother, a woman of sixty, made good use of the money she'd gathered over the years. Three stepfathers and three settlements later, Kendall had a college education and two letters of recommendation for her Bureau interview.

Getting along with the men in her mother's life had never been the problem. More and more recently, she'd been realizing how sad her mother had become. And how demanding.

Her mother didn't allow Skylar Dawn two seconds to linger or even to put the phone back on its charging station. She immediately clapped her hands, and her granddaughter jumped to her feet.

Oh my God! She's reacting like a trained puppy.

Kendall swooped in and picked up her little girl, who should need a bath from playing in the dirt. But she was perfectly clean.

"Wow. Let's go for a ride. What do you think, sweet girl?"

"Kendall, I was just getting ready to run her bath. Isn't it late to go out?"

"Actually, Mother, you might be right. But we're going

anyway." Kendall smiled and steadied her daughter back down on her feet. "Let's go see if we can find some flying monkeys."

Skylar Dawn giggled as they skipped down the hall and out the front door.

It was clear that changes needed to be made for her and her daughter. She'd set paperwork in motion the next day. She'd find out the possibilities before she approached Heath.

Six months of living with her mother instead of her husband was long enough. Five minutes down the road, she realized she'd pointed the car east toward Heath. She slowed and turned into a drive-through. Then they got ice cream and played at the park until they both really needed a bath.

It was fun. Spontaneous. She used to be those things. It was the whole reason Skylar Dawn had come to be.

It was time to find that person again.

Chapter Two

Wade Hamilton shoved the last file into the back of the box. It represented months of work and the official end of his desk duty. It had taken him almost as long to heal from the beating he'd received six months ago. But everything worked again. Both with his body and his status as a Texas Ranger Company B lieutenant.

Ready to take his place at his partner's side. Ready to get out from behind his desk. Back to handling things by the seat of his pants instead of the rule book. Doing so had landed him in this desk chair. He'd learned his lesson to slow down and think a little. He liked fieldwork… not paperwork.

Unfortunately, Major Clements had discovered Wade was good at paper shuffling. He'd been allowed to assist with a few cases as backup for Company B brothers. But the paperwork grew while he was gone.

It seemed like the rest of the office had grown accustomed to him shuffling their requests, too. Coming in early and staying late was second nature now. Why not, since he had no life?

That's where he was bright and early on a Monday morning. At work before the rest of the staff or other Rangers finished their first cup of coffee, he was shuffling papers. Almost done, the latest request for his company's support caught his eye. He knew the name of the FBI agent heading the task force. He'd attended her wedding just over five years ago.

Kendall Barlow was the new team leader of a cyber-crime task force and asking for computer and field support on the joint task force. Heath—her husband and the logical choice—had already been assigned to cybercrime. Now their relationship would need to be reviewed and disclosed. He'd been on the task force since it was headed by Jerry Fisher. But still, Murray was the best geek Company B had.

It was up to Wade to recommend someone else or okay Heath for a couple of days in the field with Special Agent Barlow.

It was also an opportunity to resolve his friend's problem. He'd been listening to Slate talk about his temporary roommate for six months. How he worked the horses, cleaned the stalls, never missed a phone call with his daughter and never—ever—spoke to his wife. Heath, on the other hand, never said a word. Wade held on to the paperwork and grabbed a second cup of coffee.

Who was he to jump in to the middle of a man's business? Especially marriage problems? But the more he tried to talk himself out of it, the more his gut told him to assign Heath to work with his wife.

Slate and Jack were both standing at his desk when he returned from the break room. Before he asked their advice, Jack pointed to the request.

"What's this?"

"You're sending him, right?" Slate asked. "It's exactly what they both need to force them to figure out what's going on."

"You think so?"

"Damn straight," they answered together.

"The man's turning into a bear," Slate said. "I might take his head off if he snarls at Vivian again."

"If the FBI put in the request, you should accommodate it," Jack stated, hanging his jacket on the rack.

"What if *she* doesn't want it?" Wade asked, already knowing that he would recommend Heath.

"Then she has a friend who is thinking along the same lines we are." Slate took his seat opposite Wade. "Maybe she's as cranky as he is."

"Who's cranky?" Heath asked as he walked through the door.

"The old man, Major Clements," Jack said, jumping in. "We're coming up with reasons he might be out of sorts. I say he's getting ready to retire. Wade says his wife might be cranky."

"My bet's on the wife." Heath winced as he took off his jacket, holding his side. "The old man's never going to retire."

The guys nodded in agreement. Slate mouthed "Bear," while pointing to Heath behind his hand.

Wade recognized Heath's movement. When his own ribs had been cracked, he'd held his side the same way. Heath had probably injured himself at the rodeo this weekend. But he'd never admit it.

Wade agreed with hiding it from the boss. If he hadn't been unconscious with an eye swollen twice its size, he probably would have taken a couple of days off and never admitted anything about the beating. Or about the woman who'd saved his life by alerting Jack to his whereabouts.

Time to put his own fantasies to rest and find the woman who haunted his dreams... Therese. If he couldn't work on that, the least he could do was help get Heath and Kendall back together.

He reached for the request, ready to recommend his friend and submit it to Major Clements. The old man would make the final decision if Company B would waive the conflict of interest. Maybe Heath and Kendall could find mutual ground and resolve their differences.

If not, then this assignment would at least help them reach that decision, too.

He completed the paperwork and sent it on its way. Assignment made.

Chapter Three

Heath held his side as he carefully lifted his arm into his suit jacket and then set his white Stetson on top of his head. The required Texas Ranger uniform wasn't what people expected when they saw the star on his pocket. Traditionally they all wore white Stetsons, but with suits rather than jeans. He even wore a white shirt and black tie today.

Good thing, since he'd been assigned to work with an FBI task force regarding potential cybercrime. The agent in charge thought a research company had some type of ulterior motive for collecting the data.

Cybercrime had a broad definition—it referred to any crime committed with a computer or through a computing device. The slim file he'd received held just the basics and an address where to meet the agent. He was curious to learn what had tipped the FBI off and what the specifics of the case were.

Why meet here in the field? It wasn't the norm. Neither was getting a last-minute request for field backup on a task force he hadn't been active with for a while. Jerry Fisher—his wife's old partner—had been promoted to group leader overseeing several teams in cybercrime. What was different now?

He waited for this mysterious agent at his truck. The older neighborhood was nicely kept up. The homes were on the smaller side for this section of Dallas. They'd eventually be sold and torn down to make way for larger lots.

It was a shame. Some of them looked really nice and were perfect starter places for couples. *Or to house mothers-in-law.* He'd been thinking about his wife the entire trip across town.

Only natural that he'd start thinking of her mother, since he half blamed her for egging on their arguments. He'd gone back and forth long into the night about calling Kendall. Even picked up his phone a couple of times. But the chicken part of himself won.

What if that phone call ended everything?

This morning he watched the sun rise while riding his mare and resolved to call Kendall today to make a date to talk. Not over the phone. Not around Skylar Dawn. Certainly not around his mother-in-law. The promise gave him peace of mind. Six months was enough time apart. He needed to try again. Speaking face-to-face would allow him to gauge her reaction. And if she called it quits?

Well, he wanted her to look him in the eye if she did.

There were several cars on the street of the address he'd been given. None of them were a government-issued sedan. He glanced at his watch—only a couple of minutes early.

If he was working with the FBI, he'd eventually have to visit their Dallas field office. He wasn't excited about running into Kendall accidentally. Or her supervisor, Jerry Fisher.

Whoever his partner from the FBI was, they were late. Unless he was supposed to meet them inside. He walked around the truck, calling Wade to see if there'd been a time adjustment to the appointment. When a black sedan pulled up behind his truck, he disconnected. He leaned on the tailgate while putting his phone away, waiting.

"Heath?" A familiar voice rang from the far side of the government car.

The car door shut, and he stood at attention for some reason. The face came into focus while his body charged out of control.

Kendall?

Dammit. He'd almost dove into the truck bed. Hard to do with his heart galloping up his windpipe like a stampeding mustang. He wanted to leap on its back and get the hell out of there.

His hands itched to wrap themselves in her wild strawberry blond mane. But no wild mane flowed down the back of FBI Special Agent Kendall Barlow. It was pulled smoothly against her head into a ponytail. A few short tendrils escaped in front of her ears, the lobes pierced with the small diamond studs he'd given her.

"Nice to see you," she said, before smiling a strained grin.

"Hey." It felt awkward. He hadn't been alone with her in a long time. He deliberately eased his shoulders, trying to relax. "Nice earrings."

She fingered a stud, as if figuring out which pair she wore. "Oh, these? I can't remember where I got them." She teased with a genuine smile now. She remembered exactly who had given them to her... Him.

The awkwardness was worth it for the smile he hadn't seen in months. "I... No one told me it was your task force."

"Can we sort through the conflict of interest after Mrs. Pelzel's interview? She's watching us out her window."

"Would you like to work with someone else?"

"Of course not." She stopped on the sidewalk, head tilted to the side to look up at him. Physically only an arm's length away, but completely out of his reach. "We can be professional about this. At least I can."

Professional? Sure. Why the hell not?

Her task force. Her lead. Her knock on the door. He

turned sideways on the porch to let her pass. The slight scent of ginger and orange filled him with memories. He recognized the smell of her lotion and was getting sentimental. Instead of pulling her into his arms and kissing her until they were both senseless, he tugged off his dark shades and tucked them in his pocket.

He could be professional. If he had to.

Kendall explained who they were when Mrs. Pelzel came to the door. She introduced him as Ranger Murray. No one was the wiser that they were married, since she'd always used her maiden name professionally. Once they were invited inside, Heath quickly discovered Kendall had been on this case for several months. Sitting on one of the most uncomfortable couches in the world, he concentrated on Mrs. Pelzel preparing large glasses of iced tea. A suddenly dry throat couldn't wait to be quenched.

Kendall looked at a message on her phone, and he wondered how they'd drifted apart. More than five years of his life had been devoted to this woman.

How could it all be gone over one wrong question? He didn't want it to be. But getting back to her wouldn't be easy.

Once again, he was close enough to touch his wife, but promise bound to keep it professional. Reminding himself to stay professional. He'd kept that way back when they'd first met. He could do it again now.

Mrs. Pelzel brought the glasses in on a tray. He popped off the couch to help, but she shrugged him off. "Please sit. I have never had a real Texas Ranger visit before. This is so exciting."

She handed them each a glass. He downed his in record time and could only blame it on nerves.

Kendall set down her glass after taking a sip, then straightened her jacket. Time for business. "Mrs. Pelzel, would you be willing to let my computer forensics team take a look at the PC?"

"Can they do that from here? I don't think I could live without my computer for a long period of time," the home owner replied. "That's how I stay in touch with my grandkids, you know."

"We could have someone out here in a couple of days," he answered. "They could check it right here."

The older woman shook her head. "Oh, wait. You know, I should have told you when you first arrived. There's really not a problem, so you'd be wasting your time."

Kendall gave him a look he should have been able to interpret. Maybe she'd just been surprised that he'd given an answer she didn't like. Maybe she thought it strange that Mrs. Pelzel had changed her mind. He didn't know, and that was disappointing since he should, being her husband and all.

"Mrs. Pelzel, what happened that made you call the FBI?" Kendall asked. Her notebook was open. Her pen was clicked to a ready position, but her casual body language told him she wasn't expecting a real answer.

That hadn't changed, at least. He could still read her mannerisms, it seemed.

"I'm afraid I'm just a silly old ninny who made a mistake," the older woman said.

Kendall turned a page in her notebook, sliding her finger across the handwriting as she skimmed the page. "You told us you had a feeling that someone was watching you through the computer's camera."

"I did," the older woman whispered.

To her credit, Kendall the FBI agent didn't roll her eyes or make any facial movement that indicated she didn't believe the older woman. "You also mentioned that the computer seemed to be running slower since they installed the Public Exposure gadget."

"Really, you should believe me when I tell you I made a mistake," Mrs. Pelzel said, her fingers twisting into the loose long-sleeved shirt she wore.

"Will you confirm that you have one of the PE monitoring systems?" Kendall's enthusiasm moved her forward to the edge of the couch. Both sets of law enforcement eyes moved toward the desk, where the older model computer sat.

"They seem like a legitimate company," he said, attempting to get Mrs. Pelzel to share more information.

"I'm not a helpless old woman who doesn't know how to research a product or service. I didn't think it was anyone's business how much time I spent online. But the money they offered was enough to buy a new roof. I just couldn't pass that up."

He'd heard of Public Exposure and their controversial social media monitoring system. The file he'd been sent from the task force stated a strong belief the group was involved in more than the good of the common man.

"I sound old and kooky about someone watching me. But I swear that the camera light comes on by itself while I'm cooking or watching television. I hear a click, and the red light pops on and off." She covered her mouth like she'd said something wrong and then looked at her computer.

Warning bells sounded, and he couldn't help glancing over to see if the light was on.

"It doesn't sound kooky at all, Mrs. Pelzel," Kendall comforted. "In fact, we've had several other residents report the same thing. But we need to take your computer to our forensic team and have them check—"

"I'm sorry. Maybe I'll have my granddaughter look at it. I was wrong to bring you here. There's nothing weird going on." Mrs. Pelzel stood and lifted her hand toward her front door. "I'm sorry, but there's nothing I can do."

"Mrs. Pelzel, I believe you," Heath said. "A start to resolving this issue would be to make certain you log out of your Wi-Fi. Turn everything off before closing the lid and unplugging it. And ask your granddaughter to verify your router has an encryption key. You might want to change your password."

"Thank you. I'll try to remember, and I'm very sorry to have wasted your time."

Kendall stood, defeat written clearly on her face. She flipped her notebook closed and stowed it away inside her suit jacket. They both stopped on the front walk when the door shut. Heath squinted at the noon sun and put his glasses on while she made a couple of more notes.

"The precautions won't make any difference," Kendall told him, following with her sunglasses dangling from between her fingers.

"You don't think this is someone trying to steal identities, like that file sitting in my car states."

"It's bigger than that." Kendall continued to her car.

"How many reports have you taken?"

"Dozens." Kendall leaned on the government-issued sedan, appearing more defeated now than she had inside the house. "And for every person who reports that their camera light is sporadically coming on, there are probably another dozen who don't."

"It's a shame she wouldn't let an expert search her computer. But if you have had that many complaints, why haven't your FBI computer whizzes found what you need from those victims?" He crossed his arms across his chest and leaned his hip against the sedan, close to her.

"What did you think of Public Exposure before this morning?"

"I've seen their public service announcements. They're a group that promotes kids playing outside instead of hanging on social media. How are they involved in potential identity theft?"

"First, no accounts have been affected—bank, credit card or otherwise. None of these complaints go further than what you witnessed. Mrs. Pelzel doesn't realize that it was me who she spoke with when she called. I take the complaints, but by the time I get to an interview, something has changed their minds and they've all made a mistake."

"All of them?"

"This makes over twenty. Oh, and they all use the word *kooky*."

"They can't all be saying the same thing. You think Public Exposure is threatening them?"

"Yes. Sometime between when the resident calls me and when I get here. All of these people withdraw their complaints or concerns and I can't move forward."

Mrs. Pelzel watched them from her window. Heath saw her drop the curtain back into place. Without moving his head, he looked at the windows of the neighbors. More than one resident peered through the blinds.

"I kind of understand about that feeling of being watched." He barely nodded, but Kendall picked up what he was throwing down.

"There's also a white van at the end of the block." She pointed a finger behind her.

He glanced in that direction. "Two men in the front seat. Just sitting like they were when I arrived."

"Want another chat?"

"I'm game."

Kendall flipped her identification wallet open and held it in her left hand, leaving her right ready to react. Her weapon was at the ready in her shoulder harness, his at his hip. She turned and they took the first steps into the middle of the street toward the van.

The engine sprang to life and the van burned rubber in reverse. It was around the corner before they could pivot and get back to the car.

"I didn't see a front license plate," Kendall said, pointing for him to get into her vehicle.

"Nope. At least we don't have to wonder if we're being watched or not." He hesitated to open her sedan's door. "My truck is faster than this old heap."

"Yeah, but this is government insured. I'd hate for our rates to go up."

He jumped inside and buckled up. That was his Kendall. Always practical.

And he loved it.

Chapter Four

Kendall concentrated on driving the car. If she let herself get distracted and think about why Heath had been assigned her case, she'd screw up. Driving or talking…somehow she'd messed up one or the other, and he'd shut down.

At the moment, his hand gripped the back of her seat and the other gripped the dash. He'd lowered the window as soon as she'd pulled away from Mrs. Pelzel's home.

"Do you see them?"

"You're about to cross Inwood. Take a right." He was grinning from ear to ear.

A definite improvement from when she'd first arrived. She'd thought he was about to throw up when Mrs. Pelzel went for the tea. She turned right as he suggested with the direction his finger pointed. For a by-the-book kind of guy, he had a good intuition about where criminals went.

"Slow down, Kendall." Heath dropped his hand and pulled his sidearm.

She tapped the brakes and followed the direction of his narrowed eyes, toward the end of the block where the van sat parked in a driveway. She couldn't tell if it actually belonged there or not. She slowed further.

"We need a better view." He rested his weapon on his thigh but kept it pointed toward his door.

"Do you think they've seen us?" She pulled the car to the curb, keeping her foot on the brake and the car in gear.

"Not sure."

"Thoughts?"

"They aren't getting out. We should call for backup. Last thing we need is a chase through a residential part of Dallas."

"Agreed. A high-speed chase isn't ideal anywhere."

"Nope."

At least he was concise. Shoot, he always had been. Heath Murray was a cowboy of few words.

"As soon as I put the car in Park, they'll take off."

"Probably. Backup?"

"I hate to do that when all we have is the suspicion they were watching us or Pelzel's house." She needed proof. Something solid to move forward with. Not a reprimand about pursuing innocent bystanders.

"They did peel out in Reverse to get away."

"True, but we hadn't identified ourselves. I just see a media nightmare when they claim we were coming at them with guns."

"Want me to ask?" His hand reached to open his door.

"Let's just wait a minute and see what they do."

She had no more than finished the sentence when two men exited the van, walked to the rear and removed paint buckets. One of the guys went and punched the doorbell, also knocking loud enough to send every dog on the block into a barkfest.

"You've got to be kidding me." She hit the steering wheel with the palms of both hands. "This is the first nibble I've had."

"Drive slow."

Kendall didn't hesitate and put the car in motion. With his gun resting on his thigh, Heath used his phone as a camera. She didn't have to watch. She was confident that he'd capture as many images as possible. She focused her gaze on the men, switching between them, watching for a weapon or any questionable movement.

They drew even with the house and the man still at the van climbed inside and quickly shut the rear doors. The one at the house knocked again, causing the dog inside to bark once more. She could see it bouncing against the window trying to get out.

"Catch the plate?" Heath asked.

"He stacked paint cans in front of it." Frustrated, she kept the car moving and pulled around the corner.

"We could wait here. See what they do."

"We'll give it a try." She performed a three-point turn, pulled next to the curb and cut the engine.

"Video call me." He plugged a headset into his phone and used one earpiece, dropping the phone into his jacket pocket. "Stay here."

"Heath, no." This went against training, but it was their best option.

"Don't worry. I don't do crazy." With those words, he was out of the car and tapping the hood as he walked around the front.

She should have been more insistent and demand he return to the car. She dialed and he answered but didn't talk. She could hear his boots on the street, his breathing and then the echo of street sounds after she heard them in real time.

He crossed the street and stood on the grass at the corner house's garage wall. The cell screen finally showed a picture other than the inside of his pocket. He lifted the phone around the corner, and she could see past the neighboring driveways.

"They're standing at the back of the van. One's talking pretty rapidly and waving his hands. Can you make out what they're saying? I can't."

"No," he whispered into his microphone.

"They're both looking in your direction, but I don't think they can see the phone. The driver is opening the doors and putting the paint back inside."

"I can have a conversation," he whispered.

"No. Heath, no. Just wait." She had a bad feeling. A very bad feeling.

Trusting premonitions had never been a strategy for her. She never looked for good luck or blamed a bad streak on chance. More than anything else, she investigated and found the answers through old-fashioned hard work.

But something screamed at her to get Heath back in the car.

"Time to pack it up, Heath."

The screen went black as she heard the driver slam the van doors shut in real time and then on the echo in the video delay. She started the car to be at the ready.

But Heath didn't return to the vehicle. She inched the car forward until she could see her husband disappearing into the front door alcove, getting closer to the van instead of coming back to her.

"Heath!" She called to him without any response. She sank lower in her seat, hoping neither man in the van noticed the car.

The van's engine roared to life.

Kendall braced herself, fairly certain that the next thing she heard would be gunfire. The van peeled out of the driveway and down the street…toward her, passing Heath and turning left. Perfect for them to follow.

"Let's go!" Heath's voice roared at her through the phone.

She put the car into Drive, stopping just as he rushed away from the house and leapt over a small hedge. Even in boots, Heath was across the concrete street and in the car within seconds.

His speed always amazed her. Riding horses, running

or taking down a suspect…the action didn't matter. His hat was in his lap, and his hands were waving to follow the van.

"We don't really have a reason to follow these guys," she mentioned as she took the next left, back to the main road they'd turned from earlier. "Why do you want to pursue?"

"Gut feeling?"

Just as she was about to open her mouth to explain how their joint task force operated—that she was in charge and he shouldn't take off like he had—the van sped up and fishtailed around a corner.

"If they really think that's going to work, I guess they don't know much about you, Kendall."

Even increasing their speed and darting around a car, she caught the smile and wink. The natural response was to smile back. So she did. It was the reason she'd fallen in love with him. His gallantry. His bravery. His…okay, everything.

Kendall stopped herself, concentrating on switching lanes and accelerating. She'd confront him later. After whatever they were doing was over.

"Watch out." Heath raised his voice, pointing in front of them.

The van went through a yellow light. They weren't running sirens. And a powder-pink sedan, heading in the opposite direction, turned left in front of them. They were going to hit each other. Kendall slammed on her brakes, as did the sedan. They barely avoided each other as they fishtailed sideways to a stop.

"Gun it. Car to your left."

She heard the words and trusted the Texas Ranger next to her. She floored the gas, trying to look for crossing traffic, getting their car across the intersection. It was a good time of day to be on Northwest Highway. No one was in their path when she heard brakes from one direction and tires squealing from the other.

The SUV they'd passed a few seconds earlier had crashed into the rear of the pink car, stopping where her sedan would have been if Heath hadn't yelled. There was a loud bang and horns.

"Great job, babe." Heath patted her shoulder from where he rested his arm along the back of her seat. "I'll check on the drivers."

She pulled around to protect the drivers from oncoming traffic and hit the hazard lights. Heath got out, leaving his hat in his seat. She dropped her head to the wheel, reaching for her phone to call the accident in to authorities and request a tow truck. She sat back as she gave all the appropriate information, letting out a long sigh.

The van was out of sight. Heath was busy with the drivers, and all Kendall could do was force herself to breathe. That had been close. Too close.

No suspect was worth what had almost happened. She had to be more careful, less reckless. Skylar Dawn needed her parents to come home. Period.

"You okay?" Heath asked, back at the passenger door.

She nodded, still a little stunned by it all.

"I can't say I'm bummed about them getting away." The corner of his mouth barely rose as he leaned on the car.

"What? Why's that?"

"Where's the fun in catching them the first day I get to work with you again?"

He said it with such a straight face that if she hadn't known him, she never would've seen that playful gleam in his eye. Yet she couldn't argue with the logic either. She would've been bummed, too.

Chapter Five

Heath wanted to take Kendall in his arms until she stopped shaking, but he'd jumped out of the car to check on the other drivers. Instead of helping her now, he spoke to her through the passenger door, keeping the entire front seat between them.

Hugging your wife after an accident was allowed, in his book. He just didn't know if it fell under the professional umbrella. He straightened, grabbing his aching ribs, worse now because of slamming into the seat belt. But he swallowed the grimace of pain, keeping it to himself. He wouldn't mention it to the EMTs who would be arriving on the scene, judging by the distant sirens.

Kendall stretched a couple of times as she stood from the car. "I can't believe they missed us."

"You didn't hesitate."

She nodded, letting the statement stand as a compliment about their teamwork. And this time, he didn't add the frightening picture in his head of a different outcome. If she had stopped to question why he was yelling a command at her... Damn, they would be pinned between those two cars right now.

But she hadn't. They were unharmed. Fine to go home to Skylar Dawn. And good enough to work together tomorrow.

"The drivers are fine." He'd walked around the hood of the car before realizing it. His hand opened between

Kendall's shoulder blades, and he might have patted her a couple of times if he hadn't seen the tears.

But he had.

Just two, but they were enough to make her curl into the crook of his arm and stand there until they heard the first siren grow close. She broke away like someone had thrown water on them.

"Traffic needs to get through. I should probably move the car." Her voice was awkward and strained as she looked around the intersection.

"I can take care of it."

"Don't coddle me, Heath."

"Whoa there, *partner*." He emphasized the last word to remind her why they were there. "I'm allocating resources. You're the better photographer. I'm going to need every angle possible before the cars move." He stuck his hand in his pocket.

Her mouth formed a perfect O before accepting his phone. Then she was back. Professional. Doing her job as the authorities arrived. Identifying herself as an agent and taking pictures.

Staying out of the way, the Dallas PD officer gave him the go-ahead to move the FBI sedan. It didn't have a scratch on it. Just as he opened the door, in a moment where no one else watched, he caught a glance between the two drivers.

A knowing glance. Like they'd gotten away with something.

It took him a few minutes to get the sedan back on the same side of the street as the rest of the cars. By the time he returned, both drivers stood with officers, giving their statements. After an initial check, they'd both declined the ambulance ride to a hospital.

The woman in the pink car was crying again, her mascara smeared like his mother-in-law's the day his world had turned upside down. It was hard not to think about it—the afternoon Skylar Dawn had broken her arm. But he pushed it from his mind.

Something was off about the accident. Maybe he'd been hanging around Wade too much lately. His friend's intuition seemed to be rubbing off on him. Everything about the SUV guy who had nearly T-boned them screamed that the man wanted to run.

It had to be the highway patrol officer in him. He'd stopped more than his fair share of antsy drivers with drugs or weapons in their cars. The SUV driver shifted his weight from foot to foot. He kept looking around, especially at Kendall.

Okay, Heath admitted that his wife was an extremely attractive woman. Nothing about her shouted married or mom. And seeing her work again was…hot. He got why men would watch her. But this guy didn't have a look like he was trying to ask her out.

Nope. Heath recognized the short glances. The slow quarter turns to keep her in his peripheral vision. The driver must not realize that Heath was a Ranger or anyone else significant. He hadn't given him a second glance since Heath asked if he was okay.

Heath leaned against the pink car's trunk, watching both the drivers through his mirrored shades. There it was again. A specific look that acknowledged the drivers knew each other. One of the man's eyebrows rose, and the woman's chin lifted slightly.

Indiscernible to anyone not watching them specifically. A look that confirmed his gut feeling that something was off. If he'd looked away for a split second, he would have missed it.

If the drivers knew each other, they must know the men in the white van. He took a step toward Kendall, who was wrapping up with the officers. But what would he tell her?

That his instinct told him these two apparently innocent victims had a connection to the group Kendall was looking into? They couldn't hold the two based on his observation. His gut instinct had gotten them into this accident by encouraging her to follow the van.

If he followed any intuition, it would be to keep his thoughts and observations to himself until they could investigate. That's what the Rangers and FBI did. They found the facts and built cases.

He'd wait.

For now, he'd make it clear about his role here. No reason to let Public Exposure know he was working with Kendall. He pushed off the trunk and marched to Kendall's side. He pulled her close to him.

When she turned to him—most likely to express her anger—he kissed her. A full-on-the-mouth, like-she-belonged-to-him kiss. For the moment...she did. Although she may not after the next time they were alone.

"I'll explain when we're alone," he whispered. Then in a louder voice, "You ready to go, babe?"

He could see the fury rising for him embarrassing her. "Gentlemen." She nodded to the officers, excusing herself.

Heath didn't back off. He kept his arm around Kendall's waist as they walked to her sedan. He opened her door and tried to kiss her again.

"No way," she said, dodging his attempt. "You better have a dang good reason for what you just did."

He ran around the back of the car, trying to come up with something. Anything other than the real reason, since he didn't want to explain himself. At least not yet.

She stared at him as he snapped his seat belt into place. "Well?"

"It was time to go."

She huffed. "That makes no sense at all. If you wanted

to go, you could have said something and not embarrassed me in front of the Dallas PD."

He let her vent as he looked through the pictures she'd taken of the scene. Once he was back in the office, he'd be able to run a full background check. Once he had information, he'd explain to Kendall.

"You aren't listening to me."

"What?"

Kendall slowed to a stop beside his truck. "I said, if you're going to get possessive because someone's looking at me, then this joint effort isn't going to work."

"That wasn't… I wasn't…" he tried. *Get your information right before you tell her.* "Professional. Got it."

The awkward pause resulted in an awkward thumb gesture indicating he should get out of the car. She lowered the passenger window from her side and waited until he bent his face down to look at her.

"I'll talk to you tonight when you call Skylar Dawn. We'll decide what our next move is and where to meet tomorrow."

"Good idea."

He stood. The window went up and she pulled away, leaving him in the middle of the street. She had a right to be upset. On the surface, he'd behaved badly.

Back in his truck, he resisted the impulse to bang the dashboard. It sure didn't appear that he'd racked up any points for moving back home. He'd do his research, and maybe his instinct about the drivers would pay off.

Drapes dropped into place at the house to his left. Blinds closed at Mrs. Pelzel's home. There was more to this case than fraud. Every instinct he possessed told him so. Kendall was keeping something from him. He knew that before being assigned to her task force.

Fraud? Or a decision about their life—together or apart? Maybe helping his wife would give them an opportunity to really talk. But now, it was time to work some computer magic to figure out what secrets the residents of Hall Street were keeping.

Chapter Six

"If I weren't a mom, I'd be cussing like a sailor right now." Kendall closed the office door behind her.

Jerry Fisher didn't look up from the paperwork under his pen. "I put in the request as you asked. You must have known there was a possibility that your husband would continue on the task force until they could find an alternate. Do I need to file a furgle conflict of interest and pull you from the case? Oh, sorry. I forgot you're offended by that word."

The witty comeback she'd expected hadn't come. Instead he'd deliberately used that stupid word. Her supervisor sounded…bothered. *Shoot.* She'd been using his listening abilities for her personal venting. That needed to stop.

The pen dropped to the desk, and he covered the papers with a file. Kendall plopped down in the lone chair near the bookshelf, emotionally exhausted. She'd only returned to the office to delay explaining to her mother why she looked like she hadn't slept in a year.

Jerry leaned back in his chair, fingers locked casually behind his neck. "Look, if it's too difficult to work with Murray, I can give this thing to Kilpatrick. It'll die a quick death, and it won't be your responsibility or be on your record."

"Kilpatrick is two months away from retirement. He

won't take it seriously." She could handle Heath and the investigation. If she couldn't…well, she deserved to be reassigned.

"We both know this investigation isn't going anywhere, Kendall. I spoke with my supervisor and the DC cyber-crime group supervisor. They're still not interested until your victims have monetary losses or receive extortion threats. It's just not a priority for them." He leaned forward, chatting like the friend he'd been when they'd first started out at the Bureau. More like he was doing her a favor by taking the case away.

Did he really believe she was wasting her time? Had he lost confidence in her ability? Or was her desire to crack a big case obscuring the reality that Public Exposure wasn't one?

"We actually had a break this afternoon. The address of the complaint was being watched by two men." She wouldn't remind him that she could manage Heath.

The fact was that Jerry Fisher drank the Kool-Aid. He'd moved up to management. He was her boss. Bosses lived by the rules. Bosses wanted successful investigations. Bosses didn't need to hear about personal problems.

If he needed results…well, that's what she'd give him.

"Were you able to question them?" He picked up the pen and tapped both ends back and forth on the manila folder.

"We were in pursuit when they— No. No questioning, yet." But the incident strengthened her resolve. She was on to something important. "I won't take up any more of your time."

"Furgle. I have time." He gestured to the files on his desk. "Believe me, I'd rather be in the field with you again."

"I bet." She smiled, in spite of his using that stupid word…again. She left more determined than ever to break this case wide open.

Jerry wasn't the only one who needed results. Climbing

the FBI ladder had been her dream for as long as she could remember. She needed a big win in her column. Someday she wanted to be the agent in charge, the boss, the person others reported to.

But, honestly, she couldn't remember why.

Did she want to be behind a desk making all the decisions without the full picture? Did she want to move and take Skylar Dawn away from her life here? And, more importantly, away from her father?

Like my mother did?

God, the realization stopped her in her tracks. That wasn't the plan when their argument started. Well, marrying and having a child had never been a part of her life plan either. She rubbed her palms together as she continued down the hallway. She needed to reevaluate her life. The realization wasn't a surprise. She just hadn't admitted it to herself before this minute.

Even though she'd wanted to have the same evaluation talk with Heath, she hadn't acknowledged it was exactly what she needed to do personally.

She needed more information about Public Exposure, which would mean a late night of research. But her first call was to the house. Her mother picked up Skylar Dawn from day care each day, but she always waited until Kendall got home before serving dinner.

"Mommy!" her daughter answered. She either could recognize the caller ID or knew it wasn't six o'clock and time for Heath's call.

"Hey, sweetheart. How did today go?"

"Bumble the rabbit died, Mommy. It's so sad. I'll miss her."

"That is sad, honey. Is your class all right?"

"Yeah, Miss Darinda says it's part of the circle of life. Like the lion movie."

"That's true."

"I drew a picture. MiMi put it on the frigeator."

"I'll be sure to look at it when I get home."

Skylar Dawn sighed long and very audibly into the receiver. "Working late again? My, my, my."

Her daughter mimicked frequent sayings of the adults around her. This particular one was used by Naomi in an attempt to make Kendall feel guilty or ashamed. Kendall already felt both, since she'd be missing time at home.

"Yes, sweet pea. I'm working late, but I'll be home in time to read a chapter from our book."

"I could get Daddy to read it."

God, she felt guilty enough without letting Heath know she was working late on a Monday. Tuesdays and Thursdays were normally spent in the office. That was Heath's night at the house. For some stupid reason, she didn't want him to know that the late hours were extending to other days of the week.

"I'll be home in time. Can you get MiMi?"

"Love you, bye-bye."

Maybe it was superwoman syndrome or imposter syndrome or some other syndrome working mothers had come up with. Whatever it was could be added to the list of things she needed to face and talk about with Heath.

Not Jerry. Not her mother. And not any other friend or coworker.

It was time she admitted she couldn't do everything.

Right after she proved that Public Exposure wasn't what they claimed.

HEATH'S PHONE ALARM SOUNDED. Five minutes until his six o'clock phone call. He swiped open the book, getting it ready to read for Skylar Dawn.

"Barlow residence."

Naomi. Not the cheerful voice of his daughter.

"Evening, Naomi. May I speak with Skylar Dawn?"

"I'm sorry, Heath. She's taking her bath. She got excep-

tionally dirty this afternoon hopping around like a bunny."
Naomi described the playful act with disgust.

"Is Kendall available, or is she in with her?"

"She's not here tonight."

"And after Skylar Dawn's done?"

"Returning your call is not my responsibility, Heath."

"Gotcha. She's being punished for getting dirty." He
waited, but Naomi didn't respond. "At least tell her I called?"

Again there was silence.

If Heath hung up, it would be the only part of the conversation repeated to Kendall. He kept the line open, waiting until his mother-in-law responded. In fact, he put the
call on speaker and looked at the book.

He heard splashing and singing in the background.
Naomi had returned to the bathroom.

"I can't stay on the phone any longer. It's time to wash
her hair." She disconnected.

"I think Naomi Barlow is in contention for the monster-
in-law of the year award," Wade Hamilton stated without
looking across the office at Heath.

"Mind your own business. Wait. That's impossible for
you, right?"

"I was commiserating with you, man. I know what that
phone call means to you."

"You're as bad as an old meddling matchmaker. Admit
it. You're the one who assigned me to Kendall's task force."
He swiveled in his chair to face Wade.

No one else was in the office. He could speak freely. He
had intended not to mention the conflict-of-interest part
of his assignment. His anger was actually at his mother-
in-law and the phone call. He should shut up. Keep it to
himself—his general policy about everything these days.

Too late now.

Wade took a few seconds to smile like a cat skimming

a bucket of milk still under the cow. Then he rolled his pen between his palms, shrugging his shoulders slightly.

"I'm not sure if I should slug you or thank you."

"Hey, I'm just looking out for my own self-interests here," Wade said, spinning back to his computer screen. "I'm tired of hearing Slate complain about your bad habits."

"I have a few stories I could tell."

He held up his hand. "God, no. I have no reason to listen to more. Instead, is there anything I can help you with?"

"Thanks, but no. I'm running some facial recognitions and backgrounds. Why aren't you going home?"

Wade shrugged again. "I have my own demons to chase."

Demons? Heath recognized barriers. Several months ago Wade had been brutally beaten, cracking ribs and almost losing an eye. He would have lost his life if it hadn't been for a woman named Therese Ortis warning another company Ranger, Jack MacKinnon.

All traces of the woman had vaporized. Was she the demon Wade chased? Too late to ask. The conversation was over.

It was a good time to step outside and call Kendall. He left a message when she didn't answer, then texted her to call when she was home so he could talk with Skylar Dawn. The light pollution around here didn't block every star in the sky. He perched against the tailgate and just looked out.

There would be rain in the next couple of days. The color around the moon had changed. His mother had taught him that. He should take his daughter for a visit. Soon. But the nine-hour drive to Southwest Texas was hard enough when two parents shared the responsibilities.

That had been the excuse, and his parents had accepted it. The last real trip they'd taken to Alpine had slowed them down further with the horse trailer to pick up Jupitar and Stardust almost a year ago. When had life gotten out of hand?

The day I walked out of my house.

Needing a pep talk, he dialed. "Hey, Mom. How's everything going?"

"It's much the same. The baseball team looks to do pretty good this year. But you didn't call to catch up on Sul Ross."

"I don't mind hearing about it." And he didn't. Just listening to his mom's voice gave him a sense of inner calm.

"Are you still living…?"

"At the Thompson ranch? Yes. And no, I haven't really talked to Kendall. Skylar Dawn is growing and getting more amazing every day. She made new paintings for everyone. I'll get it in the mail this weekend."

"No rodeo? No busting heads?"

He rubbed his bruised ribs but knew his mother referred to Kendall's mom. "That was this past weekend. Okay, maybe it happened a little tonight, too."

"Uh-huh. You're going to kill yourself and make that woman very happy."

He was pretty sure he wouldn't drop dead, but the pain was a constant reminder that he might not have too many rodeo days left. Maybe he should focus on more rides with Skylar Dawn instead.

"Mom. We've talked about this. I need the money." Yeah, he did. And one crack about his mother-in-law was all either of them was allowed.

The extra work he did around the ranch still didn't repay the Thompsons what boarding his two horses would cost. He was determined to make up the difference and not accept a free ride.

"We could help you out, but you won't let us."

"You already have three full-time jobs. A professor at the university, a wife and a nurse to Dad. You're the one who needs to slow down. I should be sending money to you. Is he okay?"

"Dad is still the same. He's giving everyone what for, doesn't remember doing it, then does it again." She laughed. "I wish we could come see you, but breaking his routine is really hard."

"I know, Mom. I should be there."

"Nonsense. You have a very important job, a family and a wonderful daughter. Concentrate on those precious girls."

"Yes, ma'am."

"I'll call my grandbaby this weekend. You okay? I should get your daddy into bed soon."

"Just that… I'm always better after talking to you." His mother's positive, can-do attitude poured out of her every sentence. "Love you."

"I love you, too, son."

Talking to at least one woman he loved gave him his second wind. He returned to his desk and began the computer searches he needed on Public Exposure. He wanted to know everything.

Making a substantial contribution in the morning would make it much harder to stop his involvement with the case. The last thing he wanted was for Kendall to play the conflict-of-interest card.

Wade finally went home.

It was too late to speak with his daughter. Too late to read to her. He had no reason to text his wife. Again.

"This can't be right." The addresses of the two drivers today weren't only on the same street in Dallas—they were on the same block.

He looked up the owners—not them, a corporation. Now the digging got fun. So fun he didn't notice the time until it was two in the morning.

Time to call it a night.

He had what he'd been searching for. A good, solid, old-fashioned lead.

Chapter Seven

Kendall opened the front door and found Heath leaning against her SUV. One hand held a donut with sprinkles, and the other had a large coffee. Skylar Dawn ran past in her pink jeans and matching jacket.

"Daddy!"

Heath set the coffee cup down on the hood and lifted their daughter to his hip. He received his hug and smooches, then set their almost-four-year-old on the ground.

"Is that for me?"

"Yepper doodles." He smiled like Kendall hadn't seen him smile in months. "Jump inside and buckle up first."

He opened the door, got Skylar Dawn settled inside and handed her the donut, complete with a set of napkins to cover her favorite blue bunny shirt she wore in honor of Bumble the rabbit.

Kendall stood there, finishing the last bit of coffee in her travel mug before setting it on the front porch. Without looking, she knew her mother disapproved behind the curtain. She didn't care.

Heath was a great father.

Their baby girl had cried herself to sleep the night before. The tearstains had been apparent on her plump little cheeks. It had been a rare occasion that Kendall hadn't made it home to tuck her into bed. Then she'd noticed her phone battery had gone dead. When she plugged it in, there were numerous messages from Heath.

They'd ranged from upset about her mother to extremely worried about where she was to wondering why she was ignoring him and offering to pull himself from the Public Exposure investigation. She'd texted that her phone had died and received a Great in response.

Of course it wasn't great. Their situation was far from great.

But watching him with their daughter made her knees melt. He showed so clearly how much he loved Skylar Dawn. It brought tears to her already puffy eyes. She hadn't slept. A recurring vision of what could have happened at that intersection had kept her awake most of the night.

"Come on, Mommy," Skylar Dawn said between bites.

"That better be a double shot, skim with a dash of vanilla," she answered from the porch before joining them.

"Why would I order you anything else?" He smiled at her, too.

But as he handed it to her, he glared at the window where the curtains moved slightly. She didn't blame him. Her mother had no right to decide Skylar Dawn shouldn't speak with her father.

That was a direction in which Kendall never wanted to head. No matter what happened between her and Heath, their daughter would never be used to hurt him. She'd made both of those points clear to her mother as soon as they'd gotten up.

"How did you know to bring the donut this morning?" she whispered as she passed him.

"I had a hunch." He cut his eyes toward the window again.

"I did speak with her about bath time."

"Ha. Like that has ever worked before," he said to her

over the SUV, then pulled at the booster seat straps to verify they were locked in place. "Mind if I ride in with you?"

Not waiting for an answer, he jumped in the passenger seat and buckled up.

He has a point.

Setting her mother straight hadn't ever done any good. The woman had a habit of behaving exactly how she pleased. Oh sure, her mother helped by picking up Skylar Dawn and spending the night whenever the job required late hours. But she never really let Kendall forget that she'd helped. Or that Naomi Barlow's way was probably the better one.

Explaining why Kendall did something a particular way didn't matter. Naomi just nodded and proceeded as she liked. It was something Kendall had accepted for years.

But not after last night.

Not after seeing her precious little girl's hitched breathing from crying in her sleep.

"It won't happen again, Heath," she said, buckling her belt. She meant it. And she'd told her mother as much.

He placed his hand over hers on the shifter. "Tell Naomi that next time, she'll have to tell me to my face." His voice was low and carefully controlled.

They were all upset. Well, perhaps their daughter wasn't any longer. Her smile had white icing and rainbow sprinkles surrounding it.

"Is that good, sweet pea?" She changed the subject instead of reassuring Heath again.

Skylar Dawn nodded, holding out the now-icing-free donut. "Want a bite?"

"No thanks, Daddy brought me my own treat."

They drove to the day care, listening to stories of Bumble the rabbit. The kids had a memorial service planned for today. Kendall tried to concentrate, but her brain—and body—kept coming back to the surge of energy she'd felt when Heath's hand had covered hers.

The split second of comfort and reassurance had done crazy things to her emotions. She missed that feeling. Missed driving together. Missed family dinners.

Missed him.

This tsunami of emotions set her dangerously close to tears as Heath walked inside the day care with Skylar Dawn. She had only a few minutes to get herself together.

Turn off the emotions. Turn on professionalism. Think professionally.

"Man, those kids are taking this bunny thing seriously," he said, getting back into the car.

Kendall pulled through the drive and was back on a major street before she tried to think of something to say. But her mind was blank. Wiped spotless like a counter top after her mother had cleaned.

"Find anything by working late last night?" he asked.

Professional.

"I eliminated possibilities, but haven't found anything specific."

"I worked late, too." His voice held a subtle tease that she recognized.

"How could you find something on the first day?"

"I didn't want to speculate yesterday. But I kept getting the feeling that the drivers of the other cars knew each other."

"I totally missed that."

"You were kind of shaken up."

A professional wouldn't admit that she'd been shaken up all night. "Did they know each other?"

"It goes beyond that. They're both members of Public Exposure. Have been for about three years."

Six years ago, she had slammed on the brakes and hugged him after a similar announcement. It had broken the ice, and after their joint case was over, they'd gone on a date. Then another and another.

"It's hard to believe they'd be that bold and try to…to…"

"Kill us? They probably would have liked those results." He took out his phone. "I have their address. They live on the same block off Wycliff, near Uptown."

Genuine excitement. They might be getting a break. She headed the SUV in the general direction that would take them north of downtown Dallas. New nightclubs and restaurants were springing up in the area all the time. Housing was sort of limited and in high demand, barely keeping up.

"You got a lot accomplished last night."

"There's more. They were both convicted of fraud. The Postal Inspection Service brought charges that stuck. The guy's still on probation. He'll see his probation officer next week."

"Why didn't you mention this yesterday? I could have saved you time and run it through the FBI database."

"I got what we needed," he said, pointing out a left turn. "I could just as easily have been wrong and wasted the whole night."

"But you weren't. This might just be the break we needed."

"Are you going to tell me why you feel so strongly about this case? What made you think there's more to it?"

"Maybe I had a hunch myself."

She couldn't admit she needed something big for her next promotion. Or that the promotion might result in a transfer. Not after the night they'd all just had. She wasn't prepared to have that conversation yet. Talk about counting chickens before they hatch.

She glanced at him during a stop light. He was waiting, patiently. Good grief, wasn't there anything bad about the man? Oh yeah, he wanted her to quit her job.

"It bugged me that this antisocial group would be paying people to monitor their social media use. Where's all the money coming from for their so-called study?"

"Have you checked on that?"

"One fund. They actually told me about that."

"You've interviewed them? Been to their offices?"

"I actually made a phone call. I don't have enough to subpoena their financial records. Maybe they thought if they told me, I'd give up."

"But it just made you more curious."

"Exactly."

"If there was an actual social media study, they'd have a variety of participants. Almost all of the people who were accepted are over the age of sixty. They're almost all single-person households and all homeowners."

"I noticed that, too. Wouldn't you want to target social media users under thirty? I mean, if you're trying to change the world and want less use. Why such weird participants? That's what piqued my curiosity. Then I found the odd complaint about being watched or feeling like they were being watched."

"What do you think is going on? You ruled out identity theft, but what else could it be?"

"That was my first guess. But the participants haven't lost money. At least not that they'll admit to me. They receive their payments from the study. I suspect that Public Exposure has a bigger plan. I just can't determine what direction to even look."

"Remember—whatever they're doing, it's big enough to want you out of the way. They must think you're on to something."

Yesterday's car incident came rushing back. "I could have gotten both of us killed."

"It was my fault, babe. I was the one who wanted to follow the van." His palm covered her upper arm, then slid up and down comfortingly before he pulled it back across the console.

"No one's to blame. I appreciate you checking them out. Seriously. Now we have a lead."

"A definite connection to Public Exposure, like you suspected." He adjusted in his seat, looking antsy and uncomfortable.

She turned the SUV a couple of times and realized they were a few minutes away from their destination. She hadn't gone by the office to verify information or follow any of her normal procedures of obtaining another vehicle. The excitement of working with Heath today and all his information had totally distracted her from her normal routine.

Even the drama at home this morning couldn't take away from the excitement of working with this particular Texas Ranger. He believed her. He trusted her instincts.

She stopped and shifted the car into Park with two blocks to go.

"You got me so excited about advancing the case, I forgot to pick up a Bureau car."

"Well, damn. There's not room for them both with Skylar Dawn's booster seat back there." He joked as if he hadn't been waiting for her to figure that out on her own.

He'd never chance someone discovering what car they drove. Neither would she. They'd have to go back. Fortunately, they weren't far from the field office.

"Look, Heath. I might have suggested that I'm totally in charge here. But that shouldn't stop you from sharing your ideas and consulting with me."

"Tell me what you need, Kendall. I'm at your service."

"Advice. Honest advice, not just what I want to hear. Last night my supervisor was getting in my head, making me wonder if this was truly worth pursuing."

The truth of her words didn't scare her. It felt good to say them out loud.

"Last night you didn't know these people had tried to kill you."

"They tried to kill you, too."

He pressed his lips together and shook his head. "I'm pretty certain they didn't know I was on the case with you. They might now, but yesterday was all about you."

"You're probably right about that." She hesitated to mention the panicked feelings she had the day before, but if they were working together, maybe he should know. But the words didn't form.

"Head to your office. Arrange for backup. Then we can bring both of the drivers in for an interview."

Was he asking a question or giving her a suggestion?

"Why do I get the feeling that you aren't going with me?"

"I don't mind taking a walk and keeping an eye on things until you get back."

"No. You're right. We honestly don't know how these people are going to react. They tried to kill us, Heath. What would happen to Skylar Dawn?"

"I see your point. We wouldn't want your mother raising her." He followed up with a laugh.

Heath had always been honest with her. Even though he'd chuckled, hard truth echoed in his words. Their daughter could not end up an orphan.

"You asked me for my honest opinion, Kendall. I gave it to you." He turned in the seat, picking up his hat from next to the car seat in back.

"You are not going out there on your own."

"I'm just going to verify the suspects are home. Just a little old-fashioned Ranger surveillance while you get things settled. If I have a problem, I'll call Jack. He's close by on assignment."

He opened his door.

"Call Jack on the way. You knock. I'll have your back from the street."

"Good idea. Let's go."

He winked at her like that had been his plan all along.

Chapter Eight

Heath made the call to Jack while on their walk around the corner. His voice sounded normal, no overreaction, no urgency. But Kendall could feel the readiness in his determined steps. In the way he moved his badge from his shirt to his suit coat. And in the way he flipped that same jacket behind his holster.

She clicked the lock button on her key ring, and the horn echoed off the gas station behind it. She looked down the block at an array of businesses on Lemmon Avenue, then back in the direction they were heading—full of renovated homes and thirty-year-old apartment buildings. Truly one of the up-and-coming parts of Dallas. One side of the street had gated driveways with stairs leading up to the front doors. The other side had parking along the street.

"This isn't a good place to follow someone," she mumbled since Heath was still talking to Jack.

"I texted the address," he said into the phone. "Yeah, we headed straight here instead of picking up a government issue. Right. No way we're letting them get a look at Kendall's regular ride. Skylar Dawn's seat is in the back... Six minutes is great. We'll be at the corner."

Six minutes. They could wait six minutes. The drivers from the previous day didn't know they were coming. Together with Heath, she could observe, make a plan, get prepared, call her office for backup.

"I can't believe I totally forgot to grab a sedan," she said once he was off the phone.

"We were talking, no big deal. Jack won't be long. This may turn out to be nothing."

Waiting on one of Heath's fellow Rangers would give them time to collaborate. But each minute ticked by excruciatingly slowly. And quietly. The more time she spent observing their surroundings, the less she felt like talking. Heath sent the pictures and information about the two suspects to her phone. She had a good image of who they were looking for.

"Good idea." She tilted her phone's screen toward him. "I can barely remember anything about how they look. Saundra Rosa and Bryan Marrone. I didn't give them a second thought."

"You can't do everything, Kendall. Even though you get close every day."

"Thanks," she whispered. Partly because she wasn't good at accepting praise and partly because of the weird feeling the neighborhood gave her.

Four more minutes.

"About this thing with your mother..."

Heath raised his hat and pushed his longer-than-normal hair back from his forehead. Then he secured his official white hat once again. It was one of his common stall tactics, waiting for her to explain or offer an excuse for Naomi. Then he wouldn't have to talk. But there was no excuse.

"It was wrong and uncalled-for. I told her as much." She did a three-sixty checking the neighborhood again. "Isn't it kind of weird that no one's around? Not a single person."

"You noticed that, too?"

"Do you feel this?" She twirled her finger in the air. "It's like that time at Fright Fest when the zombies were following me."

"Actually, watching you there was a lot of fun for me. But I know what you mean."

"You're getting that prickly sensation like someone's watching you?"

"That would be an affirmative." His voice lowered as his right hand descended to rest on his weapon. "You noticing a theme with these houses?"

They passed Rawlins Street heading to the next block.

"Either they all used the same bucket of paint for their trim…" She counted two houses without the same color. Heath kept walking but managed to turn in a full circle, checking their backs.

"Or they're all owned by the same corporation, which has an odd color preference." Most of the house trim looked the same as the apartment windows from the previous block. She'd seen that specific color every day recently in her files. "Unless you're really into Public Exposure orange."

"You think everyone who uses that color are members? Maybe it's a home owners' association thing." He shrugged. "Maybe they're just weird."

"Or part of a cult."

He cut a disbelieving look in her direction. "Let's talk with the drivers before we draw any concrete conclusions."

She wasn't sure she was off the mark, though. "I don't think Brantley Lourdes leads Public Exposure like a religious cult. But these people all listen to their leader as if nothing he says is wrong. Why else would two people be willing to crash into us, risking their lives?"

"You think Lourdes is capable of an attack?"

"I… I'm not sure." She had no facts to back up her feeling. But just like yesterday, she knew they were being watched. The unmistakable itch raised the hair on the back of her neck.

Heath grabbed her elbow, gently pulling her to a stop.

He searched her eyes like he had a thousand times before. "You are sure." He tapped one-handed on his phone, putting it on speaker. "Jack, I'm not sure what's going on here. Stay sharp."

"Hang on, I'm still two blocks away. Don't do anything until I get there," Jack said.

"Man, we've moved past the corner. If I were Wade, I'd say I have a bad feeling about this. Hell, we're heading back to the SUV." Heath hung up.

"Hang on—" She wanted to delay the retreat, but one worried glance from her husband substantiated the uneasiness racing through her blood.

"We both know something around here isn't right, Kendall. How much digging have you done into this Public Exposure group? What's not in the file?"

She faced toward the SUV and began slowly moving down the sidewalk. It was no surprise that Heath took his steps backward next to her, keeping a wary watch behind them.

"Not enough apparently." But that was something she'd correct first thing she could.

"My general research last night gave me the impression they're mostly considered a do-good organization that encourages people to get off social media and interact with others."

Kendall couldn't shake the strange, creepy feeling. Even nature seemed to be in on setting the mood. No dogs barked, no birds chirped. The air hung heavy and thick.

"Excuse me. Can I help you?" A man stood in one of the orange doorways of the corner house.

Heath whipped around, ready for an attack. "Texas Ranger Heath Murray, sir. Sorry if we've alarmed you. Everything's fine."

Heath stopped moving toward the vehicle and didn't remove his fingers from his weapon. The thumb strap was unsnapped, ready to pull.

That creepy feeling got stronger, even though the man looked normal enough and splayed his empty hands for them to see.

"We'd appreciate if you returned indoors, sir." Kendall issued the directive, but the man stayed put. She couldn't force herself to move away.

"I'd rather know what's going on." He put his hands on his hips. "I'm calling the police."

Even though he didn't have a threatening posture, the situation felt off. Everything about it shouted a scenario from training. One where she turned her back and got a rubber bullet bouncing off of it.

"That's your right. Please go inside to make the call."

"I have my phone right here."

"Don't do it. Keep your hands in the air. I'm FBI. Do *not* reach for anything." She drew her weapon keeping the barrel toward the ground, then tapped Heath's shoulder, letting him know she had his back. "My partner is going to approach and verify that you're unarmed."

He was closer, so it was natural for him to check the man out.

"Okay, okay. I'll go back inside."

"You'll stay where you are," Heath shouted. "Keep your hands above your head, turn around slowly then take a step backward."

The man seemed innocent enough, but the uneasy feeling of the neighborhood persisted.

"There's a step. I'll fall." The man stretched his hands higher and took a step inside his open door.

"Stop!" they both shouted.

Heath moved toward the man, who finally froze. A little way down the street, she saw movement—two people running then ducking behind a car. One had hesitated when they'd shouted.

"Movement at nine o'clock," she informed Heath. "It might be our couple."

"One thing at a time. Jack will be here any minute." He took a final step, reaching the man, giving him instructions and letting him know what was coming next in the pat-down.

The neighborhood was still unusually quiet. Out of the corner of her eye she caught a glimpse of a car, heard the doors shut—no matter how quietly they tried to accomplish it. Every sound seemed to echo under the dense trees.

The man now faced her. Heath had explained how he'd watched the glances of the two suspects the day before. From behind her sunglasses, she watched the man who'd gained their attention. Every so often he darted his gaze in the direction of where the people had been running.

Then a crazy gleam was in his eye and the corner of his mouth twitched—just like a person about to smile. He blinked heavily and stretched his eyebrows to relax his eyes before he noticed that she watched.

There it was again—his eyes darted quickly in the direction of a car starting.

"Heath, he's a distraction. Our couple is in a car down the street."

"You sure?"

"Ninety percent."

Heath removed handcuffs from his back pocket, locked one around the man's wrist. He quickly moved him next to the porch post and locked his other wrist around it. The man couldn't run away.

"Let's go." He turned and took off in one motion, getting several feet ahead of her.

They didn't bother keeping to the sidewalk, but simply

ran across the lawns to the end of the block. A horn blared from behind, then next to them. *Jack.*

"Where are we running to? Hi, Kendall," Jack casually said through his open window.

A car peeled out, passing Jack's big truck and heading in the opposite direction.

"Go with Jack. Follow the car."

It wasn't her first rodeo. She'd been in charge before. She should be telling the guys what to do. But Heath took off around a parked car and she jumped inside the truck. Maybe her husband had seen something she'd missed, since he wasn't heading in the direction of the car.

"What did this guy do?" Jack asked, quickly following the car down the next left.

She had one eye on the sedan and kept looking around for anything suspicious. Again, there was nothing there, just the spine-chilling feeling that they were being watched. Even while speeding down the street.

"Nothing solid. Yet."

HEATH DIDN'T HAVE time to explain why he ran in the opposite direction of the car. He'd seen the woman's pink sweater in the thick shrubbery bordering the apartment complex they were next to. At least he thought he'd seen a pink sweater. Replaying the car's hasty exit in his head, he couldn't visualize two people inside.

Only one.

So he'd taken off. Playing out a hunch.

Hell, he didn't know for certain if he chased the woman from yesterday. How should he know if she dressed in pink every day? What had caught his eye might actually be another decoy. He had no way of knowing. But the sweater happened to be the same color as the car from the day before.

And he didn't believe in coincidences.

He headed to the north side of the house, where he'd seen the top of a blond head before it ducked behind a large oak tree. *Gotcha!*

Grabbing a decorative post to keep his feet under him as he made a sharp right-angled turn, he followed the fluff of pink between two houses. His jacket caught on thorns as he barreled through the narrow path that was basically the width of his shoulders.

As a bead of sweat rolled into his eye, he twisted sideways, wishing to ditch the regulation jacket and hat. He used the sleeve to wipe his face when he slowed at the southwest corner of an old wooden home.

Dang. Rosebushes.

The woman was a lot slimmer than he was to have made it through this gauntlet without getting stuck. The thorny growth on the lattice at his shoulder might appear pretty from the street, but it kept him from scooting next to the house for cover.

Basically, he was sticking his neck out and hoping for the best. He looked around, then pulled back to a position that hid him from the street.

Slowing his breathing, he listened. He kept his movements small and again used his sleeve to wipe droplets of sweat from his face. He wasn't overheating. The humidity was high—like running through a rain cloud.

No matter how much he tried, he hadn't grown used to running in his suit. Boots, yes. Hat, yes. But suit, no. He'd run in boots and a hat his entire life. He'd always had a hat on his head. There weren't many pictures, going all the way back to before he could walk, without one.

And boots? Well, they were safer than tennis shoes where he'd grown up in Southwest Texas. Rattlers, scorpions and other varmints didn't like to be suddenly disturbed by a boy running after a horse or his father.

Funny what went through his head while chasing a subject.

Skylar Dawn on the other hand was dressed in all sorts of frills. Boots were the exception not the rule—except on weekends at the Thompson's ranch.

He missed being with her every day, helping her pick out clothes—frilly girl or cowgirl. He wanted to sit beside her bed to read, then turn out the light with a goodnight kiss. Wanting to have memories with her, but also of him. Just like he did of his dad.

If things between him and Kendall stayed good today, maybe they'd get a chance to talk about him moving back in.

Chapter Nine

Kendall pulled her phone from her pocket, ready to report what had just happened. Three streets from the original neighborhood, Jack still followed at a distance far enough back not to call obvious attention. At this time of the morning, cars and trucks flooded this part of Dallas. And they basically all looked the same.

Their one saving grace was that Jack's vehicle hadn't been on the street very long. Hopefully, no one had seen her jump inside.

"What did the guy on the porch do?" Jack asked, tires squealing as he turned a sharp corner.

"He was the distraction."

"For the guy who hasn't done anything? That's sort of— Hang on."

She grabbed the handle above the door as Jack followed the path of the car, cutting across two lanes and pulling a U-turn. The bulkier truck required some of the sidewalk.

"I thought you had that light pole for sure." She tried to joke, but her heart raced, causing her voice to shake a little.

The man they followed turned again. Jack hit his brakes, waiting two heartbeats before turning after him, but the sedan was already turning again.

"This guy is acting like he's being followed. Either he's paranoid or his aim is to make us paranoid. I can't tell." Jack securely gripped the wheel and made another U-turn.

"I bet he's doubling back. I can get there before him. We'll already be on the street and he won't know we're in position."

"Good idea." She wished she'd thought of it. She wished she could think about anything useful. Her mind kept jumping between Skylar Dawn and Heath.

Focus was definitely necessary.

Truth was, she hadn't been in pursuit of a vehicle in a while. She was out of practice. Most of her work now happened behind a desk or in a lecture hall. Sure, she completed field interviews from time to time, but that wasn't the norm. At least not for her.

Then the file on Public Exposure had landed in her lap. Mysteriously after it had been closed for lack of evidence. She hadn't been able to tell if Jerry had supported her work or not.

"There he is." She pointed to the second car in the left turn lane. "Your hunch paid off."

"This would be easier if we had some backup and could leapfrog tailing him. Anyone around Harry Hines?"

"It wouldn't help. I couldn't catch the license plate number to call it in. Did you?"

"No. It's obscured by the other vehicle. Looks like it's just us for now."

The car passed them on the left with a car between them. Kendall pressed the video button on her phone without physically turning to look in his direction. Definitely their man, and he had no clue they were following him.

Or had been following him. They went straight as he slowed to turn. The sedan waited its turn in the feeder lane for the interstate. Just her luck.

"We're in the wrong lane."

"I got this." Jack jumped the short curb of the median and pulled a U-turn without slowing traffic. "Maybe you should call this in before it gets real."

As Jack sped up to catch her non-perpetrator, Kendall gripped the dashboard, knowing that his definition of *real* perfectly matched her husband's. All she could do was hope it wasn't real yet for Heath.

HEATH TUGGED HIS slacks higher onto his thighs and knelt, without touching the stone path or garden dirt. He could manage the balancing act for a few minutes. He pulled a blade of grass an edger had missed and almost tucked it between his teeth but thought again.

Kendall wouldn't have let Skylar Dawn mimic his actions. No telling what pesticides might be lingering around. This time he sort of believed there was something in the water. This street was as strangely quiet as the first one everyone had run from.

No dogs barked.

No cars drove past.

Nothing to disturb the heaviness in the air.

Humidity churned with the gut feeling that there was a lot more to Kendall's case than she was letting on. If she ever admitted to acting on her instincts, he might actually get the whole story.

Eventually.

If he earned her trust—no, *when* she trusted him again. He could wait for her. Just like he waited for the woman in the pink sweater to feel confident enough to leave wherever she was hiding.

Two houses with orange trim were nearby. He waited. His gray suit mixed in with the red roses, and he hoped his white Stetson lost its shape against the white house.

Waiting was the only option until Kendall returned. She might have called for backup, but he wouldn't know what type of car to look for. He'd turned his phone to silent, so it wouldn't even vibrate, just after tucking himself amidst the roses.

He wasn't making the mistake of his phone giving him away after the five or six thorns he'd fought.

Waiting was his specialty. But he had little choice in the matter. It wasn't like he had cause to go house-to-house looking for a woman he wasn't certain had even been there. What was he supposed to ask? Is there a pink sweater inside?

At least Kendall and Jack were on the trail of a sure thing. Jack was good. Kendall was better. They'd make sure the driver from yesterday didn't get away.

"WATCH OUT!" KENDALL braced herself between the middle console and the door. Her feet worked imaginary pedals. She stopped and accelerated the truck as if she were driving.

"Do you see him?" Jack asked.

"I hate the sun's reflection at this time of day. I can't see the lanes, let alone a gray sedan."

"Same here." Jack moved half of the truck onto the shoulder.

She finally had a better view and tugged at the seat belt to lean forward. "Wait. See the car darting half in the lane and back again?"

"Hang on."

As if she wasn't already.

She made the calls—one saying they were following a person of interest, then another to Jerry, the boss, who wasn't pleased they were darting through a major Dallas traffic artery during rush hour.

"Even one-sided, that conversation didn't sound good," Jack said when she hung up.

"We're not to put any lives in danger."

"Understood."

Jack drove with skill, taking advantage of a shoulder or exit lane—when there was one—to illegally pass without putting too many civilians at risk. But it didn't stop her heart from climbing into her throat.

"Looks like he's heading east. Maybe I-30 or south to I-45. What do you want to do?" he asked.

"Do you think he knows we're following?"

"Can't tell." Even behind his mirrored shades, Jack's eyes reflected his excitement. "Right now, he's not showing signs that he knows. He just seems in a hurry to get somewhere. If he heads into downtown proper, we're going to have a problem keeping our cover."

"And if he stays on either highway, we can coordinate a safe stop with Dallas PD."

"Looks like it's the Cadiz Street exit. You've got your direction. It's downtown. How aggressive do you want to get with this guy who hasn't really done anything?"

"When you put it like that…" So Heath hadn't mentioned to Jack that they'd nearly been killed the day before. Or that this guy had been involved. "Before he clearly fled, he was a person of interest. We only wanted a conversation."

With the man who tried to kill us.

"I'll get close enough for a clear look at the plates."

"I'll call it in, making all departments happy."

Jack got the truck just behind the sedan as it braked to exit. She snapped a picture of the plates and of the driver as they passed. Jack turned right at the light and the driver turned left. She made her calls.

The second one was to Jerry, who still wasn't happy.

"I've sent a unit to the address you gave me. No one's on the porch handcuffed or sipping their morning coffee. Did you get the name of this supposed subversive?" Jerry shouted.

"Ouch," Jack said softly.

The last thing she needed was one of Heath's partners

cracking jokes. She shortened her breath, deliberately hold-ing an exasperated sigh at bay. "There wasn't time."

"There are two agents cruising the area," her ex-part-ner said. "No sign of Murray either. Are you with him?"

"Looks like our guy is heading for the interstate. Should we follow or check on Heath?" Jack asked.

"Stay with the sedan," she told the Ranger. Into the phone she said, "Tell them not to shoot the man in the white hat."

FORTUNATELY, THERE WEREN'T any windows on this side of the house he leaned against.

Heath wanted to move but needed to stay put. Without anyone coming around, the woman in the pink sweater was bound to feel comfortable enough to come back outside. And most likely, she'd be heading down this path back to her place on the other street.

And he'd be there. Easy-peasy, as Skylar Dawn would say.

Unless the rosebush that he'd pretty much flattened caught on his jacket and kept him from moving. Then again, it might be his stiff legs that kept him from chas-ing someone down. He pushed the brim of his Stetson up with his forefinger, then wiped the sweat into his hairline.

Kendall had shaken her head at that habit more than once. It's why he tied a kerchief around his neck when he worked outside. His straw work hats had more ventilation than the regulation white beaver-felt Stetson. He wouldn't take a chance at drawing attention to himself by digging his sweat rag out of his inside pocket.

Still…he loved wearing the big hat. He loved being a Texas Ranger and all it stood for. Sweat ran down his back. Okay, the suit jacket he could live without.

A door opened.

It had to be close. Maybe even the front door to the

building he leaned against. Light steps across the concrete porch headed in his direction. Heath pressed his shoulders closer to the wall and tipped his head back until his hat raised off his forehead.

"I'm sure they're gone now, Rita. Thanks so much for the lemonade. Oh my goodness. I don't need to wear this sweater until I'm back indoors. It's getting warm out here."

"You take care. I really enjoyed the visit. I just need one more hug. It's going to be a while before I see you again."

There were two female voices. No distinguishable accents. Then additional steps—heels this time. An outer door gently swung shut.

"You guys take care on your trip," the woman who apparently lived there said. "Let us know when you get to Del Rio. That's quite a drive."

"Sure thing. I can't wait until you'll be there, too. Bye now."

More steps. Two doors shut. Humming.

It must be his lucky day.

The blonde he'd been chasing waltzed around the corner of the porch as she swung the pink sweater over her shoulder. She looked toward the street just as she passed him, missing that he stood in the rosebush.

"Howdy," he said with his best twang. He latched onto her elbow so she couldn't run. Then as she twisted to free herself, he said, "Don't do it."

Gone was the polite woman on the porch. She made a disgusted sound, stomped her foot and slung a couple of curse words in his direction.

"Who do you think you are? Let go of me."

He was surprised she didn't have a cell phone in hand, already trying to call for help. "Saundra Rosa?"

"How do you know my name? And what are you doing hiding in the rosebushes?"

"I had a couple of follow-up questions about yesterday."

That got her attention. "What about yesterday? I've never seen you before."

"That's right. I don't think we met at the accident. Ranger Heath Murray, ma'am. We should probably move back to the sidewalk before someone calls the police." He gently and firmly moved the pink sweater lady in front of the house she'd been visiting.

"If I'm under arrest, aren't you going to read me my rights or something? I'd like to contact my lawyer before you cart me off to jail."

"Sure. Is that what you want...for me to arrest you? I was fine with a conversation."

"A conversation?" She looked truly bewildered.

"But if you want me to arrest you..." He reached for his handcuffs, forgetting they were on the wrists of a man almost two blocks away.

"No." She cleared her throat. "Not really. You just want to talk? What about?" She kept looking around, mainly up at the windows trimmed in orange.

Heath took a step sideways, blocking her view of the house behind him. "What were you doing in that part of Dallas?"

"I was delivering some items to a shelter." She stuck out her chin, defiantly, practically daring him to call her a liar.

"I promise this won't take but a minute. You told the officer yesterday that you were unfamiliar with the car you were driving. That's why you accelerated by mistake through the intersection."

"Yes. This is really about the car accident?" She lifted her hand and chewed on her short thumbnail.

"Is it your husband's?"

"What? No, I'm not married."

"Who did the car belong to?"

"Why does that matter? I'm paying for the damage to

the other car. But I'm buying the Pink Thing. That's what my car reminds me of. You know, like the ice cream."

She popped a hip to one side and rested her hand there. It reminded him of when his daughter pretended she was a teapot. Saundra wasn't four years old. The pouting, put-out actions weren't reflecting well on a woman in her twenties either.

A couple of other doors had opened, including that of the home she'd been hiding inside. No one yelled or stepped onto their porch, but he got the feeling they weren't going away.

"That's good, very responsible." He brought his notebook out from his pocket. "This is actually for my office. More paperwork for the higher-ups."

"Are we done, then?" She pointed toward the unofficial path connecting to the next block. "I really have somewhere to be."

"Yeah, that just about covers it."

"Finally." She took steps back toward the house she'd left.

"One more thing." He pointed his finger in the air to stop her, then focused on her face, waiting on a reaction. "Why does Public Exposure want to kill my wife?"

Chapter Ten

By the time Jack took the right-hand turn and drove two blocks for the U-turn, the sedan and occupant were nowhere to be found. Kendall received a call that the Dallas PD hadn't seen the car driving down or near Cadiz Street.

"We heading back to Heath?" Jack asked.

"Yes. Hopefully he's had better luck."

She dialed, but knew by now her husband had probably silenced his phone. He was excellent about calling Skylar Dawn, like clockwork. But communicating with the rest of the world…well, he answered when it was convenient. She left a message and sent a text asking for his location and informed him they were ten minutes away.

"Thanks for your help with this, Jack. I won't be caught like this again."

"No problem. I've been helping Dallas PD out with a couple of cases until Wade is off desk duty." He was relaxed behind the wheel, taking morning traffic in stride now.

"I didn't realize Wade had been injured that badly."

"Well, it's his injuries combined with the fact that he went against orders. Of course, I'm not complaining too loudly. I did get a girlfriend because of his misbehaving. Take a look in the console." He grinned, a charming smile that had been breaking hearts ever since she'd met him.

Wow, that had been six years ago. She raised the console lid, where a black jewelry box sat alone.

"Go ahead. Take a look. I'd like your reaction."

"My opinion won't mean much." She reached for it, shutting the console and sitting straight again, both excited and embarrassed at the same time.

"You're a woman, aren't you?" Jack laughed and switched lanes on the interstate. "And this is bling."

She flipped open the ring box. "Oh my, that's a lot of bling."

"I was hoping you'd react that way. I'm a little nervous. Okay, I admit it. I'm a lot nervous." He exited Oak Lawn, very close to the neighborhood where they'd left Heath.

"This is the woman you met last fall?"

"Yeah, Megan Harper. Honestly, I don't know what she's going to say. I mean, I think she'll say yes. It's the logistics of Austin versus Dallas. Who moves, that type of thing."

"No doubts about if she loves you?"

He shook his head. "There's been a zing there since the first time I held her in my arms."

Kendall didn't have any words. The ring was beautiful and she stared at it, missing the ring that normally sat on her fourth finger. She'd removed it and stuck it in her jacket pocket when she'd seen Heath on the stoop of Mrs. Pelzel's house the day before. Things had been hectic and she'd forgotten about it.

"It's gorgeous, Jack. I think she'll be very pleased. When are you going to ask her?"

"Soon. At least I hope to. Her parents are coming from England in a couple of weeks. I think I'll do the whole old-fashioned thing about asking her dad for permission."

The sweet gesture of respect was enough to bring tears to her eyes. It brought back many memories of her and Heath. She quickly closed the lid and stowed them away again.

"I didn't mean to…" Jack let the words trail off. He

didn't have to say exactly what he meant. "You're really the only woman I could trust with this. My sister wouldn't be able to keep the secret. And there's no way I want my mom knowing before the ring's on Megan's finger. She'll have the whole wedding planned out without asking either of us for our opinions on anything."

Kendall laughed and dabbed at her eyes. "I know exactly what you mean. Mom had the country club booked in less than two hours. I remember telling Heath that she'd settle down. It never happened."

"I'm afraid that's what my mom's going to be like."

"Of course, I was busy with work, so I didn't really mind. I think Heath was more disappointed that he didn't help choose the cake flavors. The man does love cake."

"I've seen him chow down at office birthday parties."

They were at a stop light, and the truck filled with an awkward silence. Jack tapped his fingers on the steering wheel. Kendall flipped her phone over, checking for messages.

Nothing.

Heath could take care of himself. But in this crazy world, she'd prefer to have his back. Or to know that someone did, at least.

"This is the longest red light ever. Don't you have lights?"

Without a word, Jack flipped a switch and a siren sounded. Cars slowed at the busy intersection long enough for them to get across.

"If he was in trouble, you would have heard from him."

"I'm sure you're right. It's just…"

"It's okay, Kendall. I get it. I remember how I freaked not knowing if Megan was okay." He pressed his lips together and shifted in his seat.

The subject made him just as uncomfortable as it did her. She wanted to believe that Heath was okay. The belief somehow made her feel more professional. And no matter what she'd said yesterday when she'd first seen him, they weren't just professionals. They were married.

No matter their differences, he'd always be the father of her child. She'd never want any harm to come to him. Period.

They were still a couple of blocks away, and Jack was driving as fast as traffic would allow. The lights and sirens were off. He'd only used them to get through the intersection. So she did what she and Heath needed to do more of. She started talking.

"You'll have to tell me what Megan's like. Oh, and when are you going to ask her? Does anyone else know? I don't want to spill your secret."

"She'll be up this weekend. We could all have dinner if you want," he said before wincing a little. "It doesn't have to be with Heath."

"It's Heath's weekend with Skylar Dawn." As if that was a real answer. She took a deep breath, deciding to be honest. "I know this is awkward. The one good thing about working together for a while will mean we actually have time to talk. We've both been avoiding it."

"That's a good plan." He pointed to her car. "See, he's okay."

He was right. Heath leaned against the brick wall of a 7-Eleven convenience store, as casually as a real cowboy leaned against anything. She was relieved and furious all at once. Thank God he was okay, but why hadn't he returned her calls?

Jack stopped and she quickly jumped from his truck. "Thanks for the help, and I'll see you soon. There's no need for you to stick around and witness me murdering my husband."

HEATH LOOKED UP from under his hat. He had spotted Jack's truck midway up the block and slid his phone back inside his pocket. He had four texts and a message that he hadn't had time to listen to, but he knew what it contained.

Kendall would be—there wasn't another word for it—worried.

"I guess you didn't catch your guy?" He stood straight, stopping himself from walking to her.

"Well, it looks like you didn't catch yours either." Her voice was controlled and deliberate.

He recognized the compressed lips, the restraints she held on herself. He'd been on the receiving end of the cool wait-until-we're-alone look a few times. She pulled the keys from her pocket, spinning the key ring around her finger and heading for the SUV.

"Um... Kendall. Wait. We're not—" He reached to stop her, but not before Saundra stepped through the front doors of the building with a cup of coffee.

"Holy cow. That's—" She pivoted, doing an about-face toward him and grabbed his arm, taking them to the corner of the building. "What the heck's going on?"

"I was trying to tell you. Saundra ran into me and, after a couple of minutes, she decided to explain something to us about yesterday's accident."

"Oh, that's such a relief."

Dammit. Her go-to phrase let him know that she was more than a little ticked off at him. But at least the words she said loud enough for Saundra to hear were cloaked in a syrupy, concerned tone.

One surprised look and Special Agent Kendall Barlow was back in charge and had herself under control. "Miss Rosa. What would you like to explain? Wait. Should we try to find some place that's a bit more quiet? Is there a coffee shop nearby?"

"I only have a minute. I've explained to Heath that this is all just a big mistake and I need to get to work. I don't really know Bryan Marrone. I mean, I've seen him driving down the street, but that's it. I don't *know* him. You see?"

"Do you want to take her in for questioning?" he asked, crossing his arms, determined to keep a straight face.

"You have to believe me," Saundra pleaded. "I didn't really *do* anything except let him crash into my car."

There shouldn't be anything funny in Saundra's explanation. She didn't know him, but she'd let him crash into her car? He'd heard a lot of explanations over the years—every Texas highway patrolman did. Hers just made his top-ten list. There was hilarious, and then just plain absurd.

"Miss Rosa, I think we'd be better off having this discussion somewhere other than the 7-Eleven parking lot." Kendall gestured toward a couple of men walking inside the store.

"Oh, no. I couldn't possibly go to the FBI building. That's totally out of the question."

"Miss Rosa, please." Kendall opened her arms. One slowly moving behind Saundra and one gesturing more toward him on the corner. "Let's at least get away from the door."

She moved. Kendall moved. He kept his back to the ice machine and glanced around every other minute, making sure no onlooker stared too closely.

"You don't really think I tried to kill you. Do you? I mean, no one was really hurt." Saundra sipped her coffee, stretching her eyes open as large as they could get.

Kendall coughed or choked like she'd swallowed wrong. Heath tried not to look at the varying shades of pink powder on Saundra's eyelids. But damn, she was serious. She really didn't think she'd done anything wrong.

If he'd had a second set of handcuffs, she wouldn't be walking around drinking the coffee he'd bought. This was the very reason they needed backup, or that Bureau-issued sedan. If they'd had it, he would have arrested Saundra Rosa at the rosebushes.

Did Kendall feel the same way, or did she want to tackle the investigation from a different angle? Standing slightly behind her, he couldn't see her face and couldn't make a judgment call on what she thought.

"Thank you for your honesty, Miss Rosa. Did Ranger Murray get your contact information?" Kendall paused while Saundra nodded. "We'll be in touch."

"Hey, Saundra. You'll be needing these." He returned her cell and ID he'd held onto during their conversation and walk.

"Oh, right. Thanks for not arresting me, Heath." Saundra power walked away from them, retracing the steps they'd taken earlier down the Wycliff Avenue sidewalk. Then she slowed, bending her head over her cell.

"I'd really like to know who she's texting right now."

"What in the world were you thinking?" Kendall turned on him as soon as Saundra was out of sight.

"What?" He honestly didn't know which way the conversation would go from here.

"You couldn't give me a heads-up that you'd not only caught your suspect, but that she was getting coffee?" Kendall vehemently pointed toward the 7-Eleven door while walking toward the SUV.

The key ring was still slipped over her finger. She clicked the unlock button and moved toward it, as if she'd suddenly remembered that she had a car. They didn't need to argue out in the open next to the trash.

Whatever reprieve he'd received from her being upset was apparently gone as they sat in the front seat. She kept twirling her keys instead of using them. She leaned forward, dropping her head on the steering wheel and taking deep breaths.

His hand lifted to drop on her back. After a moment's hesitation, he let it. She didn't shrug it off.

"I was calling you when I saw Jack's truck halfway up the block."

Kendall puffed her cheeks and blew the air out with a slow *wuff.* As much as he wanted to continue to touch her, he raised his hand and rested it on the seat-back. She turned the key, cranked the AC to high and pointed the vents toward her face.

A lot of effort was going into her movements to keep herself calm. He knew her, knew what she did when she was too upset to speak politely. Blasting the AC in her face was just a substitute for fanning herself.

"Why don't you just go ahead and say whatever it is you're trying hard *not* to say? Or maybe we could go collect my handcuffs?"

"You know that the first man is no longer there?"

"Sure. I had to walk past the house with Saundra. Is that why you're sore?"

"Good grief. No. I was—" She put the SUV in gear. "Do you want to see if the man is still in the house?"

"You tell me. It's your case."

"Is that really how this is going to play out? You take off alone, darting through houses that seem to all be part of the same organization where—"

"Yeah? Where what? Did you expect them to ambush me?"

"It wouldn't be the first time. Would it?" Kendall visibly clenched her jaw.

"Are you really going there? I'd prefer to have one argument at a time."

"If it's relevant to this particular argument then I think we—" Her cell rang and she clicked the button, connecting the hands-free. "Barlow."

"This is Special Agent in Charge Lou Grayson with the Portland office. Have I caught you at a convenient time?"

Kendall pulled into an alley separating Rawlins and Hall Streets. She took the phone off speaker quicker than his mare headed for the barn for dinner. She began to get out, but he stopped her. She could stay in the SUV while he collected his cuffs.

Heath hated to admit as he got out of the SUV that he had another bad feeling. If a Portland agent was calling about the case, Kendall wouldn't have needed privacy.

"Dammit," he muttered to himself. "What the hell is going on?"

Chapter Eleven

Kendall locked the SUV and followed thirty feet behind her husband.

"Special Agent Grayson, what can I do for the Portland agency?"

"Join us. And it's Lou. Please."

What?

His words stopped her in her tracks at the corner— a good vantage point to have Heath's back if something went wrong.

"I apologize, Lou, but now might be the wrong time. I'm out in the field—"

"I'll text you my direct number."

Heath walked up the sidewalk to pick up his handcuffs.

She needed to get off the phone. "Special Agent Grayson, I need three minutes. Sorry."

She tapped the red disconnect button and stashed the phone in her pocket. The bright silver still hung around the pole, locked in place. The neighborhood continued to be abnormally quiet and vacant for a block in Uptown. It was just weird to be outside this long and not hear a single bird or dog.

Heath was on the porch, key in hand, as he collected his restraints. No surprises. He didn't knock on the door to see if the man was inside. He did everything she'd asked. Then he retraced his steps. No one left their home. No car drove by. Her husband was ten feet away and she ran back to the SUV, dialing while attempting to be as focused on her duty as possible.

"My apologies, Lou."

"Glad you called back," he said without any irritation in his voice. "I know this might seem like it's out of the blue, Kendall, but you come highly recommended."

"I'm very flattered and honored, sir. But I didn't apply for a transfer."

"Let me give you a better idea of why you were recommended."

Lou Grayson recounted some of the high points of her last evaluation. She heard the words, knowing they were true…but…why her? *Why now?* Those words kept ringing over and over in her mind while Heath turned the corner toward the SUV.

He stopped, took his own cell out and turned his back to her. All the signs were there that her husband suspected something was wrong.

How would she explain the phone call from Portland without lying to him? Her only two options were avoid or evade.

"Kendall? Are you still there?"

Tempting as it was to claim a bad connection and deal with this another time, she didn't move through life like that.

"Yes, sir. I think I'm still a little stunned."

"As I said, this might seem sudden to you, but we've actually been considering it for quite a while."

"May I ask how long, sir?"

"Since your partner was promoted. You'd be taking over our cybercrime unit, when the group leader retires in three months. Of course, we'd like you here well before then to learn the ropes."

"I'll need time to think about the move."

"How long do you think you need?"

"As long as you'll give me. This is a big change."

"I don't doubt it. How about a week?"

"Sure. Thank you, sir."

Heath stuck his cell in his pocket and placed both hands on his hips, clearly frustrated. She waved at him to return while she exchanged pleasantries with Grayson and disconnected.

"I called for a neighborhood patrol. They'll pick up Marrone when he comes home."

"*If* he comes home. He might be on his way to Mexico."

"More like Del Rio," he said.

"Where?" She couldn't have heard him right. "Del Rio, Texas?"

"Yeah. I overheard Saundra talking to a woman on Vandelia Street. I thought she was just making up the trip. You know, as an excuse. Then again, the woman said she'd love it there. As if she'd been before. Does it mean something?"

"Brantley Lourdes has land there. It's almost compound-like." Practically giddy, she grabbed Heath's arm, shaking it with excitement. "That's where Public Exposure's headquarters are."

"Did you issue a BOLO for Marrone?"

She shook her head, and Heath dialed the Rangers. She flipped open her notebook with the license plate of the sedan they'd been following. He gave them the information needed for the all-points bulletin.

Continuing to smile, she steered the SUV toward FBI headquarters.

She was excited. No. *Ecstatic.*

The couple that had tried to smash their car the previous day definitely worked for Public Exposure. She had a connection. Together they would break this case open. She was sure of it now.

"DPS will get him if he's on a highway out of town to

Del Rio." Heath stashed his cell back in his pocket. "Do you want Dallas PD to pick up Saundra Rosa? It might be a good idea to see if she's willing to come to your office on her own. You might be able to flip her there before Public Exposure sends a lawyer."

"You mean *you* might be able to flip her. She seemed very eager to cooperate and kept looking to you when she answered. Sort of like you promised her something. Did you?"

"I've been told that women feel safer with a Texas cowboy around. I simply explained that we needed to file some reports."

"You said 'Yes ma'am, no ma'am.' And you told her we had to file reports. That made her stop what she was doing and let you buy her a cup of coffee while you waited to speak with me?"

Her husband cocked her head to the side and lifted a finger—a sure sign she wasn't going to like his next words.

"I might have asked her why she tried to kill my wife."

"And her response...?"

"Crying. Full-blown, mascara-running, fall-to-her-knees weeping. As a highway patrolman, I've seen a lot of women cry. I've told you some of the stories. But I've never seen anything like this, Kendall. She even asked me for forgiveness."

"And then she denied everything?"

"Absolutely everything. Even down to knowing Marrone, at least knowing him well. As she said, they wave at each other when they pass each other on the street."

"Do you believe her?"

"Hell, no."

"Thank goodness. For a minute there, I thought you'd totally lost it in the past six months." She pulled into the FBI parking lot. "That woman was lying through her teeth."

"Sadly true."

HEATH HATED THE idea of obtaining a visitor's badge and tagging behind Kendall as she went through her office. He'd been there, done that, and he'd felt like a puppy on a leash.

"I'll wait out here. Make some phone calls."

"You're sure? No coffee or anything else?" Kendall didn't wait long for an answer. She was already out of the SUV and walking fast. "I'll text when I'm coming down. It may be a little while."

"No problem."

Heath didn't want to draw the attention of FBI security. He had other things to think about instead of justifying why he was waiting. He kept the door open and his feet on the parking lot asphalt when all he wanted was to move and get rid of some nervous energy.

His phone began vibrating. "That was fast," he said in answer.

"Hey, Heath. Just letting you know, man. The house you wanted us to surveil has already had four visitors. I texted the pictures. No car fitting the description or plate number you issued the BOLO for."

"I owe you one, Jason."

"Not for long. My daughter wants riding lessons. When she mentioned lessons, I actually told my wife I knew a real cowboy. Me and my big mouth."

"Anytime. We can ride a couple of times and let her see if it's something she really wants."

"That would be terrific. How long you want me to hang around Rosa's house?"

Heath scrolled through the pictures—three men in dress shirts and ties, one woman. "I think we've got a start here. Thanks again."

"I'll talk to my wife and we'll make a date," Jason said.

"You've got my number."

"Let's go with a heavy patrol in the neighborhood."

Heath hung up and first texted, then called Wade at the office.

"What's up?"

"I'm at the FBI headquarters waiting on Kendall to get a Bureau-issued car."

"Thanks for checking in?" Wade asked it as a question, probably since that wasn't the normal routine. "Okay, what do you want me to do with the pictures you texted? I assume they're surveillance photos."

"You got it. I'm wondering if one of the men is Brantley Lourdes."

"Man, all you had to do was open your smartphone for that answer. He's a pretty well-known guy. But I'll run the other faces for you. While I let the program kick this around, how's it working out with Kendall?"

"It was a rocky start. Then I thought I'd done something good. Now we're back to barely speaking." Enough personal business. "Check if the others have ties to Public Exposure."

"You got it," he said, clicking keys on his computer. "You two are all over the place. Why don't you just tell her you want to move back home?"

"It's not that simple."

"Sure it is."

"It's not like I haven't tried, man."

"For a married man, you sure don't know anything about women."

"And you do? I seem to recall that you're single and haven't had a date in—"

"Yeah. Got it. Minding my own love life. The people in your pictures are all board members for Public Exposure. I'll text you their names and pertinent info. They're from all over the country."

"Question is…why are they all in Dallas? And why are they all visiting a home of a suspect?"

"Good question. When do you intend to find out?"

"Soon. See you, man." Heath hung up.

A horn honked behind him. Kendall had kept her word to be fast.

Just tell her you want to move back home.

The thought was there. The courage…not so much. He was afraid she'd tell him why it wouldn't work.

Instead, he stayed focused on their investigation. "A buddy of mine at DPD is watching Saundra Rosa's place."

"Already?" she asked.

"I had some time while you were on your call. Anyway, he grabbed a couple of pictures of visitors, and I sent them to Wade. One was Brantley Lourdes."

"We only spoke to her an hour ago and he's already making a house call?" She pulled out from the parking lot.

"It gets better. Seems most of his board of directors for Public Exposure is here in town." He tapped a knuckle against the window, giving her time to think.

"You know I'm not someone to play hunches. I like good old-fashioned investigating and facts. But every feeling I have tells me that company is dirty."

They'd played this scenario before, back when they first worked together. His hunches had proved him right after a bet that it couldn't be that simple. That bet had gotten him the first date with the love of his life.

He didn't do a lot of dwelling in the past, but working with Kendall was a constant reminder that he'd been in love from the first time he'd laid eyes on her. She'd been a rookie agent working one of her first cases and he'd been her backup at several remote locations. A little town south of Burleson serving warrants and looking for a handgun.

Following one of his hunches about the gun's location led to their first date. Yeah, he'd won the bet that afternoon and they'd both won that weekend.

"Heath? Yo, Heath!" She snapped her fingers in front

of his face. "Did you have nice trip? Ready to get back to work? So…if they're all here in town, it looks like whatever's going down will likely be soon."

"We'll need a warrant," she said.

"It'll be easier to get it through my department. You have a longer chain of command than I do."

"If I could just get my hands on some hard evidence that this is a cybercrime, they'd give me a lot more resources and a little more leeway."

"Good thing you know someone who has a little leeway then," he answered.

"You know, since we're working together, I don't mind you staying at the house."

That was sort of out of the blue. But he liked it. Riding to and from work, having dinner together… *Wait.*

"I don't want to put you out. I mean, it's only convenient if you don't stay at your mom's."

"True. I… I think it's a good idea. Especially after how upset Skylar Dawn was last night."

Did she want him to stay at the house to work things out? Or was it because their daughter was upset?

Did it really matter? Did he care why he would be waking up with his girls?

Nope.

"Sounds good. I'll even cook."

THE BOLO ON Marrone paid off. Texas Highway Patrol spotted the car and picked him up south of Waco. He could be transported back to Dallas County Jail soon after she made a request. They could interview him while he awaited a hearing for his parole violation.

Again, Kendall owed Heath for arranging the BOLO. If she hadn't been working the case for more than six months, she might begin to get an inferiority complex.

Late Tuesday afternoon, they easily procured the warrant. Hearing that their suspect had fled the city and had an outstanding violation, the Waco judge had no objections regarding extradition. They could collect it in the morning and question their suspect upon his return.

"I still don't understand why the Public Exposure board of directors met here in Dallas. It isn't the main headquarters, and none of them actually live here."

"It may just be a coincidence," Heath said.

"You've never believed in a coincidence in your life. I don't know how many times you've told me that."

"True. You want to take the munchkin out for chicken strips or pick up food on the way home?"

She smiled. This was the normal routine when it was her husband's turn to cook anything except breakfast. "I think she'd prefer to have you at home all to herself. I'll make myself scarce."

Was that a look of disappointment that he hid by rubbing his face with his hand?

A real look or one she projected onto him? She couldn't let sentiment or wishful thinking get in the way of the case.

"You seem to be thinking pretty hard, Agent Barlow. If you're trying to tell me that my cooking's not so good. Don't worry. No illusions there."

"I wasn't thinking that even if it is true. Would you mind dropping me at the house? I'll send mom home while you take Skylar Dawn to dinner. She'll get a kick out of that."

Kendall turned the SUV onto their street.

"You got it." His agreement sounded like a forced confession.

"You don't have to sound so thrilled about it."

"Not a problem I get it."

"I don't think you do." She parked in the driveway and he practically jumped out of the car faster than stepping away from a bucking bronc. "Wait…"

But he didn't hear her. And she didn't chase him. Instead she sent her daughter skipping to a fast food dinner and her mother home for the night before she could complain too loudly about it.

Then she took advantage of an hour to herself, poured too much bubble bath into the tub and soaked until the water grew cold.

Wrapping herself in her comfy robe, she promised herself the nap would only last a couple of minutes when her head hit the pillow.

And not one time did she think of a way out. She couldn't practice the right thing to say. Whatever was needed to be said to Heath—her husband and her partner on this crazy journey.

Chapter Twelve

The third day working with Heath began with him in their kitchen if the wonderful smells in the house meant anything. Kendall had never been a night owl. She'd always thought of herself as a morning person. Morning workout or run, coffee and a quick shower had always been her style. Then she'd met a man who fed livestock at the crack of dawn every day and made fun of how late she slept.

This morning she could barely roll over. She'd experienced a total lack of sleep from tossing and turning. The awesome dreams of Heath seemed short-lived, and she struggled to get back to that place where everything was happy…and perfect.

The smell of coffee and biscuits finally had her stretching across the twisted sheets and eager to find her travel mug. Her mother didn't drink coffee. Just tea—morning, noon and night.

Coffee. Coffee. Coffee. The smell beckoned her to get out of bed.

Oh, God. I slept all night.

Shoving the sheets aside, she pulled on running shorts and a sports bra. She needed a couple of miles to work out the kinks and get her blood pumping. But she could start with one of those fresh-baked biscuits—and coffee.

"Hey, good morning." She came around the corner, expecting Heath and Skylar Dawn. Taken off guard, she smiled at her mother setting a plate of food at the bar.

"I told him you don't eat like this in the morning, but he insisted."

"Morning, Mother. Don't take this the wrong way, but why are you here this early?"

"Heath called and asked me to come and take Skylar Dawn to school."

"I can handle that."

"I told him as much, but again, he insisted. He said to check your phone and that you didn't have time for any exercise. He also left you this smelly stuff." She pointed to a pot of coffee.

My hero. Heath had found their coffeemaker from wherever her mother had hidden it. After moving it to the back of the pantry, her mother had bought a single-cup coffeemaker for the counter. It was the perfect temperature for a cup of flavored tea without any mess or boiling teapots.

"Where's Skylar Dawn?" She poured the brewed java into a mug and blew across the top.

"In the tub. In fact, I need to check on her."

"Mother, I'm sure Heath gave her a bath last night," she said a little louder, to carry down the hall where her mom was already headed.

"She fed horses this morning and stepped in some—oh good Lord, you know what she stepped in out there. You should listen to your messages, darling. I'm not sure it's really time sensitive, but he said it was about your case."

Kendall laughed on her way back to the bedroom and her phone. She was fairly certain that if—and that was a big if—her daughter had stepped in you-know-what, Heath had cleaned her up. But her mother was her mother.

Another bath wouldn't hurt Skylar Dawn. She'd play

in the bubbles and smell like pink bubblegum at day care. No harm done.

She checked her messages. "Another agency—yours— served a warrant on Marrone's rental house. They found Saundra Rosa's body. Don't forget to pick up a Bureau sedan. Meet you there."

When Heath mentioned "body," she scalded her tongue, forgetting the coffee was still hot. She hurriedly dressed, pulling her hair into a ponytail. She scooped her creds, keys and phone into a pocket. Opened her gun safe and holstered her weapon.

"Gotta run, sweet girl." She blew an air kiss to Skylar Dawn. "Thanks for taking her this morning."

"I guess his message was important after all."

"Very." The door shut behind her as she ran to the SUV. *Dang it. I forgot my coffee.*

HEATH CHECKED HIS WATCH. "Special Agent Barlow is a few minutes away," he told the medical examiner, not really knowing how long it would take.

"I've got a couple of minutes. I know you want her to see the scene, but once transport arrives, I'll have to move the victim."

"I understand."

He kept taking pictures. Every angle possible from where he'd been allowed. Then more of each room he could see.

"It looks like she came for a visit and Marrone dosed her with something. We found a needle mark on her left arm." Supervisory Special Agent Jerry Fisher had mentioned his theory several times to anyone who would listen.

Too many times. An uncomfortable number of times.

There was one problem with his theory. Bryan Marrone hadn't returned to his house. Picked up south of Waco, he was dressed the same as he'd been the previous morning and in the same car. Jerry didn't know that the Dallas PD had been sitting on this house until the BOLO for Marrone had been canceled.

Absolutely a setup.

Yeah, that bad feeling had returned.

Heath kept avoiding direct conversation with Kendall's supervisor. Besides the fact that he just didn't care for his wife's former partner, he didn't want to give the agent an opportunity to tell him his services were no longer needed.

The two players they had connected to Public Exposure were accounted for. One dead—honestly, he was sorry for that. Maybe if he hadn't spoken to her or bought her a cup of coffee… It sounded heartless, but he hadn't killed her. The only justice he could give was to find her killer.

And it sure as hell wasn't Bryan Marrone.

He left the house with orange trim and saw Kendall walking through the police and onlookers, credentials in hand, "FBI" coming repeatedly from her lips.

"Morning. Glad you could make it," he greeted her without saying what he really wanted to say. Okay putting that into words right here wouldn't have worked. But a guy could think about it.

"Any theories as to how she was killed?" she asked, continuing her power walk up the sidewalk.

"Plenty. I'll let you decide for yourself." He stayed put. No reason to crowd the small house with one more body.

She turned, taking a backward step. "Did Skylar Dawn really step in you-know-what?"

He laughed and nodded. "I bet your mother had her in the bath faster than the wicked witch melted."

He stared after his wife, liking the way she flashed her creds at the other staring officers. There had been plenty of times after they were first married that he'd watched men looking at her and simply pointed to his wedding ring. She was definitely a beautiful, confident woman worth admiring.

Returning to his phone, he looked carefully at the body of a totally different type of woman. A young woman who loved pink and had unaccounted-for visitors yesterday.

"Why did you run, Bryan Marrone?" he asked under his breath. "Who were you afraid of?"

"Who's afraid of whom?" Kendall asked, coming to stand next to him. She tipped her head slightly to look at him before blocking her eyes with her sunglasses. "Oh. Well, Jerry's wrong."

"Yep."

"Is anyone checking out her house?"

"Yep." He pointed to three houses down, where a do-not-cross tape had been hung.

"Darn." She snapped her fingers like she'd missed an opportunity. "I don't suppose…"

He nodded. "I took a look at it earlier. Everything looks comfortably messed up."

"'Comfortably messed up'?" she asked with a tweak of her head.

"Like someone looked for something but didn't want us to know they were in a hurry. No phone. No laptop. But the TV was still there." He handed her his phone.

"Oh. I suppose you got pictures?"

"Yep." He stepped aside for the gurney that would remove the body. "I have a different adventure for you."

"The pink car?" She looked at him above her glasses and smiled.

That was the super smart agent he'd fallen in love with—one step ahead of the rest. "It's probably nothing."

"But an adventure nonetheless." She winked. "My car or yours?"

"You drive. Swing by my truck for my laptop. I'll call Jason at DPD and find out where they towed the Pink Thing for repairs."

IT TOOK THEM a good hour to drive to the repair shop. That in itself raised a red flag.

"Why would someone who lived in Uptown have their car towed to McKinney? That's just not logical, unless you have family or someone's doing you a favor." Kendall pulled on gloves before she began looking through Saundra's car. "And Saundra didn't have family."

"No one who works here has seen or heard of our victim. I didn't get the impression that any of them were lying. Did you?"

"No. Darn it. They seemed genuinely upset when you told them she'd been murdered."

"Um. I think that was because she owed them for the work they'd already started."

Kendall flipped the glovebox open. "Papers. Owner manual. Looks like she owned the car."

"She definitely liked pink." Heath continued to take pictures of sneakers, a sweater, T-shirts and running shorts, all in varying shades of pink.

Kendall leaned down to look under the passenger seat. "Candy wrappers, twenty-seven cents and an eraser."

"Eraser?"

"Yeah, it's Betty Boop. A fat Betty Boop, but I recognize the cartoon character." She set it on the seat cushion.

"Can I see that?" Heath asked after taking pictures.

Kendall handed it to him, and he pulled the head off to reveal a USB. "A flash drive?"

"*This* I can work with." He smiled from ear to ear.

"I bet they were looking for this at her place. Perhaps it's a connection to Public Exposure."

Heath took something from his jacket pocket and

plugged it into his phone. Then he plugged the flash drive into it.

"I should probably warn you that we shouldn't look at the evidence yet." She waved at him to let her see the screen, too. "You're one of the only guys I know who carries a flash drive attachment for his phone."

"Hey, I resent that remark. I picked it up this morning from the ranch. This case is about computers." He shrugged. "Why wouldn't I?"

"That looks like a complicated encryption. Do you think you'll be able to break it?"

"Looks like it's going to be a tech thing after all. Yours or mine?" he asked.

"This time, I think I have to go with mine. They have a bigger department. If we connect Public Exposure to cybercrime, they'll put a rush on it. DC might get involved."

"Then our adventure would be over."

With the exception of one major thing—they needed a shred of proof for the big leagues to come on board. She didn't know why that was important to her. Maybe it was justification that she hadn't wasted six months of her time and taxpayer resources. Maybe it felt strange, and she wanted a solid explanation.

Or maybe she wanted a big break to boost her career. She couldn't tell. It was probably a little of all of the above.

"Maybe not yet. I'd like to flash this in front of Bryan Marrone to get his reaction."

"It's a long drive to Waco." He bagged their evidence.

"I asked Dallas PD to extradite him. He'll be here in the morning. Honestly, did you think I wouldn't?"

"Nope. Just hoping for more time with you. My couple of days is officially up." They spoke to others in the garage and waited on local law enforcement to take over the car.

"We make a pretty good team, Barlow." He touched the small of her back to guide her through the door first.

"That we do, Murray."

THE OFFICIAL CALL came that Heath would be continuing with the case. The city of Dallas wanted someone local representing their interests.

Avoidance. Who was worse? Him or Kendall? Both of them took the opportunity to talk with as many other people as possible. Right up to the time they were in the SUV and they went over their plan to interview Marrone.

"I like watching you work. I always have." Blocks away from the house…his mouth finally caught up to his heart.

"Right. We only worked one case together."

"Hey, I watched from home."

"Right."

That tone…one of disbelief. Normally it was a good reason to stop and walk away to avoid what would follow. Not today.

"Kendall, I need you to believe me that I don't want you to stop working. Wait a minute before you do the psychological profile and get angry."

"Okay."

"See, I probably did mean it six months ago. But I don't know why. My mom has worked every day of my life. If it wasn't for her, things around me would never have happened. I know you're capable of handling everything."

Seconds ticked by but she wasn't angry. The emotion would have shown up in her movements.

"Then why?"

"I was scared. For you. For Skylar Dawn. Don't get me wrong, I wanted another kid for the right reasons, but I wanted you around to protect all of us."

"Your dad?"

"Yeah," he squeaked the word out. "Things happen that

are beyond our control. Dad is gone because he fell not because he chased criminals through the street."

"I wish you'd told me this earlier. Maybe…"

"It's hard for a man in my line of work to admit he's scared. Even though we know the risks."

They were in the driveway and in a good place. As much as he wanted to stay…she needed time.

"See you in the morning."

His wife waved from behind the wheel without looking at him. He didn't press for an answer just got in his truck. For the first time in months, he might get a good night's sleep.

Chapter Thirteen

KENDALL BEGAN HER questions from the door and slowly moved closer, taking a chair and inching it even closer to invade Marrone's space. Several people watched from the two-way mirror. It was a classic technique.

"Come on, Bryan. We understand if you're scared." Kendall was an excellent interrogator. She had the Reid technique down pat. She'd planned this one down to the minute, or cue. "I mean, they killed your friend. Who wouldn't be scared?"

After she moved in close, after she commiserated, then Heath would enter and say they found proof that Marrone was guilty. They'd discussed exactly what he was to do while returning from McKinney the day before—and again this morning.

"Bryan, you've got to give me something to work with."

"Are you sure Saundra's dead?" He gulped. The young man's Adam's apple moved up and down his thin neck.

"Yes, hon. I may be alone in thinking you're not guilty." She placed a hand on his knee. "None of my coworkers believe that you left town right after you saw us yesterday morning."

That was Heath's cue.

A light tap sounded on the door. He let himself in, and Kendall withdrew her hand with a guilty look.

"Special Agent Barlow, there's no reason to continue

the questioning. The techs found this in Saundra Rosa's car. It proves that Marrone here is guilty. He has one, too."

Bryan might have been watching him toss the evidence bag onto the table, but both him and Kendall stared at the young man's reaction. Everything about his face screamed that he knew what was on the flash drive.

Then he relaxed. He sank down in the chair and acted like he couldn't have cared less what evidence they had. He knew. Whatever was on the flash drive, Marrone knew. It's what he'd been looking for in the apartment.

Kendall's tactics changed. She jumped up from her seat and grabbed the bag. "You know what this is, don't you?"

"You don't have anything on me 'cause you can't read that thing without the key. You'll never get the algorithm before we kick some ass around here."

"You'd rather go away for murder than tell us?"

"I'm innocent."

"Your fingerprints are on the syringe and once we—"

"No. They're not." He tried to bring his arms above his head, but the handcuffs jerked his hands back to the table. "I think I'd like my lawyer now."

They'd gotten nothing definitive. Kendall would be upset.

He wasn't. No one had called to tell him to remove himself from the investigation. That meant another day working with his wife.

Another day to work up the courage to tell her he wanted to come home.

"What do you say? Ready to go home?" Heath asked.

Not Kendall. She was ready to rework everything she had on Public Exposure. "What do you think he meant by 'before we kick some ass'?"

They left the county jail, changed cars and headed out. It was the first time she'd walked to the passenger door and let him drive their SUV home. But it was a silent ride while she scoured her notes, flipping page over page over page.

He didn't bring it to her attention that they'd arrived home. He grabbed his hat and made it to the steps before his daughter threw open the door.

"Daddy, make me fly." Skylar Dawn took a running start and leapt into his arms.

Heath had completely forgotten about his injured side. When she hit his ribs, a smoldering burn kicked into a bonfire of pain. He hid it as best as he could before he lifted his daughter into the air and spun her around like an airplane, complete with sputtering propeller noises.

It didn't last long.

"Hey, sweetie. Let me grab some jeans, then I can play in the backyard with you." Heath used his key and opened the front door.

"Skylar Dawn, come get your bunny and jacket," Kendall called from the car.

Maybe…just maybe she hadn't seen him. Either way, he needed a minute to catch his breath.

He rounded the corner, heading for his bedroom closet. He barely had his shirt unbuttoned and an old pair of jeans thrown on before his mother-in-law appeared in the doorway with laundry.

"Oh dear Lord. You scared me." The stack of clothes fell to the floor as she grabbed her chest with one hand. "What in the world are you doing here? It's Wednesday."

"It…it is my house, Naomi."

"No. You used to live here. It's not your night. Does Kendall know you're here?"

"You know we've been riding together." He bent and scooped up Kendall's laundry. "You're spoiling her by keeping everything together."

It was meant as a half-assed thank-you, but her expression turned deadly.

"I have the right to help my daughter and spoil her if I want. Someone needs to treat her nicely."

"I think I should head back outside." He tried to scoot around her, even with the laundry in his arms.

"I am dead set against you staying here. We have an arrangement and you're breaking it."

He dropped the laundry onto a dresser and turned back to the door. "I don't have an agreement with you, Naomi. There's not even a formal agreement between me and Kendall."

"I beg to differ."

"You can beg all you want, but as long as Kendall's comfortable with me at home, I'm staying. Now step aside, or I'll have to force you."

She did, cowering at the door as if he'd really threatened her.

Five years. For five years he'd been in the house, been around her. He'd never hurt her, and he hoped she knew that.

"I'm truly sorry you don't want to be around me. After all this time, nothing's going to change that." He returned to his walk-in closet, jerked an old T-shirt out of a drawer. "I'm going to play with my daughter now. You can go talk with yours or complain. Whatever you want."

She moved to Kendall's dresser. With her back to him, she began refolding the laundry. He couldn't let her obvious hatred bring him down. Tonight was a plus. An extra night to see his daughter. More time with Kendall, with the possibility of a discussion.

Skylar Dawn was putting things away in her bedroom as her mother had instructed. He wouldn't interrupt her. Pulling his phone out, he texted his own mother. He hadn't appreciated her enough for accepting Kendall as part of their family. He had it pretty good.

His dad may not be capable of remembering things,

but his mom was a rock. Just a simple Love you went a long way with her. The return text was a smiley face and heart emoji.

"Your ribs are cracked, aren't they?" Kendall appeared with an armful of kid stuff, probably from various places throughout the house.

"Did I forget to mention that? Yeah, it happened Sunday." He raised his shirt and let her see the darkening bruises. "It's getting better. How did you know?"

"You winced when Skylar Dawn jumped into your arms." She playfully acted like she was about to leap into his arms, too. "Bulls or broncs?"

"Bronc. He caught me off guard. I was thinking about something else."

"Dare I ask? I've seen all those rodeo groupies." She leaned against the doorframe and shook off an offer to help. "Never mind. It's none of my business."

"Wait a minute." He lowered his voice to avoid little ears. "I have never—okay, I can't say never. But since I've met you, I haven't been attracted to anyone else. What about you?"

"Oh, it's not like no one's asked," she teased. "It's just... there's something about touching the person you're in love with. That same kind of touch doesn't come from anyone else."

She smiled thoughtfully. Or maybe wistfully. Words weren't his thing. He'd always used as few as possible. But he'd never thought about what she'd said before. He liked it. She was exactly right. No forbidden fruit was better than a touch from her. No one affected him like she did.

His baby was done putting away her toys. He rushed in the room, squeaking like a monkey. Then he acted like the Wicked Witch of the West from *The Wizard of Oz*, quoting some of the famous lines from the movie. Skylar Dawn quickly imitated the monkeys and wanted to fly like them.

Kendall joined them by cackling and doot-da-do-da-doing the witch's theme. They all collapsed on the twin-size bed, tickling each other. Naomi walked by without a smile. No longer angry, he was simply sorry she couldn't find joy or happiness. He recognized the feeling.

When he wasn't with his family, he felt the same way.

THE EVENING WENT off without a hiccup—not one phone call about Marrone's questioning or Saundra Rosa's murder. No additional complications from Naomi, who left for her own home before dinner. And no last-minute inquiries from work, for either of them.

Heath glanced at his girls, his ladies, his loves. He slid the bookmark into *The Wizard of Oz* and snapped a picture of the page to be able to pick up the story if he read from his place.

Dammit. This was his place. Not the room he used at the Thompson's ranch.

Kendall didn't stir when he picked Skylar Dawn up from her arms. He tucked his daughter in bed, making sure the night-light wasn't blocked by a Lego tower. He kissed her forehead one more time before leaving her door cracked a couple of inches.

She'd be four years old next week.

And he'd missed six months of the past year.

To get to the guest room, he had to cross through the living room again. Kendall had slid down the leather couch and curled into a ball. He reached for a blanket but then tossed it into the chair he'd vacated.

Cracked ribs didn't deter him from lifting her into his arms and carrying her to their king-size bed. He left her dressed, but pulled a light blanket on top of her. He kissed her forehead and got a smile—he could see it from the night-light she now had in their room.

And because he couldn't resist the beautiful temptress

in front of him, he brushed her lips with his. He wouldn't be sleeping now. He could sit in her "perfect" chair that matched the "perfect" color of chocolate paint on the walls. Or he could lie down beside her.

Thunder rolled in the far distance as he watched the woman he loved sleep.

Chapter Fourteen

Kendall woke with something all too familiar wrapped around her… Heath. Lightning flashed. A crack of thunder followed.

At some point, Heath had moved them to the bedroom. She'd slept through it. Well, she might have missed him holding her earlier, but not now. His strong arm dropped from her shoulder to her waist.

Perfect. Her world right that minute was perfect.

"You okay?" he whispered close to her hair. His voice was so soft that it wouldn't have woken her. "Want me to go?"

"No. It's too late," she whispered. "You'd just come right back first thing. Stay. But I should check on Skylar Dawn."

"I got it." His warmth left her side as he rolled off the bed behind her.

Heath yawned, using a lot of his vocal chords, as he often did. It always made her smile. His bare feet slid across the carpet, then *tap-tap-tapped* down the hallway's wooden floor. Minutes slipped by. She closed her eyes, trying to reclaim the dream she'd been in. Heath returned, gently closing the door.

Another lightning bolt struck. The thunder answered more quickly. He sat in the chair they'd specially ordered to match the paint and bedspread.

"I don't mind sleeping on the couch." He crooked an

arm behind his head, supporting it. He still had his white undershirt on along with the rest of his clothes. Another bolt of lightning gleamed off his championship-roping belt buckle.

Kendall pushed into a sitting position, letting the cover drop to her lap. "I need to get out of this blouse and bra."

"I could help with that if you're too tired." He was back-lit by the glow of lights outside, so she relied on experience to know he grinned from ear to ear.

He wouldn't make the first move. He wouldn't say the first word, opening a conversation about what they really needed to discuss. When she'd suggested counseling six months ago, he'd told her talking had gotten them into this mess. Then he'd asked how it would get them out.

So far their week had been full of polite comments and—*dammit*—professionalism. Just like she'd insisted. God, she wanted to kiss him.

Wanted to lie next to his long body and be wrapped in his protectiveness. In five years, she'd never wanted to sleep alone. Before Heath, she'd never considered herself a cuddler. But she was. At least with him. And she missed it.

She threw back the covers and went to change. Their bathroom was in the opposite corner from where he sat. She didn't need the light to find the door or her things. Her pj's hung on the hook. She slipped them on and crawled across the giant king-size bed back to her side.

If she'd walked over to her husband—still sitting in the chair—she would have sat on his lap, tucked her legs to her chest and wrapped her arms around his solid-as-a-rock chest.

But she hadn't. She pulled the covers up to her breasts, just wishing she had. Wishing for a simple way to get out of the mess they found themselves in.

"You'll be grumpy all day tomorrow if you sleep in that chair."

"I promise not to be grumpy." Heath's nail scratched the stubble on his cheek before running his fingers through his golden brown hair. It was a familiar movement that made her shiver in anticipation. She knew what his chin felt like against the softness of her skin.

"If you don't want to sleep on your side of the bed, just say so." Okay, that came out a bit snippy, but at least she'd gotten it out.

"You scared of the dark now?"

"Oh, the night-light? Your daughter has been coming to sleep with me. I think it's because you let her sleep with you."

Heath cleared his throat. The sound of fingers moving across his scalp seemed super loud in the silence.

"I'd probably be better off on the couch if you don't want me to touch you. I won't be able to make any promises to stay on my half of the bed." His voice was husky and, ironically, full of all sorts of promises.

"I don't recall asking you for any."

"Good. 'Cause I ain't giving any."

The click of the door locking got her hopes up even further. She felt his tall, lean body move through the room instead of heading for the couch.

Kendall covered her mouth, concealing her happy grin. She heard the boots hit the floor—first one, then the other. Another pause where he removed his socks. Heath stood in front of her, pulled his undershirt off, then dropped his old, torn jeans.

He'd lost weight if they fell off that easily. Lightning flashed, outlining his excellent physique. Anything he'd lost had turned to muscle.

"I'll never get back to sleep," she said as he dove over her to land in the middle of the bed.

"Do you need more sleep?"

"Don't you?"

The rain started then, and not a gentle spring sprinkle—it came pounding as hard as her heart. Light from the storm hung in the room long enough for her to see his jaw clench.

"I don't think sleep's in the cards tonight."

God, she hoped not.

They faced each other, both with an elbow propping them up, arms curled around a pillow. She waited for him to make the first move. Had he been serious? Or just teasing? He shifted on the bed, and yearning shot through her entire body at the memory of him lying there.

His free hand reached toward her to catch one of her pajamas' bowed strings. He playfully tugged. Untied, the front of his favorite silky pajamas would fall open like it had many times before. She hadn't thought what that night mean by way of an invitation when she'd hurriedly tugged them on. And now? Now she wanted the invitation to be loud and clear.

An excruciatingly slow pull finally had her top gaping open. The soft glow from outside the windows and the occasional burst of lightning showed her white breast right down to a hard nipple poking the green silk.

She wanted to roll Heath onto his back and take over. He'd let her. She could do what she wanted. But the exquisite turn-on of his exploration was as good as the very first time they'd made love.

She already ached and wanted out of her clothes. She wanted him. And under his boxers, she could tell he wanted her, too.

He gently rubbed the back of a knuckle across her nipple, sending a current through her body. One knuckle turned into four skimming back and forth, making her breath catch.

A half smile brightened Heath's face as the back of his hand slid across her belly, then a veiled touch moved across the inside of her arm, making her shiver. He laughed—a small sound that was full of the fun from torturing her.

She began to do the same to him, but he stopped her pulling her fingers to his lips and kissing them one by one

"That's not really fair."

"Nothing about this is fair," he mumbled against the inside of her wrist.

"Hmm? I'm relaxed now and think I can drift off again."

"Is that a challenge?" he asked, already moving to a sitting position and then to the end of the bed.

"Oh, I don't know." She deliberately yawned and lifted her arms above her head while turning on her back. "I'm seriously tired."

His hand wrapped around first one foot and then the other, dragging her entire body to line up with him at the end of the bed. "Toss it over here."

She slapped her hand backward on her headboard until she landed on the lotion bottle. Flipping it to him one-handed, she grinned to herself at how she'd obtained her foot massage.

Heath wasted no time kneading her tired feet, rubbing each part until she'd melted into the mattress.

"Would you relax?"

"I'm a marshmallow," she mumbled against the pillow.

"Only if the marshmallow's been in the sun and is all dried up." He tugged on her toes, wiggling them back and forth. But he was right. His strokes lengthened into long glides up her legs, with feather-soft kisses on the way back His calloused fingers skimmed across her skin, exciting her entire body.

He stretched over her, capturing her hands above her head. Nuzzling the base of her neck, barely touching her with his lips, he then dragged the tip of his tongue to her shoulder. She wanted to squeal with delight at the way he caused her body to react.

She tugged at her hands and he let her go. She first pushed at his chest, then began to remove her pajama top. But his hands delayed her action, gently pushing her shoulders to the mattress.

All the while, the storm raged outside the thick-paned window. The lightning was more rapid now, followed by almost-constant rolling thunder. Rugged fingertips traced the outline of her pj top, dipping between her breasts to tease the delicate skin.

"You are absolutely beautiful." He fingered an errant strand of hair from her cheek. "I've missed you."

She parted her lips, about to quip that he'd been with her for four days, only to have Heath pull her quickly to him and slash his mouth across hers.

The temptation had been there each time they were close, but she'd held back. She'd missed kissing him. She didn't have to miss it anymore. They could figure out what would happen in the morning.

This very minute, she really needed him. All of him.

She stretched her arms around his back, wanting skin. Lots of skin. His body stretched on top of hers. He ran his hands down her sides, latching on to her hips and bringing them up to meet him.

He traced her collarbone with his mouth. "I love your legs. Love the fit of you against me." He emphasized his words by dropping his pelvis against hers.

Her mouth opened again and his tongue was there to pleasantly invade, dancing a dance that had stood the test of time. Without words, he invited her to join him.

Or maybe she'd been inviting him all along? She didn't care. She wanted her handsome man, and it was evident he wanted her. She slid her arms higher along his back. He quickly pushed himself up, taking the pressure of his chest from hers and lifting his back out of her reach. She immediately missed his warmth, his weight and...his everything.

His mouth seized her nipple through the silky material. He scraped his teeth gently over it, then captured her sensitive skin again. She bucked into him, wanting more. It didn't work. She could only accept the teasing and absorb the wonderful sensations building inside her.

Lying next to her again, he nudged her chin to turn with his knuckle. Once more he held her close, kissing her hard and excitedly, then soft and invitingly. Her breathing was fast and ragged. She forced her mouth away, letting the scruff on his chin rub her cheek. She hooked a finger on each side of his boxers and inched them lower on his hips.

Distant thunder. A gleam of far-off light. He quirked an eyebrow, questioning her, stopping his own exploration through her silky pajamas.

Keeping her eyes locked with his, she moved her hands to skim the light dusting of hair across his ruggedly hard chest. Again he stopped her. Was that her hand trembling or his?

"It's okay," she crooned, trying to convince them both. Convince them that everything would be fine for him, and that she knew what she was doing.

"I can still walk away, Kendall. I won't think a thing about this. Well, that's not true. I'll be disappointed, but I can still make it to the couch right now."

"I don't want you to go," she whispered. Then she kissed him, a long luxurious kiss that she had a hard time pulling away from.

"Will you let me stay?" he asked, his voice cracking with emotion.

Stay? As in…stay more than just tonight? As in, come home? Her mind shouted at her that they needed to talk, but her body drowned out the argument.

What really mattered was that she needed him. Wanted him. Loved him.

"Stay."

Chapter Fifteen

Kendall looped a toe in the waistband of Heath's boxers and tugged them off his hips. He drew his breath, stupidly about to object, until she placed her fingertips across his lips.

"Shh."

Then came cool, confident kisses across his chin and shoulders and collarbone. His arms were getting weak supporting himself above her body. The look on her face told him she felt him tremble. The teasing Cheshire cat smile that followed issued a challenge.

It didn't take much to knock his arms aside and force him to drop on top of her. She surrounded him with her arms, using her nails to scrape his flesh in a sexy way only she could accomplish. Immediately, she soothed his skin with the soft brush of her fingertips.

God, her touch charged him with energy, rejuvenating his soul.

His hands grasped both sides of Kendall's hips to remove her pajama bottoms, then quickly shot to cup her face as he got caught up kissing his woman.

His. Everything about her was his. Missing her kept him up at night.

Their tongues tangled a brief moment before Kendall twisted and sat on top of him in the blink of an eye.

"Now, where was I before you distracted me with all that luscious kissing?"

Her hair was still in the tight ponytail like it had been every day recently. He hadn't seen it loose, felt it flow over him, in what seemed like forever. He reached and pulled off the holder.

He captured her surprised mouth and attacked her lips. When she moved, the long lengths of her legs caressed him like the silk of her pajamas.

He grasped her slender hips, his thumbs inching their way to her intimate secrets. She urged him to please her, and when she begged for release, he hesitated, savoring the magic of the way she looked.

Darkness seemed to penetrate everything in the room, but it was the first time in months Heath felt surrounded by light. It followed Kendall wherever she was—especially now. Her eyes were soft, her breasts lush, and the tip of her tongue peeked out between her lips. One last touch, and she cried out her release. The first of many, he hoped.

Lightning flashed, and he soaked in every long curvy line of her. Determined he would take his time, he savored every second of them together. But as the thunder rolled closer, shaking the windows with its intensity, Kendall guided him inside.

He was home…all he could do was feel. An overwhelming amount of love rushed through him, taking him to the only place he wanted to be.

"Don't move," he told her. "Just give me—"

She moved.

In a single motion, he flipped her to her back and let her pebbled nipples rub against his chest. Their hands were everywhere. Roaming, searching and exploring after being apart for six long months. He wanted to memorize every subtle change, wanted to feel her hair—

Kendall tried to move to one side, but he kept her where

she was. With very little maneuvering, he slid into her again until the rhythm took care of itself. Kendall pulled him to her until they climaxed like the first days they were together.

Satisfied beyond words, Heath shifted to his side of the bed, bunching a pillow under his head. Kendall turned on her side, propping herself half on him and half on the mattress.

"Storm's moving on." He noticed the lightning flashes were fewer and farther apart.

"I suppose you're tired."

Was that another invitation? He softly dragged his fingers up and down her leg. He loved her soft skin. "Not really."

She nuzzled his wrist. He nuzzled her neck in return. He laughed, and the sound was short but deep from his core. It was an excellent new start, even without an official apology from either of them. But there was plenty of time for that. Now that he would be around every day again.

"What did you have in mind?" he asked after she twined her legs around his.

"We could make up for lost time."

"Actually, I need some food before we go a second round." He twisted a little to get a look at her. "We didn't have dinner. Aren't you starving?"

"Oh." She pursed her lips together in a short pout and kissed him. "Mister, you talk entirely too much. Do you know that?" She turned over, scooting her body into a spooning position.

He'd missed his opportunity to make up for lost time. She was ready for sleep. His right arm was tugged over her body as she pulled her hair out of the way to rest on his left biceps. "Okay, yeah, I get it. You want to cuddle. I can handle that."

A deep type of hunger had been satiated by Kendall.

He could wait until morning breakfast with Skylar Dawn to satisfy the other. No food was worth moving away from his wife. He enjoyed her this close.

Life was complete.

IT WAS MUCH earlier than anyone normally got up, but Heath didn't mind. He woke up and decided to run home for a different suit. But that didn't work. As soon as he was out of their bedroom, he heard Skylar Dawn reading under the covers.

Whether she was actually reading was still a mystery. She at least had the book she'd memorized last year with a flashlight pointed at it. She was reading all the parts with different voices for the mommy, daddy and little girl.

Since neither of them could head back to bed, he decided to make breakfast. He still had clean shirts hanging in his closet. Who needed a different suit when he had an opportunity to spend time with his daughter?

"Does MiMi have to pick me up?" Skylar Dawn asked between bites of scrambled eggs.

"Yes. Mommy and I still have to go to work." He flipped a Spanish omelet for Kendall.

"But I like it when you pick me up."

"Why? Want to get dirty?" He gently tapped her nose with his knuckle.

"No, silly." She pointed her fork at him. "We go see Stardust. I love my pony. Can we go today?"

"Sure thing. But we have to go to work first."

"I don't work." She giggled.

"You do your work at day care."

The oven timer began to ring in an old-fashioned buzz. He'd have to replace that ancient thing before long.

"Biscuits ready!" Skylar Dawn shouted.

Heath stuck the spatula over his lips. "Hey, Mom had a late night."

"Biscuits," his daughter whispered, pointing to the oven door. "I want cotton jelly."

"Cotton jelly it is." He laughed. Cotton was short for apricot. They'd all called it that since Skylar Dawn had first asked for it that way.

He spread the jelly on thick, and Skylar Dawn had it on both sides of her cute little mouth when Kendall came into the kitchen.

"What's this? Everybody's up so early." She kissed their daughter's forehead, swiping a finger of jelly off a sticky cheek before turning to him. "You made breakfast."

"Daddy made it special." Skylar Dawn pointed to the stove.

Heath rushed to the pan, pushing it off the burner before the omelet burned. "It's not much."

"I think it's super." She wet some paper towels and cleaned up their baby girl.

Why did he get the feeling something was wrong?

"Everything okay?" he asked, almost afraid of the answer.

"Go make your bed and brush your teeth. Then you can watch TV until it's time to go." She helped Skylar Dawn off the barstool and watched her leave the room.

Heath set down two plates with half of a badly formed omelet on each, then two cups of the single-serving coffee. Then he sat down himself. Kendall leaned against the wall leading to the open living room.

"Going to eat?"

"I'm not really hungry."

"We've got a full day today and might not have time for lunch. You might—"

"I can decide when I want to eat, Heath."

No need for guessing. She was upset. Maybe even angry.

He accidentally dropped his fork on the floor. He bent

to get it, but Kendall beat him. She walked it to the sink and didn't turn around to face him.

"Maybe you should take your own advice and just tell me what you want, instead of writing a book in your head to find the best words."

"Okay." She spun around. "I've been offered a promotion. It's an opportunity to lead a cybercrime group."

"And it's in Portland." He should have known.

"How did you know? Oh, the phone call."

"Are you taking it?" His knees hadn't buckled. That was good.

"I… I don't know."

"Are you telling me about it or asking?"

"What do you mean?"

He pushed away from the bar, scooped up the plates and headed for the garbage. He no longer had an appetite either.

"Telling me means you're moving and asking me for a divorce." He rinsed and placed the plates in the dishwasher. "Asking me means you'd like me to come along."

"I haven't… I don't know yet."

"Are you asking or telling?" he pressed again.

He couldn't look at her or he'd lose it. Really lose it. As in yell that she couldn't go. He watched her reflection in the window as she covered her face with one hand and wrapped the other tight around her waist.

Exactly where his arm had been all night.

"If last night hadn't happened, how long would you have waited to tell me you were leaving?"

"That's not fair." She swallowed hard and faced the counter—away from him. "I need to think."

Fair? Think? What about his life had been fair in the past six months? He'd said what he felt at the time, before thinking it through. Before realizing that it hadn't been what he meant.

He wanted Kendall to quit work when *she* wanted to

quit. He wanted her only to be happy. As many times as he'd told her that before he'd left, she obviously hadn't really believed him.

Heath didn't have words. How could they work with this hanging over their heads all day? He didn't know what to do.

The hell he didn't. He was taking the day off.

"You know, Kendall. I think this is the perfect day for Skylar Dawn to play hooky. Tell your mom she's got the weekend off."

"You can't—"

"Darlin', I can." He left the kitchen, calling to his daughter. "Skylar Dawn, change of plans. Get your boots, darlin'. Let's go see Stardust and Jupitar."

He got his daughter out of the house quickly by throwing a few things into her backpack and setting her on his hip.

When she asked, he told their girl that her mommy wasn't feeling well. It wasn't a lie. He was pretty sure that Kendall felt real bad about springing it on him like that.

Last night had been a natural reaction. Something neither of them had expected, but they'd both wanted it. Maybe she'd been conflicted. Maybe they shouldn't have made love.

He didn't have the answers, and apparently neither did Kendall.

Chapter Sixteen

"Are we really staying here all weekend, Daddy?" Skylar Dawn kicked the ribs of her pony to keep up with his mare.

"Yepper doodles," he said in a bad cartoon duck voice.

She laughed. "And I get to ride Stardust every day? And not go to school? And I get to stay at the ranch house? And we get to order pizza?"

"Yeppers on everything, but I think Mama Thompson is making the dough. Then you can make your own pizza in her oven."

"I can put as much cheese on it as I want?"

"I'll leave that to Mama Thompson to decide."

"This is fun, Daddy."

"Yepper doodles."

She laughed at him again.

They'd gotten to the Thompson ranch early. He'd taken care of feeding the other horses and had let Skylar Dawn feed the chickens. The Thompsons had come to the paddock to say hello and get their order for lunch.

Both adults had seen through his excuse that Kendall wasn't feeling well. They told him several times they'd be hanging around the ranch all weekend if he needed help. They'd had a short, knowing look with each other, then Slate's mom had told him she'd make all his favorites.

"Is Mama Thompson my grandmother?"

"Not really, darlin'. But she loves you like a grand-daughter."

"I like it here."

By "here" she meant the Thompson ranch, large fields surrounded by trees that cut them off from the housing developments. A secret little stock pond full of catfish. Far enough away from the major roads a person couldn't tell they were twenty minutes from the Dallas suburbs.

He slowed Jupitar to a stop, letting Stardust have a little break. Tipping his hat, he shoved his hair back from his face. Maybe they should go for haircuts this afternoon. Or fishing. Skylar Dawn usually screamed and giggled at live bait, but she was surprisingly patient for an almost-four-year-old.

Shoot, she'd be four in nine days.

Skylar Dawn imitated him by taking off her little straw cowgirl hat, shoving her bangs back and securing it again on her cute little head. He'd been corrected more than once that she was a girl, not a boy.

"Fishing or the barber shop? Which do you want to do after pizza?"

He'd let Skylar Dawn decide. This was her day to play hooky and his to wonder about their future.

"Pizza, then Mr. Craig at the candy shop."

The old-fashioned barber pole looked like a candy cane. He didn't bother to correct her. It didn't matter. How many days would they have like this if Kendall moved them to Portland?

His wife would transfer, get the promotion she'd longed for. He'd have to seek out a new job in law enforcement. Go through more training, be reduced to rookie status—man, he didn't look forward to that.

Dad-blast it. He'd have to give up the horses. Moving them would be too hard. Paying for them even harder. His daughter was just getting the hang of riding, too. They were almost at the edge of the property.

Where had the time gone? Out of the corner of his eye, he caught Skylar Dawn rocking in the saddle. This was probably the longest she'd been in it. No matter, he'd let her ride with him on the way back. That would help.

"My, my, my," she said, sitting back in her saddle like him. "Have you and Mother had another fight?"

"What? Since when do you call Mommy 'Mother'?" He knew the answer. His mother-in-law always said "my, my, my," so this had to be her insistence on proper English. Never mind that. He needed to answer the real question. "Why do you think we had a fight?"

"You're acting funny, Daddy."

He guided Jupiter to face both Skylar Dawn and her little pony. What could he say to make her feel better? No lies. He refused to do it. But he also refused to make his daughter's life miserable.

"Hey, baby. Sometimes things go wrong. So, yeah, Mommy and I argued. But that doesn't mean we don't love you or each other. Remember that time you had a fight with Stacy? What was that about?"

"Bumble. She said he had a stupid name. We aren't supposed to say *stupid* in school."

"That's right. But you still went to play at her house that Saturday."

She nodded her sweet little head. "You and Mommy are still friends, too?"

"Always. No matter what."

"Okay." She shrugged, pulling the reins to go around him.

Dammit. No matter what happened…

Friends, lovers, parents. They'd always be all of those things. There was nothing else to think about. He'd follow Kendall to Portland. He'd live with her or live next door—

whatever she wanted. Not just for Skylar Dawn. He'd be there for his wife until she told him differently.

"Daddy?"

Heath wiped the bit of raw emotion from his eyes. Putting a smile on his face, he looked Skylar Dawn in the eyes. "What, honey?"

"What's that?" She pointed behind him.

He turned in his saddle and saw a dust cloud.

Dust? After all the rain they'd had last night? Not dust. *Exhaust!*

"I don't know, sweetheart."

Woah. Engines. The sound of all-terrain vehicles echoed off the stock pond's built-up back containment wall. There were several of them. The Thompsons had only one.

This was not good. Something was off.

"Hey, baby girl, I think you need to ride with Daddy for a while." He guided Jupiter next to Stardust, then reached down to lift Skylar Dawn. Setting her in front of him, he looped his left arm around her.

"You're squeezing too tight, Daddy."

"We're going to go fast, baby. You like fast, right?"

"Yes!"

Excited, she grabbed Jupiter's mane, ready to fly. Now if he just had someplace to go. At the edge of the property, there weren't any back gates close by. Even if he had wire cutters in his back pocket, he couldn't cut the barbed wire before those four-wheelers caught up with him.

He kicked Jupiter into motion. The mud might slow down the men headed their way, but not his mare. She was as fast as the lightning that had cut across the sky in the early morning hours.

"Hang on, baby!"

He'd loped horses with his girl sitting there a couple of times, but not as fast as this. He tugged her to him even closer. There wasn't any doubt the vehicles were following them. Thank God he knew what he was doing.

Riding this land every day had him knowing just where to go. He could make it harder for them to follow. Lead them into small ditches that might be bogged down with mud.

"Stop before you hurt your daughter!"

What the hell?

A gunshot pierced the sound of the galloping hooves. He couldn't slow down enough to tell if they were really aiming at them or not. Mud shot up from Jupitar's legs. The wind whipped their faces as the sun beat down, warming them. His mare darted to the right, causing him to rise in his saddle.

Skylar Dawn screamed. "Daddy, slow down!"

"I can't, baby. I can't."

Public Exposure! The information they'd obtained must have scared them into going after all of Kendall's family. It was the only explanation. He hadn't been on any major Ranger cases. No one was after him. It had to be Brantley Lourdes.

"Haw!" he shouted to Jupitar.

No use trying to get his cell out of his back pocket. Both hands were occupied controlling Jupitar and holding on to Skylar Dawn.

If he could just make it back to the house…

That's when he saw another vehicle. He hadn't turned around to see how many four-wheelers had followed. They'd split up, boxing him in.

He could try to jump the fence, but Jupitar wasn't a jumper. More likely, she'd dump them over her head by coming to a full stop. The vehicle got closer. Two hooded men rode it. One carried a shotgun.

No choices.

No options.

"Whoa, girl." He pulled Jupitar to a stop.

"Daddy?"

He might have halted, but he didn't ease his grip on his daughter.

"First things first. Toss your cell on the ground. Careful-like. Make sure it's face up, and no monkey business." The voice was full of authority and came from behind him.

He slid his hand down the reins, lengthening his grip until he could reach behind him. He tossed it, forcing the man to get off the back of the ATV in front of Heath and pick it up. The man cracked the case, removed the SIM card and then threw it over the fence.

Jupitar startled. He whistled to get her under control. The man with the shotgun jumped off the ATV and pointed it at the horse. *No! Them.*

Skylar Dawn was between the barrel and his chest. There were too many, and he was unarmed. "Down on your own or we can pull you off of there, Ranger," the guy behind Heath said.

There was always the slim chance that the Thompsons had seen the ATVs come up the drive. A slim chance... but a chance nonetheless.

"I don't know who you are, but point the gun away from my daughter."

"There's one way this is going to go. Mine. If you do as I say, we'll be glad to point our weapons at only you. Now, get down," the guy behind him directed.

"I'm scared, Daddy." kylar Dawn had a death grip on his arm. "Why can't we see their faces?"

"It'll be okay, sweetheart."

"Only if you do as I say," the guy doing all the talking said.

"I can get him down," said the one still straddling the ATV in front of Heath.

"Come on, Heath, get off your high horse." A second

man behind him chuckled. "Listen to me, or I'll have to kill you in front of your kid."

"Trauma does weird things to kids, man," a third voice said from behind him. "Just look at all of us."

They all laughed and agreed. Skylar Dawn began to cry. He couldn't turn around to see who was there. But looking toward the house, he could tell no one would come there in time to stop these men from doing what they wanted.

No choices.

No options.

Unsure exactly how much his daughter understood, Heath switched her around to face him. "Hold on to Daddy, hon." Her little hands latched behind his neck, and he kicked his leg around until it looped around the saddle horn. It was a tricky place to balance, especially with a small child.

"Steady, girl," he instructed Jupiter.

His left arm held his shaking daughter—who was holding it together much better than he'd ever thought possible. The other held the edge of his saddle. He needed something. Some type of defense. His fingers searched for his rope.

"Whoa there, partner," one of them said. "Keep your hands where we can see them."

"I have to get down, right?"

"Want me to get the girl, boss?"

"That's not necessary. Heath Murray is a champion cowboy. I bet he can slide to the ground from where he's at."

Heath's boots hit the ground, and his horse didn't move. He was out of stall tactics, out of ideas. What did they want? Was it a ploy to scare him or did they—

Stardust came into view, being led by yet another man in a mask. That made six he could now see. Three ATVs with two men each. None of them had identifying marks.

No unusual clothing. He couldn't even tell skin color. They either had on goggles, or the skin around their eyes was blacked out like superheroes on TV.

"That's right, Heath. You're surrounded and have no options. Get her." The main guy pointed to one of the men and then to Heath's daughter.

Heath wanted to back up, to run. But the leader was right. He was surrounded.

"Hold on now!" he shouted and put Skylar Dawn's back toward Jupiter's neck. "Why are you doing this? What do you want?"

"Hell, Heath. I thought we were pretty clear about that. We want your daughter. We made a special trip out here and everything," he joked.

"Whatever reason you have for doing this, just tell me. We can come up with some kind of a deal."

"A Texas Ranger like you? Married to an FBI agent? I don't think so." He pointed again—this time at the man holding the shotgun. "Shoot the pony." The man swung the gun from Heath to Stardust.

He tried covering his daughter's eyes, but her little fingers tugged at his hand. She screamed. She twisted.

"No! Stop! Daddy, don't let them hurt Stardust!"

The man pumped a shell into the chamber. It didn't matter. He'd never drop his daughter. How could he?

Three men got to Heath. Two tugged his arms. The third tore his now-hysterical daughter from him. She screamed, "Daddy! Stardust! Don't you hurt them! Stop! Daddy! Help!"

One man locked Heath's arms behind his back. Another hit him. He threw them off. Tried to get to Skylar Dawn. She kicked and twisted herself and bit the man's wrist until she wiggled to the ground and ran. Heath ran after her but was tripped.

He fell, eating mud, as he yelled for his daughter. She

was scooped up, her little legs still running through the air. Her hands in little fists beat on the leg of her attacker.

One of the men kicked him in the back of his head. Then again in his sore ribs. White-hot light radiated through every part of him as he heard the rib crack on the second kick. He tried to get his feet under him, but again the toe of a shoe hit him in the side. He began coughing, unable to catch his breath.

The ATV engines revved to life. He couldn't hear his daughter. Maybe because they had gagged her, or maybe because a buzzing sound was shooting between his ears.

One by one the engine sounds faded. He coughed, choked. He couldn't see because of the mud covering his face. Could feel only the pain from his heart breaking.

"Skylar Dawn," he called.

He wasn't alone. Something moved through the brush close to him. One of the men was still there—their leader. He grabbed Heath's shirt, dragging him to his feet and hitting him. How many times, he didn't know.

The world was just pain. It was worse than being trampled by a bull. Much worse. The leader shoved him to the ground. Heath couldn't move.

"We'll be in touch," the bastard said over him. "Follow our directions or you'll never see her again."

The third engine roared loudly to life and then faded across the field. Heath used his shoulder to get a bit of the mud from his eyes. He rolled, taking a long while to get to his knees.

"Oh God." He fought through the pain. Fought to stay awake.

If he could just get to Jupiter. And then what? He tripped over something on the ground and fell hard, taking the brunt of the fall with his chest. He couldn't scream. Couldn't call out. Could barely breathe.

His eyes focused on a small straw hat near his face.

"I'll find you, baby girl. And those bastards will pay."

Chapter Seventeen

"Where is he? Come on, Heath. Pick up." Kendall looked at her phone as if it had the answer. Then she dialed Slate's number and quickly hung up when Jerry walked up.

"Glad you could get here so fast, Kendall." Jerry did a finger gesture pointing to her cell. "Is there something wrong? Having trouble with Heath?"

"No. Did you find something on the thumb drive?"

"Look, I was your partner a long time. It sounded like you were looking for your husband. Is he MIA or do you know where he is?"

"I'm sure everything's fine and he's not answering because he's knee-deep in muck at the ranch."

"Okay. There's nothing yet on the encryption. I came over to see how you were and tell you that you're needed in the conference room."

Jerry left but the creepy feeling didn't as she walked to her summons. Something was wrong. People could call it whatever they wanted, but she just knew something was off.

"Thanks for coming in, Special Agent Barlow." Steve Woods opened the door to the conference room and gestured for her to sit. "Is Ranger Murray not with you?"

"No, sir. He had…obligations today." She hoped those obligations would allow him to call her soon.

"I wanted to introduce you to Agent Therese Ortis.

she'll be taking over the Marrone interrogation. It seems our local complaints have backed into her ongoing investigation."

"Of Public Exposure?"

"Yes," Agent Ortis said. She stood at the other end of the room, arms crossed, mainly looking into a two-way mirror. "I can't go into many details. Sorry about that. I know how frustrating it can be."

Kendall had known from the beginning that the company she'd been investigating had ulterior motives. She just hadn't been able to connect anything except the local dots.

"We wanted you to know that Marrone was released late last night. His lawyer argued it was an illegal stop." The second-in-command of the Dallas field office took a step to the door.

"What about the parole violation? Didn't we have him on that?" She looked from one agent to the other. "This would be one of those things I can't know?"

"You did a good job," Agent Ortis acknowledged.

"Then why do I feel like I'm being punished?" She shook their hands. "Am I off the case?" she asked.

"Therese might have additional—"

"Actually, I'd like to work with Special Agent Barlow—that is, with your permission—wherever I can." She crossed the room with her hand extended. "There are some things I won't be able to fill you in on. At least not yet."

"Thank you. I'd be glad to help." Her phone buzzed in her jacket pocket. "Is that all, sir?"

He nodded, and she left the room to answer. She returned to her desk and redialed Slate Thompson.

"Kendall?"

Finally. "I've been leaving messages everywhere. I need to talk—"

"Hey, yeah, about that. I got your messages and called

the ranch. Mom took a look and found Stardust, Skyla
Dawn's pony. She returned to the paddock. Alone. The
Jupitar ran up. I'm on my way there now. I'll call you a
soon as I know anything."

It all happened in slow motion.

Kendall looked up to see agents running toward he
She hadn't realized she'd dropped to her knees, taking
stack of files to the floor with her.

Skylar Dawn was gone or hurt? Where was Heath
She'd known something was wrong. She couldn't speak
Her throat seemed to be connected to every part of he
body and it was all shutting down, vital organ by vita
organ. Someone helped her to stand, and she felt a chai
at the back of her knees.

Voices talked over one another. Someone called for as
sistance. The room filled with men and women. All th
dark suits seemed to fade to black.

Kendall took it all in, struggling to think. She stare
at her colleagues. None of them could really help. Sh
couldn't keep her daughter safe. Heath might be hurt.

"What happened?" Jerry asked. "Someone call a para
medic."

"Something's wrong. What if they took Skylar Dawn
Heath's... I don't know what's happened and I have a ter
rible feeling."

"Someone find out what she's talking about. And wher
the hell are the paramedics?"

"I'm not hurt. I have to get to the ranch." She shove
herself to her feet, rolling the chair backward, hittin
someone who stood behind her.

"Kendall, you aren't making sense," someone said. Sh
didn't know who, and didn't have time to figure it out.

She moved through a throng of agents, all clueless hov
to help. She did an about-face. "I need my Glock." Sh
ran back to her desk and slid her weapon into its holster

"You aren't going anywhere alone. I'll drive you. That's not a question. You aren't leaving without me." Jerry took her elbow and guided her from the building.

Again, time passed at a snail's pace. Couldn't Jerry drive faster?

Where was the fast-forward button? It had been only a blink of an eye since her daughter was born. One little skip, and now they were planning her fourth birthday party. She needed time to move at the same rate now.

Her phone vibrated in her pocket. "Heath?"

"It's me," Slate said. "Heath's unconscious. We've called for an ambulance."

"And Skylar Dawn?"

"She's not here."

"Are you arranging a search party?"

"Kendall, Heath was attacked. He's really bad off. We found tire tracks."

"Are you saying my daughter was kidnapped?"

There was a long pause. Jerry flipped the lights to warn cars to get out of the way.

"I'm on my way."

SITTING ON THE PORCH, Heath listened as Slate tried to issue orders indoors. Jerry Fisher and Major Clements were arguing. Both wanted their respective agencies to be in charge of the investigation. Law enforcement officers searched the area, but they wouldn't find anything. He'd told them that.

Skylar Dawn had been kidnapped by Public Exposure. No doubt in his mind about that. Two hours had passed, and still no word. Drained, his body ran on autopilot, sipping a cup of coffee Mama Thompson had put in his hands.

The idea that someone would hurt his daughter kept replaying in his mind, caught on an endless repeating loop. He couldn't stop it.

"Yes, Ranger Murray is conscious, but the kidnappers wore masks. He said there were six men." Slate was speaking to someone in the living room.

Heath had lost track. Everyone was involved. Local PD, Rangers, Public Safety, FBI Dallas and surrounding departments—they were holding off on issuing an Amber Alert. And he sat there…doing nothing except holding a cup of coffee. He couldn't bring himself to even drink.

"The paramedics said you should go to the hospital, son." Slate's dad laid a kind, gentle hand on his shoulder.

"I'm good."

"You need X-rays. What if you've punctured a lung or something? What good will you be to your little girl then?"

Heath took a deep breath, letting it out slowly. His eyes met Kendall's. "Nope. I'm good."

He hadn't really spoken to Kendall. He hadn't told her he was sorry for not protecting Skylar Dawn. He took a sip. The breeze across the porch was cool today.

"Did someone find her hat?" he asked. The words came out, but he thought they sounded weird. Maybe it was a weird thing to worry about. "She's going to want her hat."

Kendall moved to sit next to him. "Her hat is with the little bit of evidence they found."

"I told all of them they didn't leave anything."

"They took seven sets of footprints, the ATV tire tracks. But nothing that will point us in the right direction."

"No one knew I was here, Kendall. I should have been working with you. Slate and his parents saw me this morning. That's it. I asked them not to mention us if you called. Sorry about that."

She shook her head.

"Why do you think it was Public Exposure?" Kendall's voice dropped to just above a whisper.

"It's logical after this week. They were organized. They listened to one guy. We know something's happening in their organization. You have the flash drive. They obviously don't want you to discover what's on it. Then they kidnap our daughter."

A cell phone rang. From across the porch, they heard Slate answer. "Ranger Thompson."

Slate ran over to them. "It's the kidnapper. He'll only talk to Heath. No speaker."

The bastard had his daughter. He wanted to curse, rant, say a hundred things, but he kept his mouth shut. Slate placed the phone in his hand.

"Ranger Murray?"

"I'm here. What do you want?"

"Your daughter or your wife. You choose."

During the long pause that followed, Heath wondered if the man had hung up. "You must choose, Ranger. Your daughter? Or your wife? Which will it be? I'll telephone again."

"Wait! Is Skylar—" The call disconnected. "Dammit!"

"What? What did he... Is she okay? Did she say anything?" Kendall stayed next to him.

Others gathered close. He wanted to tell Kendall that everything would be all right, but he didn't know if it was true. He desperately clung to whatever courage he had left. Courage that kept him from collapsing like a desperate father, while Kendall held it all together. Another mother would have fallen apart long before now.

"He wants me to choose between you and Skylar Dawn."

"There's no choice." Her gaze held his.

"You're damn right! I can't choose. I won't."

Kendall cupped his face. "I'm not asking you to. I already have. We're doing everything exactly as he says. We have to if we want to see Skylar Dawn again. She needs to be safe."

Half of him knew she meant it. The other half of him

couldn't believe her logical, matter-of-fact response. None of him believed she would've asked such a thing of him.

"Right. How do we convince them?" He nodded toward the men scattered all over the Thompsons' lawn.

"Tell me again what he said. Word for word."

HEATH SAT ON the porch and repeated the short phone call word for word. Then he sat in the living room and repeated it. Then he repeated the conversation in the dining room. He answered all the questions they asked with an "I don't know." He couldn't take it anymore. He grabbed Kendall's hand, leaning on her a bit more than his masculinity preferred.

They left the porch and the crowds. Kendall released his hand and draped his arm around her neck.

"Thanks. Not keeping my feet under me is kind of embarrassing."

People kept reminding him there'd been six men and a gun pointed at his daughter. Hearing it over and over didn't help.

"Where are we heading?" she asked.

"The barn. I don't think anyone's unsaddled Jupiter and Stardust."

"Okay." She didn't try to change his mind, but she did wrap her arm around his hip and take more of his weight.

They walked together and he gained more strength. It was better than sitting around, listening to the different law enforcement agencies argue about who was in charge. Bottom line—he and Kendall would decide how to move forward. Skylar Dawn was their little girl.

"It's going to be hard to fight the bad guys in my current physical condition."

She released him to lean on the corral rail, then pointed to his horses at the water trough. "I don't think you can unsaddle, feed and rub down both horses. But I bet Mr. Thompson would care for them."

"I'll ask him." He reached for his cell. "Dammit, they destroyed my phone. It's somewhere in the neighbor's field, or collected for evidence."

"Sorry, the FBI took mine to trace any possible incoming calls."

"You know that I'm... It was my fault. I'm the one who's sorry." He cupped her face with his hands, staring into the sadness in her eyes. "If only I hadn't brought her here. There just wasn't anything I could do when they showed up."

She wrapped her hands around his wrists, holding him where he was. "I know. We all know. My God, Heath, there were six of them. You're lucky to be alive."

"If anything happens to her..."

"You heard what the kidnappers said. They wouldn't have said anything about me unless I'm the one they really want." She cupped his cheeks like he still held hers. "Promise me you'll go after Skylar Dawn. You do whatever they tell you to do and find her."

She looked at him expectantly. He nodded. The promise just wouldn't come. He'd find a way. He had to.

"Do you hear that?" he asked.

"It sounds like a cell phone. Wait here."

Kendall ran into the barn. Then grabbed Stardust, leading her inside. He waited. The barn had been cleared by three agencies. Nothing would harm her there. It was easier than attempting to catch up. Physically, he felt better than he had two hours ago, but he needed time to recover—something they didn't have much of.

"Heath!" she called.

He limped his way through the door and heard the cell phone. It was tucked under the edge of Skylar Dawn's saddle.

"There are clear bags in the tack room." He pointed.

"Do you think it's them?" She ran, shouting over her shoulder.

"It has to be. None of the men clearing the scene would have left their cell."

Once back, she carefully slid the phone from the pony as he lifted the saddle.

"We have a choice here, Heath. We answer it and move forward, possibly on our own. Or we let the FBI set up the trace and answer it the next time it rings. And to be honest… I don't know which is the best way to go."

"Does it say there are any missed calls?"

"Not that I can see, but that doesn't mean anything, Heath. It might not be programmed to show that. How could all those agents have missed this?"

The phone stopped ringing. He shrugged while looking into the corners of the barn. He couldn't see anything. There were too many places to look for hidden cameras. But he knew.

"They're watching us, Kendall. I can feel it. They were here." He pointed to his feet. "Probably here in the barn. They waited for one of us to come here to the barn to call."

"You can't be sure—"

The phone rang again. He stretched for the plastic-covered cell.

She met his hand with her own, reaching across Stardust. "That was the FBI agent talking. Kendall Barlow trusts you." She scooted the ringing phone out of the plastic enough to push the green answer button and then speaker.

"It's about time," the same voice from earlier said. "I've got a couple of errands for you. There won't be another call, so you better remember. You with me?"

"Yes," they both answered.

"There are no exceptions. Keep this phone. I'll call you tonight to give you further instructions. You'll need a black suit and a bright red dress. No exceptions. There's a wedding reception at the Anatole Hotel tonight. Be there."

The phone went dead, and they stared at each other.

"They'll never let us do this on our own."

"This guy didn't even ask us not to involve the cops." As inconspicuously as possible, he looked around the barn again.

"It would be impossible to assume we wouldn't find a way."

"Kendall, he didn't ask for anything."

"Except me."

The grip they both had on each other's hand was rock solid. They hadn't been unified in a long time, but there wasn't any question they were now. They'd follow the kidnapper's instructions. They'd get their little girl back.

And somehow, he'd save Kendall, too.

Chapter Eighteen

Fancy red dress? Check. Black suit, white dress shirt? Check. Boots for the suit? On Heath's feet. Small clutch purse with the Cherry Bomb lipstick she'd bought ages ago to match the dress? Check.

Jeans and T-shirts for them both…just in case. And a change of clothes for her daughter. Red high heels?

"Mother, where are my red high heels?" In a flash, she remembered that Heath had given those to Company B to attach a tracker. "Never mind."

Everything was beside their bag. Just like it was supposed to be. She went over the list a second time, unable to accept that it was complete. It was a simple list and a simple task. Her mother had pulled everything together and laid it out on the end of Kendall's bed.

Their bed—hers and Heath's.

In spite of checking the list twice—make that three times—she had the nagging feeling that she had forgotten something.

"You're forgetting your jewelry," her mother said, coming up behind her and sniffing into her tissue. "You really shouldn't go to a wedding without any jewelry. It will look odd."

"That's it." She removed her wedding rings and walked to her vanity to put them away.

"I meant that you can't attend an evening wedding without jewelry, darling. Not to take your rings off."

"I don't want to lose them."

She dropped her ring set on the porcelain hand Skylar Dawn had given to her. Or, more accurately, Heath had given it to her for her first Mother's Day gift.

"Would they do that? They'd not only kidnap your daughter, they'd steal your wedding rings?"

"I don't know what they'll do, Mother. This is a first for me, too."

Her mother gathered the extra clothes she'd set out, placing them in a garment bag. Kendall couldn't remember owning one. Taking a step toward the door she stopped herself. She'd been heading to Skylar Dawn's room again.

It was silly how long she'd just sat there, staring at the half-built Lego castle. She wanted to finish it for her daughter. But they were working on it together. She couldn't touch a piece without Skylar Dawn telling her where it went. That was the rule.

Kendall returned to her vanity instead and reapplied her eye makeup. It was getting close to the time Heath's partner would pick them up. She should go check on him. But twenty minutes ago, he'd drifted fitfully off to sleep. Obviously still in pain, but refusing to take anything that would impair his judgment.

Her mother watched from the doorway of the bathroom. She was sighing a lot, a cue that she wanted to say something.

"Thanks for staying here, Mother. There will be agents outside. You'll be perfectly safe."

"I'm not worried about that." She lifted a finger, indicating that Kendall should join her in the bedroom.

A sinking feeling hit between her shoulders. She wouldn't like what her mother was about to say. "Are you sure this can't wait, Mother?"

"You've got plenty of time, I think. Heath isn't awake yet."

"It might be better—"

"I need you to promise me something, dear."

"I promise I won't do anything stupid." Used to this promise, Kendall said it without thinking much about it. Her mother required it every week or so. Did it matter that this time she didn't believe that anything would truly keep her out of harm's way tonight?

"No, dear. I need you to promise that when you bring my granddaughter back to me, you'll finally restrict that man's visitation to supervisory visits only."

She could only stare at her mother.

What?

Helpless. Stunned. She couldn't think of words. Her daughter had been taken in order to draw her out without a fight. She might not ever see her baby again. Might not see anyone again for that matter. The demand from her mother struck her as ridiculous.

"I don't understand, Mother."

Naomi Barlow perched on the edge of the chair, prime and proper with her hands on her knees. "You can't trust that man. This would never have happened if Skylar Dawn had been here, where she belonged."

"They would have taken her from day care or even here. There's no telling how many additional people would have been hurt if that had happened. This is not Heath's fault. How can you blame him?"

"He comes and goes as he pleases."

"It's his house."

"I know he spent last night in this room and not the guest room."

"This is not the time, Mother."

"He took our girl without even telling you where he was going, disrupting her routine."

"Getting her dirty?" The deep voice came from the doorway.

Kendall sent a look telling him to cool it. But she didn't blame him. A lot had happened. Just a few days earlier, her mother hadn't allowed him to say good-night to his daughter. And before they could bring their baby home Naomi wanted her to commit to what? A divorce?

Heath did a one-eighty and left. She wanted to follow, but enough was enough.

"Heath is my husband, Mother. He's the father of my child. If anything happens to me tonight, he has the right to limit your involvement in Skylar Dawn's life. And frankly, I wouldn't blame him. I can't believe you could even think about cutting him out of our lives. How could you?" She headed for the door, but her mother's sobbing stopped her.

"Oh my goodness. I… This can't be happening. It just can't be happening." Her mother cried for real now.

"But it is, Mom. It's not Heath's fault. There were six men attacking him. He could have been killed." She lowered her voice, almost choking to get the words out. "I… I thought he was dead. I would never have forgiven myself."

She turned quickly to hide the tears. Her gaze fixed on her engagement ring. She'd never planned to marry. Everything about her life had been about joining the FBI. As a little kid, she'd always thought she'd find her father. She'd quickly outgrown that idea as she went through high school and college, each course chosen as a precursor to joining the academy. Every extracurricular activity was carefully chosen for the same reason.

She'd run cross-country for stamina. Even been on the college wrestling team. She'd been in such control of her future, securing the job with the FBI. Then she'd met Heath, and everything had changed.

No more rigid control. Instead, there was joy. Fun. He made her laugh. He made her live. When Skylar Dawn had joined them, she couldn't imagine anything that might be missing. And now...

"If something happens to her, life won't be possible."

"It'll be okay, dear." Her mother gently patted her back. "I shouldn't have said anything, but I know you'll bring our darling girl home safe and sound."

"You don't know that," Kendall whispered.

She'd been in such control of her future, of her life. Now she was helpless. Absolutely helpless.

Facing her mother, she closed her eyes for a second to strengthen her resolve. Now wasn't the time, but her mother had pushed the issue. When she looked at her mom again, Naomi was crying.

It was totally unexpected. Her mother didn't cry. Not real tears. She sniffed, stayed stoic and normally didn't show emotion.

"Mother, what's the real reason Dad left?"

Naomi looked taken off guard. "I don't believe that's any of your business. Especially right now."

Kendall didn't want to tell her why the thought had popped into her head. Or that she'd known there would never be an answer. It had been a foolish thirteen-year-old's dream to find him. That hope had long been abandoned.

At first she'd blamed herself, but soon her disappointment had shifted to acceptance. Heath had once asked her why she tolerated so much from her mother. Kendall had never pinpointed the answer until right that minute.

Without her and Skylar Dawn, her mother was alone.

Sitting here, listening to her hatred of Heath... Kendall couldn't take it anymore. No matter what happened, he'd always be Skylar Dawn's daddy. Clearly upset, her mother sniffed then patted her eyes with the tissue again.

"I... I'm sorry, Mother. I really do appreciate all the help you've given us—"

"That's what I'm here for, dear."

"Let me finish." She took her mother's hand between her own. "Because of your anger and bitterness, I almost threw out the best thing that ever happened to me."

"That's not true. *He* left. He walked out on you. And now—"

"I'm sure Heath's going to get your granddaughter back home safely. Like I said…if anything happens to me, Skylar Dawn is his daughter. You might want to rethink how you treat him. I know I am."

"Even if he runs to his mother when things get rough?"

"What are you talking about? Are you saying that you overheard him talking to his mother about us? About our problems?"

"I told you that, dear." The tears were gone as if they'd been calculated the entire time.

She wouldn't have gone that far. Would she? Had she deliberately said the one thing she'd confided that hurt Kendall the most? All these months she'd believed Heath had been confiding in another Ranger and shared their problems with the world instead of her.

"Fair warning, Mother. Things will be changing around here when this is all done. You should begin getting used to that idea."

"It's time to get ready," Heath said from down the hall. "Slate's on his way."

HEATH TAPPED ON their bedroom door, slipped inside and retrieved his suit. Kendall had been right. It wasn't the time to talk. But there would be a discussion when Skylar Dawn came home.

First and most importantly, his focus had to be on his daughter. The kidnapper said he'd have to choose between them. He'd spent the last three hours staring at the ceiling, his head throbbing, his side screaming that he shouldn't move. His mind was caught in a loop that there was no choice.

No man could choose between his wife or daughter.

Maybe it would be easier to think about his mother-in-law problem? But that didn't take much thinking. Naomi Barlow didn't believe he was good enough for her daughter. A simple cowboy from a failing Southwest Texas ranch would never be good enough.

A Texas Ranger who loved her daughter and granddaughter more than his own life would never be good enough. Not for her. He couldn't change her mind, and he needed to accept it. If he didn't, he'd lose Kendall.

If he didn't lose her today.

Stubborn and smart, his wife would do everything in her power to return home.

She wanted a promise that he'd do whatever the kidnappers said. He couldn't and wouldn't make that promise to her. He trusted that he'd know what to do when the time came.

He was stubborn and smart, too.

After dressing, he opened the front door and checked on the Rangers from Company F, one in a truck and one on the porch. But the man on the porch wasn't in the traditional suit and tie. Tonight Bryce Johnson was dressed in jeans so he'd blend into the neighborhood.

"Just wanted to let you know that Slate's on his way. I assume no one's been sneaking around or watching the house. You guys need anything?"

"We've got you covered, Heath. Don't mind us," Bryce said, standing and shaking his hand. "You guys were there for Major Parker when the twins were kidnapped. Don't worry about anything here."

"I meant to ask when you got here. How's everyone doing in Waco?"

"We're all good. You let us know if *you* need anything.

We're here for you, man." Bryce pumped his hand again, and also clapped him on the shoulder.

"Before I head back in, you got the cell numbers of my team. Right?"

"Wade supplied us with everything we need to keep apprised of the situation. If you need any help, just let us know. Otherwise, I can guarantee you that no one's getting in this house."

This time Heath slapped Bryce on the back. "I don't think we've caught up since that advanced computer stuff in Austin two years ago. We should compare notes again soon."

Bryce nodded.

Heath was ready. At least, he was cleaned up and dressed. He hadn't retrieved his black boots from his closet yet. He rarely wore them, except for special occasions.

He stumbled into the wall, his breath leaving him suddenly. Like he'd been hit again. Skylar Dawn had been kidnapped. He shook himself to regain control. He couldn't lose it. Not now. Not until it was over.

"Are you okay?" Kendall asked. "Do I need to call the doctor?"

Damn, she was beautiful. Dressed and ready to go, with the exception of her shoes. With that dress she should have a smile on her face. Her look of concern seemed out of place—but warranted. He was pretty certain he looked like he needed a doctor.

"No, thanks. I got it." He stood, grabbing his midsection, letting her believe the panic he'd experienced was just his sore ribs. "I got a look at my face, though. Looks like the beauty will be attending the reception with a beast."

He pointed to the split on his cheekbone held together with Steri-Strips. The bruise around it had already begun to blacken. He tried to joke, but he honestly couldn't have laughed if he tried.

God, he hoped he could do whatever was necessary tonight. *No!* He would push through the pain and get it done, no matter what it took.

"How much did you hear of the conversation with my mother?"

"You were right. This isn't the best time for that particular talk." He stood straight, keeping his breathing as shallow as possible. "Right now, I need to switch to my dress boots. These look weird with this black suit."

"Sit down. I'll get them."

As soon as she left the front hallway, he hobbled to the couch and eased himself onto it. She returned faster than he could move and caught him just as he leaned against the cushions.

"Maybe we should get a stand-in for you."

"That's not happening, Kendall. I'm resting now, but I'd never forgive myself if something happened and I stayed on the sidelines. You know you'd feel the same."

"It was worth a try. But you're right. I would push through all the pain to do my part." She dropped the boots on the floor. "There is one thing I can help with—getting these boots off and the others on."

"I won't let you or Skylar Dawn down, Kendall."

"No matter what happens, I don't and I won't blame you." She slipped the first boot off. "This is the result of my investigation, not yours. It's exactly what I feared most."

"I remember the multiple conversations about not having kids because we both had dangerous jobs. I meant every word back then just as much as you." He caught his breath from the pain as he forgot to brace himself when she tugged the second boot free. "I don't regret the decision to have our daughter, though. No matter what happens."

She took his hand into hers. "Neither do I. Never. And I'm sorry for what Mother implied."

"Later. But while we have a moment—"

"Ding-dong," Slate interrupted, letting himself inside. "How ya doing, partner?"

Heath waved him off. He wouldn't answer every person who asked him that question. Otherwise he'd be reliving the experience every other minute. It was better to concentrate on the task at hand—rescuing Skylar Dawn.

"Did you bring the phones?" Heath asked.

"Phones? We only need the phone he left in the barn." She looked to both men. "What did you have in mind?"

"This guy is probably going to ask you to drop the phone he gave you. Why not drop two that are old and useless?" Slate said.

"That actually makes a lot of sense. I spent some of the time Heath rested moving pictures off this thing." She set her cell on the coffee table. "That's really smart. Thanks, Slate."

"I wish I could take credit. Totally your husband's idea after his was destroyed." He handed her a grocery sack. "Here are your shoes. Best the techs could do quickly."

"I'm still against this idea. It's likely that the kidnapper will have a wand or something."

Heath raised an eyebrow. "Whatever it takes?"

"Right." She slipped both shoes on her feet. "It's worth the try. They may not actually be as smart as us."

"So what we did is clone your phones." Slate pointed to the two older versions. "If the kidnappers call your number instead of the phone they left, we'll still be covered. And just in case they allow you to keep the phones, we have you covered with a tracker. Reception begins at seven. Are you guys ready?"

"Give us a minute."

"Sure, man. I'll be in the van."

Heath waited for the door to click closed. He pulled both boots almost all the way on, then stood, slipping them on the rest of the way. When he was done, Kendall threw her arms around his shoulders.

"No matter what—" she kissed his cheek "—I love you and Skylar Dawn more than anything in my life. You two are the most important things in my life. The best things that ever happened to me."

"You took the words right from my heart."

Chapter Nineteen

"Want to dance?" Heath asked her to ease the tension be-ween not only everyone watching them, but the two of hem. With his injuries he could only sway. Kendall gen-ly wrapped her arms around his neck. Maybe they'd have a moment to finish talking about the thoughts that had un through his head while he'd been in the living room and van.

"Dammit, Heath, you can't take off like that," Slate said rom behind him.

They both ignored him. Kendall drew a deep breath and said, "I need to say something."

He looked at her seeing no one else. Beautiful eyes illed with tears but didn't overflow. Then she blinked hem away.

"I'm sorry."

"What?" He was confused. Why would she be sorry? He's the one who lost their daughter.

"Before you moved out, Mother told me she overheard you talking about our problems on the phone. I was angry you'd talk with someone else and not a counselor."

"Just Mom."

"I realize that now. I should have known."

"I should have told you."

They swayed into the middle of the temporary dance loor at a wedding reception they weren't supposed to be

attending. Thinking about wedding vows really hit him i
a vulnerable place. No way would he admit that to anyone
But the reminder did its job. Who was he to decide which
of their careers was more important?

If she'd have him…he would move to Portland. He ben
his head, kissing her neck sweetly, just to remind her h
was there. She tilted her face, her eyes closed. For a mo
ment he forgot where they were as his lips softly capture
hers. He meant it as a comforting kiss, almost a farewel
in case something happened to them.

But Kendall changed it. She kissed him longingly an
then drew away, breathless. His body was on fire from
the brief encounter.

"You shouldn't kiss me like that," he said into her hair

"Uh-huh," she mumbled with her head on his shoulder
her breath softly caressing the small hairs on his neck.

"I wish Skylar Dawn was safely at home. Then I coul
spin you around the dance floor until we forgot all ou
problems," Heath whispered in her ear. He turned and
brought her body closer still, holding the small of her back
firmly under his hands.

"I don't need a dance floor to forget," she said, barely
loud enough for him to hear. "I want to be a family again
Heath."

A tap on his shoulder stopped his reply. Slate inter
rupted, handing him a cell phone.

"It's on mute. But this is our guy. He called me instead
of the burner or either of you. He knew it would take u
longer to get a lock on him."

They all moved off the dance floor. Slate tactfully
blocked anyone from approaching so he could answer the
call in semi-private.

"This is Murray."

"Drop your phones in the lobby fountain. A cab's wait
ing for you. You have four minutes to be at the northwes

corner of Elm and Houston. Don't speak or signal the others with you at the reception. Keep the line open, Ranger Murray. You don't want to endanger your daughter."

"Where do we go?"

"I don't repeat myself, Ranger. Take this phone with you and don't disconnect. I'll be monitoring your progress to verify you're following my instructions. Drop your cells in the large fountain on your way out the door. You have four minutes."

The line went silent. Heath was careful not to push the end button. He grabbed Kendall's hand and pulled her toward the lobby.

"That was him?"

"Yeah. We have four minutes to get to Elm and Houston." He dropped the old cell Slate had given him into the fountain. Kendall took her fake phone from her clutch purse and did the same.

"Where are you going?"

He pushed through the revolving door and asked the doorman, "Do you have a cab waiting?"

"I have one for Heath and Kendall."

"That's us." Heath turned to her, pointing to the cell screen to show that the call was still active. "We agreed to do everything exactly as he said. We have four minutes to get there." He put his arm around her, tugging her close. "We might make it if we're lucky."

"One swipe with a wand and the shoes are blown," she whispered close to his ear in order not to be picked up by the phone.

"The guy told me Elm and Houston," the driver said. "Any particular corner?"

"Northwest. There's extra if you get us there in three minutes," Heath told the driver.

"No problem if you let me drop you. The actual corner requires me to circle 'round."

"Fine. Why did he give us only four minutes to get there?" he asked softly. He dropped a twenty on the front seat.

"He had to be watching us. Now we don't have time to contact any of the agencies watching us." Her eyes went to the cell in his hand.

"He told me not to disconnect." He listened to the phone. "Nothing. He's listening and keeping us from contacting anyone."

"He'll probably have another cell waiting for us. We'll jump to another location. He'll try to lose our tail before we can do anything about it. Did you recognize his voice? Could it be Marrone? A high-paid lawyer got him released."

"No, it was the same guy as this morning, but not Marrone."

In a louder voice Kendall asked the cab driver, "How far are we?"

"Just two more turns. You sure are in a hurry to see the grassy knoll."

"The grassy knoll?" they both asked.

"Yeah, man. Elm and Houston is where Kennedy got shot," said the cab driver.

"I didn't recognize the street names." Kendall pressed her fingers to her temple. "That means people, as in tourists."

"Very good, Ranger," said a distant voice and Heath brought Slate's phone to his ear again. "Continue on Elm. The phone's under the tracks. Don't forget to leave your partner's cell in the cab."

"This is going to sound strange, but we need to continue on Elm and be dropped on the other side of the rail overpass," Heath repeated to the cab driver.

"I can't stop there, man. It's a blind curve." The cabby stuck out his hand waiting for extra cash.

"Pull up on the sidewalk," Kendall told him. They left the cab and the phone. "What else did he say?"

The sky was clear, and he could see a few of the brightest stars in the sky. They crossed the dangerous street as fast as they could. Their four minutes were up.

"Hey!" a man shouted from the opposite side of six lanes. "Are you Heath and Kendall?"

"Yes!" they shouted across the busy six lanes of traffic.

"This guy on the phone said to head for the stairs back here." He lowered a cell onto the ledge and pointed toward the way they had come. "Damn. I'm calling the cops. That guy said he'd kill me if I didn't yell for you."

Avoiding oncoming traffic, they moved further into the underpass and ran across Commerce and Elm streets.

"Good grief, the stench." Kendall covered her nose with her hand.

"It smells like a hundred elephants from the circus relieved themselves."

"I can't believe you're making jokes."

"I thought I was being factual." He guided her along the narrow sidewalk toward the cell.

"We're sitting ducks, you know. The kidnapper has cut us off from our backup with all these one-way streets. We're on a dark walkway that might as well be a tunnel. The car trailing us passed without ever slowing down. We can't be sure they saw us at all."

They exited the semi-tunnel. How many times had he driven through here and not taken a serious look. They both drew clean air deep into their lungs. Heath searched Dealy Plaza on the edge of the city of Dallas. Very few people walked the sidewalks, but the kidnapper could be any one of them.

"How long 'til they realize we're not in the cab?" she asked.

"Until the cab stops for the FBI. Slate will be trailing

your shoes. They'll hang back long enough to make it loo
like they lost us."

The phone rang as they approached the ledge, makin
it easy to find.

"Walk north through the parking lot, turn east, cros
Houston Street, and follow the light rail on Pacifi
Avenue. Make your way to the West End Marketplac
Don't borrow any phone along the way, Murray. We'
watching."

"This way." Heath guided Kendall past a picket fenc
to the parking lot for the Kennedy Museum.

Mental pictures of President Kennedy's assassinatic
invaded his thoughts. If the kidnapper wanted to give the
a feeling of doom, he'd succeeded.

"He more than likely is watching us. What now?" sh
asked.

"We're to go to the West End."

They began the trek, following the kidnapper's instru
tions. The light rail street was closed to cars and had n
pedestrians.

"At least he can't hear us now," Heath said.

"You hope." She nodded toward the phone. "Try th
yet?"

"Password protected. I can answer, but can't dial."

"Figures." Kendall stepped around a shattered beer bo
tle. She grabbed his hand, causing him to stop and loo
at her. "Remember your promise to let me handle the kic
napper. You get Skylar Dawn to safety. That's the onl
thing you need to do."

His tug on her hand got her walking again. "That dres
is beautiful. I haven't seen you wear that since we had
night out three years ago. Wow. It's really been that long?

At his change of subject, she dropped his hand. "Yo
promised, Heath."

"Not exactly. I told you I wouldn't choose. Let's get
ere and find Skylar Dawn."

He caught her hand in his, seeking anyone out of the
rdinary. People walked in both directions. It was a beau-
ful spring evening to be strolling the West End. And it
eemed like everyone was.

They rounded a corner onto Market Street, which was
ull of people. They headed toward an open courtyard
here a band played. The phone rang, slicing through the
ull roar of the street noise. Before he could pull it from
is pocket, Kendall stepped in front of him.

"There is no choice, Heath. Skylar Dawn needs you. I
now how to handle this creep. Leave him to me."

Keeping his eyes on her face, he brought the phone to
is ear as it rang. "Yeah?"

"It is time to choose, Ranger. Your wife or your child."

"Where's Skylar Dawn?"

"She'll be safe for twenty more minutes."

"Damn it, man! What do you want?"

"Your wife. I can see you both. Send her to the Dallas
quarium. I'll call again to tell you where the girl is when
have your wife."

The line went dead.

"Did he say where Skylar Dawn is?"

He shook his head, frustration keeping him momen-
arily silent. "I'm supposed to stay here, wait for his call.
e'll let me know where to pick up Skylar Dawn after he
as you."

"Don't worry about me, Heath. I'm trusting you to find
ur daughter."

"He wants you to start walking toward the aquarium,"
e said, pointing behind her toward the building.

They'd taken Skylar Dawn there several times. Seeing
e endangered animals section was her second favorite
ing to do. The first was riding Stardust.

"You can do this." She squeezed his hand, pushing the phone to his chest.

"I'm not worried about me. He's…"

There wasn't enough time to explain what he wanted her to know. He should have answered her before they left the dance floor. She was walking straight into the hands of a madman, with a strong possibility they'd never see each other again.

"Come back to me, Kendall."

She turned to walk away, but he caught her off guard and pulled her into his arms. His lips claimed hers with the hunger of a starving man, the desperation of a defeated one. He'd never known a kiss so transparent. He'd never experienced a kiss filled with regret and longing. Regret for what might have been and longing for what might never be.

His wife pulled slowly away, her free hand cupping his cheek.

"I wish you had a gun or I could send backup. Something." His voice rose in frustration. "I can't just let you turn yourself over to him."

"He's watching. I've got to go, Heath. Find our girl."

She lifted his fingers from her arm and kissed him one last time. Then she put one foot in front of the other and walked away from him. Stopping himself from following was pretty much the hardest thing he'd done in his life.

Chapter Twenty

Heath stood there until she was out of sight. He shoved the phone in his back pocket then ran into the crowd gathered and enjoying a night out. A couple walked toward him and he didn't hesitate—no matter what the kidnapper had insinuated earlier.

"Excuse me, do you have a cell phone? This is an emergency. My daughter is missing."

"Oh my God. Here," the woman said as she handed him her phone.

"I can't tell you how much I appreciate this. Could we walk?" He didn't wait on an answer. Just turned and heard them follow. He dialed Wade's number on the woman's phone. "Come on, pick up," he murmured.

Continuing to move, he ignored the man trying to sell him a bouquet and hit End. He punched the number again. The couple continued to follow.

"Heath? Kendall?"

"The kidnapper split us up. He sent Kendall to the aquarium," he shouted into the phone, looking at the people around him. "Once he has her, he's calling a burner with my daughter's location. Get to the aquarium. Fast. I'll meet you there."

"Where are—"

He heard part of Wade's shout as he clicked the phone off.

"Thanks for your help." The phone was barely back in

the stranger's hand before he pushed his way through th
crowd, running to find his wife.

But she was gone. No bright red dress anywhere.

Nervous energy kept him running toward the aquariun
A van pulled up next to him.

"Get in!" Slate yelled. "We're tracking Kendall. She'
already heading north."

Heath jumped with his three friends and fellow Rang
ers. Then Slate pulled back into traffic. They were a bloc
away from where he'd been told to stay before he suddenl
remembered the phone in his back pocket needed to sta
put on that corner. "Pull over." Heath waved the phone a
his partners.

"What? Why?" the three Rangers shouted.

"Hell, he's probably tracking you through that thing.
Wade said, taking it from his hand.

"Once he has Kendall, he said he'd call and tell m
where Skylar Dawn is."

"Who do we go after? It's totally your call, man. Jerr
Fisher is standing by, along with a host of other FBI agents
Then we've got the Dallas PD. The other Company I
Rangers are posted around the city," Jack said.

"Whichever you choose, I'm with you. I'm your part
ner. We've got your back," Slate confirmed.

They wouldn't try to change his mind. Not about stayin
with him to find his daughter and not about chasing afte
Kendall. The team would do whatever he asked.

"I can stay here, wait on the call. That way the tracke
doesn't move," Jack suggested from the front seat.

"You might want this." Wade handed Heath an earpiec
communication device, a cell phone and a Glock.

"I can't do this. I can't choose." Heath was torn.

Wade looked at the tracker. "We've got a few minute
before we know where he's sent Kendall. But we don'
know what hoops he's going to make her jump through

I don't know if the tracker will remain intact. She might even ditch it herself. She was against it to begin with."

Kendall wanted him to rescue Skylar Dawn. He had to rescue them both. One without the other was still failure. How would his daughter ever forgive him if he let something happen to her mother? The Rangers didn't do failure.

Wade rested his hand on his shoulder. "What do you want us to do?"

"We're going after Kendall." He looked straight at Slate, handing him the phone. "I'm trusting you with my daughter's life."

"I won't let you down."

Thirteen minutes later they'd followed the tracker to the Galleria Mall. Slate had stayed behind with a plan to forward the call and for Heath to speak to the kidnappers himself. Then they wouldn't know he was closer to them than they'd hoped.

Wade dropped Jack, then he drove to the opposite end of the mall to drop Heath. The phone he'd given to Heath rang.

A text from Slate stated the company phone was set with the forwarded call and he should just answer it.

"Murray."

"Kendall has arrived, and I'm a man of my word. Your little girl loves roses as much as you do."

The phone disconnected.

"What happened? Where is she?" Heath yelled.

The phone rang again. "It's Slate. Do you know what he's talking about?"

"It...it has to be the house on Vandelia Street off Wycliff, where I caught Saundra Rosa. It has bloodred roses on the south side. Orange trim around the windows and doors."

"I'm closer. I'll take a police unit with me," Slate let them know.

"I should be there."

"Kendall needs you. I'll get Skylar Dawn. You can count on me."

Silence. Wade waited to move.

"The bastard didn't give any instructions. His real target has always been Kendall, just like we thought." Had he done the right thing?

"Let's go get her." Wade faced forward and put the van in gear.

Heath slammed the panel door and ran. He hoped and prayed his wife would forgive him for coming after her and leaving Skylar Dawn's rescue to another Ranger.

KENDALL STOPPED AT the mall entrance and threw her shoes in the trash. She didn't want to jeopardize anything by letting the Rangers rescue her before she had her daughter's location.

The private car had obviously been sent by the kidnappers. She'd been locked in. No borrowing the driver's phone or talking to him. After the car arrived, the driver had stood at his door to watch her go inside. He'd simply stated that her party would be on the fourth floor.

They knew she was here.

But so did the Rangers.

Now if she could just find another way to let them follow her. The only thing she had in her clutch was that tube of Cherry Bomb red lipstick and two five-dollar bills. She'd refused any fancy gadgets except the tracker in her shoes.

Barefoot and in a tight, short dress, there weren't too many options left. No bread crumbs to leave behind. She leaned on a post on the way to the escalators. Maybe there was something...

Taking the lipstick, she drew a thick *H* on her heel. *H* for Heath. It was worth a shot.

At the bottom of each level of escalators, she left a

Cherry Bomb *H*. At the top she'd limp to a bench, discretely reapply the lipstick and then limp to the next up escalator. When she pressed her heel, she left a red spot at each level.

Once on the fourth level, she reapplied and waited on the bench. Good thing she sat down. Her insides were jumping around, making her glad she hadn't eaten. What if Skylar Dawn hadn't eaten? She had to focus, be confident. The Rangers would rescue their daughter. Heath had promised. He never lied. Bringing down the kidnapper was her job. She could do this.

Please, Heath, find our baby.

Chapter Twenty-One

"Special Agent Barlow, you've lost your shoes. And you're limping."

When she turned her head, following the familiar voice, she had a moment of pure rage at his release from custody. The man who'd turned her life into a shambles sat beside her like her best friend. The gun sticking in her ribs came as little surprise.

"Bryan Marrone. Public Exposure sent their favorite lackey, I see. I guess I shouldn't have believed you were innocent yesterday." She didn't explain why she was barefoot. Maybe he hadn't seen her with the lipstick.

"True, Kendall. It didn't take much to avoid the cops and kill Saundra. She was a sweet kid, but enough with the pink already. I prefer a lady in red any day."

"I'll put you in jail this time and throw away the key. Where is my little girl? This was supposed to be an exchange of me for her. If anything's happened to her I'll—"

"Stop being so damn dramatic." He poked the gun into her ribs until she began moving to the side of the escalators. His jacket hung over his arm, hiding the gun. To onlookers, he looked like a polite escort with his hand on her back.

"Where's Skylar Dawn?"

"I told your husband." He pushed her toward an alcove. "Don't worry about her. Do as I say and nothing will happen."

"You phoned Heath? Is she here at the mall?" Why didn't Heath recognize this man's voice? "What do you get out of this? Who's in on this with you?"

"Do you actually expect me to tell you everything? I'm not stupid, Kendall. Move to your left. I need to pat you down."

Kendall moved as slowly as she could. The lipstick on her heel smeared a little on the floor. He yanked up her foot, looking at the light trail behind them.

"Dammit, Kendall." He snatched the lipstick from her purse and tossed it into the throng of people, then yanked her out of the group of shoppers. "Show me the bottom of your foot. Your attempt to leave a trail might really get you killed. Do you have any electronic devices that are going to make me angrier?"

"Of course not. We didn't have time." But she did have the side of her other foot. *Thank God.*

"And I'm supposed to believe you?" He rubbed his hands up and down her body. "You know, ever since you rubbed my leg I wanted to return the favor."

The shiver that crept up her spine was accompanied by acid from her stomach. Marrone's hands lingered over her breasts and hips. Her stomach soured more...if that was possible.

"Oh, wait. Our modern times make detecting electronic devices easy. Put your hands on your head."

There, in plain sight of dozens of people, he pulled an EMF detector from a backpack and waved the wand close to her body. He smiled and made lewd gestures at a couple of men, who snapped a picture or video.

"I knew you were a smart woman. You wouldn't do anything to jeopardize your daughter. Wipe your foot off. You sure you wouldn't prefer money over the cowboy?"

"Give me my daughter."

He'd made a mistake. One of these people would surely

post something to social media. That would help prosecute him. But more importantly, if he made one mistake, he'd make another. That's when she'd make her move, but she needed him to reveal where they were holding Skylar Dawn.

"Head toward the service hall. That way." He shoved her to a back entrance to some of the shops.

Kendall tried to think of ways to stall for time. Surely the Rangers had followed her, but there was no guarantee.

"What did you do with my daughter?"

"Your daughter is safer than you. Those freaks may be weird, but they aren't going to hurt a kid. It'll take some time for the Rangers to determine her whereabouts. Too bad the top brass wanted you out of the picture. I could have saved the day, been a real hero."

Skylar Dawn was okay? Not in danger? Before entering the service hallway, she spun to face him. "You know, every single time a creep on the other side of the table claims they do it for the money, it makes no sense to me. Please tell me there's more to this. Some great cause or reason."

"There's a cause. Huge cause. But you wouldn't understand." He jammed her side once again. She couldn't defend herself against the gun when it was this close. "Turn and walk, or I'll pull the trigger in spite of how long Brantley Lourdes wants this to last. Of course it's about the money."

"Public Exposure is paying you to keep me away from the investigation, and you don't really know anything?"

Another jab. Another sharp pain. "Walk."

His cool, unhurried attitude worried her. Did he really think she came alone? Why didn't *he* think that the Rangers would be here any minute?

HEATH SLAMMED THE entrance door into the wall and instantly drew the attention of everyone entering or exiting the high-end mall. "Damn. Sorry."

"Your wife tossed her shoes in the trash can," Wade

aid. "Just like we thought she would. They haven't moved ince we arrived."

Where would she be? It had taken three minutes after he tracker stopped for the kidnapper to spot Kendall be- ore he called back with his cryptic message. That was the nly clue they had. Skylar Dawn better be at that house.

"Where would he try to take her?" he mumbled, but his arpiece picked it up.

"We've got the closest exits to where she entered cov- red," Jack said.

"There's too many of them. We need more units," Wade dded.

"No. Units outside might put her in jeopardy. Kendall's mart. Look for something. Listen for anything unusual," Ieath told them.

The place was packed. Heath searched for a bright red ress on his way, but didn't see one. Lots of dresses, lots f suits, hats, boots, tennis shoes, shorts…but no bright ed dress or bare feet.

Maybe he could see from the top. Before he went to he next floor, he had to stop and catch his breath. *Damn ibs.* He leaned on a pole, his eyes scanning for someone vith no shoes. There on the floor was an *H.* He bent and viped the mark. Lipstick.

How many random *H*'s would be on the floor of a acked mall? It had to be Kendall. She'd left a trail of read crumbs…or red lipstick, in this case.

Several minutes behind her, he rushed as much as he ould without pushing people out of his way. If Kendall's rail played out, he might be able to catch up. He looked bove his head, barely able to see the escalators to the ext floor.

"Stall, Kendall. Stall."

Heath followed the *H* marks at the bottom of each es- alator. On the fourth floor, the lipstick led to the hallway with the elevators. "I'm on her trail, near the ice rink elevators. No doubts. I just don't know how far ahead they are.

After he punched the down button again, he slammed his fist into his hand, wishing he were hitting the maniac who had Kendall or Skylar Dawn. The thought of losing either of them forever propelled Heath on. He punched every button, tapping the wall, waiting for the doors to open, checking each floor for her now smeared lipstick mark.

By now they should have police units ready to move in. Hopefully. Except…there was a hotel and bar near taxis or ride-share pickups. Dammit. That was how this guy would leave. "Guys? He's heading for the hotel."

"Are you sure?" both asked.

"Yeah. There's no way he'd use his own vehicle. He's got Kendall for insurance, but he's already admitted he doesn't have Skylar Dawn."

There was no time to wait. The lipstick imprint had been getting fainter.

"YOU SEEM LIKE a smart guy, Marrone." Kendall slowed her pace again until he shoved her forward. "How in the world did you get mixed up with Public Exposure?"

Marrone yanked her around a corner. "Money. Lots of money. There really isn't any other reason. Some of those people are 'true believers'. Freaks. Just remember—I will pull this trigger. I can get away while they're trying to keep you alive."

"We could stop right now, if you'd like." The light quip accompanied by a forced smile took control to deliver. The horrifying hatred in his eyes didn't have her feeling lighthearted or in control.

Leaving the elevator, he gestured toward the men's restroom. Ahead of them, Kendall could hear the sounds of loud music and people. A bar? It should be packed at this time of night. The wheels turned furiously in her mind.

The small bathroom space was empty except for one man washing his hands. He left, giving Marrone a sly smile.

"Should I call you Marrone? *Perp, kidnapper* or *suspect* probably won't go over too well in public."

"Neither would blowing a hole in your gut." He leaned on the door. "I noticed you limping slightly. Heath give that to you while dancing?" he asked with a smirk.

"I'll be fine." She wasn't actually limping, but she wasn't about to correct the jerk. Rolling to the side of her foot, she occasionally left a mark of lipstick. It was her only hope that someone could follow them.

She wanted to scream at him to stop this stupid charade and tell her Skylar Dawn's location. The longing to see her baby girl again wouldn't allow her to lose it. Instead, she needed to get him talking, bragging, something to give her a clue where her daughter had been taken. Or what other men were involved.

"Well, you won't be feeling any pain in a few hours. You'll already be dead when people discover what Public Exposure is really up to. Before they bring Dallas to its knees with the destruction and mass casualties." He said it coldly, with no emotion, as if killing people was an everyday occurrence.

Kendall knew he spoke the truth…and believed it. "Just tell me where Skylar Dawn is. You can go. I won't say anything to Heath or anyone else."

"In the last stall you'll find some clothing. Please leave the door open and change." He made a grand gesture like a butler, then backed up against the door again to keep others out.

The sloppy T-shirt wasn't too bad. The overalls were very large and made moving her legs difficult. The dirty-blond wig needed a good shampoo and brushing. She left the cherry-red dress on the stall door. As she emerged, he dangled a pair of handcuffs in one hand.

"Are the cuffs really necessary?"

He tossed them at her. She felt like an idiot snapping them on herself.

"Most definitely. Consider it payback." He pulled a small sweater from his pack. "Cover the handcuffs. wouldn't want to alarm any of the patrons."

The door opened and she stumbled as he pushed her through. Angry enough to take off his head, she had to calm down and think. She had to stop him before he could escape. She couldn't trust he told Heath the truth. If he hadn't they may never find their daughter.

The hotel bar was crowded and dark. People were squished together, attempting to get from one side of the bar to the other. It slowed their progression, giving her a chance to work on Marrone.

"You should be in a hurry," she said, attempting to sound completely confident. "The Texas Rangers are prob ably hot on our trail."

The loud music didn't drown his demonic laugh. Kend all wouldn't allow it to upset her. She used it to strengthen her resolve instead. This was the last time the creep would harm anyone.

Before he shoved her into another person to get her walking again, she made her move. She waved, then shouted, "Over here!"

He snatched her wrist from the air.

Pulling him forward, she kneed his groin hard enough to make the manliest of men cry. As he doubled over, she brought her knee up under his chin, throwing his head backward. His arm tangled in the links of the cuffs and caused him to bring her to the floor with him.

Several people cushioned their fall. Everything in the bar ground to a halt. She tried to push him from her, but he brought her hand across her throat, pressing the metal against her windpipe. By grasping the cuffs, he successfully held her, and then hit her temple with the butt of the gun.

With an excited smile forming on his thin lips, he pressed the barrel next to her ear. "That wasn't very nice, Kendall. Come with me or I open fire."

Still dazed, she allowed him to pull her to her feet. She splayed her hands and warned the men approaching, "Stay back. He'll shoot you. Stay back."

"Let the lady go!"

They both crashed back to the floor. She hadn't gotten a look at what—or who—had hit them. Through a fog, she saw a man in a black suit lift Marrone off her and raise his fist.

Heath. He'd found her. Thank God for Cherry Bomb red lipstick. He landed his punch, sending Marrone crashing into a table.

Wait! Why was Heath here? The music still blared and the lights from the dance floor flashed, but most of the women were watching Heath.

She didn't blame them. She liked watching him, too. The attempt at standing didn't work well. She settled for leaning on an elbow and watching her husband work.

"Did they find Skylar Dawn? Where's the gun? It must have gone flying."

"You okay?" he asked her.

Heath lifted Marrone by his shirt collar but let him crumple back to the floor. Heath knelt and frisked him. "He's out cold. No keys. Just a cell phone."

"We got him covered for you," a man with the bar's logo on his T-shirt said. "He ain't going anywhere. Look after your girlfriend."

"Wife." Heath yanked Marrone's backpack off finding nothing of importance.

"You sure did give him what for," someone said, slapping him on the back.

Another man with the bar's logo rolled Marrone face-down and cuffed his hands behind his back. "I knew these would come in handy one day." He grinned. "I called the cops."

Heath flipped Marrone's phone open. "Dammit. Needs a password."

"Nice flying tackle, man. She need an ambulance?" the bartender asked, pointing to Kendall.

"Can you sit up? You okay, honey?" He helped her lean against him. "Helluva stall there, Kendall. Your eye's already swelling."

"You haven't answered me, Heath. You were supposed to get our daughter. Did you find her? Is she safe?"

All the adrenaline left her body with just his look. His rescuing of her would mean nothing without their daughter. Panic pulled her fully to her senses.

"Oh my God. Wake him up and do whatever's necessary to him. We have to find out where they've taken her."

Security guards entered the bar. "Everyone stay where you are."

"He gave us a clue. Slate's heading there along with Jason's DPD units. We should know any minute. Just rest and I'll get us out of here." He kissed her quickly and stood.

"You should have gone for her."

"I'll explain later." He grabbed his broken ribs and sucked air through his teeth, hissing.

But he wasn't the snake. Brantley Lourdes and all of Public Exposure were the cold-blooded creatures who had taken their little girl.

"We're going to be a family again, Kendall. I didn't get to answer you before. Take the transfer to Portland. If that's what you want…then go for it. I'll come with you and stay home with Skylar Dawn until she's okay. We'll figure out how to do this."

Chapter Twenty-Two

Heath handed the phone to Kendall. The next phone call would be the most important of his life. The seconds ticked by as they waited. Wade arrived and then Jack, who swiped on his phone as he came through the bar door.

"Major Clements hasn't heard anything either," Jack said.

The phone rang with an old-fashioned bell. Heath froze. They all did except Kendall. She answered and immediately switched to speaker.

"I've got her. Skylar Dawn is safe and unharmed."

He heard the words and sank to the floor next to Kendall. No matter what their status—separated, together or moving—they were both her parents.

"Man, that was intense," Wade said, relieving a little of the tension.

Heath helped Kendall to her feet. "Let's go get our daughter." Then he looked at Wade and stuck out his hand.

"Here's your badge. I thought you might need it." Wade placed it in Heath's palm.

Then Jack nudged Wade. "Keys. He's waiting for our ride. But it might be faster if you bring it around to the bar's outdoor entrance. In their shape, it might take them an hour to walk to wherever you parked."

"Good idea," Heath and Kendall both answered.

"Let me get you some ice." Jack headed behind the ba▸ to the men who had helped earlier.

"Your eye's going to be spectacular."

"Why did you come after me, Heath? You were sup▸ posed to save Skylar Dawn."

"We did save her. I told you I wouldn't choose. I ac▸ cepted a plan that worked to save you both."

"What if it hadn't worked?" Kendall's eyes filled with tears.

He wanted to hold her, not debate his decision. He'▸ argued with himself every step of the way to finding her▸ What if this…what if that…

"I won't argue about it. You're both safe. That's the only outcome I need to think about."

Jack gave her a bar towel full of ice for the side of he▸ head. Kendall was in good hands. Heath walked away straight through the outer doors to wait on the sidewalk▸ Now wasn't the time to disagree. He needed air. He showed his badge and found the Dallas PD.

"A white panel van is on its way to pick me up. Ca▸ you make sure someone lets it into the drop-off circle▸ Thanks."

He was resting on a short cement barrier, when a set o▸ very lovely arms wrapped around his chest.

"I'm sorry." She kissed his neck. "And I'm grateful.▸ She kissed the other side of his neck then moved around t▸ look him in the eye. "And you're right." She took his han▸ between her own. "We're safe. That's all that matters."

Jack joined them and Wade pulled around. The min▸ utes seemed like hours until the van pulled onto Vandeli▸ Street. Kendall jumped out, meeting Slate for the handoff▸ Heath moved a little slower, but was right there in time t▸ answer Skylar Dawn's questions.

"I lost my hat, Daddy."

"Mommy found it, baby. It's okay."

"That mean man didn't hurt Stardust, did he?"

"Nope. She's safe and sound with her momma. Just like ou." He kissed her forehead. "Let's go home."

"Can we go to McDonald's first? All those people had vere carrot sticks."

"Sure, baby, we can do that. Let's go home."

'OH, MY DARLINGS. I can't believe everything turned out okay," Naomi said as they came through the door. She ugged them all. Even Heath. "She is okay, right?"

"Maybe a little dirty and in the same clothes, but she's ine." Heath wouldn't let his mother-in-law take his girl rom his arms.

"I'll run a bath." Naomi ran from the room, a tissue covering her mouth.

"I'm not telling her to leave tonight."

"I didn't ask you to. It's safer if she stays here, with the vatchdogs out front."

"What do you think?" Kendall asked, looking away from he Rangers' unmarked cars sitting in front of the house.

"We can rest easy. No one's getting through all the Texas Rangers parked around this house."

"No, I meant…" She gently lifted a strand of hair from Skylar Dawn's face and looped it around a cute little ear.

"We've both had the training, sweetheart," he whispered. 'You know that we need to find her a good counselor, talk his out, answer her questions. But from what she's said, hey dropped her off at that house and she played."

They caved and let Naomi give her a bath, parking hemselves at the open door. Skylar Dawn had lots of bub-bles to play with. His mother-in-law would have a mess to clean up, but no one cared.

"I keep going over what Marrone said." Kendall backed up to his chest and lifted her mouth so he could hear her lowered voice. "I thought at the time, this was all a plan to get me out of the picture."

"That was my first thought when he gave me the location to pick our girl up."

"Whatever Public Exposure has been working on, it's happening soon. Marrone said there would be mass casualties. I need to talk with him."

"Call Jerry. Let him handle it. She needs us both right now."

She looped her arms carefully around his neck. "I need you both, too. Maybe you should shower while I get her dried off and dressed for bed."

A breath separated their faces. He wanted to kiss her. He shouldn't kiss her. He was dying to kiss her.

He kissed her.

And she definitely kissed him back.

The perfect fit. The perfect taste. He slipped into the memory of her in his arms, in a sexy sparkly dress with a strap that didn't want to stay on her shoulder. He'd wanted to kiss her from the moment their eyes had met. Even on an investigation, he hadn't waited long. Before the week's end, they were in each other's arms, close enough to melt into the other's soul.

Tonight was no different. It was as if the years had all slipped away last night. His body felt alive again, on fire. He wanted her badly enough that it ached.

A caress across his face slipped down to his shoulders and pressed him away. But his last intention was to stop. They had been close to losing everything. He needed more of her, craved more from her lips. Desire was like an infection in his blood, surging with every pulsing beat of his heart.

But a small giggle from Skylar Dawn reined in his longing. She was laughing at them. They drifted slightly apart then he lifted her between them.

"I'll only be a minute."

He laid loud, sloppy kisses on both their foreheads and transferred their daughter to his wife. No matter what… they were a family.

KENDALL USED A giant fluffy towel to cover Skylar Dawn. She put her in pink pj's and braided her hair after brushing it. By the time she was finished, Heath was done and had collected *The Wizard of Oz* from the living room where they'd left it.

She heard Heath begin reading and jumped in the shower. He'd taken a cloth and a bottle of water, then washed her feet clean while they'd waited on transport home.

Scrubbing hard, she scoured every place the filthy Bryan Marrone had touched her, then tossed the exfoliating sponge in the trash. Maybe it was a good thing they wouldn't see him tonight. She might tear his head off for what he'd done.

Tomorrow was soon enough.

She dressed and braided her own hair before slipping into bed with the loves of her life. Then the what-ifs began. Heath's arm was around Skylar Dawn, and he slipped his fingers through hers.

"You can't do that to yourself," Heath whispered. "No one's to blame. We're good. All safe and sound."

How did he even know she blamed herself? Maybe because he'd already had time to do the same?

"It's no one's fault. I…"

"Kendall," he squeezed her hand, "we deal with this tomorrow. Not tonight. Maybe for a while we can just forget."

"You're right," she said, staring at the ceiling.

"Again?" He laughed softly. "This being right thing goes straight to my head. I think I like it."

"Shh, you'll wake the baby." She used her free hand to tuck the light blanket around her little girl's shoulders.

"She's not such a baby anymore," Heath whispered again. "Her birthday's just around the corner. Get some sleep."

He turned off the headboard lamp. She closed her eyes and tried—really tried—to sleep. It didn't work. She switched on the HISTORY channel, clicked the mute button and tried again. She was still wide awake.

The TV glowed, casting eerie shadows over the garment bag. It hung over the chair Heath had sat in only last night. She rolled to her back, stretching muscles she'd forgotten she had.

The room suddenly went dark. She swallowed the moment of blind panic, preparing for an attack.

It took a minute for her to realize she'd moved against the remote, clicking the off button. She wished she could laugh. There was no immediate threat, but for a split second, terror—a too-familiar and unwelcome emotion—had suppressed her intelligence. She cautiously moved from under the covers.

Public Exposure would make a move soon. She hated not doing anything, but their daughter needed them. Needed to know that she was safe.

But was she? Public Exposure was still out there. Planning.

Was anyone safe? Was Marrone telling the truth about a catastrophe? If he was, there weren't many hours left to get the details from him. Who was working on it? Would he talk to them? She should be there, watching the interrogation. It might trigger something she'd forgotten.

Kendall couldn't sleep. She tried to place bits of information into logical categories in her mind. But her mind had other plans. It kept burning the image of Heath's face on the backs of her eyelids.

The image of him smiling as he got on one knee and proposed. He really was gorgeous. Possibly the most handsome man she'd ever met. Her cowboy. It didn't seem possible he could have grown more handsome, but he had.

Some of the cockiness she'd noticed during their first assignment together was gone. Strange how she missed it. Maybe not strange, since she hadn't thought about working with him in years. But he was much more than that. Even though she'd withheld answers, he'd accepted and offered his help.

Skylar Dawn was so much like him. She had his eyes, his thick hair and that cute little attitude when she slipped on a pair of Western boots. Even the way she stubbornly held her mouth. On Heath it was sexy. But on her darling little girl, it had always been a constant reminder of who her father was.

God, she missed being a real family.

Before she'd met Heath, the closest she'd gotten to settling down was having the same apartment for more than six months. Her mother had encouraged her every step of the way, and she'd accepted the help. But the looks her mom had been sending Heath's way this week were wrong. It was time for Naomi Barlow to accept her son-in-law.

If she wanted her life back—and she did—Heath and her daughter had to come first. She just couldn't imagine life without Skylar Dawn. And the past six months proved life without Heath wasn't a life either. She'd been simply existing. Not living.

In order to protect them both, so they could get on with living properly, she couldn't dwell on what their future might be. She needed to determine who had attempted to kill her...and why. Then catch the bastard before he succeeded.

They had a life to live.

Chapter Twenty-Three

Giggles and the smell of strong coffee awoke Kendall—followed by her daughter's attempt to sneak back into bed. Then came lots more giggles and a few shushes from Heath.

"Ready?" her husband whispered. "One. Two. Three."

"Surprise!" Skylar Dawn shouted in her sweet voice. "Wake up, Mommy. We made toast and omelets."

"Oh my goodness." Kendall pushed pillows behind to prop herself up.

Heath set the tray across her lap, immediately moving the hot coffee to her bedside table. Skylar Dawn twisted around on her knees, grabbed Heath's pillow and carefully plumped it behind her to match her mommy's.

They all sat in bed eating off the same plate until Kendall took a sip from her mug.

"We forgot my coffee, Daddy. My, my, my, what are we going to do with you?"

The "my, my, my" belonged to Skylar Dawn's grandmother and was flawlessly reenacted. Her husband carefully moved from the bed so he wouldn't disturb the tray of food. He bent at the waist and began backing out of the bedroom.

"Your wish is my command."

Coffee for their daughter came as warm cocoa. It had to be in a mug that matched her parents'. Skylar Daw eached across her and fiddled with the paper towel Kendall used as a napkin. She took her own and tucked it into xactly the same place on her pajamas.

"Do you want cotton jelly for the toast, sweetie?"

"Yes, please."

Kendall handed her the jelly-covered bread. The exhange went a little wonky, the toast flipping jelly-side own from Skylar Dawn's hands. It made a mess on the omforter they had draped over their laps.

"Oh furgle, furgle, furgle."

Kendall's heart stopped. *Jerry?* Her daughter was imiating a man she'd never met?

"Where did you hear that?" She turned to her daughter o fast it scared her.

"I'm sorry. I'm sorry." She began crying and grabbed endall's arm. "I know I wasn't supposed to tell anything."

"What's happened? She okay?" Heath asked, returning the room and setting down the cocoa.

"I didn't mean to scare you, sweetie. I'm not mad." endall pushed the tray past her feet to the end of the bed.

"They said I couldn't ever tell or we'd get hurt. Bad urt."

She held on to her daughter, wanting to forget everying. But she couldn't. *Those bastards.* "They can't hurt s, honey. I—I—I promise. Just tell me where you heard at word, okay?"

"I don't know. I think it was the house." Skylar Dawn niffed.

"What house?" Heath asked.

"The one I didn't like. Please don't make me go back." he turned and buried her face in her daddy's chest, then ulled the covers over her head. "I'm sorry. I won't say it gain. Promise."

"It's okay, baby. No one's making you go anywhere. ou'll stay right here with us."

Heath looked over their hidden daughter's shape. Kend all moved her breakfast to the bedside table, then scoote close to her family. She and Heath soothed Skylar Daw until she fell back to sleep. Heath tucked her in tight an nodded his head toward the doorway. Kendall joined hir at the open door.

"I promised Skylar Dawn she wouldn't be alone." H lowered his deep voice. "Will you wake your mom up t sit with her while we talk about this?"

"I should check in and see if they've discovered any thing." Her mind was spinning. *Jerry? How could that be*

"Check in with who, Kendall? The only man we know who says *furgle*?"

"There has to be a different explanation. What if sh heard it after he arrived? He's an FBI agent and used t be my partner. He can't be dirty."

"Agents can be bought just as easily as a store clerk Who better to point your investigation in the wrong di rection?"

She turned her face into his chest. "He knew ever move we were making. Oh my God, Heath. Jerry kid napped our baby. What are we going to do?"

"We're going to send that bastard to jail."

"How? Who's going to believe us?"

"We'll need a plan."

"Still, Heath. We have no real evidence. How can w convince someone he's responsible because our daughte learned a new word?"

He pulled her into his arms, surrounding her in lov and confidence.

"I know three men who won't hesitate to have faith."

Chapter Twenty-Four

With another long day ahead of them, Wade wished he had someone to call and talk to, like his fellow Rangers. Maybe it was because his three best friends each had a special someone now. He had watched Skylar Dawn go into her mother's arms and wanted…something. Anything.

"He's quitting," Slate announced as he walked through the office door.

"Who are you talking about?" Jack asked, right behind him.

"You mean Heath," Wade tried to confirm.

"Yes, I mean Heath. The guy I've been calling partner since I came to Company B."

"This is about you?" Jack said. "Not the fact that he almost lost his daughter and wife?"

"It's not for personal reasons." Slate sat on the corner of Jack's desk, looking at everyone around them. "Kendall has an offer in Portland, and he told her he'd quit the Rangers."

"How do you know this?" Major Clements asked, coming from his office.

"He said it to her after he knocked Marrone what's-his-face on his back."

"Through his comm? That was private." Jack frowned.

"I can't help it if you guys didn't listen after they left the club and I did." Slate shrugged.

"You're not supposed to know this. He hasn't resigned yet, Slate." Major Clements waved everyone back to work. "It ain't over until he actually does it."

"Yeah, he's going to. I know how much he wants to be with Kendall and Skylar Dawn. He's been moping around here for six months," Slate said.

"Hell, you're the one who's been complaining about how horrible he's been acting." Jack replied by pushing Slate off his desk.

"We have work to do, boys. We still need to find out what Public Exposure is up to. Why did they need Kendall out of the way? What had she discovered, and why did Bryan Marrone say a lot of people would be finding out what they were all about? Do we have a ticking clock?"

"As in a bomb or something?" Slate asked.

"We have no idea when, or if, this threat is actually going to occur." Jack began looking at his computer. "How are we going to narrow down what this event could be?"

"Right," Wade said.

"So we have access to Kendall's notes?" Major Clements paced between the desks.

"I don't, but I think we have something better now." He pointed at the door, and the couple who should have been at home.

"What the hell are they doing here?" their commander semi-yelled, but hugged Heath and Kendall as they entered. "We're glad you two have Skylar Dawn back safely. You guys should be home with her. We've got this covered."

"She's actually bouncing back pretty well. And she's in excellent hands. Josh and Tracey Parker brought their twins up to play." Heath wrapped his arm around Kendall's shoulders. She didn't pull away.

"Actually, Tracey brought the twins. Josh brought three Company F Rangers. They're at the house and not leav-

ng until this is all behind us." Kendall laced her fingers
with Heath's free hand.

Wade leaned back in his chair. The question on his
mind was which Ranger called which Ranger. Josh offering to keep an eye on them was probably a safe bet. He
probably didn't count on both Heath and Kendall coming
back to the case.

"Why do you think we can't handle this without you?
And why didn't you take this to the FBI since it's your case,
Kendall?" Wade crossed his arms, waiting for the bomb.

"Because the FBI is in on it." Kendall dropped the
words like an explosion.

"My office. Now," Major Clements commanded. "Slate,
bring chairs for these two."

Wade grabbed the back of Heath's rolling chair, and
Slate grabbed his own. They exchanged glances, and true
to form, Slate smiled—most likely at the possibility of
saving someone. He loved to be a hero.

In the major's office, Heath didn't hesitate to sit. The
beating he'd taken trying to protect his daughter had left
him with two broken ribs and a hell of a lot of bruises.

Kendall waved off the chair and rubbed her bruising
cheekbone. "I prefer to stand, thanks."

The last one inside the office, Jack closed the door.
"Maybe you guys should start at the beginning."

"Agreed," Major Clements said.

"For months I've wondered how Public Exposure always seemed to be one step ahead of me. I could never get
a break." Kendall paced, but kept her eyes on the major.
"I was handed this case by my former partner. He'd been
monitoring it, but kept saying nothing was there as the
complaints grew. There was an immediate reluctance to
give me resources or support."

The major sat on the corner of his desk. He'd known
Kendall almost as long as they all had. He'd been at the

wedding and at the hospital when Skylar Dawn was born
He'd cursed right along with all of them when she'd been
kidnapped.

Wade didn't have to wonder if everyone believed Kend
all. All they were waiting for was enough proof to act on it

"I know now that Jerry Fisher, the supervisory spe
cial agent, asked to waive the conflict of interest
regarding Heath helping the task force," the major said.

"He bet on us being at each other's throats and not mak
ing any progress," Heath said.

"Right. The thing is—" Kendall looked at him with ad
miration and love "—Heath's a damn good detective. We
made headway that Jerry wasn't counting on. That's why
he arranged to distract us by abducting Skylar Dawn."

"Distract?" Jack asked.

"Heath said from the beginning he thought the whol
thing was a ruse to really get Kendall," Slate said.

"It was. Bryan Marrone stated he was instructed to keep
me under wraps—"

"Or dead," Heath interrupted.

"—or dead," Kendall agreed.

"Other than his assignments, you haven't mentione
why you think Supervisory Special Agent Fisher is work
ing with Public Exposure," the major pointed out.

"This is the part that's really thin." Heath wrapped his
arm around his midsection and took a deep breath.

He and Kendall looked at each other. "Paper-thin," she
agreed.

"Skylar Dawn has a habit of mimicking people she'
around." Heath twisted in his seat to make eye contact
with everyone. "For instance, she says 'my, my, my,' when
imitating my mother-in-law. Or 'that's a relief,' which is
something Kendall says."

"That's true. She even does my mom and dad after rid
ing," Slate threw out.

"She hasn't been around Jerry since she was born. He's never been to the house. I've never taken her to work," said Kendall.

"And what's she saying now?" the major asked.

Kendall moved to stand behind Heath again. "Furgle."

"Paper-thin," Major Clements mumbled. Then he looked straight at the couple. "We can't march into the FBI headquarters and arrest a man because he says 'furgle'. What does that even mean?"

"I'll let you look that up, Major. It's an obscure word from *Catch-22*."

Heath stood. "Agreed, sir. But without him," he continued, "my family isn't going to be safe. I believe Marrone knows something, but I also think he'll never tell us. He talks about freaks being true believers. Yet he's bought into whatever they're selling."

"We know we're the only people who can get Special Agent Fisher to admit he was behind the kidnapping." Kendall moved to stand closer to the major. "He was one of three people who knew where Heath was on Friday. I remembered that early this morning. The other two are in this room. Slate wouldn't even tell *me*."

"In my defense, Heath asked me not to."

"I appreciate your loyalty. Even if it almost got my husband killed." Kendall laughed halfheartedly.

At least she could joke about it. Things could have gone in an entirely different direction if Slate hadn't called his mom to check on Heath and Skylar Dawn.

"Paper-thin," Major Clements said again. "If we get the warrant to search Special Agent Fisher's apartment for a device to read the flash drive…then and only then will we move forward."

"I suppose you two have already determined a plan of action?" Jack asked.

They both nodded. Kendall put her hands on Heath's shoulders. It was good to see them together. Really together.

"Kendall and I will go to his apartment and see if we can find the information," Heath began. "I could grab the devices, but then the encryption key might also be in the apartment—we'll have to make sure the warrant covers looking through items, etcetera."

"You don't need to do this. Any of us can plug in a flash drive," Slate said.

"When it comes to computers, I'm the best this Company B's got. You've all come to me for help. Sorry, but I'm not leaving it to one of you guys."

"Now all we need is the flash drive," Slate said. "There's no way Jerry will relinquish that into our custody," he added.

"I think I know a way." Kendall paused, and everyone looked in her direction. She looked only at Heath. "I didn't have a chance to tell you that the Public Exposure case has been moved to another agency. The agent in charge said she'd work with me if possible."

"Great. How do you contact her?"

"I'll need to contact Assistant Special Agent in Charge Steve Woods, and hopefully he'll tell Agent Ortis to contact me."

Agent Ortis? It couldn't be the same woman. The rest of the planning had lots of discussion and objections on both sides. Wade didn't hear much of it, until Slate punched him in the arm.

"What's up with you?" he asked behind a cupped hand. "Are you really going to let these two go after yesterday? That's a good idea?"

"Was I able to stop you or Jack from finishing what you started with your girlfriends? This is Heath's wife, his daughter. If he can walk, he's going to see it to the end."

Everyone looked at him. Yeah, everyone in the office had heard him.

"Damn straight," said Heath, Kendall and Jack while Major Clements nodded.

Wade leaned against the door, waiting. He opened it for Kendall when she stepped out to call Woods, and he stayed in the doorway of the break room while she dialed. She raised an eyebrow, silently asking if he wanted something. He did.

He couldn't think straight until he knew if this Agent Ortis was the Therese he'd been looking for since last year.

Kendall finished up with a smile on her face. "He's going to pass along the plan and see if they go for it. He wasn't surprised about Jerry. I wonder if they already knew."

"It might make the warrant easier if they did."

She pointed her finger toward the major's office. "Is there something else?"

"First…is Skylar Dawn okay? Do you guys need anything? I could watch the house after Company F leaves."

"We'll have to see, but thank you. Today, my mother promised to spend every minute with her. I think she's okay. Josh Parker's twins were kidnapped, and they took them to a counselor. They're calling a couple of people for recommendation."

"That's good. That's good." He scratched his chin while Kendall looked at him strangely. "This might seem out of the blue but I was wondering…is the agent who took over the case *Therese* Ortis?"

"Yes, do you know her?"

"I believe we've met a couple of times."

"Small world, isn't it?" She scooted past him. "I should get back in there. Special Agent Woods said he'd have an answer pretty soon."

She turned around a few feet from him. "Would you like me to tell her to give you a call? That is, if I see her. She seemed a little on the top secret side."

"No. No. That's okay. She knows how to find me."

Chapter Twenty-Five

Kendall entered Jerry's high-rise apartment building and issued the warrant to the supervisor. Heath entered covertly through the basement. They each took a different way to Jerry's apartment door. Major Clements was meeting with Steve Woods at the Dallas field office.

None of her coworkers had known the details of how they'd gotten Skylar Dawn back. They had to be right. It had to be Jerry. Therese hadn't reacted with surprise, and had been instrumental with the warrants coming through so quickly.

Everything inside Kendall told her Jerry worked for Public Exposure. It hadn't been easy, but they'd managed to get through most of the morning without tipping him off. Hopefully.

"We're keeping it quiet," Heath reminded her. "Remember, if he comes back before we're done, we wait for backup. No heroics. And no bashing the jerk's head in for what he did."

"Are you reminding me or you? Public Exposure can't know we've got him. I agreed to the plan, Heath. I'm fine with it. Even if I want to rip the man's head from his shoulders."

Once inside the apartment, the laptop was in plain sight. The password took a little longer to find. Heath pulled out desk drawers and looked on the bottom of small statues.

in holders, the stapler and tape dispenser until he found he current version inside a notebook.

"How did you—"

"A guess. He seems like the kind of guy who would use omething complicated. But he doesn't seem like the type vho can keep it in his head."

He began to access the information on Jerry's computer. he touched his shoulder before leaning in close to see vhat he found. With each screen, she was sure they were etting closer to arresting one of the men responsible for idnapping their daughter.

"There it is," he said with an exaggerated sigh.

"That's a direct email from Brantley Lourdes. We've ot him." She almost giggled in delight. "Are there any thers?"

A noise in the hallway brought her back to earth super ast.

"Dammit. That's a key. Make the call."

Heath dialed his phone, connecting with Wade.

"What are you doing in here?" Jerry said as soon as the oor swung wide. "I thought you were giving your state- ents. Why are you on my laptop?"

Kendall looked at her friend, her boss, her former part- er. There wasn't any reason to pretend. Not any longer. Why?"

"Why what?" Jerry asked innocently. But the recogni- on was there in his eyes. He knew they were on to him. You have no right to be in my home."

Heath nodded in her direction, poised to plug in the lash drive. Hopefully the laptop would decrypt the file.

"Actually we have a warrant for your personal computer nd cell phone, and to search your residence. Someone's t your office." She stuck out her left hand, leaving her ight on her Glock. "I think I'll take your weapon while m at it."

"Slow down, Kendall. Are you going to arrest me? O
what charge? You have no proof anything's been done,
Jerry spouted as he looked back into the hallway.

Maybe. But at least with those words he sounded guilt

Kendall flexed her fingers for him to hand over hi
weapon. "Heath and I already tossed a coin to see wh
took you down. Too bad for you that I won. Hand it over–
now. Or I'll drop your face onto this expensive Italian tile.

Heath pulled his weapon.

"Okay. Okay." Jerry raised his hands.

"You messed up, Jerry," she told him. "While I wa
waiting on Heath to call me yesterday morning, you inte
rupted my phone call to Company B. You pointedly aske
where I thought he was. You were the reason I stayed at th
office instead of looking for him. And then you insiste
on driving me to the ranch putting you at the scene so yo
could plant the phone."

"You're right, babe. But I think Jerry's smart enough t
know that's all circumstantial. But wait," Heath nodde
"As hard as you might have tried, there was a fingerprin
on the cell phone left on Stardust."

"Not yours, unfortunately," Kendall continued. "Th
kid who placed the SIM card inside and activated the bogu
account? Turns out he's in the system and was oh too will
ing to pick you out of a photo lineup."

They might have been gloating. Just a little. But the
had a right to be proud for doing their job. Both of the
could have stayed home. They could have buried thei
heads under the covers and just been thankful they wer
all alive.

That wasn't what men like Heath did. Because he wa
a better man, he made her a better person, too.

"I really don't understand how you got into bed with th
vile piece of slime. You stole my daughter, Jerry." She a

anced a step, really wanting to plant his face in the floor. 'Hand over your gun or I'll consider it resisting."

"Don't do anything stupid, Kendall." Jerry splayed is hands. He drew back his jacket and took his service veapon from its holster with two fingers. "There's defi-itely been a mistake."

"We know you were one of the kidnappers."

"Skylar Dawn mimicked your idiotic use of *furgle*," Heath threw out. "Got it. I'll have files open any minute. The file might take longer."

"Okay, okay. I was hired by Brantley Lourdes. You hould be thanking me for saving her. They wanted you oth to disappear. At least I put the kid someplace safe."

"She was safe with me." Heath stepped from around he desk.

"We've got him, Heath. All of them."

"I don't think you know exactly who or what you're up gainst. This won't end with you taking me to the Bureau. Public Exposure is bigger than Brantley Lourdes."

"Save it for later." She took handcuffs from her jacket ocket. "We'll nail Brantley Lourdes *and* Public Exposure. You should start worrying about the deal you're going to roker."

He turned around, but only one hand came behind his ack. Before she could say furgle, he'd reached out and grabbed a hidden snub nose revolver. He spun again, aim-ng it at her head.

"Drop it, Heath. Or I swear I will shoot out her con-rol center and your kid will have a vegetable for a mom f she's not six feet under."

Heath dropped his gun on the desk.

"Now, pull the flash drive and join your wife." He di-ected them toward the open door. "Uh-uh. Keep those ands up."

Their backup would be there any minute. But Heath's

phone that was relaying all the information to them wa
still on the desk. Moving as slowly as possible, they mad
it to the elevator.

"How could you have betrayed us? Betrayed your coun
try?"

"There you go getting all dramatic again, Kendall
Money, and knowing where the nonextradition countrie
are." Jerry laughed. "Basically lots of money."

Heath looked from Jerry to her and reluctantly backe
onto the elevator when the doors opened. Standing clos
est to the panel, Jerry pushed a button, and then pulled
second gun strapped around his ankle to point directly a
Heath's chest.

"No." She moved between Heath and the barrel. Jerr
might be reluctant to shoot her, but not her husband.

The elevator began its descent. Heath's hands were o
her shoulders, trying to push her to the side. She stoo
firm.

This was her fault. She hadn't cuffed him soon enough
Could he get to the second Beretta under her jacket she'
put there for just this reason? She crossed her arms to dis
guise any movement he might make.

"Don't try it. Keep your hands up exactly where I ca
see them, Heath. Turn around and put your hands on hi
shoulders, Kendall." Jerry held his gun steady.

She turned her back to the traitor and held Heath
steady gaze. The pressure in his hands exuded trust an
confidence. Jerry pulled her gun and his cell, then stuc
his snub nose into her back. She continued to look int
her love's eyes.

"What are you going to do when we get to the groun
floor?" She meant it for Heath, not Jerry. She'd need hi
help to take this bastard down before he shot both of them

Heath frowned and pressed four fingers into her righ
shoulder, then three, then two… He'd understood her ques

on. She needed to know what floor they were on if they
ere to do this together.

"You are the only *one* for me, babe," she said to let him
now when they should act. Now they just had to survive
ie ten-floor descent.

"Believe it or not, Kendall, you've brought this on your-
:lf by being too damn good at your job," Jerry said. "If
ou had just walked away. I gave you a lot of opportuni-
es to shut the file on this thing."

Heath's fingers pressed into her shoulder, counting
own the floors. It was risky, but the close quarters could
ork to her advantage. They had to act before they reached
ie basement.

"I'm afraid I'm going to have to get rid of you both."

The basement floor indicator dinged.

The doors began to open. She let the rage, terror and
ove all mix together to create a surge of energy. She leaned
orward against Heath and kicked backward, hitting Jerry's
hest. Heath shoved her aside, and she hit the wall as he
immed the traitor in the chest. The momentum carried
ie men down, and they fell to the hard elevator floor, be-
veen the doors, keeping them from closing.

The gun blast made her ears ring. Heath pounded Jer-
y's wrist against the floor until the gun skidded down the
ick garage floor. Heath kept Jerry down with his weight.
he added his strength to hers, but soon pulled back, tak-
ig Heath with her.

Jerry didn't move. He was out cold. Heath pulled them
way from the traitor. He checked for a pulse, then rolled
:rry to his stomach, pulling Jerry's arms behind him and
:sting his knee and body weight there.

He stretched out a hand and pulled her close for a hard
uick kiss, then his hands were searching her arms. "You
kay? You weren't hit or anything, were you?"

"I'm fine. His shot didn't get you?"

"No, I'm good." He gave her another quick kiss.

"You really are." She pulled her badge and pointed t her Glock as the second elevator doors opened, and a se curity guard ran toward them. "Special Agent Kenda Barlow. He's a Texas Ranger. Could you direct our backu down here? We're taking this man into custody."

The guard didn't move, but the second set of eleva tor doors opened again and Heath's team was there fo the save.

"Took you guys long enough."

"Did you find the elevators kind of slow here?" Sla said.

"Did you get all that on tape?"

"Right up until you left the apartment."

Heath put an arm around her, pulling her farther awa "First off, I regret not getting to hit you for what you di to my wife and daughter. And basically the hell you've pu me through. Keep that in mind before I get on that eleva tor to escort you upstairs."

"Heath," everyone cautioned.

"You've got one chance, man. Where is Public Exposu attacking this afternoon, and where is Brantley Lourdes? He lowered his voice so that only Kendall and Jerry coul hear. "One shot to answer, or you're mine. Alone wit me for as many floors as this building has, and then bac down."

Chapter Twenty-Six

Heath let the Rangers talk around him and over him in the apartment garage while he sat in Wade's truck. He was actually too tired to think about anything. He didn't know whose back seat he occupied. He just needed to close the windows and not move for a month.

He was too exhausted and in too much pain. He'd been holding it together on aspirin and having his ribs bound with an ACE bandage. But damn, he and Kendall looked as bad as they felt for once.

"Here, take these." Kendall dropped two extra-strength somethings in his palm and handed him a bottle of water. "It's all I could find. I think you could still take a painkiller the doctor prescribed when you get to the house. Wade and Slate both volunteered to take you home."

Bruised and broken physically, but not down and out. They'd won. They had Skylar Dawn. They had the man who had orchestrated her kidnapping. So why didn't he feel that it was over?

"What's wrong with my truck?" He pushed himself to a sitting position, waiting for her to explain. Images of someone swiping it raced through his head.

"We're in no shape to drive, remember?"

"I'll wait around until you finish. We should both see Skylar Dawn together."

"That's just it—"

"One down, one to go." Slate swooshed his hands together like he was dusting off. "The threat of being alone in the elevator with Heath really scared the pants off your boss. He talked a little, but lawyered up."

"I'm sure all the Rangers standing behind Heath helped convince Jerry to disclose where Brantley Lourdes was staying."

"What do you mean, 'one down, one to go'? Are they arresting Brantley Lourdes?" Heath looked at Slate for the answer.

"You ready to go, or should I let you guys talk?" Wade pointed toward his truck. The one Heath was currently using.

"Were you trying to get me out of here before you took off to follow another lead?" Heath turned to Kendall. "Are you trying to question him without me?"

"Actually, you're both heading home," Major Clement informed him. "You have only two options—the hospital or the comfort of your own bed. Which is it going to be?"

Heath slid across the seat, attempting to hide the winces and groans.

"Give up, Lieutenant. You can barely stand. You won't be any good out there if you pass out. Time to go home to your little girl," the Major said.

"He's right." Kendall extended a hand to help him from the truck.

He had to admit defeat by sitting on the edge of the seat. "What about you? Somehow I'm getting the impression that you have different plans." He wouldn't let her go without him. "At this moment, Lourdes is still out there and you're at risk."

"I'd be fine, but I told them I need to head home. They're sending the new agent who's in charge of the case here. She has a couple of questions."

"Why didn't you say so?" He tried to push himself to stand on his own.

"We've had a couple of interruptions," she whispered.

Most of the time he was a tough guy. Now…not so much. Wade and Slate each claimed a side, ready to help. Wade's fingers began clenching his biceps as a dark-haired woman walked into their circle.

"Kendall. Heath…if I may? I'm Special Agent Therese Ortis." She stepped forward to shake his hand. "I have a few questions for you both. Then you can head home. I'd be glad to catch you next week for your full statement."

That look. The shy moment when two people who know each other try to keep it a secret. It happened between Therese and Wade. Heath had a hunch, but he'd respect their bare acknowledgment of each other.

"What can we do for you, Agent Ortis?"

"I'd like to face Brantley Lourdes with a little more knowledge of his group. Why did you think the word *furtle* was so unusual?"

"Jerry used it on Kendall more than once when he was her partner." Heath's dislike of the man had begun as soon as they'd looked up the meaning.

"It's a word used in the book *Catch-22*. Jerry always used it out of context, and I didn't appreciate it," Kendall said.

"We found the book upstairs in his bookshelves. But you never reported him for his actions?"

"She told me, but she took care of the problem herself," Heath answered.

"Did Special Agent Fisher read a lot?"

"Not really," Kendall said.

"Would it surprise you to know we found at least thirty top literary titles?"

"Yes. He doesn't talk about reading. I'm not certain what that means, though." She thought of something im-

portant. Her mouth formed a perfect O before she pulle
out her phone. "Heath, what's your password to you
backup file for your phone? You know, the one wher
your photos are stored automatically."

"The same as it's always been." *K-n-H-4ever*. He sti
believed that could happen. "What did you remember?"

"The pictures you took of Saundra Rosa's crime scene
There's one." She rapidly swiped through the picture
"There's the other."

She flipped the phone toward Agent Ortis.

"They have the same books. This is great. The books ar
their key. I can work with this. Good work. I'll be in touch.

"Let's get out of here." He lifted his arm and waited fo
Kendall to dip her shoulder under it to hold him stead
while they walked to his truck.

Once out of the apartment garage, they continue
around the block to where he'd parked and his partner
were waiting to drive them home.

"You made the agency come to you," he said once the
reached the truck. "I didn't think you'd ever walk awa
from a case."

"One thing I think we've both realized this week is ho
important our family is. We're needed at home."

He handed her the keys and she helped him into th
passenger seat.

"Did you see the way Wade looked at Therese Ortis?
Kendall sounded lighthearted and teasing by the time sh
had her door shut. "I swear, I think he's got a thing for her.

"She has to be the informant who saved his life afte
that beating he took. Before we left, Jack told her tha
Megan would be in town this weekend." He could pla
along and avoid the all-important question of which room
he'd be sleeping in tonight.

"Oh my gosh, so much has happened that I forgot t

ell you Jack is supposed to propose. I guess those plans
re on hold."

"Good for him. He's been head over heels for Megan
ince they met."

"What about Slate and his new love life?" Kendall
urned onto the highway, heading home.

"Vivian wants to get back on her feet, but they're still
exclusive. Is that the word nowadays? I've been away from
hat rodeo for a while now and was never that much into
t before I met you."

"Really? Come to think of it, you've never mentioned
ny old girlfriends. Surely you had a girl in every city."
His wife smiled. Teased. Winked and smiled some more.

He shook his head, afraid to break the relaxed atmo-
phere inside the truck's cab.

"Not even in college?" she asked.

"I think I told you things got hard about that time. I
worked at the ranch in Alpine every spare minute I had.
Mom needed my help so I lived at home."

"Unlike my mother, who has never needed help. Some-
imes I wonder…"

"Wonder what?"

Kendall stopped at the corner of their street. "I wonder
f she did…you know, if she needed someone, she might
actually find a person who makes her happy."

THERE WERE FOUR Rangers guarding her house and visitors
nside. Kendall hesitated to drive the truck into the drive-
vay, wondering how to tell Heath she needed a little time.
He reached over and took her hand. Maybe he'd sensed
her hesitation. Maybe she needed some type of explana-
ion for how well he knew her.

"I need time to figure this out. Alone. My emotions
are all mixed up."

"Take all the time you need. Moving is a big decision for all of us."

"I'm just an emotional wreck right now," she finished with a long involuntary sigh, shutting the engine off in their driveway.

"I get it." He caught her hand, bringing it to his lips and making her smile. "Wait. Before we go inside, I've been trying to say this all week. So bear with me."

"I just need a little time—"

"Sweetheart. It's my turn. I'm going to respect your time, but I think I need to move back in for a while. I love you and Skylar Dawn more than life. I thought my biggest fear was if something happened to the two of you because of work."

"But it was my job."

"Just hear me out." He scratched his chin. "I found out that's not my biggest fear. That would be living without you."

"And Skylar Dawn."

The squeals of children at play inside the house brought her statement home.

"Honestly, she'll always be my daughter. Nothing will be able to take that away. No matter how far away she is or whether or not I live in the same house. I don't want to grow old without you. And believe me, I'm feeling the creaking bones earlier than I thought I would." He rubbed his ribs with his free hand. "You don't have to say anything now. I'm sorry for all the assumptions and for leaving you alone. I should have just told you that a long time ago."

Her hand shook. "For one of those strong, silent cowboy types…you know just what to say."

They got out of the truck. He stood on his own, not needing her help. She liked helping him, enjoyed him leaning on her—literally. It was a reason to touch him and feel safe.

More sounds of children playing had her feet moving the steps. She waited at the top for him.

"I'm going to talk to the guys before I head inside. ut—" His brow crinkled in concentration.

"What?"

He stepped up and pulled her into his arms, kissing her ke it was the first time. Exploring her mouth, accepting er passionate response.

"I love you, Kendall. I always will."

He waited as she turned and quietly opened the door d then clicked it closed. No one heard her come inside. he let him go without telling him. She leaned against the or with her hand on the knob about to return to him.

"Real pretty speech." Bryce, the Ranger who had stayed the corner of the porch, had hung back until she'd come side. "She'll come around."

She waited. There was a long pause before Heath re-onded. "I don't know. There's been a lot of space be-een us in the past six months."

"I have the first shift on your porch tonight before your artner takes over. He's ready to take you to the ranch. If at's really where you want to go."

"Need. Not want."

"Like I said, she'll come around before you know it. ee you in the morning."

She ran down the hallway away from the door, away om Heath.

Did she really need to think about their situation? She as emotional and out of control. Waiting was the logi-al thing to do. And she'd always been logical. Waiting to ake a choice—that was the way to go.

So why was her heart breaking again without him by er side?

Chapter Twenty-Seven

Why had he come to the rodeo? He'd gotten up early t feed the horses after a restless night of tossing in his be alone. But he'd needed to get away from the ranch. Neede to get away from everyone really. Needed to be with peo ple who weren't worried about him.

His parents' house was too far away to visit and be bac to work in a couple of days—if he could concentrate c anything. It had been less than a full day. He couldn't g by himself, and he didn't want Kendall to think he wa pressuring her for an answer. Instead, he reassured h mom that he was okay via text…about every three hour

Hell, maybe he *should* pack up Jupitar and take a tr home to see his mom and dad. The major had looked hi in the eye and told him he'd put him on desk duty for s months if he showed up for work sooner than a week.

But the major didn't know Heath was sleeping on th couch. Officially…he didn't have a home at the momer Maybe that was the real reason he'd come to help at th rodeo. He didn't want everyone to know he wasn't wit Skylar Dawn and Kendall.

Dammit, he was a chicken after all. Even his mornin ride had lost its appeal.

"What are you out here for, Heath? Did that bronc thro you a little softer than we thought last week?" the manage of the rodeo asked.

"Afraid I've got some broken ribs, Bobby Joe."

"And you're spending your free time here? Don't you ave a life, kid?" He cupped Heath's shoulder before he alked off to the next thing he had to do.

A rhetorical question that shot straight through his eart. He didn't want to think. His thoughts would only nd on Kendall. And who knew how long she'd take. He ight not know what to say or when the right time to say was…but she always needed time to think.

And he always gave it to her.

"So what do you say, cowboy? What are you doing after ou're finished?" asked a sweet voice he recognized but dn't expect to hear.

Heath dropped the edge of his Stetson to block the sun om his eyes. "Kendall?"

"I had to come down here to make sure the rodeo group- s were behaving themselves." She wore her tightest, low- t-cut jeans and had her shirt tied in a knot just under er breasts.

"I'd let out a howl but it might draw attention to you."

"And that's bad?"

"Sure it is. No way do I want to share your company."

"Oh. Really?" She turned to face him.

"You can't be surprised."

"I'm just… I'm not very good at flirting anymore."

He looked around, searching for their daughter. She was ith the Parkers, heading for the stands. Two additional angers from Company F flanked her and his mother-in- w. Bryce hung back, waiting on Kendall.

Her shy mannerisms reminded him of his ability to t tongue-tied. He tried not to crowd her when cowboys ssed by and needed more space. But he liked crowding close to her.

"I see Skylar Dawn found her hat," he said, tipping his a little to see her better.

"Actually, Josh's twins asked to visit Stardust. You

know they have their own horses. I agreed because
thought you went to the ranch." She stuck her fingers in
the front pockets of her jeans, but they didn't disappe
very far because they were super tight.

It had been awhile since he'd seen her in his world. Jea
and boots looked great on her. The wolf whistles wou
start pretty soon if he didn't get her shirt untied from und
her breasts and tucked into her waistband.

"Anyway, we went out there this morning. We mig
have to get her a bunch of farm animals after what th
Parkers were telling her about baby pigs and chickens."

"We?"

"Dammit. I'm going to sound crazy, but I don't nee
time to think about whether I love you or not." She thre
her arms around his neck.

"You sure? You seemed to have a plan to wait yeste
day. Waiting is sort of your thing."

"That's ridiculous. If I knew what I was doing, don
you think I'd be doing it right now? I'm stumbling arou
in the dark."

She switched her hands into her back pockets, drawi
even more stares from the cowboys.

"Hey, babe. It's kind of chilly out here. Do you have
sweater?" Heath didn't wait for an answer, he took his je
jacket off and draped it over her shoulders.

THE MEN BEHIND them laughed. Kendall waved, flirting
little more by dropping the jacket off one shoulder. The w
whistles ensued. Bryce covered his laugh behind his han
Heath glared then looked up toward their daughter to smil

"Changing the subject, Skylar Dawn seems to be doi
okay. She's walking around without you and laughing." H
waved at the stands.

"Jackson and Sage have talked a little about how scary
was to be kidnapped. They've been a big help. Our daug

ter is bouncing back faster than I thought possible." She turned to wave at everyone in the stands.

"Enjoy the show, Bryce. I can take care of my wife for a while," he said in a louder voice. "Maybe we should go somewhere we can talk?"

"Home?" she asked.

"I was thinking about a walk around the pens. That is, if you don't mind the smell." Heath wrapped his arm around her waist and guided her behind the staging area.

Kendall tugged his arm to head to a secluded corner. "What do you say, Heath? Will you give me another chance to get this right?"

"I don't want to go through life without you, sweetheart. I love you."

"I love you, too. And I'm *asking* you to help me decide about our future."

Heath took off his hat, circled it in the air and let out a big cowboy holler. He grabbed his ribs and winced, but not for long before he pulled her into his arms and kissed her.

When he let her up for air she told him, "I'm ready to ride off into the sunset, cowboy."

* * * * *

COMING SOON!

We really hope you enjoyed reading this book. If you're looking for more romance, be sure to head to the shops when new books are available on

Thursday
12th July

To see which titles are coming soon, please visit
millsandboon.co.uk